Loves Clashing

lorraine
annette
wheat

Published by Bookish & Lovely
Los Angeles, California
www.bookishandlovely.com

Cover design by Zoe Zheng
Interior design by Bookish & Lovely
First edition: 2025
ISBN: [Insert ISBN here]

DEDICATION

To all my family and friends that would read my poems, my short stories, my unpublished pages, so many unpublished pages.

PROLOGUE

zoey flipped through her high school yearbook on the verge of having a panic attack.

What's it like attending high school with the chosen ones, the trendsetters, the geniuses, the royalty even? Highly stressful, at least for her. And it shouldn't be. Attending Christian Leadership Arts and Science High, the most prestigious academy in the world should be super fun. Filled with celebrities, arts, and innovation. Only those destined for greatness attended.

"Destined for greatness," she recited over her yearbook as if she were chanting a spell. CLASH embossed white on a fancy blue leather cover. Sometimes CLASH merch felt magical, making her feel powerful and fancy by touching it. But no matter how much she stared at her yearbook with its fancy blue cover and its sans serif white letters, no matter how much she tried to manifest confidence, she couldn't shake her fear. It wrapped her like her orange maxi.

What if this year, her junior year, was just like last? All those horrible rumors. People laughing at her, the viral social media videos–that egregious nickname. She groaned, flipping through her yearbook. Barely any signatures covered the pages, and the few that did referenced her horrible nickname. Frog Legs. She absolutely detested that nickname. She slammed her yearbook close. *I'd rather die than graduate CLASH known as Frog Legs.*

She didn't care what it took. Her legacy would not be Frog Legs. She crossed her bedroom, channeling Miraculous Ladybug, Beyoncé, Sailor Moon, a tiger, all the powerful feminine energy she could muster. She needed the strength of the universe to submit her fear. That way she could show up to school orientation with the energy of a tigress.

Her phone buzzed with a text from her bestie.

Ian: Dying in the heat waiting for you.
Zoey: Coming.

She tossed her yearbook under her bed. She wasn't bringing that thing with her even though everyone usually brought their yearbook to summer orientation. It was one of CLASH's many traditions, but that book was filled with memories of her old self, a person she could not be if she wanted to redefine her legacy.

"Mom. Dad," she called. The house was quiet. The lights were out. She looked in their bedroom, then the living room, and then finally the kitchen. Mom and Dad were long gone. A wrapped egg sandwich on the counter was the only sign they left behind. Zoey swallowed the sandwich in three gulps, feeling guilty. She had completely missed Mom and Dad leaving. And this was a really big day for Dad, his first official day as CLASH principal. And she missed sending him off with a big hug because she had been so busy having a panic attack in her room. They had probably left early so Dad wouldn't be late. Guess a text would have to do:

Zoey: Happy first day. Dominate CLASH with excellence.
Dad: Thank you, Baby Girl. You on your way?
Zoey: Kinda ...

If kinda meant about to leave. She texted three orange hearts, hurrying into a heat that scorched her flesh. It was hot. Southern California blazed spicy. Her poor bestie Ian glistened sweaty, his Latin skin reddening while he waited against her red corolla. The sun melted his freshly cut black hair, his wet edges fading into a mini mohawk.

She ran to him, unlocking her car so they could slide into air conditioning.

"Thank you," Ian breathed, buckling up before grabbing his yearbook from his book bag. "Did you grab yours?" His was purple, with metallic stingrays dotted all over it. Academy replaced the word High in the name even though everyone called it CLASH. CLASH sounded cooler and less pretentious, which probably wasn't the vibe the Bautista twins were going for when they created their special edition. The Bautistas were the king and queen of CLASH. They loved organizing fundraisers for the underprivileged, hence the special edition yearbook they sold for about a month to raise funds for their family scholarship foundation. And, like always, Zoey had missed out because she hadn't known. And her bringing her standard blue yearbook would remind everyone of her loser status.

"I don't have time to grab it."

"You sure?" Ian's face said it all. She'd be the only one without her yearbook.

"Yes." She pulled out of the driveway and loaded up the Google Maps. It would take thirty minutes to get from Compton to Bel Air. They'd have to hurry when there was no space to hurry. The 405 was packed, making it impossible to bob and weave through traffic. She had to edge closer to Bel Air inch by inch.

This is my life. She groaned.

"You know we could skip if you don't want to go." Ian flipped through his yearbook. The margins were filled with signatures, and every photo of him was stunning. He was the tall, lean muscle to her short and curvy figure. Photographers loved snapping photos of him rehearsing in dance studios, leaping across stages, and getting fitted for costumes. He looked like he was revolutionizing the dance department. The one photo of her was a black and white symbol of her lonely dedication to craft. She stuffed pins into a lace costume under harsh lighting, surrounded by black. It chilled her how truthfully the photo captured the essence of her social life—correction, her old social life.

The gaslight popped on. Her heart clenched.

"You didn't get gas?" Ian asked.

"Sorry. I completely forgot." She had been so stuck in her head this morning. The fears about school orientation completely wrecked her to-do list. She groaned, turning off the highway onto Sunset Boulevard. They still had a ten-minute drive. She crept through Brentwood as if driving slower would save her gas, passing gas sign after gas sign, looking for something under five bucks a gallon. Gas prices were high, and they only increased the closer she got to Bel Air. She would not find cheap gas in this suburb filled with mansions and country clubs.

Her car slowed to an uneasy stop. *Oh no.*

Ian eyed her. Seriously?

"I know. I'm so sorry." She banged her head against her headrest. They were going to miss orientation. And not showing up was just what CLASH-mates expected of her. Only losers didn't show up. Why would they? That's what made them losers. Or worse, disrespectful. A disrespectful daughter that didn't even show up to her dad's speech.

Ian patted her shoulder. "It's okay." He hopped out of the passenger seat and onto the hood of her car, googling restaurants within walking distance. "We can grab froyo. Our favorite place is a fifteen-minute walk."

"I don't want froyo!" She climbed into the heat. Her FOMO made her hotter, and she didn't have sunblock. What could she do now? She couldn't bother Dad when he needed to focus on his CLASH debut. Texting Mom was also out.

Mom never kept secrets from Dad. That left walking. She started away from the car. "Let's go."

Ian's mouth dropped. "Are you sure?"

"One hundred percent. I'm not quitting."

"If you were not my day one." Ian slid off the hood and started behind her.

They walked past landscaped yards dotted with lemon trees, her shame as bare as the streets. There wasn't nearly enough foliage to hide behind. She could become another meme or a news story. Someone could look out their window, spot that she and Ian didn't belong, and call the cops. *Stop, stop, stop.* Sweat trickled down her thighs. All the negative thoughts weren't exactly helping. She rolled the cotton maxi to her knees, imagining a cool breeze, the water sprouting from the school's stingray fountain, the blue auditorium cushions at her back. Her Google Maps showed only six more minutes, and then they'd be out of this scorching heat. She could do it.

A black Escalade glided past her. And she wouldn't have thought anything of it if the Escalade didn't suddenly lurch to a hard stop as if someone inside that car knew them.

Please don't be a CLASH-mate. Ian sent her a questioning glance, suspecting the same. *Please, please, please,* she begged, hoping God, Fate, The Universe would open a portal and transport her to a realm where this wasn't happening. She hoped with all her heart it wasn't a CLASH-mate, maybe a teacher, maybe a friendly neighbor. She'd even take a cop. But if it had to be a CLASH-mate, then please, God, let it be anyone but a Bautista. She could take any CLASH-mate but the Bautistas.

The car edged forward, braking, backing up, lurching forward, then backing up. It felt so meta watching the Escalade's indecisiveness as if trapped between two powerful forces yelling, 'Do this–No! DO THIS!'

Dread filled her body, her suspicions increasing. She hoped fate was on her side, and then Ian laughed, killing her hopes. Ian didn't have to speak his thoughts. She could see the guess in his eyes.

The car slowly backed up. Her heart quickened, the thumps drowning Ian's laughter. Please let Ian be wrong.

The tinted window lowered.

Anyone but a Bautista.

Four gray eyes focused on her. She stopped praying, embarrassment wrapping her tighter than the sweat dripping from her pores. Why the Bautistas? Did God hate her? Did the sun hate her, transforming her into a sunburned mess and wearing off her deodorant? Had the sun somehow lassoed a gravitational pull around the Bautistas' Lyft and navigated them to this exact spot to witness her suffering?

She felt like she was at her worst, icky and needing a shower. And the Bautistas? They looked flawless. Vega's thick, black hair styled into a lob, bounced around her shoulders. And Sebastian looked like the cool breeze Zoey craved even though he was the last person she wanted to see. Oh, and look. How nice. Fate even brought a camera crew to film her pain.

She remembered stalking Sebastian's feed and discovering he was starting production on a dance series. The post had explained Sebastian's desire to tell a story about his family legacy. And how beautiful for him, but for Zoey? She stayed calm, knowing any dramatic occurrence would lead to her becoming a plot point in his docuseries. No need for the entire world to know her life was a mess.

Vega raised her purple phone, snapping a photo of Zoey and saying nothing. It was Sebastian who leaned over his evil twin and asked, "You guys need a ride?"

Zoey wished Sebastian wasn't so helpful. He was probably the one who demanded the Escalade return to help them. But she didn't think it was safe to accept his help. Not with Vega in the car. Vega hated her and was the sole reason people scribbled frog jokes in her yearbooks. And she would be the reason that if Zoey attended orientation, she'd sit in the back with no friends. Thanks, but no thanks.

"We're good. My dad's bringing gas," Zoey said.

Ian's eyes grew big. "You sure?"

'Yes!' she mouthed, hoping he got the message. She needed his support. Compton before Bel Air always.

Sebastian looked confused. "Wouldn't you miss your Papá's big introduction?"

"She'd rather die of heatstroke than be a good daughter," Vega groaned. "Let it go."

"That's not it!" She wanted to support Dad, but she couldn't trust Vega.

"We're grabbing froyo to cool off and then sitting with the car so we don't get towed," Ian said. "You know how it is in West Hollywood."

"I'm so sorry you and Frog Legs are stuck in this mess." Vega's tone softened towards Ian.

Disgusting. Zoey turned from the cameras so they couldn't film her face.

"Since you guys won't be at orientation, want to sign yearbooks now? Might as well. It's tradition." Vega extended her special edition out of the window, along with a purple pen. "Sebastian, get yours."

Zoey backed away from the car, knowing she wasn't invited to the special edition party. She watched the tradition unfold like a lonely outsider. Sebastian and Ian flipped through the glossy pages, writing their notes fast while Vega took her sweet time. She reminisced over the photos, reading aloud as she wrote in a singsong voice, "Love you lots, Ian. You're a phenomenal dancer that'll dominate this year. XOXO, heart, heart." Sebastian and Ian didn't read their notes aloud, seemingly aware of Zoey's pain.

Ian shoved Vega's special edition back into the Escalade. "Catch you guys later."

Vega wasn't ready to go. "We have to take photos." She hopped out of the car wearing a silk bohemian dress that made her five-foot-ten, too-thin body look ethereal.

Zoey recognized the dress from Teen *Vogue*'s cover and instantly regretted her orange maxi. What was she thinking?

Her outfit was too safe when she was at war with Vega. This wasn't David and Goliath. She had to go bigger, bolder.

Sebastian didn't budge from the car, not in the mood for photos.

Vega shoved her phone at Zoey, turning to Sebastian. "Come on. It's tradition."

Tradition. Sebastian was a stickler for tradition, an aspect that made him attractive and regal, like CLASH. And his love for tradition would be the reason this moment stretched on longer.

Zoey's mouth dropped when Vega shoved her phone into her chest. It was freaking ridiculous that Vega thought she should take their photos, but she couldn't refuse. She had to be the happy CLASH-mate who was so willing to maintain a tradition that she couldn't participate in because of Vega. She snapped photo after photo of Vega, Sebastian, and Ian posing with their perfect bodies and flawless faces. *Please save me.* She glanced at the camera men filming silently.

"That's enough," Sebastian finally said, turning to Vega. "Unless you want to pay her."

Thank you.

"Thanks, Frog Legs." Vega snatched her phone back, sending Zoey fifty bucks. "Hope that's enough. Want me to sign your yearbook as well?"

"As some kind of payment? Wouldn't that break tradition?" Vega hadn't signed her yearbook last year and probably didn't want to now. More like she wanted to mock her for not owning a special edition. Vega sent a group text

X

about the special editions, hoping only the "cool kids" would get the memo. And, well, Zoey? Sorry, not sorry. "I left mine at home anyway," she shrugged.

"Such poor planning." Vega returned to the Escalade. "You'd be the only one without a yearbook, so I guess froyo's better for you." She blew kisses at Ian. "Enjoy your bestie date."

Sebastian threw deuces at Ian and extended his hand to Zoey. She took it. At least Sebastian was a decent human being, unlike Vega. His hand was soft, firm. Her breath caught when he pulled her forward, his body swallowing her up. He was as tall as Ian, six-foot-two, with a muscular physique molded by the dance program. She folded into his body. Cool and smelling sweet, he became the chocolate froyo to her hot stickiness, his touch satisfying her cravings.

"We're about to be late," Vega shouted.

Like she cared about being late.

Zoey was glad Sebastian ignored Vega, hugging her tighter while his sister seethed. Maybe Sebastian hugged her to annoy his sister. They only had one class together, French, and rarely talked then. All he had to know about her were Vega's lies. For him, hugging her was akin to hugging a mentee, but for her? Everything. She spent years daydreaming about Sebastian, his arms around her waist, her head against his chest, he feeling strong, his face signaling his Spanish heritage, his black hair brushing a lean jaw with a cleft in his chin. She fought the urge to press her index finger into the groove, meeting his eyes. He looked at her like a teacher looked at a struggling student. Not like a boy-friend. But what did she expect? She didn't know him, and he didn't know her. She was always too afraid to get to know him, knowing deep down he'd only date someone as brave as himself. Someone that brave wouldn't let Vega bully and shame them out of attending orientation.

She watched Sebastian climb back into the Escalade, wait-ing until the car had turned a corner. Then she continued walking. Vega wasn't winning. She was being brave like Sebastian and showing up at orientation.

Ian rushed up beside her. "I thought we were grab-bing froyo."

"I lied."

"Are you sure you don't want to skip orientation?"

"I'm not quitting."

"Check your phone."

"Why?"

"Vega's post. We look a hot mess."

What post? How did Vega have a post? The memory of Vega snapping a photo flashed in Zoey's mind. She released the biggest sigh. This is my life. Raising her phone, she shud-dered. *What did he mean WE look a hot mess?* He wasn't in the photo. She was alone on the road, looking oily and starved for water. Vega's caption, 'When your priorities are off,' was horrifying but so fitting.

Ian commented, 'Sometimes froyo has to be priority number one.'

Ha, ha.

CLASH-mates were leaving laugh-face emojis in real-time. Someone tagged her in a story of Dad greeting students with the words, 'Daddy-daughter where?' She hated how Vega could make a fool out of her so easily, destroying her whole day. She hated Vega's wealth, and her sexy lob, and her ballet figure. She hated Vega's dress, its simple extravagance. How it hinted of summer and teased of fall. How the V-line showed off Vega's clavicle, persuading the eye to travel the lines of her bony body. And here Zoey was wearing a boring maxi. She hated that Sebastian wasn't following her account but saw the post anyway cause he was following Vega. His comment, 'Be professional,' was as much an attack on her as it was on Vega. If she had professionally prepared for orientation, she would have gotten gas the night before and prepared a stunning outfit to rival Vega. But no! She was failing at life. And she was tired of failing. She was going to do whatever it took to win this year.

"I'm not dressing safe on the first day of school!" she yelled.

"Good. CLASH hates safety." Ian stuck out his hand. "I'm really sorry this is happening."

She stared at his palm. "Why are you sorry?"

"You're my day one. I want you to win."

She stared into his brown eyes, feeling guilty. None of this was his fault. She smashed her palm against his. *And I can't hate him for playing the social game with Vega either.* Life at the bottom of the social pyramid sucked, and her love for him was bigger than her misery. "I'll win," she whispered. *Somehow.*

Zoey flipped on the lights in her sewing lab as soon as she got home. She was lucky to have the place. Mom and Dad spent their vow-renewal money on her lab so she could have a space big enough to contain her creativity. And she had painted the walls orange and hung pictures of the Eiffel Tower alongside stickers of Sailor Moon and Miraculous Ladybug. She passed her sewing machines, going to the back where she hid her scandalous creations. Women dancing in Latin clubs inspired her boldest designs. They were creative but mediocre. For some reason, she couldn't capture the women's sexiness, how they challenged norms and weren't afraid of vulnerability. Like Sebastian.

Sebastian wasn't afraid. And neither was Vega, and Zoey didn't want to be anything like Vega, but channeling her enemy's audacity was a must. She found the beginnings of an orange vegan leather mini, a dress she envisioned so skintight it'd cling to her existence, but wearing such a revealing dress on the first day of school was scary. One drop of insecurity and her classmates would label her thirsty for attention instead of a boss proudly displaying her curves and talent. It was why she never finished the outfit.

She laid her palm over her thumping heart.

CHAPTER 1
ZOEY

self-humiliation sucked, but it taught her a lesson. Be bold. Seeing Vega's orientation outfit while stranded in Bel Air changed her worldview. She couldn't win a war against Vega playing safe. Not when she had to soften hearts made of gold.

She spent the rest of summer finalizing her outfit, hand-stitching an homage to Miraculous Ladybug. She even crafted a beaded choker with Tikki's face in the middle. The orange dress looked luscious against her wild, curly hair, dark eyes, and caramel skin.

She flipped on her television, scrolling through YouTube to find her favorite makeup tutorial, following along to line her lips with gloss and enhance her eyes with sparkling eyeshadow. She'd glitter it up as much as possible for the first day of school. Batting her lids, she moved on to her hair, knotting her curls into two puffs at the bottom of her skull.

Her look was complete, and she looked fire. She hoped everyone at CLASH took in her outfit and forgot about that seventh-grade rumor Vega spread. She'd done nothing to deserve the cyberbullying, but Vega loved preying on the weak. Decent human beings needed food to survive. Vega feasted on ruining people's lives. Well, Vega needed to find someone else to eat cause Zoey was fighting back.

The makeup tutorial faded to black, and the melody of a familiar song rose in volume. Zoey bounced, her eyes flickering to the television mounted to her peach walls.

A Fear of God logo glowed white against the screen's blackness, signaling the start of the advertisement. The screen transitioned to Sebastian dressed in black and white fleece athletic wear. She watched him dance ballet across the rooftop of a downtown skyscraper, turning when he turned, flicking her wrist when he lifted his arm, and pointing her toe when he lifted his leg. The camera pushed closer as his turns quickened. Breathing heavy, she turned faster, stopping when he stopped. His gray eyes burned through the screen, challenging her to buy Fear of God and join him on a rooftop.

Tingles shot through her body, wishing she could swipe her credit card yes. She'd love to dance with him on a skyscraper. The commercial was cinematic, and Sebastian was perfect for it. His fashion sense focused and as minimalist as his wdedication to craft, the complete opposite of hers. She'd describe her taste as edgy but fun and colorful.

She stiffened. Sebastian was ballet De Stijl. Her back-to-school outfit was Les Arts Décoratifs on discount. She should have stitched an oversized sweatsuit adorned in black and white. That's what Sebastian liked. Not exactly eye-catching, but couldn't she have found a balance between eye-catching and minimalism?

She grabbed her cell phone, calling Ian.

He answered on the fifth ring. "You're stranded and dying in the middle of nowhere."

"Sebastian'll hate my outfit. Have you seen his Fear of God ad? He's wearing the same style he's worn since fifth grade–so not me, but I should have designed balletcore De Stijl."

"ZZZZZZOOOOOOEEEYYYYYY, it's five a.m., five a.m., and you're calling me about that fake?"

"I need your help." Zoey tried to get Ian to stay on the phone a little longer. "Just watch it and help me come up with some ideas."

"You better be happy I'm madly in love with you."

"No, you're not."

Ian didn't answer, too focused on watching the ad. Finally, the music faded. "You will not grab Sebastian's attention with balletcore De Stijl. Are you kidding? He sees that every day. Stick with Miraculous Ladybug revamped orange."

"Are you sure?"

"Yes, see you in two hours." Ian hung up before Zoey yelled, "Two hours is way too late."

She grabbed her handmade bookbag and carefully hurried down the stairs to the kitchen. Mom was at the stove wrapping up a final batch of pancakes while Dad finished packing their lunches.

Zoey's stomach gurgled. Okay, maybe she didn't have to rush to snatch Ian out of bed. She reached for a plate.

"So that's your big first-day look?" Mom cut Dad a look with her eyes, warning him not to criticize.

Dad concentrated on tucking the turkey sandwiches into plastic bags, struggling for the right words. He obviously didn't like Zoey's choice, but she didn't expect him to get it. He was in his forties, conservative, and an expert on school administration, not fashion.

Mom spoke up to help Dad out. "Love your look, but don't you think you should save it for your salsa nights? It's a little tight."

"No, orientation taught me I can't be safe."

"You were close, but you didn't quite make it to orientation," Mom said.

"I had a run-in with Vega. And she inspired me to go big, and I wish I could go fancier, tighter, but you know," Zoey shrugged. "Time's a thing."

"That doesn't sound right at all. Isn't Vega the girl who disrespects you? I don't think she has your best interest at heart. Maybe you shouldn't listen to her."

"I don't listen to everything she says. But she's right about this. I can't hide."

"But," Dad interjected, handing her and Mom their lunches. "Don't you want to exude comfort and professionalism? It's first-day impressions. You want to dress for success and surprises."

"My outfit's the surprise. People'll love my bold take on pop culture."

"For sure, but what do you love? What do you want to be known for?"

"Fashion that's fearless. That's why this is my outfit." She turned to Mom for help.

Mom raised her spatula in surrender. "Look, I don't agree. But you're sixteen, and it's your body and your self-image. If you love it, I love it. Just don't bend over."

"You mean don't even look down." Dad grabbed his briefcase, kissing Mom and then Zoey on the cheek. "You can have this outfit as long as you're not late. Call Ian and tell him to hurry up, or you'll finish your first day in a turtleneck and jeans."

Eeewww. She didn't work this hard to end up in jeans and a turtleneck. She checked the map on her phone. Two hours of traffic. Typical of a Monday morning. She wished her family could afford Bel Air so she didn't always feel like she had to rush in the morning. She wolfed down the pancakes in chunks, running out the door to grab Ian.

When Dad announced that he was CLASH's new principal, she spent an hour researching home prices, dreaming as if Dad's new paycheck was big enough to accommodate her dreams. It wasn't. Dad definitely didn't make enough for Bel Air, and even if he did, he'd never leave. Compton had flowed through the Raines family veins for five generations. They grew up attending the same schools, shopping at the same grocery stores, and playing football in the same parks. Mom and Dad got married at the Compton library. Compton held too many memories for Mom and Dad to leave, but Zoey felt differently.

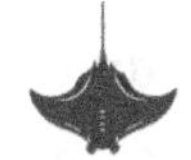

CHAPTER 2
IAN

"so you're not a complete commitment-phobe." Mahogany looked up from where she lay on his chest, jealous. "You stay loyal to Zoey."

Mahogany's jealousy was just as hardcore as the sex, sending intense ripples through his body, but he didn't actually love Mahogany's jealousy. He preferred cuddling, her skin mashed against his skin, not arguing about Zoey. "I'm literally her only friend. I have to stay Zoey stuck."

"Why don't you sleep with her then?" Mahogany grabbed the remote.

He had already. He fought the smile. Remembering those freshman months always made him laugh. Zoey had been freaking out that no guy would ever find her attractive, and so he proved to her that was a total lie. He even dated Zoey for a month before she demanded they stay besties so that she could focus on maintaining her perfect GPA. He loved Zoey too much to let heartbreak destroy their friendship.

Besides, ghosting Zoey was impossible. She lived next door to him, and her parents were his godparents.

He could tell Mahogany knew he was thinking about Zoey. She removed her body heat, crossed her arms, and flipped through YouTube, casually surfing as if she never intended to land on Sebastian's channel.

"Come on." He tried grabbing the remote before she clicked on a video of Sebastian touring his pa's company in Madrid.

Sebastian walked halls lined with windows peaking into ballet rehearsals, stopping at the one with his pa, disrupting practice to ask his pa boring questions about being the director of the Nacional Compañía de Baile. Only a nepo baby could interrupt a company rehearsal for an interview.

"I don't get why you hate Sebastian so much." Mahogany laughed at Ian's expression. "He's the only reason you can afford CLASH."

"Ouch. Say something meaner. I love it when you're mean." There were so many reasons to dislike Sebastian. Like the requirement to audition for the Bautista dance scholarship every year when it was the only scholarship that made its recipients audition annually. Or the fact Sebastian could rely on his family's success while he worked his ass off for second rank. He could coupé jeté en tournant in his sleep. Did Sebastian want fouette turns? 32? He'd *Swan Lake* for the money. Unlike Sebastian, he needed scholarships. His list rolled on with reasons, but Mahogany's list was shorter. She was Sebastian's pas partner, which maintained her rank as number one for females in their class. What were the faculty or Fear of God's reasons for liking Sebastian? Were they blind? Sebastian's dancing was so stiff … so inhuman. "It's like watching my ma boil oatmeal."

"Jealous?"

He yawned, stretching. "A little. I mean, Zoey's always talking about how much she loves watching Sebastian dance. And I wish she'd talk about me like that."

Mahogany threw the remote at him. It hurt. He rubbed his chest, exaggerating the pain while Mahogany pulled on her baby blue panties and matching bra.

"You know I'm teasing, right?" he asked. "Zoey's a friend. I'm addicted to you."

"You're addicted to everything. That's why you can't choose who or what to love." Those words hurt way more than the plastic remote, unsettling him the more they simmered in his mind. Was Mahogany making fun of his friendships or attacking his commitment to dance? He loved his family, he loved dance, he loved Mahogany, and he showed that in his own way. And most of all, he loved being himself. CLASH oppressed his identity, leaving him desperate for fun and freedom. And Mahogany's kisses, her cuddles, kept him from losing himself. "I'm addicted to you and making this the best year–"

"Great!" Mahogany interrupted. "Just don't make this year the same as last."

Make this year the same as last? "What?"

Mahogany yanked open his door, revealing his padres mid-knock. Ma stood there with her tech-nerd boyfriend, Jonah, and Pa stood with his hippie girlfriend, Portia. Portia was also dating Jonah. It was complicated, and Ian didn't expect people to get his padres' marriage. Sometimes, the way his padres loved blew his mind, but he thought it was fun, so he didn't try too hard to understand why they needed Tech and Hippie Nerds. Mahogany, though, thought it was weird. He could tell by her face.

"Breakfast's ready," Ma said.

"Sorry, Ian killed my appetite." Mahogany pushed past the bathroom.

He couldn't let Mahogany leave angry. Not on the first day of school. She could be angry on the second. He jumped out of bed, running after her.

Ma jumped out of the way. "You got ten minutes to kiss and make up and be downstairs for breakfast. Zoey'll be here any minute."

Ten minutes was all he'd need.

CHAPTER 3
SEBASTIAN

mamá and papá built a beautiful dance studio for him and his twin sister. It was a stone building placed at the side of his parent's three-story house. He could plié on sprung flooring and look out giant windows. His backyard was endless, filled with purple jacaranda trees. But no amount of beauty could convince his sister to show up to rehearsals on time. Vega believed she was too beautiful to be on time.

He wasn't nice, but he was patient. He rarely asked Vega to wake up at four a.m. just cause he liked to train in the dead silence of black mornings. But today was the first day of school, and the faculty requested they perform a waltz at the welcome-back assembly. Vega had flaked all summer on rehearsals, but she had promised to join him at four a.m..

The clock ticked and tocked to his échappé sautés. His sweat dripped to the rhythm…six a.m…now seven a.m… Vega had lied. She flaked again.

"Hulu! Yes, Hulu wants us! Yes! Yes!" his producer Amy Pak screamed, entering his studio. She was ecstatic that they had found a streamer before completing the docuseries.

That's how much their investors believed in him and his sister, even though Vega never showed up. From TikTok influencer to Hulu docuseries. He had made so many sacrifices, saying no to friends and dating, saying no to anything but dance so that he could grow their follower account and land the brand sponsorships that earned them an eight-episode docuseries. What sacrifices had Vega made? He felt so alone and disappointed that he didn't want to hear Amy scream about how happy she was about the Hulu creative execs.

"We can totally handle three more cameras and an extra sound mixer," Amy said.

Maybe he could. Vega? What if she messed up? There would be five cameras instead of two filming their horrible performance. He shuttered, bouncing up into a grand jeté that felt off.

Amy confirmed they would have five a.m. call times to capture his morning workouts. He wanted to tell her he didn't want a camera crew there before nine. Early mornings were when he was at his weakest, and he didn't want the world knowing his jeté en tournants weren't always perfect. Like now, when he landed off balance and winced in pain.

Amy paused. "Are you okay?"

He hated Amy's pity, that he messed up, and that his sister had flaked again. Barging past Amy, out of his studio and across his backyard, he hurried up his winding staircase.

Vega laughed behind her bedroom door. He slammed it open, disgusted.

She sat on her bed, eating cinnamon chips, dressed in the signature student government khakis and collared shirt, video chatting with her boyfriend, Gregory. She had prioritized Gregory over him again.

"Come in, Love," Vega said sarcastically. She looked at him in her mirror. They looked almost identical, with the same straight, black hair, gray eyes, and round but narrow Spanish noses. That's where the commonalities ended.

"We had a four a.m. rehearsal," he continued.

"We've rehearsed a million times, and Greg needs my help with his speech. Sorry."

Gregory waved from the phone. "What's sup?"

He leaped towards Vega, ripping the phone from her grasp and ending the call.

"Hey!" Vega shouted. He was three inches taller than her, so she hopped onto her bed and then jumped on his back.

She smacked him while yelling for her phone. He pushed her onto the bed.

"Mamá," Vega screamed, rushing out of her room.

Sebastian followed her down the stairs and into the kitchen.

Mamá video-chatted with Papá at the kitchen island, sipping a coffee while Chef Ramón served her a tostada con tomate. Vega didn't even care, interrupting Mamá's call with, "Tell Sebastian to give me back my phone."

"We have a dance in front of the entire school," Sebastian said. "And she's chatting with Gregory instead of practicing like she promised."

Mamá sighed. She had his gray eyes that always cooled him when he felt like he was burning alive. Even though he could never refuse her, she positioned the phone so he saw Papá clearly. *"Dale su celular a tu hermana, por favor."* Please hand Vega back her phone.

He swallowed his shame, tossing the phone on the counter.

Vega snatched it up, leaning over Mamá and blowing kisses at Papá's digitized face. Papá also had gray eyes and dark hair. But unlike Mamá, looking like Papá was a burden.

"How's the weather in Madrid?" Vega softened her voice, leaning into the phone's camera.

"Why aren't you practicing?" Papá replied.

Sebastian cut in with, *"Vega's busy with her couple goals."*

"I practice tons. Sebastian's a liar." Vega curled her lip. Knowing how much it would disappoint Papá, she'd never admit the truth, choosing instead to leave the kitchen so that Papá couldn't question her more.

Mamá bit into her tostada. *"What Vega desires is just as important, and you must respect that."*

Respect that? He sacrificed his social life to make Vega successful, and she didn't appreciate him. He wished he could tell Papá just how little Vega practiced. Whenever Vega did practice, she made him feel like he was failing himself and his parents. Pressure built within. He cracked his knuckles, thinking he'd soon fail CLASH by dancing the worst waltz ever.

"Don't even bother coming to the presentation," He whispered to Mamá, leaving.

"Hey!" Papá called.

He faced the phone, struggling to meet Papá's gray eyes even though the screen size made Papá look smaller.

"Happy first day of school. Love you. You'll dance amazingly."

"Sure, Papá." He glanced at Amy typing away on her cell phone. She'd been sitting in the back the whole time, jotting down possible storylines for Vega and his relationship. This is what having five cameras on his every move would feel like. His loneliness on display while his sister danced around his misery, making him feel worthless. His muscles grew tense, his hands making fists.

He felt Mamá's hand. She was warm and smelled like fresh coffee. She had ended Papá's call so that they could talk.

"I can't do this show with Vega," he admitted.

"She's your sister."

"She hates me, and I don't want the world to know it."

"It breaks my heart you believe that."

Sometimes, Mamá made him feel like he was six years old, weak and crying at everything. Then he discovered he could move across the stage like Mamá, a champion ballroom dancer, and Papá, an international movie star, so he consumed himself with dance and left the tears behind. He felt like his sister didn't care about their legacy.

Mamá turned to Chef Ramón. *"Prepare two eggs and potatoes with onions and pepper for Sebastian, please."*

He watched Chef Ramón breaking the eggs into the skillet.

"You're being so mean to yourself and your sister. Remember your mission, to show the world how much you love your family legacy. Your sister's a part of your legacy."

He'd have to compensate for Vega's mediocrity and dreaded doing that in front of the world. He didn't feel like explaining that to Mamá, so he pushed away the breakfast Chef Ramón set before him. *"I have to get ready."*

He headed up the stairs and into a cold shower. The icy sting kept him from drowning in rage. Vega flaked on her responsibilities, and now their dance might not meet expectations. People expected perfection from him, and he delivered. Otherwise, he was wasting people's time.

He dressed in khaki pants and a black-collared shirt with matching sneakers. Vincent showed up wearing the same, except his shirt was brown, and Gregory dressed for the student assembly, sporting a blazer and dress pants. He buzzed about his opening speech, but Sebastian turned his back on Gregory. He couldn't forgive him for hogging Vega all summer.

Vincent bragged about his summer basketball camp in Madrid, flaunting his new Spanish skills. Sometimes, Vincent's tongue rolled the sounds awkwardly. But this meant the world. Finally speaking Spanish with his best friend,

Sebastian asked about the foods and the museums, stuff he already knew, just to keep Vincent talking.

"*Vi un show en el teatro de tu Papá,*" Vincent said. I watched a show at your papá's theater.

Sebastian's smile faltered. "*Guay.*" Cool.

The camera crew arrived at seven, filling the kitchen with the scent of mud and oil. Sebastian didn't care about their names. He lowered his head and used Vincent and Gregory as shields until he felt confident.

Amy showed him the new car he would have to drive, an electric Jeep Wrangler painted in CLASH colors. He recognized Vega's jealousy. She wanted a new car even though she hated driving.

Amy announced, "You guys have to share. It'll make getting shots easier."

His heart ached a little, remembering how much they used to share until Papá moved back to Madrid. Vincent's joking about their lack of sharing only made his heart hurt more. The crew had fitted the car with GoPros, so Sebastian let his friends talk while he drove to school in silence. He tried to prepare for their big performance by visualizing the Viennese Waltz. Peso Pluma booming from his speakers made it hard. He didn't want to ruin the vibe, so he didn't tell Gregory to shut up about class president, or ask Vincent to stop bragging about his "Spanish skillz." And he didn't demand Vega get off social and focus on visualization. When Vincent asked what his plans were this year, he forced out the words, "Dance dominance and funding one more kid a full ride to CLASH."

"The scholarship's not all you," Vega pointed out from the backseat. "I contribute."

"The bare minimum," he muttered. Cause you hate dancing with me.

CHAPTER 4

ZOEY

she stormed out of the front door, planning to drag Ian out of his bed, and stopped, shocked.

Ian was already hugging it out in the front yard with his two sets of parents and Mahogany.

She used to think her mom and dad were married to Godmom and Goddad Cruz. They always hung out, celebrating holidays, sharing gossip, and attending church together. Churches didn't like non-monogamous couples, so that meant they always had to find a more accepting church. But, when she turned ten, her godparents started dating what Ian called "the tech and hippie nerds." She and Ian had hated Tech Nerd Jonah and Hippie Nerd Portia, and one Fourth of July, that hatred boiled over. When Mom and Dad threw their annual Cruz and Raines barbecue, they proposed inviting Tech and Hippie Nerds. They're family, right? Wrong. Zoey and Ian cried until their parents got them to confess, 'We don't want you to divorce.' Their parents had laughed so hard Fanta spurted from Dad's nose, and Godmom Cruz toppled over. Eventually, they felt guilty for laughing and agreed to keep the barbecue just between them that year.

After the Cruces returned home, Mom and Dad explained they believed in monogamy while her godparents believed in that other stuff. Dad had wanted to go into some long lecture about diversity, but Mom had cut him off. She simply put it like this, 'People are different. People are weird, and so am I. I get down with the weird, so I don't question.' Mom's words had stuck with Zoey. She tried her best never to question her godparents or Ian, no matter how much his sexual habits irritated her.

Godmom and Goddad Cruz made room for her to join the group hug. She tried to stay present, ignoring the nagging question, isn't this hug a bit too long?

Mahogany was the brave one that cut it short, dashing off to her Lexus while yelling, "We're going to be so late if we don't leave soon."

Zoey wanted to blast straight out of Compton like Mahogany, so she jumped into her Corolla, spun up the engine, fastened her seatbelt, and then . . . and then she waited for Ian.

He was Saturday strolling to her car.

She lowered her windows. "Can you walk a little faster?"

"Nope. I'm taking you in." He slid into the passenger seat. "You look so sexy."

She figured she could be a little less annoyed with him. "But not cheap, right?"

"Never. You don't make cheap."

"I'm just so nervous." She backed the car slowly out of the driveway, waiting for all the middle schoolers hurrying past towards Malcolm X Primary at the end of the street. Dad used to work there with Mom until he earned CLASH principal.

She seized an opening, driving down the street lined with houses cut into crooked squares. They barely turned off Poplar when Ian said, "Let's grab donuts."

Her jaw dropped. She couldn't believe it. "We can't be late on the first day."

"Please! Let's own this day with chocolate and sprinkles."

She rolled her eyes, glancing at the clock. She decided to just give in. There was no way they would be early with this traffic, so she weaved down North Matthisen Avenue. The Compton of today was so different from the eighties and nineties when N.W.A was rising to fame, and Compton was the deadliest city in all of California. Over-policing and drugs had either put her parents' friends in jail or forced them out of the neighborhood. Neighbors become faces and cultures Mom and Dad didn't know, but then Godmom and Goddad Cruz moved next door. A couple of years later, Zoey and Ian were born. Life improved, and Compton became the boring Compton Zoey knew.

She parked on Rosecrans in front of Ian's favorite donut shop.

Ian jumped out of the car and rushed inside. She breathed in the smell of dough and coffee, fighting her growing irritation while Ian chopped it up with Señora Lopez for a full ten minutes before returning to the car with a bag of donuts. He handed her a glaze covered in orange icing and black hearts.

"I told her about your outfit, and she gave you this for free." He winked at her.

She took a big bite and turned onto the 405, her car inching towards Bel Air. The slow pace intensified her anxiety, reminding her that life changed slowly when she needed her social life to change now, no starts and stops. Each push on the brakes reminded her of feeling stuck and how she could feel stuck and alone all junior year. She turned to Ian. He hummed content, chewing his coconut-covered donut. She was a hot mess, strangling her poor steering wheel.

The CLASH sign emerged, looking intimidating. *This is it. Don't freak out.* She eased into the parking lot. There were so many CLASH-mates, all Vega loyalists trained to be Zoey haters.

She should have never accepted Vega's bet to steal that frog from their seventh-grade science class, but Vega had promised Zoey a spot at her lunch table, next to Sebastian. And she'd stomach an hour of Vega to spend her lunches with Sebastian, flirting, forming a friendship, and possibly becoming highschool sweethearts. Her dream.

All she had to do was prove she was fearless. Then Vega would welcome her into the inner circle.

Vega had wanted her to steal the frog they were dissecting when Mr. Rogers wasn't looking. She snuck the frog inside her lunch bag, on edge but excited, thinking about Sebastian. They'd share food and plan dates filled with magic. And deep down, she wished she and Vega were friends, Vega with the body of a supermodel and the personality of a queen. So fun to style. They could have girls' nights filled with glitter. Those were her thoughts while approaching Vega's lunch table. She had pulled out the frog, expecting Vega to shout, "How cool" and make room. Instead, Vega tossed her lunch and screamed, "Zoey eats Mr. Rogers' dead frogs."

Sebastian had jumped up mid-burrito bite, eyeing Zoey, disgusted. She'd never forget his face. How his lips curled, and his nose scrunched. He thought she was gross. As if she were covered in frog juice. Everyone pulled out their phones and recorded video, the lunchroom chanting, "Zoey eats Mr. Rogers' dead frogs." She threw the frog in Vega's face, and Sebastian looked at Zoey as if he'd never touch her.

The memory left Zoey shaking. She couldn't go through with this. Her outfit was too tight, and people would call her thirsty. Crying on the first day of school would be the worst. She turned to Ian. Somehow, he made his donut last the drive to school, and he was finishing his last bite. "We can wait until the bell rings."

He licked his fingers. "We're not waiting till the bell rings, not when you created this flawless masterpiece."

"But I don't know. My outfit's a little much."

"And I'm always a little much. We can be too much together."

Ian did make a great accessory with his gorgeous mohawk haircut, bronze skin, and perfect dancer body. He was hot, and she felt lucky to have him. Freshman year, she had made the mistake of letting him run wild out of the friend zone. Even though she loved him, she would never make that mistake again. Shoving Ian back into the friend zone had been hard, but he forgave her. He'd stick by her if her outfit turned out to be a total fail. At least she could cry against his six-pack while he reminded her she was beautiful. "Okay, let's do it," she whispered, unsure.

That was enough for Ian. He jumped out of the car, grabbing her books.

She entered the summer fashion show that was CLASH. Luxury vehicles sprinkled the parking lot. Bugattis paired with matching Bottega Veneta handle bags. This was her moment.

She took a tiny step forward, knowing her steps couldn't be too big or her dress would rip. She was owning her outfit and the way it hugged her curvaceous body. So when some redhead pulled out her phone and started recording, Zoey winked in her direction.

Ian was always the star in any crowd. He kissed cheeks and gave hugs, switching between Spanish and English depending on who grabbed his attention. Being Señor Popular was his norm; today, it would be hers.

A girl screamed, "Oh my god, Miraculous Ladybug! I love it! Can I take a picture?"

Zoey's heart swelled, leaning cheek-to-cheek for the selfie.

Her phone blew up with mentions. She jumped when Vincent Dixon popped up in her likes. "Vincent follows me!"

"Vincent follows everyone," Ian replied.

"Yeah, but he actually liked my photo–" she shoved her phone in his face.

He pulled the phone closer. "Now Sebastian liking your post's a big deal. He doesn't like anything."

Sebastian liked her post when he didn't follow her. He was one of those people with millions of followers only to follow ten, and today, she was number eleven. She jumped for joy, jumping behind Ian's back when she spotted the real Sebastian. He stood with Vega and the student government posse, AKA SG.

Ian turned his back to SG, facing her. "Do you think they see me?"

"Vega's literally waving at you right now," Zoey sighed.

"Great. Fun time's over." He code-switched into dancer jock mode so fast. She hated dancer jock mode. It made him elitist and super standoffish, but that was SG's vibe.

"You deserve an Academy Award." She took her books from him.

"I know." He blew her kisses, heading to where no unpopular kid could venture.

Zoey felt amazing even though she had to walk the halls alone. All those summer days spent at home sewing her back-to-school outfit had paid off. She glided into the audi-torium, confidently scanning the rows. A jock smiled and waved at her. He was cute. Maybe she'd sit there.

"Frog-Leg Zoey," the jock yelled, singing, "Miraculous, up to the test–"

"Or not," his friends chimed in, laughing.

"Ha, ha. I pass every test." Her voice stayed light, nearly avoiding an ego-dripping argument when CLASH-mates were GPA-obsessed maniacs.

She found a seat in the back, feeling stupid. One outfit wouldn't change people's impressions. She'd need at least a dozen to revamp her brand, so much work, but she couldn't lose hope.

Dad–Principal Raines emerged from the curtains to stand at the podium.

"Hello, Innovators! Hello, Leaders," he shouted.

She used to fear Dad working at CLASH would destroy her chances at popularity, but Ian reminded her Dad would be too busy learning CLASH-isms to destroy her social status. Transitioning from the principal at Malcolm X Primary to CLASH would not be easy, but if Dad could go from Compton to Bel Air, she could go from social disaster to elite. Like daddy, like daughter.

CHAPTER 5
IAN

ian often talked about CLASH during dinners at his god-parents'. Essentially, every CLASH story starred Zoey as Ladybug and him as—he hated cats so …he ran through a list of shows Zoey forced him to binge–Tuxedo Mask. He was code-switching to hide his identity. They fought tears by moonlight and struggled to win friends by daylight, hoping they could impress so-and-so enough to get back-doored into their dream lives, no strings attached. He'd end their stories complaining about how much he felt like he was losing his soul to Queen CLASH and wanted to quit. Zoey hadn't yet reached the point of quitting, and Tuxedo Mask did not abandon Sailor Moon.

'Focus on your loves!' Pa Raines would reply. 'Stop wor-rying about everyone else, blah, blah, blah—' brilliant advice for someone not Ian. He walked with the giants that could make his dreams happen, so he exuded giant energy. It was a ton of pressure, and he thought Pa Raines was too Compton to understand.

He was wrong.

Pa Raines might have played the daddy figure all those dinners, but he wasn't fool enough to bring his every day to Bel Air. Standing center stage of the Spears Theater, he code-switched the heck out of his Compton vernacular, delivering his speech on CLASH history like an NFL news correspondent. He was playing the social game. Good for him. Playing the game was survival.

Ian was playing it by sitting with SG, even though he preferred sitting in the back with Zoey. SG was supposed to inspire students to take an interest in school policies, but it was a social club that reeked of old money. Greg and Vega came from celebrity families; Mahogany's father owned a talent agency; Vincent was born into a family of athletes. Polly and Marc were international royalty, representing their countries through dance. And, of course, Sebastian, with his low social aptitude, was a walking brand magnet at the sweet age of sixteen. Ian was the only average human in SG.

He didn't belong in SG, but one crazy night at a party freshman year changed his social life. Dancing with Vega led to them hooking up and she gifting him with an SG committee position. Before SG, he had a few dancer friends plus Zoey.

Sometimes, he really missed them. His old friends had cared about what he thought. They didn't force him to wear polos or go to parties. They didn't assign him tasks, and they didn't talk through student assemblies.

He grew annoyed with SG, wishing they'd shut up about their summer vacations and listen to Pa Raines. History was unfolding before their eyes, and SG didn't care.

"I worked at my ma's Latin Club in Long Beach," he replied to Mahogany's question.

She was trying to include him in the conversation, but his summer was boring compared to their global adventures to places like Madrid and Abu Dhabi.

"Why don't you invite me to El Famoso more?" Mahogany asked. "Maybe we can all go dancing."

El Famoso was his only sanctuary away from CLASH. He'd die before he let them colonize it. "You sure? You hate Zoey. And Zoey's always there."

Mahogany rolled her eyes and turned away from him. "I'm rooting for everyone Black."

Sure, he believed Mahogany was rooting for Zoey to succeed as long as that success didn't interfere with her plans. He loved Mahogany, but she was so possessive. Such an SG trait. If Mahogany wasn't monopolizing his time then it was Vega. Pleasing them was as stressful as monogamy, utterly exhausting, and not to mention an identity killer. He needed space. He was never inviting them to El Famoso.

"This year is an exceptional year," Pa Raines announced. "Because our school is the film set of Sebastian and Vega Bautista's docuseries. Every student attending today had to receive permission from a parental guardian."

That or find another school. Ian slouched further in his seat. He couldn't abandon Zoey, so he had his padres sign the paperwork.

Greg stepped onstage, and SG stood, so Ian stood. He clapped even though he didn't want to hear Greg recite Vega's words. She sent the speech for their feedback, so Ian knew she was the brains behind every metaphor leaving Greg's lips. She should be onstage. Not Greg.

He glanced down the row at Matthew, a second-string soccer player who drove an SUV. Matthew grinned.

Ian felt his phone vibrate in his pocket.

Matthew: You look bored.
Ian: I'm so bored.
Matthew: How can I change that?

Ian glanced upward as he thought of a fun reply. His eyes flickered backstage, and he caught sight of Sebastian and Vega arguing behind the curtains. There was something beautiful about the angry Bautistas. Their skin reddened, their eyes big, their lips snatched backward. Ian leaned forward, wanting to hear their verbal attacks, especially Vega's.

Sebastian peered at the audience, then stepped behind the curtains.

A colossal wave of FOMO swallowed Ian whole. *Man.* He slumped back against the seats, grabbing his phone.

Ian: Down for a quick hook up?

Matthew: Leave now?

Ian: Meet you at your SUV.

CHAPTER 6

SEBASTIAN

he was tired of arguing with his sister, but Amy loved it. He could tell. She whispered for the cameras to capture close-ups, but Sebastian shoved them back with his eyes.

"It'll take five minutes," he begged Vega. Less than that to run their waltz. Their change steps into the reverse turns were off, and he could correct that, but Vega wouldn't step away from the backstage curtains.

"It's the waltz, not *Swan Lake*," Vega snapped. "We don't need to go over it a hundred times."

"We haven't gone over it enough."

"You're a crazy addict. Go away." Vega turned her focus back to Gregory.

Gregory looked powerful, commanding the stage, encased in blue lighting. What a fraud. Vega had picked out Gregory's outfit, wrote his speech, and coached his enunciation. She had poured so much energy into creating this illusion, and no one would ever know cause Vega didn't write a personal thank you in her speech.

"Pathetic." Sebastian gave up.

"You're pathetic," Vega yelled.

He found a seat in a corner where he could create his dancescape. It took a while for his mind to relax. The pressure from the cameras and sound lightened. Gregory's voice became a hum. The images of the Viennese Waltz fell away, replaced with memories of him and Vega at age thirteen, Papá still living with them in California. Papá used to wake up the entire family so they could drive to dance on the beach. Vega never complained then about waking up early. They would practice ballet on demi-pointe with the sands massaging their soles. Sebastian used to love dancing with his sister. She knew enough to anticipate his movements. Then they turned fourteen. Their abuelito died, and Papá returned to Madrid to oversee the family's ballet company. Papá became someone he watched in commercials and in movies. Then Papá released a memoir about the Bautista legacy. It became an international bestseller, opening the door for Sebastian's Hulu docuseries. And to think he couldn't finish the memoir. Each story about him and his sister united in dance stung, agitating wounds that wouldn't scab. Vega wouldn't let him heal, wanting him as broken as she. She made dancing, his only love, unbearable. Ugly.

The crowd clapped.

Sebastian opened his eyes, catching a camera lens zooming in. The stage manager waved him towards the curtains. He approached, masking his emotions so that he could look the part as much as he dressed. He wore a black tailcoat suit with a blue shirt and pocket handkerchief that matched Vega's ball gown. Saygrace's *You Don't Own Me* poured from the speakers. He would have never picked that song, but Vega said the song declared her individuality.

He held Vega in an offset position, applying upward pressure to her palms, gliding her forward. Everything went well. She sidestepped on two, swaying on two three. He tried to lead her into a reverse natural turn, and she stepped on his right foot so hard it hurt. He bit the inside of his cheek. Her form worsened, and her breathless counting didn't help.

He couldn't risk turning her again, so he kept their steps basic till the song ended. He spun her into a bow. She was all smiles and glowing eyes. As if she had danced the best dance of her life.

He hurried away from Vega, from Amy, from the cameras and sound recorders. He burst into the air, his right foot throbbing from Vega's misstep. He was done with her, her insults, her flakiness. Not another year. He was finding a dance partner he loved.

CHAPTER 7

ZOEY

zoey had studied social dancing since she could walk, so she knew Vega and Sebastian were struggling. *How wild!* The entire school was watching, not to mention cameras filmed, and they looked like they hadn't practiced together.

If she were Vega, she would have worked her butt off to make Sebastian look phenomenal. She would spin in big circles with him, relishing his touch. He the prince to her princess. They'd be royalty, and no one would call them Frog Legs.

She winced when Vega stepped on Sebastian's foot. That looked painful, but Sebastian didn't miss a step, gliding Vega back on beat. Good for him. She would have needed the curtains to drop so she could limp off stage for the school nurse. Sebastian remained in control, reminding Zoey of the bachata dancers at Ian's family studio. When she wasn't working there, she was dancing, losing herself in the rhythms, coming alive with each twist of her body. Her partners grounding her feet, guiding her into each spicy, delicious move. It was so thrilling. Dance brought every human life, so maybe Vega wasn't human but a corpse in a ballroom dress.

Poor Sebastian. He loved dancing, and he was stuck dancing with a corpse.

Everyone clapped, startling Zoey out of her head. She'd been so caught up thinking about Vega, the corpse, she had missed the end. That was the worst waltz ever, and probably no one else would think the same.

Instagram confirmed her theory. People were commenting that Vega's performance was everything. Zoey clicked on her own profile. A CLASH-mate had posted her back-to-school outfit, tagging her in it. There were so many likes. Hearts and smiley faces galore. And people still called her Frog Legs when her social handle read Fashionista Zoey! She'd have to create a miracle to erase Frog Legs from CLASH history. Meanwhile, Vega could embarrass a prodigy in front of the whole school and get nothing but love. Life was so unfair.

Zoey stomped to first period, pausing when she felt something loosen at her back. She reached around, running her fingers over the back of her neck. She could feel the zipper but couldn't tell what was wrong. She needed a mirror. Rushing into first period, she headed straight for the wall-to-wall mirror in the back. Her eyes went huge. Her dress was ripping apart from the zipper. A total fail. She had to fix this.

She slammed her bookbag on a nearby desk, stretching to the bottom for her sewing kit. It had to be here. She flipped the bag over when she couldn't feel the hardshell case. Notebooks toppled out with colored pencils and erasers, but no sewing kit. She rubbed her forehead, flustered. Where the heck was her sewing kit?

"Already making a mess?" Mrs. Sehar called from the front of the sewing lab.

Zoey hadn't even noticed her teacher sitting behind the desk. "Happy first day, Mrs. Sehar." She hid her panic, not wanting her favorite teacher to know the embarrassing truth. She messed up her dress. If Ian could earn an Oscar for codeswitching, she was about to earn hers for pretending she was fine in the middle of a disaster.

"Happy first day." Mrs. Sehar finished pinning a butterfly barrette to her purple hijab and waved Zoey to her desk. "A Hip-Hop re-imagining of Miraculous Ladybug. Love it."

"Thank you!" Zoey crossed her arms, hoping that would hold her dress up long enough to survive this conversation. She wanted to slip away, but Mrs. Sehar kept talking.

"Junior year, you've finally made it. And this is a big year for you. I want you to push yourself beyond your comfort zone so you can get into your dream program."

Already doing that and failing. She feigned excitement. "I want to study in Paris."

"Really? Did I tell you I studied at the Paris College of Art? I keep in touch with my professors and can be a reference."

Zoey screamed. That would be huge. She threw her hands over her mouth. Her future was becoming a masterpiece, just like she dreamed.

Mrs. Sehar handed Zoey her syllabi. "Can you help me pass these out?"

She needed to save her dress, but she couldn't say no when all she could count on was her role as the teacher's pet. It was a highly coveted position. CLASH-mates competed for it shamelessly, but Zoey had all the time in the world to earn teacher's pet. Arriving students tossed her dirty looks once they saw she was already tasked with handing out syllabi. *Sorry, not sorry.* Zoey squashed the thought. Sophomore-year her would have flaunted her teacher's pet status in their faces. But she wanted friends, so she stayed humble, smiling at the first student she handed a syllabus. Then she skipped to the next.

Marly, who was usually late, rushed right through the door and into Zoey. Syllabi scattered everywhere.

"Oh my god, I'm so sorry." Marly went on hands and knees to help.

Zoey bent over, her zipper bursting open. She popped up to save a dress that was nothing more than trash swinging in the air conditioning. Embarrassment flooded her body, her hands and arms shaking. CLASH-mates pulled out their phones. 'Zoey eats Mr. Rogers' dead frogs' flashed through her head, and suddenly she was staring at Vega. Big, fat, laughing faces closed in. The classroom became the cafeteria, extremely cold and unwelcoming. Zoey crossed her arms, bending her body to protect her lingerie from the cruelty.

She felt sick, her legs shaky. Was she in the cafeteria or her sewing class? She struggled to remember seconds before. Her thoughts hazy, overwhelmed by the laughter and the phones pushing closer to film her shame. This would be all over social media. They'd make memes about her, and she'd have another stupid nickname.

Mrs. Sehar yanked a tablecloth from her storage closet and threw it over Zoey's panties and bra. They were Lady Bug-inspired, remnants of her disastrous outfit. "Head to the front office and ask for clothes."

Zoey couldn't move.

Mrs. Sehar shoved her past the exit, yelling, "Put your phones away now," and slamming the door.

CHAPTER 8
SEBASTIAN

shame smothered him. CLASH-mates gave him half-hearted fist bumps and sent him pity-filled looks. 'Stop staring! People mess up!' he wanted to yell. Even though he didn't believe that. Others messed up, not him. He had a flawless reputation. Then Vega stomped on his foot. Shame built in his throat like vomit.

Ballet III was about to begin, and if he danced this angry, he'd hurt himself or his CLASH-mates. He found a spot at the back of the studio. Inhaling and folding into a butterfly stretch, pressing his forehead to the floor. Blackness filled his vision. Blackness was his happy place, or it could be if Vega wasn't so close, if he didn't have to listen to SG lie to her about how great she danced. *Why are they so close?* They weren't having a student government meeting.

"Can you guys back off?" he snapped.

Vega and Ian looked stunned, Marc, Polly, and Mahogany hurt as if the studio wasn't big enough for him to have personal space.

40

Maybe he should spell it out for them. He pointed across the studio. "I need space, and there's space for you guys over there."

"So now you're in charge of space distribution?" Vega asked.

A countdown set off inside him. He jumped up. Ten seconds till meltdown. That's how long they had to move. He felt the cameras' giant eyeballs on him.

"Sebastian," Mrs. Agnes called.

He snapped his head in her direction.

"Please lead the barre routine."

Mrs. Agnes just saved him, or rather SG, from getting pummeled. His teacher's small, muscled frame dressed in forest colors was enough to ease the overwhelming madness brewing within. He forced a deep breath, forcing his feet to the center. The cameramen pushed close, making the studio claustrophobic even with its enormous windows. Those windows usually gave him a sense of freedom, but today he felt stuck, trapped inside a loser's body.

Polly's awkward attitude snapped him out of his mental hell. He hurried to lift her knee so it was in line with her toe. He repositioned Marc's arm while he relevéd. Vega's foot sickled in dévelopé, which wouldn't happen if she did the strengthening exercises he recommended.

He adjusted her foot, and she kicked his hand away. Squashing the sensation burning his stomach, he tried a different tactic: lead by example. He unfolded his leg into dévelopé first position, demonstrating the point of his foot.

From hip bone to pointed toe, his line was as straight as the barre. All Vega had to do, for once, was mimic him.

Vega turned her head to piss him off. He knew her thoughts as if they were his own. She thought he was trying to make her into him. Wrong. He was pushing her to perfection. Perfection was the bar for the Bautista family. It was in her genes.

Mrs. Agnes squeezed Sebastian's shoulder. "Relax," she whispered before leading him and the rest of the class to the center for the across-the-floor routine.

What was Mrs. Agnes talking about? He was relaxed.

The cameramen filmed Mrs. Agnes, and he watched her dark skin form lines emboldened by lean muscle. Like always, he drowned in her movements, only finding ground when she called the first group of dancers to move across the floor.

Ian and Vega volunteered to go first.

He wished Vega had chosen to dance with someone else. Ian's command of movement made Vega look like a beginner struggling to match Ian's ability to play with tempo. Sebastian felt sick watching her wasted talent, knowing his family had dedicated their lives to dance for generations. Their grandparents owned a ballet company in Madrid where Vega had trained every summer. They had traveled with their papá to learn the professional life of a celebrity dancer. They rehearsed long hours with their mother, so they knew what it took for their mamá to be a WDC World

Champion. Yet all of that knowledge and promise meant nothing to Vega.

"Can we talk?" Sebastian asked Vega after class. He tried to sound friendly so she wouldn't fight him.

Vega glanced back to SG waiting at the door. Ian wanted to watch them fight, but Mahogany, Polly, and Marc were used to their arguments, so they waved and told Vega they would see her at lunch. Mahogany dragged Ian with her, leaving Vega behind.

Sebastian promised to keep their conversation short. "I just want to talk about this morning."

"It's history," Vega groaned.

"Not really."

"I need to spend all of lunch picking a theme for the Back-to-School Bash. Greg's announcing he's running this year, and it needs to be epic, so I don't have time for this."

He could see Amy waving the cameras and sound closer, but he wasn't going to give Amy the emotion she wanted. He took a deep breath, cooling the fire burning in his chest. "You know what this docuseries means to me, right? We're Bautistas. Our family has been dancing for generations. And everything we do is bigger than social media; it's bigger than ad deals. We'll represent our family this year at our Fall Showcase, showing the Bautista commitment to excellence in dance. So I need you to be better than you are."

"Great, dream big," Vega started, "Love it, however, I'm not spending twenty-four hours a day in a dance studio trying to achieve your version of perfection."

"How about one hour a day after school?"

"No, I'll give you a couple hours on the weekend."

"That's not enough."

"That's all I got. I'm running Greg's campaign. He needs me." Vega tried to walk around him, but he wouldn't move.

"Find the time."

"Move." Vega pushed him, but he grabbed her hands, refusing to let them go even though she kept pulling.

"Find the time, or I'll replace you."

"You can't replace me. Who would want to dance with you? I'm the only reason you have any friends."

"Like I said, choose what's more important, running Gregory's fan club or being my dance partner." He released her.

She stumbled backward onto her butt. He instantly felt terrible. She swatted his hands whenever he tried to help her stand. "I helped you build your fame," she yelled. "You didn't do it all by yourself. You're such a jerk. And no one wants to dance with an obsessive jerk."

Not another year. He wasn't enduring her mess for another year.

Barging into Mrs. Agnes' office, he slammed the door behind him. But, oh yeah, privacy was no longer a thing now that he was making a doc. Amy squeezed through the door. Two cameramen and the sound guy followed.

Mrs. Agnes held him with her gaze, her eyes soft and kind. She let him breathe until the flames burning his stomach cooled.

"I've thought about this long and hard," he said. "Vega hates dancing with me, so I'm dropping her."

Mrs. Agnes massaged her hands in lotion. "Watching you and your sister reminds me of dancing for the Opéra National de Paris." Her French accent was still thick even after five years of teaching ballet in America. "There's a lot of pressure. Very little room for failure. It feels like the world is on your shoulders. And that emotion, the desire to succeed, can blind you to what matters: blood. You and your sister love each other deeply."

"*Aimer, ce n'est pas se regarder l'un l'autre, c'est regarder ensemble dans la même direction,*" Sebastian quoted from the famous children's book Le Petit Prince. To love is not to look at each other. It is to look together in the same direction. He loved that quote. He had first heard it at his Aunt Adrianna's wedding in Alsace. It was a popular wedding quote, so he guessed Mrs. Agnes would recognize it, and he had guessed right.

She smiled, very sad. "You know you'll hurt her feelings if you simply drop her instead of working to find a compromise?"

He didn't want to compromise. He wanted Vega to be great. As it stood, her mediocrity was squeezing every drop of joy from the one aspect of his life that gave him purpose. He had found his love, and all he needed to do was find someone who loved dancing with him. Like his papá found Mamá. That was it. Dumping Vega would free him to find a partner who loved dancing with him as much as he loved dance.

"You've made up your mind, I see," Mrs. Agnes said. "Do you know this one, 'Ce que femme veut, Dieu le veut,' from the French poet Alfred de Musset? It's my favorite."

"What a woman wants, God wants," Sebastian replied. "Sounds like a challenge. Défi relevé, Dieu." Challenge accepted, God. He made a cross to a God he didn't believe existed. Outside of the classroom-led prayers, it was the first prayer he initiated that year.

"Wait?" Amy asked, so confused she broke the fourth wall. "That's it?" She searched Sebastian for signs she misunderstood the conversation, her eyes then begging him to change his mind. "She's central to the story. Remember all those conversations we had all summer?"

Many of those conversations were Amy chatting away while he focused on dancing. She was excited about leveraging the success of his papá's book so that they could tell a story about the next generation of Bautista dancers. He'd usually tune out most of what she said. Sometimes, she'd take him to grab pho. Amy was Korean, but her comfort food was pho. In those moments, he'd eat his beef pho and try to get her to talk about anything but the docuseries. He'd ask what it was like being a third-generation Korean American, why she moved to Los Angeles, why she liked the chicken pho instead of the beef, why summer rolls were summer.

"I remember the summer rolls," he finally replied.

Amy grabbed her cell phone and exited, very upset, knowing he was dropping Vega.

CHAPTER 9
IAN

he always felt imposter syndrome when he walked into the CLASH cafeteria on the first day of school. It gave startup tech vibes with its blue walls decorated in donated murals. A reinterpretation of Bach as trap music played from the speakers, an ode to CLASH's first Black principal. Not the average school cafeteria. Attending Malcolm X Primary up to third grade taught him that much.

He breathed, his imposter syndrome eased by fried chicken, macaroni, and … deep inhale … banana pudding, smells that reminded him of Thanksgiving at his Godparents' house. Looks like the culinary students prepared a soul-food-inspired menu to go with the trap music. Fried chicken salad with a yam puree, honey-drizzled corn-bread, pure torture when he knew he wouldn't be able to eat any of it.

SG never wanted to eat the cafeteria food, always buying lunch, running up their parents' credit cards without asking permission. And what was another thirty bucks spent on him? Another way to shout, money didn't matter.

He headed to the SG table. CLASH faculty designed the lunchroom to encourage engagement, but SG didn't care. They chose a bench in the center, using the adjoining benches for their bags so no one could sit too close.

A brown bag waited for him. He sat down, opening it. A plant-based burger sat at the bottom. Today must be Polly's day. She was vegan, and the only one who would force veganism on him. Vega always wanted sushi. Vincent tried to order from minority-owned businesses, and Greg and Marc loved anything fried, while Sebastian only ate healthy. He hated it when Sebastian and Polly ordered his lunch. Mahogany always asked. She was the only one who did, and that's when he stole the opportunity to buy cafeteria food. He really wished it was Mahogany's day.

"How about techficial?" Polly chirped, her South African accent coating her words.

Ian stared, confused.

"Like technology and official. We can dress up like business execs."

Oh, they were pitching themes for the Bradfords' Back-to-School Bash. It was just another platform for the Bradfords to showcase their wealth and announce that one of them was running for student body president. The Bradfords had four generations of boys, with Greg being the youngest. All the Bradfords had been president, and now it was Greg's turn.

Ian wondered if now was a good time to ask if Zoey could make the invite list this year. She was trending on social. People loved her outfit. Maybe that could go in her favor.

"How bout GOAT?" Marc suggested.

Did people still say that? "I like techficial," he said only because he didn't want to spend his lunch listening to them brag about how they were the "greatest of all time." He got it. They were all rich–except him–and gorgeous. Next topic. "Is the guestlist finished?"

"Not yet." Greg smiled.

"I'm thinking Zoey Raines."

They fell silent, knowing that was his bestie even though it was an unspoken rule, no besties outside of SG.

"Let's get Vega's thoughts on that," Greg replied.

Coward. Ian glanced at the door, searching for signs of Vega's purple heels. Thirty minutes left till lunch and Vega still wasn't there. If Sebastian made Vega miss lunch, Greg would have the time to create an excuse for why he couldn't add Zoey to the guestlist.

His phone vibrated with a text.

Matthew: Want to meet up and finish what we started?
Ian: Want to but can't.

He had to wait for Vega even though he wasn't sure she'd make it. He finished his sandwich and, feeling the strongest urge to stress eat, looked at Polly's sweet potato fries. "Can

I have some?" She said, "Yes," and he scooped them up. The salty sweetness eased his stress only a little.

He caught sight of Vega barging through the double doors, straight to their table. She was flustered red, her hair slightly messy, less polished, her lips bruised from nibbling. Fighting with Sebastian made Vega more attractive and less out of reach. He loved it. Normally, he'd make a remark, pushing her to spill the tea, but he couldn't set her off even more. Not yet.

"Did you guys pick a theme?" She reached for her sushi tray, a California roll surrounded by sashimi.

"Techficial," Polly replied.

Vega made a face. She didn't get it. "Next."

Ian cut in with, "I liked your Next Gen Leaders idea from last year. That was lit." Vega loved it when he championed her ideas. And he needed her to love him so she'd be willing to consider Zoey.

"We need to top last year's theme."

"How about Black Violin?" Vincent asked.

Ian grew excited. "Black Violin, a vampire ball. We could all get vampire teeth, dress in couture, and play classically remixed compositions," and the Bautistas could confess that they were vampires posing as humans.

"Love that. Let's do it," Vega said. "Polly, can you create a post with the theme, hinting that the party invites will come out this Friday?" When Vega smiled at him, Ian knew he earned the privilege to bring up Zoey.

"I'm wondering if we can add Zoey Raines to the guestlist?"

Vega chewed her sashimi. "I don't know. She might sneak a frog into the party."

"That's mean."

"How so? Vega shouldn't have to invite people she hates."

Ian shot Mahogany a look. There goes rooting for everyone Black. "I thought we were about inviting innovators."

"How exactly is Frog Legs an innovator?" Vega asked.

"Her back-to-school outfit is an insertion of herself into a pop culture moment, modernizing and making it new." SG loved his statement, voicing their agreement. Mahogany was the only hater, claiming, "It was loud."

Vega looked almost persuaded. "Did she post her outfit?"

Polly whipped out her phone, clicking to Zoey's handle and laughing. She shoved her phone at Vega.

"Oh my God," Vega gasped. "Poor, Frog Legs."

Ian went straight to TikTok. Personally curated for his viewing pleasure, a feed of one-minute renditions of Zoey standing naked in the middle of a sewing lab. His face went hot, a warm sensation brewing below his stomach. Zoey was eye candy, her hips curving to boobs he loved squeezing. He let his mind play for a second, slamming his phone down. This was a setback.

"Zoey's matching panties are fire," Vincent said as if that would make things better.

More than a setback. This was horrifying. CLASH-mates sucked the life out of gossip as if every drop increased the likelihood they'd survive their gruesome studies. And his bestie was the worst kind of gossip, exam relief porn. What better way to cheer up a friend on exam night than to text them a screenshot of the loser with the nice body? His chest tightened, thinking about all the people benefiting from Zoey's pain. Standing, he grabbed his phone.

Ian: Where are you?
Zoey: Hiding in the chapel.

"Latin lover to the rescue?" Vega asked.

"We picked a theme. Greg killed his speech. What else do we need to talk about?"

"Frog Leg's outfit. I'm impressed. Maybe if she can overcome this social disaster, I'll consider it an achievement and reward her with guestlist status."

That would take a miracle with Vega's high standards. If he told Zoey that, he would be playing with her emotions. "I'll send her your love," he winked, deciding to be the good white bitch to her evil black bitch. He grabbed his books and ran to the chapel.

He found Zoey splayed out on the third row, her hands covering her face, shielding her from the eyes of the white baby Jesus smiling down from the multicolored glass mural. She must have spent moments before thrifting through CLASH's Lost and Found, which was on par with the Bel Air Goodwill. CLASH-mates were notorious for wearing an outfit twice before "dropping it at the L&L." Zoey had cut the gray sweats into baggy shorts, pairing them with an oversized jersey she cut into a crop top with a shoulder strap.

"Love how you always find gold in the L&L." He poked her legs till she made room for him.

Zoey groaned, rolling up into his arms. "This is the worst day of my life."

"Are you sure?" He scanned his memories. There was that time when they got sick and puked all over themselves at Magic Mountain. There was also that time they got a ticket for being out late in Long Beach and had to do community service at their neighborhood YWCA. That was miserable. They had to clean bathrooms and fax papers. There was also that time he got invited to the Halsey pre-album release party because Vincent's cousin had invited Greg, and he couldn't take Zoey even though she loved Halsey. "I feel like we've lived through so many horrible events together."

"I can't make a comeback from this. They're calling me Sexy-Panty Zoey. The video has a million views. I'm dying." She held the phone close to his face. Her social embarrassment played on loop.

"I'm so glad you went the extra mile and designed matching bra and panties. You look so good."

Zoey glared at him. "I need honesty from you, not compliments."

He pressed his lips together. How could he inspire Zoey without making her think she had a chance with Vega? "The truth is your outfit almost worked. I asked Vega if I could bring you to the Back-to-School Bash, and she was impressed."

"Until she saw all the social posts and decided I'm too embarrassing to invite. Yay, me."

"Yeah, but you were so close. You have all the talent you need to wow people. You don't need Vega and Greg's stupid party. You don't need CLASH." He looked around the polished chapel with its dark wooden benches, freshly painted blue walls, and White Baby Jesus. A rainbow sign plastered on the front read, 'All are welcomed,' but he didn't feel welcomed. This wasn't his church. His church had a Latin Jesus with faded walls and ancient Bibles. The CLASH chapel was a museum, not a church, and it wasn't a place for Compton kids like them. "We might go to CLASH, but we're not CLASH," Ian said. "We have so much talent, but we're not like them, so people don't see it."

"People see you, Ian, and you promised that you'd help me get seen." Zoey grabbed his hands. "You said this year you were going to help me become popular and that we were both going to kick ass and earn a scholarship to Paris. That's why we're suffering through French."

Yeah, he remembered promising that. Back when she had a nightmare that inspired a back-to-school panic attack. They were months from returning to school, and the only way to calm her was to make a promise that inspired her to stay committed to her loves. And he had to remain committed to Zoey. They were best friends, the only ones from Compton.

Compton before Bel Air always.

CHAPTER 10

ZOEY

marly made a how-to-sew TikTok using Zoey's nudes. The audacity, when Marly was her dress killer, her bad karma The Universe delivered as punishment for … for sex outside of marriage. Although if God cared about that, Ian would have no limbs. And he stayed gorgeous and sexed up. It was Zoey who suffered. And she couldn't think of one thing she did to deserve getting her work critiqued by a C-student like Marly.

She ground her teeth. Marly wasn't even using the correct terms. Bottom stitching? Did she mean understitching? And Zoey hadn't used a serger for the hems cause guess what, Marly! Vegan leather doesn't fray.

Zoey tossed her phone in her bag. She was fasting social media. People were driving her crazy. She'd work so hard on that outfit. And the fabric cost her a hundred bucks, money that was now nothing more than recyclable scrapes that she donated to the fashion department. She needed a pick-me-up. Froyo or the Alumni Corridor. Both were great, but the Alumni Corridor was calorie-free, and she needed a treat that inspired.

The Alumni Corridor was a hallway of success, located near the principal's office. She walked the blue marble tiles, eying the stingray mural painted on the ceiling. A sense of awe bubbled through and around her body as if she were underwater. She passed the cases, holding trophies and gold medals. One day, she'd have a trophy. Slowing to a stop, she faced the portraits of successful alumni. The jewels of CLASH. One day, her portrait would hang there.

Her eyes settled on her fave. Forty-two-year-old Sloane Magnolia wearing a gold romper with matching shoes, posing in full-body glory. Zoey wanted her portrait to be just like Magnolia's. She wanted to be Magnolia, a self-made businesswoman with three global fashion lines. Magnolia didn't come from money. Zoey remembered as much from when the designer spoke in her Fashion Design and Art II class sophomore year. Wanting to cherish the moment forever, Zoey recorded Magnolia's speech and posted it on YouTube. Thank goodness she had. She was hungry for the motivation.

She replayed the video, listening to Magnolia describe a shocking lesson she learned in fourth grade. Returning home from school, she had discovered her next-door neighbor sleeping on their couch. "It was a tight fit. We owned a one-bedroom apartment in Koreatown," Magnolia said. Her mom had scaled down so she could open a food truck. "I'm this nine-year-old stuck living with a single mom and a broke artist. And I attend school with wealthy kids. I thought, man. I'm worthless. I don't have any money. My mom doesn't have any money. And my neighbor's an artist who can't even keep a roof over her head. Maybe I should become an engineer."

No, you shouldn't. Engineers are boring.

"Mom moving in my neighbor was life-changing for me. My neighbor was a painter, and she showed up to her easel every day. She didn't let emotions get in the way. She had a vision of success, telling me once, 'My art is important. If I don't create, who is, for our culture?' And I thought to myself, what excuse do I have? My neighbor's broke and homeless, but she still shows up. I remember becoming this easel, molded by my neighbor's dedication to her craft. And in exchange, my mom and I became her business coaches. We pushed her to apply for grants, network, learn to animate so she could fund her painting. Our family collaboration launched my first business. And I tell you this story cause I want you to walk away with the same lesson I learned: Create for yourself, for people you love. Collaborate with artists that inspire and challenge you to love the world through your art. And one day, you'll look up, and every area of your life, including your art, will overflow with money and love. And that money and love will transform the universe."

Zoey lowered her phone, her eyes moist. This was the calorie-free inspiration she needed. She might have failed to love people through her art, but she couldn't quit and join the tech department. She had to keep designing, for the love if not for herself. One day, she'd create a masterpiece that'd blow everyone's mind. That's what she craved.

She dragged her feet down the hall. Any day now, she'd turn her life around, just like Magnolia. Vega would hate her winning. What she wouldn't give to throw success in Vega's face, proving she wasn't weak. She'd sell her soul.

Sorry God, but this was war.

She stopped, noticing a blue flier hanging on the wall. That was against the rules. CLASH treated the Alumni Corridor like a sanctuary. Only the chapel had more status. No one was allowed to hang their announcements. Feeling protective, she reached to snatch it down, hesitating when she saw Sebastian leaping across the flier. Of course, he'd get permission. 'Co-Star in my Hulu Doc,' was in sans-serif, the perfect typeface for his minimalist personality. 'Dance auditions in Studio D115 immediately after school every day, Aug. 7 to Aug. 25.'

But you already have a co-star. She reread the poster, confused. Does this mean Sebastian dropped his sister? His twin sister?

She couldn't believe it. She had prayed for this moment, yes, but it was so unlike Sebastian. She read it again, pressing her hands to her temples, amazed. Sebastian stayed loyal to Vega, surviving her drama with the intensity of a Blood surviving the streets for a Blood. And Sebastian's commitment to his family was so sexy. Loyalty mattered. Family above all else. That was the Compton mythos in a neighborhood where people died for each other. But now Sebastian was dropping his sister?

Zoey laughed uncontrollably. Was this a plot twist? She searched the corridor for cameras hiding to catch the CLASH-mate thirsty enough to fall for this setup. Television producers intentionally planted plot twists to boost entertainment. And Zoey was thirsty, but was she thirsty enough to become a plot twist?

She tilted her head, eyes rolling upward. Should she audition? It would be unexpected, and CLASH loved surprises. And she really needed a surprise to redefine her. Fashion might not be enough. Today was proof of that. She shuddered, thinking about her dress. Dance might just be the brand makeover she desperately needed. And she was a sexy dancer. She danced salsa and bachata since forever. Ian could help with ballet.

If she auditioned, Sebastian would be her prize. She fingered the flier, rubbing the glossy ink. He was the human embodiment of Sloan's advice. He'd inspire and challenge her, and she'd create fashion around him, finally exploring minimalism in her work. She could manifest her life plot twist, a fashion rebirth.

A rush bloomed in her chest, and Zoey felt like she was smashing through waves. She imagined Vega crying tears of jealousy, reading all the posts celebrating her rebirth as the Fashion Ballerina.

She ripped the poster off the wall. She was taking Vega down.

"Good. You haven't left yet."

She spun around.

Dad squeezed his briefcase and empty lunch bag, looking like he had been in too many meetings.

"I was waiting for Ian. He hasn't texted yet," she replied.

"Let Ian drive your car to El Famoso so we can ride together."

She became suspicious. Dad never liked Ian driving her car. "Okay."

"I want to talk to you about today."

I'd rather not. She hunted for an excuse, and when nothing came, she texted Ian and followed Dad out to his blue jaguar. The school got it for him so he wouldn't be caught dead driving a five-year-old minivan.

He made a stop at her favorite taco restaurant, Mami's. She waited for him, mentally preparing for Dad's speech by chanting, "I'm not going to cry," under her breath. Zoey attended church with her family, and over the years, Dad had learned to mimic the bravado of his pastors, spinning every life obstacle into a sermon. And those sermons always made her cry, but she didn't feel like crying again over her outfit. She wanted to think about how good it would feel when Sebastian chose her as his co-star, and she could throw it in Vega's face.

He returned to the car with a fat carne asada burrito.

"I want you to know how proud of you I am," he said, pulling onto the 405. Dad kept calling her beautiful and smart. "When you brought home your final design last year, that Maya Angelou *Still I Rise,*" embroidered cap with the matching dress decorated with literary quotes, I thought, I birthed a genius."

"I know you saw the video, Dad." Gold grease dripped from her burrito and onto the napkins covering her thighs. She sipped horchata, letting her tongue swish in the sweet milk. "I'm okay. We don't have to talk about it."

"We do. This is LA. And I'm sorry, baby girl, people in this city are cruel and will seize any opportunity to boost their social media followers without caring about the impact on another human being. But you're not people's inhumanity. People do what they do out here. But you keep rising, baby. Just keep your head high and rise."

I'm crying. I'm crying.

Dad pulled into the parking lot. His words simmered inside her, filling her belly like the carne asada burrito. She stared at El Famoso, a three-story Latin club. It had been her daycare, her wild night outs, her first part-time job, and it would soon be her training camp.

CHAPTER 11
IAN

zoey: can you drive my car to el famoso?
Ian: Sure.

He was too distracted to ask why they weren't riding together. The CLASH hallways were filled with energy. People laughed, and music played as if there were some kind of party. He didn't know why, and that bothered him. Shoving through the bodies, he reached for a flier. 'Co-Star in My Hulu Doc,' the headline read. Sebastian danced under the bold letters. The poster was cheesy, but the message was clear. The Bautistas had broken up.

He gaped, remembering the Bautistas arguing in Ballet III. They were always arguing, but was this now the end? He balled up the paper, tossing it in the trash. Honestly, this wasn't a surprise. Everyone knew they had a toxic relation-ship. Vega was a talented dancer but mediocre, caring more about Greg and SG than dance. Sebastian's only love was dance, and he would die alone, buried with his ballet shoes.

A horrible match. Now that they weren't dancing together, they were free to argue less.

Ian would miss the arguments, Vega's feisty looks and messy hair, Sebastian's intense snarls. They were so hot when they fought, better than television. And CLASH loved making a big deal out of drama. Everyone was probably conducting an investigation into who dropped who. He hoped it was Vega sticking up for herself, but he didn't care enough to stick around. He strolled to the parking lot. It wasn't his problem. He tossed his bookbag in the back-seat of Zoey's Corolla, mentally prepping for the traffic. It'd be killer.

The SG group message went off.

Polly: Emergency meeting at Greg's.

Polly was probably standing somewhere with Vega looking at the fliers.

Ian: Can't. Have to work tonight.

And sad face emojis just to make them think he was sorry for missing out, which truthfully, he wasn't.

He drove past the UCLA campus and turned onto Interstate 405, heading South.

El Famoso reminded him of the ancient temples in Teotihuacan, Mexico. Three stories high, with each floor looking down on the one below. There was a restaurant with an outdoor patio on the second floor. The third floor had two dance rooms that also doubled as rehearsal spaces. Oscar D'Leon boomed from the third-floor dance studio where Ma shouted, "One, two, three … five, six, seven" at her students.

The class focused on styling, and Ma pushed the salseros past their limits, and that's what Ian loved the most. Unlike CLASH, El Famoso was a safe space where he could push past his limits. He felt free to move in ways unexpected. He joined the Tech and Hippie Nerds at the front of the class and quickly learned Ma's dance for the night. Years of ballet had dressed up his salsa so that he lengthened his arms and smoothed his turns. The regulars knew he was the teacher's son, so few stared in awe as he danced.

He started making his rounds, stopping to help a short blonde in a mini-skirt struggling to get the turn right. Then he corrected the muscle head stepping on four instead of holding for five. He helped the dancers in the back, slowing the trickiest steps for people to copy. There was always a sudden rise in energy when the last song played, and people gave their all. Then, they'd linger to record Ma performing the routine before class ended. The students yelled, "Thanks, Tanya. See you next week," and headed into the night.

Drenched in sweat, he felt so alive. This was the love he was looking for at CLASH, a love he'd never find there inside that stuffy academy.

He hugged Ma and, feeling amazing, he hugged Tech and Hippie Nerds. He had hugs for days.

"How was your first day?" Ma asked.

"Crazy." What news should he drop first? Zoey. She was more important than Sebastian. He raised his phone with Zoey's TikTok loaded. His padres crowded around to watch. The mood soured as Zoey's pain stretched from his tiny cell phone and hugged them, squeezing tight. He felt sadder watching Zoey's colossal fail with his family. Maybe because they loved Zoey. At school, CLASH-mates were pricks, only wanting a good laugh.

He let Ma take his phone and bring it close to her face. As if that would make it easier to process Zoey's shame. "I have to call Janet," Ma said. "Did Frederick say anything?"

"Nope." His godparents didn't say a thing. Not to him at least. He wanted to move on to Sebastian's flier. That news burned his chest, and he tried to get Ma's thoughts. But Ma was heading out of the studio, shouting, "On social media naked and not even getting paid!" He was not getting Ma's attention back for the rest of the night. She'd spend the next hour talking with Ma Raines before cutting the call short to teach her next class. And once that class wrapped, she'd jump back on the phone with Ma Raines. That left Tech and Hippie Nerds, and he didn't vibe with them enough to share his thoughts about Zoey or the Bautista family. They felt more like Ma and Pa's lovers than padres. And he had rules. Rule number one being, don't divulge secrets to the fuck buddies.

Work could begin, he supposed, looking around for the broom mop. His padres would expect him to have the studios swept and his homework completed by the end of the night, a difficult task. Gliding the broom mop over wooden tiles calmed him, making him less sad about Zoey. Bachata music thumped. Whenever an image of Zoey tried to bring down his mood, he fought hard to stay connected to the music, popping the beats from muscle to muscle. Damn, he could turn broom moping into a choreography, but his thoughts stayed on Zoey. Her situation felt hopeless. And it wasn't like his bestie didn't invest in the social game. She was up against the school's champion competitor, Vega. The game was designed for Vega to win. Rule number two, know the rules and accept them.

Zoey needed Vega just like he needed Vega. He wasn't lying to himself. If it weren't for Vega, he'd still be the average middle-class kid with a Bautista scholarship. The broom mop stilled while he studied his reflection, his bronze skin and fresh cut. Six-foot-two with a muscled, dancer physique. Born to dance, talented as hell, that was his resume, and still Vega had to co-sign his success. Vega did her vampire magic thingy, and his yearbook pictures doubled, rumors about his F-boy status became positive press, and he cemented his spot as rank two in the dance department. Before, he bounced from two to three, losing sleep whenever he ranked three. Those quarters always broke him. He became like Sebastian, obsessively training, reducing sleep and sex while increasing stress eating. He wasn't cut out for such a lonely life filled with pressure. And no matter how hard he worked, he learned being great at school did not improve his social game. It would be the same for Zoey. She could be the best fashion design student in the department, and CLASH would hate her for outranking them until she found some impossible way to make everyone forget she was a social disaster. Getting Vega to co-sign Zoey would help, but Vega saw Zoey as prey, so that wasn't an option. Beating Vega was a better option.

Zoey could audition. That could give her a win. *If Sebastian chose her.*

He pushed dirt crumbs into a pile, pouring the pile into the trash. He didn't want to share Zoey with Sebastian when he already had to share his class schedule, the number one dance spot, his financial situation. Now he'd have to share Zoey? Unbearable. He lengthened into a tendu, stretching big as if claiming ownership of his safety. No, Sebastian couldn't have Zoey. He wouldn't even mention the auditions, praying this was one more piece of juicy gossip that Zoey missed. The broom became a sword he whipped overhead. Spinning into a pirouette arabesque, his leg lowered into coupé before slowing into croisé devant.

He heard applause, drawing his eyes to Zoey's reflection. Her adorable, huggable body drew him across the studio. He scooped her into his arms.

"Your mom's downstairs gossiping about me to my mom." Zoey snuggled against his chest. Her body felt warm and soft. "I guess you told her about the social media disaster."

"She was going to find out anyway. She's always on social."

Zoey handed him a white bag stained with grease. He pulled out the half-eaten carne asada burrito.

"Thanks. I'm starving." He claimed a spot on the floor, taking a bite. It was delicious. "This is why I love LA."

"LA loves you and hates me." Zoey collapsed beside him, spreading her arms wide.

"Don't say that." He rested his head on her stomach, hoping Zoey would play with his hair. Girls couldn't resist playing with his hair, but Zoey always took a while. "How'd the daddy-daughter talk go?"

"Dad was so sad. He kept telling me I'm beautiful."

"You're so beautiful."

"Can you not?"

"Not what?"

"Compliment me all night. I want to live in my miserable reality."

"But it's not real. Those people create these shitty ideas of you that don't mean anything."

"They hate me, and they laugh at me, and I just want to do something wicked so that they don't anymore."

Ian took another bite of the burrito, letting the juices from the steak calm his nerves. He wanted to say, 'Screw those skinny, rich bitches. They don't get us,' but he knew Zoey wouldn't listen. She wanted an invitation into the "in crowd," so he pretended to want the same for her. "What wicked thing are you planning?" he asked.

She unfolded Sebastian's flier, having folded it so none of the creases would ruin Sebastian's face.

His nightmare was coming true. "What about fashion?"

"I'll do both."

He laughed. "Sebastian'll consume every minute of your life, and you'll hate it."

"I hate being Frog-Leg Zoey or Butt-Naked Zoey."

"So you're going to quit on fashion?"

"No, I'm refocusing my energy so I can finally make friends. Why can't you get that?"

"It's not like I don't know what I'm talking about. I've been in every class with Sebastian since fifth grade." Sebastian didn't want a little; he wanted the whole. Sharing Zoey with Sebastian meant giving her to him, entirely. And then he'd also have to give Zoey to SG, with purple gift wrapping and a card. And knowing Zoey, she'd invite SG to El Famoso. And SG would colonize El Famoso, taking over his safe spaces. Vega would make Zoey into her mini-me, and El Famoso would become Club SG. He shuddered, the nightmare blackening his mood. Anxiety built in his chest and his legs. "Can't we just lean into who we are and launch influencer careers? We can create fashion videos. If you want to dance, we can dance salsa and bachata. You've been doing that all your life. We'll land brand deals and make a ton of money. People will love you for your money. Problem solved, and you don't have to suffer dancing with Sebastian."

"People don't care I don't have money."

Was she crazy? Did she not notice how everyone flaunted their wealth? It wasn't just their cars and clothes; it was their invite-only parties. It was their conversations about their privileged lifestyles they had around him even though they knew he didn't share the same experiences. It was the way they threw away their food, and their clothes, and their electronic devices. "I promise you, if you were a rich Black girl from Compton, you'd be the next Mahogany."

"Really?" Zoey grew annoyed. "You're like a God. You're super good looking. Everyone likes you."

"Cause of Vega."

"Exactly! Vega destroyed my life. Frog-Leg Zoey's the reason I don't have any friends. I need to do something amazing to revamp my brand."

"And what if Vega comes after you?"

"Bring it on like the nineties movie! I refuse to graduate CLASH as Frog-Leg Zoey." She had that obsessive look, the same one she had when she made him promise they were going to graduate and move to Paris.

He didn't want to help her audition, but what choice did he have? Zoey would never forgive him if he didn't help her win.

CHAPTER 12

SEBASTIAN

amy's dream was dead. Sebastian killed it, and he would have felt like a murderer if it weren't for her dream keeping him from living. Her sadness filled his third-floor gym. And it felt like he was benching a hundred and fifteen pounds at a funeral. Every time he took a break, his eyes floated to Amy, glued to her phone, reviewing all of the posts she had made about him and his sister. Pictures of them dancing a pas de deux on Rodeo Drive or along West Hollywood storefronts around the Grove. So many candid moments that positioned them as the loving duo modernizing ballet. He killed that lie, bench pressing his guilt to nothing.

Amy was heartbroken. She may have worked for him, but she identified with Vega, having studied ballet till she got hurt in college. A hip injury forced her out of ballet and into public relations. She climbed up through agencies until Papá hired her. She loved telling stories about him, but she saw herself reflected in Vega. Vega was her dream. Amy told him once she wanted to land a deal with Reese

Witherspoon's Hello Sunshine, and they both knew he was more Lionsgate than Hello Sunshine.

"It's alright," Amy coached her heart. He'd never seen her this sad.

He put the barbell down, sitting up. Cameramen moved for a close-up.

Amy kneeled in front of him, staring into his eyes. "How do you feel?" she asked, a trainer asking, 'How many more reps?' Not a mentor, not a friend. She wasn't interested in knowing how he felt. She wanted to gauge how much she could push him. Maybe even bring up Vega again.

"I feel ready for lats." He selected twenty-pound free weights. He might have looked invincible, but he felt crappy. Vega's constant rejection, her choosing Gregory over him, hurt. He wanted her to love their family legacy as much as he loved it. Their family got money from running textile factories in Europe, but his abuelitos took their inheritance and invested in dance. They raised his papá to become an international ballet powerhouse. They funded the family ballet company in Madrid. His papá married his mamá, and dance was central to their marriage. That's what Vega should have cared about, not Gregory's stupid campaign.

Vincent knocked on the door. *"Que tal?"*

Amy jumped back behind the cameras.

Sebastian felt his muscles relax.

Vincent began hammer curls, smiling at Sebastian in the mirror. *"Suda duro, juega duro, crece."* Sweat hard, play hard, grow. That was their motto. They begged their parents to let them tattoo the statement on their backs at the end of Sophomore year, a symbol that they were in the struggle together. Vincent also had to uphold a legacy: his abuelo and papá were basketball players, and his mamá was a sports journalist. That meant hours spent fighting for perfection. It wasn't easy, but at least they had their friendship.

"You snuck out?" Sebastian asked, knowing Vincent's papá made him practice every night and wouldn't let him sleep until he completed a hundred free throws.

"Man, you're out of the loop," Vincent said. "SG's holding a meeting in the living room. Vega sent me to fetch you."

SG was worse than dancing with Vega, sucking the love from his life. "I'm not going."

"You should. Vega's pissed off."

"Not my problem."

"She's your twin. Don't you guys have some super connection like mind reading?"

They did. "Vega uses her powers to crush me."

"She's in there saying you're the problem," Vincent said. "She's saying you pushed her on the floor and told her she needed to drop SG so that she could dedicate all her free time to dancing with you. She's calling you 'Male Chauvinistic Sebastian.'"

"Lame. Give her better names."

"I'll defend you all day. But you know how these things go. You need to show up at this meeting cause if Vega spread rumors around school? You know how this school pops off on social. Those stories incarcerate for life."

"How bout I make the rumors true?"

Vincent pressed his palm into Sebastian's chest. "You want to breathe a second?"

"I'm tired of fighting with her." He felt the cameras closed in on him. "She makes me feel like crap, and I want her to stop."

"Alright, man." Vincent held up his hands, surrendering. He had grown up next door to them and watched their sibling love sour. They had once been the twins that never fought. Vincent had dubbed those days the Bautista glory days. Back when they shared dreams, food—he could live without sushi—books. They'd leave critiques in the pages for each other, and he'd text the funniest critiques to Vincent. They had liked early morning surfing trips at Will Rogers Beach. Before they got their cars, they used to book the same Lyft. Then Vega started dating Gregory Sophomore year. Vincent claimed that was the beginning of the end of the Bautista glory days. But Sebastian disagreed. The end had come when Papá suggested Vega join in on Sebastian's success. He had been dumb to say yes. He had wanted to make Papá happy, and he honestly wanted to showcase his sister, but that meant Vega would have to practice more, and Vega rarely practiced. Papá had moved, and that rarely changed to never. Sebastian would argue with his sister about flaking. She was never there for him when he gave his all to her. She was the bad guy. Not him.

He rushed down the steps to the first floor, barging into the living room. The toxicity hit him, a thick, unwelcoming fog. Vega sat on a burgundy settee, queen of the Macbook roundtable, complaining, "Sebastian doesn't have time for SG. He never takes us seriously, and his behavior's proof." She noticed him and the camera crew at the entrance.

Polly chirped, "I'm so sorry. We should vote him out," while Mahogany kept her thoughts to herself. Gregory sat silent when he should have been defending him. That hurt, watching them all attack him, no ally coming to his defense. He thought these people were his friends, and now he knew the truth. "I'll save you the trouble of voting me out," Sebastian spoke up, drawing the Macbook roundtable's focus. "I'm dropping SG to clear up my schedule and focusing on finding a new partner."

"No one's voting you out," Vega snapped. "You have responsibilities you can't just toss aside cause–"

"I have to run dance auditions and train whoever I choose to pick up your slack. You can pick up some of mine."

Vega gripped her Macbook, shaking. "I guess that means no one here can audition, not having the time to do both." In other words, it was her or him.

Fine. He was sick of dancing with people who didn't care about him anyway. Polly couldn't even look at him, and Mahogany? They were in sync, but he didn't want to make her choose. Forcing people to choose was draining. He would instead find a partner who would stare alongside him in the same direction.

He didn't have any friends there, so he left. He'd be like Papá and search for a partner like Mamá. His phone vibrated in his back pocket. Mahogany texted him two blue hearts. He replied with three black ones.

CHAPTER 13
ZOEY

she and ian were supposed to train for Sebastian's auditions, but where was he? She searched El Famoso, the empty studios, the rooftop, the bathrooms. No signs of Ian. She checked her phone. No texts, nothing. She threw her arms up, exasperated. They should have rode here together after school, but as soon as class had ended, Ian texted her, 'Cody'll drop me off.' Translation, 'I'll be late.' Cody was Ian's hookup buddy. And Ian liked to take his sweet, lovely time with Cody, forgetting all about her, waiting desperately.

Her chest tightened, panic flaring. She wasn't a ballet dancer. To impress Sebastian, she'd have to work harder, and Ian understood that, but nothing mattered more to Ian than a hookup.

She gripped her chest. The world was spinning out of control. With eyes squeezed shut, she forced her thoughts to Ian's good traits. He's her best friend, and he always had her back. He let her cry on his six-pack when he'd rather be clubbing. He binged Miraculous Ladybug and *Sailor Moon*, and he didn't like those shows. He sacrificed his tastes for her tastes. He always shared his plantains and pineapple.

The world felt less topsy-turvy. She took a shaky first step, testing her steadiness. Her panic was gone. Mania avoided. She breathed, relieved. Ian was driving her crazy. She had to find a distraction. Wandering downstairs to the first-floor front desk, she'd peoplewatch.

The salseros arrived, dressed for class and potential hookups. Men sported fresh haircuts. Women wore form-fitting Lululemon, showing off their abs. She wanted their bodies and their wallets. And if Sebastian chose her, she'd earn enough money from co-starring in a doc that she'd be able to swipe her own credit card.

She couldn't wait to be Sebastian's partner. They'd take the cutest selfies, wearing matching gym clothes like the couples walking by … or maybe not. Fluorescent blue wasn't exactly Sebastian's style.

Zoey followed a matching couple up the stairs to the restaurant. A bartender made her a watermelon agua fresca with no alcohol, and she took it to the patio. Picking a table in the back, she watched the matching couple. That couple could be her and Sebastian. The sun set. The evening wind blew. Sebastian could hold her left hand, flirting with her, and she could eat chips and guac with her right. Her dream. And it'd come true if Ian actually showed up to rehearsal.

A waiter passed her table carrying grilled chicken with plantains and black beans. Her stomach grumbled, but she resisted the urge to order food. She couldn't eat another meal, at least not just yet. The french fries she ate for lunch were still digesting, and she didn't have room for the extra calories if she wanted to lose thirty pounds and get a body like CLASH dancers. CLASH dancers were thin like Vega or muscular like the salseros. Sebastian could have any one of them. Why risk his number one spot on her body?

Zoey found a scale in an empty studio, stepping on it to estimate the time she'd need to get a ballerina's body. 'One hundred and forty pounds' screamed at her. Big, red letters, criticizing her hips and her thighs. She cuffed her breasts. If the dance department held a boob contest, she'd win. And her curves gave Dorothy Dandridge and Marilyn Monroe. Her body gave Megan Thee Stallion and Cardi B. A body made for advertising boobs and curves. She'd hate to see them go, but sacrifices were necessary to win Sebastian. She held a moment of silence, massaging her bra with her thumbs. Bye bye, boobs. Her fingers slid down her stomach and between her thighs. Chocolate froyo made these thighs. *Bye bye, chocolate froyo. I'll give salad and water my love.* She just hoped salad and water could love her back. There were lots of salads in Los Angeles, avocado salad, mango salad, carne asada salad with tortillas—Her stomach grumbled angrily, still mad at her for passing up chicken with plantains and black beans.

She was so hungry and irritated. Where in the world was Ian? Drifting to a studio where Goddad Cruz taught, she hoped to find a complicated lesson to kill thoughts of

Ian. She stepped inside the small studio, keeping to the back. Goddad Cruz taught hip rotations to a guy with a mind-body disconnect. And still, Goddad Cruz smiled big, patient. Goddad Cruz never had a bad lesson. He loved teaching, no matter how bad the dancers danced.

Would Sebastian be as loving as Goddad Cruz? Would he break down each step? Would he touch her, guiding her legs and back muscles to the correct posture? What would Sebastian smell like, salsa or ballet? She frowned, knowing she'd get her answers if Ian would show up for rehearsal. Where was HE!?!? It was like he was sabotaging her. She whipped out her phone to text.

Zoe: Do you want me to audition?
Ian: Duh.

He's lying! Ian hated Sebastian and probably would die before he helped her become Sebastian's partner. What if he was secretly trying to keep her from Sebastian? She squashed the thoughts, feeling the claws of another panic attack. She couldn't lose control. Pressing her hand on her heart, she breathed.

"I didn't know you were here."

Zoey spun around, locking eyes with Godmom Cruz. "I'm waiting for Ian. We're supposed to rehearse."

"For how long?"

"Almost an hour. Not that long."

"Has he texted?"

Zoey didn't want to admit that she was in the middle of being stood up. No man would ever bail on Godmom Cruz. She was a total MILF, all muscle with salon-layered, black hair brushing her back.

Godmom Cruz pulled Zoey close and whispered, "Never wait for a man for anything, no matter who he is."

"I'm not really waiting."

"My son's gorgeous, and I love him, but I must be honest. When he's late, he's probably off somewhere screwing."

The truth hurt, wanting to believe that Ian valued her more than hooking up, but Ian really loved sex.

"Come dance with me." Godmom Cruz tugged her upstairs and into her evening salsa class. Dancers waited in six rows of seven.

Godmom Cruz turned on Marc Anthony's *Aguanile*, smiling as big as her husband. And Zoey chose a spot in the front, figuring Godmom Cruz would call her out if she tried to hide in the back.

The music washed over Zoey as she matched Godmom Cruz's step ball change into a pirouette. Shimmying her chest, she played with the tempo, adding an extra step or, even better, a little pose with her arm extended.

She grinned at her perfect form in the wall-to-wall mirror, suddenly thankful to Godmom Cruz for all those childhood lessons. Godmom Cruz had treated El Famoso like a day-care when she and Ian were growing up. So many hours of training. Her technique was sexy, fabulous even. She was so ready to impress Sebastian and slay Vega.

The class ended. Her breathing was heavy, but she felt powerful. A sweaty, beautiful mess.

Godmom Cruz glowed with love. "You're amazing." She rushed to hug Zoey. Their sweat co-mingled.

"She is," Ian agreed, entering the studio with Cody, his boy toy.

Seeing Ian with Cody ruined her dance buzz. She could tell those two had been screwing in the back of Cody's Corvette, forgetting all about her. And Ian threw the pieces of his broken promise in her face by bringing Cody to what was supposed to be a private rehearsal. While Godmom Cruz lectured Ian for being late, Zoey snuck off with the other departing dancers, hoping to get to her car before Ian noticed.

"Where are you going? We have practice," Ian called, chasing her down the stairs.

"I have homework due tomorrow." Mrs. Sehar had assigned an embroidery project, and she might as well head home and begin work on that.

"Come on. I'm sorry I'm late. I had to convince Cody to come."

"Ha, ha, pun intended." She stopped just at the exit, crossing her arms. "You're literally glowing orgasm."

"I'm good at what I do," Cody said. "Maybe next time you can join."

"No thanks." She hated that Cody's hazel eyes could see right through her bluff. Cody was hot Black excellence and just as bisexual and gorgeous as Ian. When she and Ian spotted him at a Juneteenth party in Leimert Park a couple years ago, they had spent most of the party talking about how hot he was, working up the nerve to speak to him. And when they did, they had discovered Cody's dope personality and were sold on a friendship. Ian had upgraded his friendship to include more benefits, while she kept hers at hugs. She wasn't hooking up with Cody for a new hobby. Unlike Ian, she still had hope for monogamy. "Why's Cody even here?"

"I want to help you win," Cody said.

She shriveled inside, feeling like Ian disclosed her dirtiest secret. Dancing in front of Cody would be like dancing in front of CLASH after Ian told everyone she liked to masturbate to Miraculous Ladybug's opening theme. It'd feel judgy. No. She wasn't dancing while Cody watched. He was a celebrity dance coach. She didn't need his harsh critique killing her spirit. Thanks, but no thanks. She exited to her car.

Ian and Cody rushed up behind, hooking their arms under hers, carrying her kicking, back into El Famoso, to the closest studio. She tried to run when they set her down, but Ian blocked the door.

"You need all the help you can get," he said.

"From you, not the whole world."

"Relax, this zone is judgment-free," Cody said.

Yeah, right. Judgement-free didn't land Cody his own studio in North Hollywood or fly him all over the world to dance. Harsh critique made Cody's career, and she wasn't ready. Not the first rehearsal.

Cody bluetoothed rap music through the sound system, breathing. She gulped down air. This was happening. Ian blocked the exit. There was nowhere to run. Cody swiped his hand over his fade, spinning on one foot and landing squarely in a wide stance. "Let's start with some popping and locking," he said, nodding to Ian. "You want to lead the ballet?"

"My specialty," Ian said.

Zoey rolled her eyes. And sharing secrets.

Ian joined Cody in the center. They stared at her, waiting.

She swallowed her fear. There was no point in fighting. Cody and Ian were bigger, stronger, and faster. And they looked ready to work. She pushed her legs forward. Her limbs felt heavy, the music fighting hard, the tension gripping her body. She'd taken tons of Cody's classes for free but made sure to dance in the back where he couldn't see her in the crowd. But there was no crowd here. Cody's eyes stayed on her, absorbing every awkward roll, every missed step. She couldn't read Cody's face, but he had to recognize hip hop wasn't her thing. Even after all those free classes.

The song ended. *Thank God.* "It's eight," Zoey pointed out. "I have a ton of homework." She'd embroider to Miraculous Ladybug and forget this night happened.

"We'll start at the barre," Ian replied, ignoring her. He took over the music. Piano and strings floated through the speakers. Somber, like her mood. When she didn't move, Ian promised to keep it simple. He was such a good liar.

She struggled to keep her knees straight. Ian called out French terms. Her mind recognized each one, and her body hated them. Oh, no, she was the lousy dancer with the mind-body disconnect. She searched for the happiness she felt earlier in Godmom Cruz's class. That happiness abandoned her.

Cody lengthened beautifully in the mirrors. He wasn't even a ballet dancer, and yet he could be. Her unease heightened. She was such a beginner compared to Cody. Her mind couldn't grasp the movements, her toes fighting against the unnatural foot positions, her core resisting the disruptions to her balance. What was unnatural to her was perfectly made for Cody, for Ian. And each time she tried to push herself, her feet cramped, her knees caved, and gravity won.

She toppled out of her pirouette, glancing at the time. They'd been dancing for three painful hours, and she felt each hour in her aching muscles.

"How are you feeling?" Ian asked, sweat dripping from his chin.

"Tired, hungry. My legs hurt. Maybe I should be realistic." Ian and Cody made her feel like she had never danced in her life. The dancers at CLASH were on their levels. What would make Sebastian choose her?

"I don't know—you sure you want to give up fashion?" Ian asked.

"I'm not giving up fashion!"

"You can balance both," Cody said, ignoring Ian's dirty look. Did Ian want her to quit? "But you have to train hard. Lots of caffeine and energy drinks."

"Thank you, Cody, for saying that." Ian better get like Cody cause she wasn't quitting. She didn't care how much coffee she had to drink.

CHAPTER 14
IAN

he wanted zoey to fail hard. That lie bubble his bestie stayed dreaming inside, bursted.

Zoey had the best imagination, creating a world where she thought she could balance fashion and dance, but the reality wouldn't be chocolate froyo and pineapple pizza, with dance on Tuesdays and fashion on Mondays. That's not how it would work. Zoey would end up sacrificing her love of fashion to dance with Sebastian.

Ian didn't know how to burst Zoey's bubble without bursting her spirit. So he had to support her crazy obsession. And he hated it. Acting fake around SG was easy. He didn't care about them knowing his truth. Acting fake around Zoey ate at his happiness, but he could win awards for faking happiness.

His padres took their pool money and built him a dance studio in the backyard. It wasn't as big as Sebastian's, but it had the wall-to-wall mirrors with the sprung flooring. He maintained a corner with freshly rolled towels and a mini-fridge stocked with coconut and plantain chips so he could stress eat whenever he felt overwhelmed. And he was chewing through his plantain chips, watching Zoey wobble on relevé.

She was flexible, she could complete her splits in all directions, and she had great timing. He could enhance her strengths, but Sebastian would want, at the bare minimum, ballet arms that never lowered and feet that didn't sickle. Correcting sickling feet was tough, requiring a knowing of the body that came with time. There was not enough time. He doubted he could help her improve. She'd embarrass herself again, but this time it'd be his fault. And as much as he wanted her to fail, could he sabotage her and keep their friendship? Losing her was scary. He finished his plantain chips and reached for some coconut chunks. This was too much pressure.

Zoey stretched into cambré derrierre, exhausted and sweaty. She needed a break.

"Take five minutes," he announced, grabbing his phone.

She fell against him, and he shared his coconut while scrolling to catch up on his missed messages. A bunch of hookups had texted. Ignore. He texted Mahogany a red heart. She was coming over tonight. Awesome. He browsed the SG group chat, freezing when he noticed Sebastian had left.

This was bad. Should he tell Zoey? That would distract her and turn the rest of the night into storytime, discussing Sebastian and Vega's endless hatred. It was better to keep Zoey focused. The less she had to worry about, the less chance she made a fool of herself in front of his enemy. Sebastian's auditions demanded the best. His enemy would sit on his vampire throne behind the audition table, ripping Zoey to shreds with his eyes. And if Zoey danced subpar, Sebastian would shred Zoey's ego with feedback. His poor Zoey would need therapy. Ian had to protect her.

Deleting his hookup requests, he cleared his schedule. They'd have to rehearse every night until she auditioned. No sex. No fun. It'd be stressful—his head hurt at the thought—and he'd suffer withdrawals, but he had plantain chips and coconut to help him survive.

Zoey tried to go home, but he forced her to dance until his phone buzzed with Mahogany's text.

He loved that Mahogany wasn't afraid to drive to Compton at night even though she wasn't from there. She grew up in Bel Air, but she had a love affair with his city. She thought Compton was a misunderstood training ground for talent. Not only did her pa's agency represent a bunch of Compton celebrities, but she once told him about the Compton Cricket Club, the only American-born exhibition cricket team that won the British Cup twice. The cricket club surprised him, but he had known about the horse-riding Compton Cowboys. Sometimes, he would look out his window and see the equestrians riding.

He lifted Mahogany out of her Lexus. She smelled like fresh cucumbers, the same ones swirling in her baby blue water bottle. "Watch my routine," she whispered between kisses. "I prepared it for Sebastian."

"You're auditioning?"

She jumped out of his arms, pulling him into his studio, and he sat against the mirrors to behold Mahogany's core belief, using dance to remember her ancestors' struggles. Her movements were never delicate, light, or fluttery, and she had no desire to dance like a princess. She leaped into a temps de poisson, arms a crown shaping her head. Then, she spun into three pirouettes, rolling onto the sprung flooring before finishing in a powerful second. She was all the precision that Zoey wasn't.

"Wow." He felt sick. His two favorite women would destroy their social statuses for a stuck-up, D-list influencer with a docuseries no one would watch. He didn't want Sebastian to have any of them. And now he was sacrificing his happiness to help Zoey audition only for her to be outdone by Mahogany.

He could see Zoey's strengths. Zoey was delicate and responsive while Mahogany was all power. She could play with tempo in ways Mahogany couldn't. But, he doubted Sebastian would see Zoey's strengths if her technique couldn't match Mahogany's.

He didn't want to betray any of them, so it was better if he found a way to talk them out of auditioning, for his sanity and their own. His relationship would change with them if either one became Sebastian's partner.

He kissed Mahogany's sweaty shoulder, her sweat becoming vaseline on his lips. "I love watching you dance. Sebastian doesn't deserve you."

Mahogany leaned into him, her warmth becoming his warmth.

He loved kissing sweaty Mahogany as much as he loved watching her dance. Undressing her as soon as they got in his room, he played with her sweet spot, and she played with his. His eyes absorbed her dark eyes, her thick, curly hair. She was beautiful, calm. He felt safe enough to mention how risky it was to audition. "Aren't you scared of pissing off Vega?"

"I love Vega, but for real, Julliard will not care that I'm a SG secretary. And I might not even go to college. If I'm lucky, I'll convince my dad to fund me a role on Broadway."

"All right, Miss. Rich Bitch."

"I'll hire you." Mahogany kissed his neck, ready to go again.

He gripped her hips when she climbed on top. "You can probably kiss these little nights goodbye. Sebastian will not give you any free time. And maybe Vega will come after you."

Mahogany climbed down from him. "Why don't you want me to audition?"

"Hhhhmmmm ... why do you want to trash your social life?"

"Normally, you'd push me to go for things like this. Dancing with Sebastian would catapult my career. You know that."

"I'm jealous. I'm tired of sharing you." Mahogany was already Sebastian's pas partner. They had the makings of a modern Ginger Rogers and Fred Astaire, her chocolate skin a striking visual against Sebastian's skin.

"I have to share you with the world, with Zoey," Mahogany said. "You should be going hard for me like you go hard for Zoey as a thank you for my loyalty."

"Like Zoey? My best friend."

"Yes, but harder. I want you to commit to me and put me first like you put Zoey first."

Mahogany did not want to be treated like a bestie. *Whatever.* He didn't feel like arguing about how illogical she was when the important issue was Vega. "Again, Zoey's my best friend. We're not best friends. We're lovers."

"I want more–"

"And you and Vega have been best friends since kindergarten. She's your entire social circle, and you're throwing that away by going behind her back to audition for Sebastian."

"I'm hoping Vega will stop hating Sebastian enough to see this docuseries as an important step in my career."

"That's not likely." He snuggled Mahogany when she tried to pull away from him. He could feel the truth settling throughout her body.

"It drives me so crazy," she whispered. "They're twins. They're supposed to be best friends, and they are so against each other. Did you notice Sebastian's no longer in SG?"

Exactly what he'd been waiting to talk about. "How did Sebastian drop SG?"

"He just showed up late to the meeting and said he wouldn't have time. He's like a historian. All he does is take photos, so we all know he did it to irritate Vega."

"He wants Vega to feel like nothing. And Vega will strike back at Sebastian and anyone who joins him. Really think about this."

CHAPTER 15
SEBASTIAN

everyone at school was talking about him. They whispered whenever he passed in the halls, pressing their phones closer to their chests. He felt their judgment in his stomach, so heavy and nauseating. The cameras filmed their gross smiles. The sound recordist captured their insults. Amy called shots, waiting for him to react so she could note it on her iPhone.

He didn't eat lunch with SG, making this statement clear: He wasn't a part of their tribe anymore. The gardens looked empty, so he chose a spot there, hoping to scarf down his food and leave quickly. Level III dancers ruined his plans, filling his table while he was mid-bite. They bombarded him with questions. How did he feel about Mrs. Agnes, about dancing *The Nutcracker* in The Fall Showcase, about today's latest rumors? Was it true?

He looked up from his salad. "Is what true?"

Michael looked shocked. "You haven't seen the TikTok? Vega made it."

"Shut up, Michael," Francesa yelled from the end of the table.

"I don't do social media unless it's for work," he replied. He squashed any curiosity surrounding the video, knowing Vega wanted him to obsess over it. That's how she destroyed people at CLASH. She'd spread a rumor to all her followers, and that rumor would break the person's confidence, one piece at a time.

Vega wanted him to crumble. She watched him in all of his Level III classes, checking for any sign that he had looked at his social media, but he refused. He wasn't playing her games when he was a champion. Look at all he had accomplished with his film crew and millions of followers worldwide. What was Vega's follower count? A couple hundred thousand? She needed her loss. He mattered more.

The bell rang, signaling the end of his last class. Gregory waited in the hall to pick up Vega, waving as soon as he saw Sebastian. "Guess you're not coming to my party Saturday?"

"That's up to you." He glared at Gregory. "Are you playing neutral?"

"This isn't war," Gregory yelled at his back. "Apologize and come back to SG. We're friends–"

He laughed at that. Being friends with SG was like being friends with his reflection, all appearances with no depth. He was tired of that. He wanted real friends who loved him as much as they loved their wealth, and their social media profiles, and their scandals.

The camera crew followed him out of the main building and into the dance school, down the hall to studio D120. Mrs. Agnes stretched in second at the barre while he prepared to rehearse *The Nutcracker* pas de deux with her. Amy coached the camera ops and the sound guys on the types of shots that she wanted.

He wanted to feel safe, so he imagined the cameras forming the walls of a Spanish cathedral around him. Papá walking him and his sister down Calle Gran Vía formed in his head. The Oratorio del Caballero de Gracia towered strikingly, the smells rich, and the silence comforting. There was his peace. Mrs. Agnes floated through his memories. Spanish words buttered with a French accent, soothing his body and releasing his endorphins. He timed his lifts to her words, his fingers digging into her bones whenever he pushed her upward.

He settled her gently on the floor. She fluttered away before returning and pressing her hand against his hand, staring into his eyes. Mrs. Agnes' gaze was always encouraging, kind, the complete opposite of Vega's. He wanted his sister to look at him with love and admiration. They were blood. They were supposed to be a home for each other, but they weren't. That's why he left her and SG.

Is that why Mrs. Agnes left her home? He knew she had given up dancing with the Opéra National de Paris to immigrate to the States. "Why'd you leave Paris?"

"I tired of straightening my hair," she laughed, patting the thick Afro on her head.

"What does that mean?"

Mrs. Agnes reached for her bag, pulled out her scarf, and wrapped it around her neck. "You know what it's like to be a minority, I suppose. You're a cis-gendered, straight male trying to redefine ballet as a safe space for masculinity, but the thing you have going for you is you look like America's definition of success. I ask you to imagine yourself pursuing this career if you didn't, maybe a Chicano covered in tattoos, or maybe Ian, but a little less good-looking." She pulled him close, pointing at their reflections. "And imagine your corps de ballet, your soloists, your principals, all beautiful, all the same, but no one looking like you. How would you feel?"

He took a moment, imagining himself an uglier Ian. That was hard. Whenever he thought of Ian, he thought of Ian showing off his looks and competing for the principal roles in every audition. He thought of how Ian practiced way less but always seemed to outshine his CLASH-mates, which annoyed him. It wasn't the point of the exercise, so he tried hard to imagine Ian, the only brown skin, black-haired Chicano, surrounded by Level III dancers. He moved Mahogany from where she was posing next to Vega and Polly so that she was next to Ian, but that didn't help. Mahogany's outfit overpowered Ian's. He could dress Mahogany in the most bland leotard ever, but he would always know that Mahogany was dancing in Savage x Fenty while Ian was dreaming of dancing in Fenty.

"Lonely, unbalanced," he said, erasing the image in his head.

"J'ai dû quitter Paris pour retomber amoureux de Paris." I had to leave Paris to fall in love with Paris again.

He shuddered, hoping he would never feel that way about dance. Dance was all he had, so if he left it, he'd have what? The absence of purpose, of happiness, of love? He walked Mrs. Agnes to the school entrance. The nothingness she had to feel rebuilding her life in the States. The nothingness he felt now. How it made him feel unwanted.

Mrs. Agnes told him not to stay too late, and he didn't tell her he wouldn't. Tonight was the first night of auditions, and he planned on staying as long as required. He entered studio D115, expecting people to fill the hallways. There was no one. He frowned, looking left and then right. A long, hollow hallway of nothingness, mirroring his emptiness. This didn't make sense. He was the best dancer in the school. People should beg to be his partner.

Someone squeezed his shoulder. He looked. It was Amy. He'd forgotten that she was even there filming.

"It'll all work out." She sounded like she knew something he didn't, as if she had noticed a foreshadowing of disaster on the feeds landing in Frame.io on her phone.

He thought back to all of the gossip he had noticed this morning. Had Amy discovered something? Had the cameramen? The sound mixer steadying the boom?

"How come no one's here?" He stared at Amy even though he was asking all of them.

"How do you feel about this?"

He grew annoyed. "Like I'm burning."

"And?" She wanted him to open up in front of the camera and start talking about his inner world, something he struggled with.

"There's no one here. I need tons of people here, and why aren't they? You know, right?" He pointed at Amy. "What do you know?"

Amy crossed her arms, apologizing with her eyes. "It'll all work out."

He stared down the hallways. Lacking humanity, just like Amy's answer. She couldn't make him feel better. No one could. That's why he taught himself to convert the nothingness he felt into pliés and pirouettes. Lifting into four pirouettes, he bounced into a pas de chat that climaxed into a grand pas de chat. The more pain he felt, the higher he reached, hoping he'd fly into joy. He landed, head lowered. He didn't feel happy; he felt heavy. And those empty halls would crush him. No one had come. Maybe Vega was right about his personality, his high standards. They wouldn't have fought all the time if he accepted her mediocrity. He shuddered, the cold studio amplifying his sadness. He detested second best, and Papá did too. Their family had set the bar so high they needed an aircraft. And without Papá here coaching them, Vega settled for dancing in the dirt. Settling wasn't in the Bautista DNA.

Sebastian wished Papá was here. Vega was better when Papá was here. He was better. Life wasn't so depressing, but Papá chose Madrid over them. Sebastian's jaw tightened, fingers gripping the flooring. Papá couldn't carry the

Bautista legacy forever. Eventually, the world would expect him to lead. He forced one leg straight, then the other. He had to stay ready for his turn, so he shook off the loneliness gripping his body, mentally shifting to The Fall Showcase. So what no one came. He could rehearse *The Nutcracker* and even review Papá's performances on YouTube. If he could stomach how much he missed Papá. Watching Papá was hard sometimes, but Mamá never made him sad. He'd watch her sugar plum pas.

He raised his head, eyes rising to the entrance. Mahogany waited, her bag at her feet, her dark brown eyes focused but soft. He blushed, embarrassed. How long had she been standing there? How pathetic did he look? "Why didn't you say anything?"

"I love watching you." She glowed, approaching him when he didn't move. She wrapped her arms around his neck.

He gave in to her warmth and her smell, four hours of training and deodorant. He loved that smell of hard work. And even though he felt weak, he was happy she was here. His pas partner was everything but mediocre. Strong, pretty, the only dancer in Level III that worked as hard as he did. She was perfect. If she'd only dump Ian, then they could be like his parents.

Mahogany laid a full-length body shot on a table in the back of the studio. "So I want to make this easy for you. Give me the part now, and we can talk to Vega together."

"And then we move to another school?" He imagined all the lies people would say about them. 'They must be hooking up,' or worse, 'They're so fake. Why'd they waste people's time?' As if he put the posters up knowing he would select Mahogany anyway. CLASH-mates would make up hurtful stories, but no one was crueler than Vega. He tensed. Vega was a gossip mastermind, and she would find the perfect story to spread about Mahogany. "Are you done with Vega?" Mahogany didn't have friends outside of SG.

"Dance is everything." Mahogany shrugged, her eyes lowering. "I'm hoping she'll understand."

"She won't. Maybe you should reconsider."

"Maybe you're right." Mahogany grabbed her photo, leaving.

His heart ached, Mahogany's footsteps echoing with each step towards the door, each step stomping his chest. Trying to reduce the pain, he gripped the table.

"You know what, screw it." She ran back, banging her hands on the table. "We're friends, too."

He laughed, relieved.

"You should see your face. You actually think I'd leave you. We're day ones. And I stay loyal. You must have me confused with the rest of these CLASH-mates."

His face went red. Pain made him forget. "I'm sorry."

"I want extra points."

"You can have anything you want from me."

Her left eyebrow arched, spinning to connect her phone to the speakers. "If Ian heard you say that."

"Isn't he poly? Doesn't he like sharing?"

Mahogany paused, jutting her right hip out in a super-woman stance.

He laughed, and she laughed, knowing the truth. Ian did not want to share her with him.

"Can I get in the right mental space to do this audition?" Mahogany asked.

He held up his hands. "Don't worry. I'm not picking fights with Ian. I don't steal, and you stay loyal. He's safe. Drama averted."

She threw up a peace sign, pointing at him and then herself, repeating the motion. "This is why we're day ones."

"Forever day ones, never twos."

She laughed, turning on classical music infused with hip-hop beats. Dropping her phone and her bag, she rolled her head in slow circles that grew bigger, consuming her shoulders and her hips. She stretched her right foot tendu derriere and lifted upward to penché. Her movements were slow, building with the tempo and transforming her into a warrior queen on pointe. She was so inspiring that he couldn't resist jumping over the table and joining. Her energy filled him, her body moving against his as if she wanted inside him. She looped her leg around his waist, her hands curling in his hair. He lunged backward. They panted.

He loved holding her. She filled the emptiness he'd been carrying deep inside until she pulled away, and it became all business.

"Any feedback?" she asked.

"None," he said. "You're powerful." He didn't know how to explain that he wanted her presence to fill him so that he never felt empty without stressing her out. She had Ian. And he didn't want to ruin their friendship. They were forever day ones, and that's what made them great pas partners. "Can you call in the next person?"

Mahogany pushed open the studio door, leaning into the hall. "There's no one else."

He had to check for himself, taking in the blue lockers reflecting the sunset. The silence seeped inside him, growing bigger and bigger.

"Why do you and Vega hate each other so much?"

That question came out of nowhere. He stared, confused. "What do you mean?"

"Everyone was talking about this in Modern." Mahogany loaded her social media, showing him a video of Vega crying. Her mascara ran, snot dripping from her nose. She complained he was an abusive brother who berated her, calling her dancing mediocre. He made her feel inferior, and then he had just dropped her. She warned her brother would treat anyone who auditioned the same. "Don't do it," she cried. "You'll be promoting abuse."

He collapsed to his knees, his mind racing. He didn't abuse Vega. He pushed her to be better, loving her too much to watch her settle for second best. And Vega repaid him by embarrassing him in front of the world, knowing he worked hard to create his reputation. He curled into a ball against the door frame, hiding his face with his knees.

"It's a lie." Mahogany massaged his back. "You're not this person. I know it."

He was demanding with high standards, but their family had high standards. They had to meet them. Why didn't Vega get that? He wasn't trying to hurt her, not like she hurt him. He stared into the empty halls, the moonlight making pools on the floors. Mahogany rested her head on his shoulder.

CHAPTER 16
ZOEY

sebastian wasn't abusive. no, he couldn't be. She ignored Ian whenever he paused rehearsal to show off Vega's TikTok. "I'm not watching it." She fought off every attempt, growing weaker with each time he asked. He had to mention that video a hundred times, beating her willpower to a pulp.

She returned home, exhausted. She lay in bed, losing a wrestling match to her curiosity. It was like fighting the urge to eat chocolate-covered pineapple when a bowl was sitting in front of her. Succumbing to her desires, she grabbed her phone.

Vega had filmed her TikTok laying on her purple, queen-sized bed. "Sebastian's so abusive, trust me," she kept crying. Streams of mascara mixed with snot dripped down her chin.

Zoey didn't trust Vega, but the more she listened, the more she pictured Sebastian yelling at his sister and then yelling at her. Vega might have been a horrible person, but she was a beautiful dancer. The absolute vision of a prima ballerina, and Vega still didn't meet Sebastian's expectations.

Zoey shuddered.

Sebastian could yell at her. She couldn't dance as grace-fully as Vega, and Vega was a speck of her brother's talent. That's how he broke her. Mean, heartless Vega. Now she was crying on TikTok, warning people not to become the next victim.

Sebastian could easily make Zoey his victim. He could crush her with his ballet shoe, brushing her off like a smudge. And she wouldn't have a million sympathizers liking her post. CLASH-mates would watch her TikTok and call her stupid for not listening.

Vega could be lying. The thought was a weak, small hope buried under a mountain of fear. It was all so stressful.

She tossed her phone on her dresser, choosing sleep over Vega drama. She dreamed of Sebastian's harsh gray eyes and lean muscles wrapped in black leotards. He danced around her, revealing fangs and biting her neck. He drank her orange blood and then dumped her for Mahogany cause Mahogany had the black blood that matched his outfit.

The dream rattled her, haunting her even when she sat down for breakfast. She told Mom and Dad about it. Dad was stressed about a school strategy meeting. He barely lis-tened, muttering she had a great imagination before rushing out the door. That left her alone with Mom.

Mom sipped her coffee, writing a red B+ on a piece of paper before asking, "Do you think Sebastian could suck your life force? Or overpower you, like a dream about power dynamics?"

Mom's interpretation terrified her so much she ended breakfast early, running to her car and waiting there till Ian slid into the passenger seat. She didn't even wait until she was out of the driveway before telling Ian her dream. "He bit my neck like a vampire, the *Vampire Diaries* kind, not Twilight."

"Sebastian's definitely a vamp," Ian replied, making her feel worse. "But, more *Dracula 2000*."

"Eeewwww." That was her least favorite vampire movie.

"I bet you he eats Vega's flesh at night."

"That's so dumb. She'd literally be dead."

"She is. They're both vampires."

Zoey imagined auditioning for the immortal Sebastian, his eyesight enhanced, spotting poor technique before she executed a move. He was already intimidating enough without nightmares. Now, there would be the rumors blackening his reputation.

CLASH opinions moved quickly, faster than a social feed, and Zoey had experienced the blowback from Vega's rumors, going from the awkward fashionista to Frog Legs all in a day. Social status decreased from five friends to one. The same would happen to Sebastian.

She entered the school, following Ian to his locker, listening to CLASH-mates call Sebastian an "ego manic with bad leadership skills," a "pretentious fake" that was too stuck up for even his own family. "He should go to jail," a student said. Sebastian was no longer the beloved prodigy. And all cause Vega had dropped a TikTok.

"Poor Sebastian," Zoey whispered.

"Rich bitch, Sebastian, you mean."

"Stop being so mean." She pushed Ian. Vega had done so many cruel things, while Sebastian had maybe made a girl cry in eighth grade cause he didn't want to be her girlfriend. She couldn't think of anything else Sebastian had done to hurt people. "What if Vega's lying?"

"Oh my God, desperate much?"

"Sebastian just dumped Vega. This could be revenge." Zoey lowered her voice just in case people were listening to her as much as she was listening to them. Vega stood with SG, a few lockers down from Ian's. Her signature purple sweater vest and khakis were wrinkled. Her hair was combed into a messy bun that screamed emotional breakdown. "When has Vega's outfit ever been off? The wrinkles scream, 'pity, please,' when her outfits always stay wicked. You know that."

Ian glanced backward. She could tell he wasn't entirely sold on Vega's act, knowing her tactics since he hung out with her. "True or not, Sebastian's a jerk." He transformed into a prosecutor, defending Vega intensely. All those years of sharing classes with Sebastian provided him with ample evidence. "Sebastian made Lucy cry in third grade and some nobody that doesn't go here anymore. I bet he left because of Sebastian."

Zoey's mouth flopped open, struggling to defend Sebastian's case. She had nothing. It was a known fact that Sebastian was strict, not nice. Rumors about him had even made it to the fashion department. He outworked everyone, genius being his mode of operation. That informed his leadership style. And everyone accepted Sebastian's dictatorship cause who didn't want to be great like Sebastian? At least, that used to be the question.

Sebastian walked in their direction with Vincent Dixon. His camera crew floated behind. His producer watched the feeds on her iPhone, reporting notes in her earpiece. He looked like the vampire in her nightmares, scary, easy to hate. She tensed when Sebastian noticed her and Ian's stare. She looked away, feeling his approach. It took everything in her to force her eyes to reach his.

Sebastian raised his head, throwing his shoulders back.

Ian did the same, standing to his full six-feet-two. They both were so tall and she so small. It was like they'd bare fangs, and their eyes would turn red before an impending fight to the death. She waited for one of them to say, 'Hey' or high five, play the social game, but Ian refused to be player number one, and Sebastian glared. Should she be player number one? She raised a trembling hand, her throat dry. Sebastian wasn't even looking at her. She'd make things awkward if she spoke. She lowered her hand. It had to be Ian. He was player number one.

He refused the position.

Sebastian continued past without glancing down at her.

She lowered her eyes, feeling devalued.

"That's exactly why people believe Vega." Ian slammed his locker shut.

"You weren't Mr. Nice Guy either," Zoey said.

"It's hard to be nice to a guy who thinks his shit tastes like cinnamon."

"He hasn't bought a pill for that? Shocking."

"You'd suck his shit through a straw."

"No. Boundaries, please."

"Transparency, please. I'm completely sex shaming you. Your infatuation's clouding your judgment. You want to give up fashion just to be with him."

"Stop saying I'll have to give up fashion!" She lowered her voice when CLASH-mates looked at her.

"Whatever you think about Vega, she wasn't lying when she said Sebastian wanted her to choose between SG and dance. Sebastian trains a lot, and he will not care that you have a project due. You'll have to meet his standards or get dumped. Are you willing to do that?"

"I just want to be seen." She wanted Sebastian to stand side by side her, his hands moving over her body, his eyes locked with her eyes. She wanted him to see her and push her to be better. "I want to create art with someone that's committed and says yes to what they love."

"Unlike me," Ian said.

How is this suddenly about you? "That's not what I said."

"You're so desperate to be seen you'd sacrifice everything that you love."

Ian didn't understand. People saw him. Just moments ago, Sebastian engaged with him in an eye battle to the death. Then, Sebastian didn't look to her as his next opponent. She wasn't worthy. He continued on, treating her like the tiny human she was in the big CLASH universe. A universe where Ian was a glittering star, and she was dark matter nobody could detect.

SG called Ian so they could walk to first period together. And Ian answered the call, leaving her to walk to class alone. Again. Becoming Sebastian's partner would at least give her friends to walk to class, so she didn't have to do everything solo when Ian wasn't available.

She entered Mrs. Sehar's class, sliding into a desk just as Mrs. Sehar clapped her hands. Her blue hijab had an embroidered stingray on the front. It called attention to itself, and that made Zoey suspicious. Mrs. Sehar only called attention to her fashion choices when she wanted to highlight an assignment.

"Start getting your presentations ready," Mrs. Sehar said.

What in the world is she talking about? Zoey scanned the room. Everyone pulled out embroidery hoops canvased in quilting and stitched with yarn. *Oh no.* She had forgotten about this assignment. She hadn't had time to think about anything other than preparing for Sebastian's auditions.

"Zoey, would you like to go first?" Mrs. Sehar asked, probably thinking that she would.

Zoey's tongue was heavy. "I don't have it."

Mrs. Sehar looked confused, and Zoey repeated, "I don't have it."

"You can turn it in tomorrow." Mrs. Sehar moved on to Marly.

Marly jumped from her seat, rushing to the front, beaming excitedly about her design. "It's inspired by LA's Chicano fashion." She showed White Baby Jesus snuggling a lamb wearing sunglasses and gold beads.

Zoey didn't even want to watch Marly's presentation. It was missing the actual edge of East Hollywood, places people like Marly never hung out. Zoey had spent weekends with Ian walking the Boyle Heights sidewalks, eating street tacos, and passing the murals painted on businesses. That was her moment, not Marly's.

I'm such a failure. She slouched lower each time she watched one of her CLASH-mates present. She would have been ready if she hadn't spent so much time practicing for Sebastian's audition–Ian's warning slapped her erect in her seat.

What if Ian was right and she couldn't balance dance and fashion?

sebastian was no longer the CLASH savior. He could get his chance in the spotlight. Thank you, Vega.

He loved her shameless TikTok, the messy close-ups showing half her face, the Sebastian insults. Every word was accurate. And he was proud of Vega for her bravery. She stripped Sebastian of his flashy brand deals and shiny legacy, leaving only the naked truth. Sebastian was an asshole. Now that the truth was out, Ian expected things to change in the dance department. Mrs. Agnes would have to toss Sebastian aside, giving him a chance at leading barre routines. He ranked second, always a shadow behind Sebastian, but not for long. Tingles twirled up his body. Rank one would be his. Sebastian would be so mad he'd probably drop out. And a CLASH without Sebastian would be heaven.

He entered Ballet III, pausing, his excitement dying down. It all seemed too normal. Sebastian prepared his barre routine, timing pliés to Adolphe Adam's Giselle while his camera crew filmed. Mrs. Agnes reviewed her lesson in the mirror. Nothing had changed. Vega assumed her position at the barre with Mahogany, Polly, and Marc, not even questioning Sebastian's dictatorship.

No, this wasn't happening. He wasn't letting Sebastian continue to lead every warmup when Sebastian wasn't even the best dancer. Sure, Sebastian had great technique, but he lacked the emotional ability to transform technique into storytelling, making Sebastian a gymnast, not a ballet dancer. This was not an Olympic sport.

Ian joined Vega at the barre. "You going to show Mrs. Agnes the video?"

"She can watch it herself," Vega replied.

"Yeah. That'd be a little much." Mahogany's opinion filled Vega with doubt.

His eyes widened, surprised. Mahogany always took his side, but was she team Sebastian? He swallowed, studying her dark skin, her brown eyes, her lips. She was so close he could kiss her, and he wanted to but wasn't sure if she'd like his kiss. She stood behind a piece of glass labeled property of Sebastian the vamp. Ian was sick and tired of the dance department treating Sebastian like he was flawless when the dude needed a personality check. He wanted to take a tissue and scrub away the dance faculty's rosy vision of Sebastian. Vega's TikTok would do exactly that. But maybe Mahogany didn't want that, valuing her status as Sebastian's pas partner more than their love. Hurt, Ian looked away.

Sebastian clapped for their attention, turning the music higher and leading them through tendus from first.

Ian anticipated Sebastian's approach, flexing his core. He felt Sebastian's hands at his shoulders and back, finding spots that forced him to lift taller. He didn't even know how Sebastian spotted an imperfection in an almost flawless posture, but that was Sebastian the vampire. Always spotting the human weakness.

Sebastian counted them through dégages from across the room, closing in on Vega. The ball of her foot kept missing the beat by a split second.

Sebastian clapped, trying to nudge her on beat. When Vega ignored him, he clapped louder until her dégages matched the tempo.

"Tighten your buttocks," Sebastian reminded her. "It'll help."

She ignored him.

And that set Sebastian off. He lasered in on Vega's mistakes, missing Marc slipping out of retiré too early and Polly turning her head the wrong way in second position frappé. Ian was so engrossed in watching Vega and Sebastian's little dance of hatred, he couldn't focus on connecting with the floor. That deserved a call-out, but Sebastian was all Vega this morning.

Vega trembled, her eyes moist but unwilling to listen.

Sebastian's anger flared.

Ian tried not to laugh. Their similarities made them the perfect enemies. Sebastian was demanding, highly critical, and driven, and so was Vega. It just so happened she wanted the exact opposite of what Sebastian wanted. And watching polar opposites clash? It was like watching an MMA fighter go against his reflection, breaking glass and flesh and drawing blood but ignoring all the pain and self-destruction.

Sebastian relevéd to arabesque, trying to persuade Vega to imitate his posture. When she didn't, he lifted her back leg higher.

She yanked her leg away. "Back off."

"Your form's off," Sebastian snapped.

"You're bullying me!"

Mrs. Agnes placed her hand on Sebastian's shoulder, gazing at Vega. "Why don't you take a moment?"

Vega looked like a hot mess. Everyone was staring at her, not Sebastian, wondering why she was reacting the way she was, but Ian understood the immense pressure Vega suffered. She wanted to just be, but she couldn't, not with Sebastian demanding perfection. Crumbling from the stares, Vega ran out of the room. This wasn't a safe space. Not for her or Ian or anyone. No one could be themselves under Sebastian's reign. That's why he had to persuade her to reclaim her power.

Ian snuck out when Mrs. Agnes led the class to the center for the across-the-floor routine.

He found Vega in the girls' dressing rooms. She sat in a ball under the counters, where she couldn't see her reflection. Her face dug into her knees. He crawled to her, rubbing her shoulders. *"You have to show Mrs. Agnes your video."* He spoke in Spanish, knowing she preferred it whenever they were alone. *"She's always going to take his side if you don't."*

"I'll show her as soon as class is over."

"Show as many teachers as you can. They all need to know how cruel he is. You're his sister, and all he does is embarrass you. He even dropped you from his show."

"I'm not his sister. I'm his enemy. He doesn't care about what I want. I want to go to Stanford and study law, but if it's not ballet, so what?"

"Fight back. Don't let him bully you." He hugged her. She was tall but slender, a firm line against him.

"Thank you for choosing me." Her face was like a baby doll smiling. She looked strong even with tears wetting her cheeks.

"Team Vega all the way." He meant it. *"You should have kicked him out of SG before he had the chance to drop you."*

Exactly what she wanted to hear. She mounted him, shoving her tongue down his throat. She wasn't afraid of dominating him, and he would never turn her down. He lifted her up, carrying her to the bench.

Vega might have been a tall, lean body made for runways, but she was a huntress with gray eyes constantly searching for prey. Make no mistake, she wanted to kill the weak and have their egos for dessert. She didn't hide her desire. It was all over her face. Unlike Sebastian, who feigned the white savior while hiding his need to kill your spirit. Such a prick. Ian preferred Vega in all her glorious evil. He nibbled her lip, her mouth as delicious as sin. He only had sex with Vega once. They had been drunk. It was rough, and it was fun. And this time would be more fun.

He played with Vega even though he only had minutes. She needed a laugh, and he didn't want to rush. Contrary to popular belief, sex wasn't always about whamming and bamming. Brushing his fingers down her waist, he discovered her sensitive spots. She was ticklish around her belly. Her laugh twinkled as she shoved at his hands, looping her legs around his, their sex becoming nothing more than wet, sloppy wrestling.

He grunted, surprised when she thrust her hips and forced him on his back. Her devilish grin beamed.

"You should take up jujitsu. Screw ballet."

"And you should enroll in love school. Become a love doctor." She squinted at him hard, analyzing him. He played with her hair, waiting for her assessment. *"You know ..."* she bit her lip.

He didn't. Just say it.

"Thank you for this, for being so fun. Sometimes I'm jealous of Mahogany—Frog Legs is not even worth my jealousy—but Mahogany's so lucky to have you. I don't know how you do it. Keep things fun when they're not fun."

If only she knew the truth. Most of the time he wasn't having fun. Physical touch was his fun. Dancing minus Sebastian was his fun. Mahogany despised his need for fun, demanding he endure the chaos pure and saintly like her.

Vega pulled away, squishing her face to fight the tears. He didn't want her to move when she obviously needed to be held, but the mood was over. And they had to return to class before Mrs. Agnes came after them. He grabbed his crumpled leggings and pulled his shirt over his head. Vega regained her visage of the huntress, and he knew not to touch her while returning to Ballet III.

Mahogany shot him the dirtiest look. It was like she could smell Vega on him. She didn't want to stand next to him. Bodies parted them, but he could feel her disappointment squeezing him, making it hard to focus. He was supposed to learn the across-the-floor routine. Mrs. Agnes rehashed the steps. Her feet looked fuzzy, his mind unable to grasp the movements.

Mahogany didn't have a right to be mad. He told her he wanted to love like his parents loved.

He wasn't ready when his turn came. Stumbling into a group of six guys, it took a second to decipher the choreography. He observed Sebastian, jealousy festering. It was like God designed each step for Sebastian, and gravity was an angel boosting Sebastian's leaps. Ian danced around the other guys, his focus on the vampire. He pushed higher, forced his limbs longer. The vampire stretched into a pirouette à la seconde, and so did Ian. One by one, each guy fell off. His heart pounded, hip aching. His body begged for rest, but he wouldn't be weak like his CLASH-mates. He didn't stop spinning, matching the vampire turn for turn until slowing into a deep lunge fourth position.

Ian raised his arms to third arabesque. He locked eyes with Sebastian's in the mirror. *Jerk.*

"Relax," Mrs. Agnes said. "Breathe; the world is not on your shoulders."

He studied his reflection, replaying his steps in his head. He had tried hard to relax through each movement while maintaining an image of masculinity. But maybe he had been too masculine, like Sebastian.

"You shouldn't let my sister distract you." Ian looked at Sebastian in the mirrors. "She can screw up, but you're on scholarship."

"What does that mean?"

"*Necesito decirtelo en español?*" Sebastian asked. Do I need to say it in Spanish?

Ian shoved Sebastian.

Sebastian shoved him back, waiting for Ian to punch him.

Ian would have if he didn't catch Vega in the mirrors. She entered Mrs. Agnes' office with her phone pulled out. Let Sebastian's fall begin. He turned away, grinning.

"I hope you're happy," Mahogany whispered, shoving past him and walking to debate class without him.

CHAPTER 18
ZOEY

she never forgot her homework, and this feeling of failure was the worst. Mrs. Sehar had looked so confused when Zoey told her, 'I don't have it.'

She stuffed pineapple in her mouth, walking to third-period French. She wished she could dip her feelings of failure in pineapple juice, eat it, and poop it out. If only getting rid of failure was that easy. Thankfully, Mrs. Sehar pitied her enough to let her turn in her assignment late. She had till Monday to embroider a masterpiece, and that still wasn't enough time. Her weekend was packed. There was prepping for Sebastian's auditions and then preparing an outfit for Greg's Back-to-School Bash. Maybe she shouldn't audition. Then, she could focus on school and prepping for the party.

She hadn't landed an invitation yet, but she was manifesting. Whenever she had a spare second, she envisioned Greg's mansion glittering in the night, filled with alcohol pouring, sweaty bodies dancing, and faces gorging on food. There would be bathroom sex and weed and leaking of obnoxious social posts. No one would hold back because everyone knew normalcy was just an alarm clock ring away. They could beg for forgiveness on Sunday, and for once, she wanted to be the one begging for forgiveness.

She was determined to get invited, but 'how?' was the big question stressing her out. Third period would have to be a brainstorming session. She hoped Ian could come up with a brilliant idea. All she had was volunteering to work on Greg's waitstaff. At least that way, she wouldn't be the only one come Monday without a story to tell. CLASH-mates expected Frog Legs not to get invited, and then, surprise, surprise, she could add something spicy to the gossip. People would view her differently, as if she had value.

She entered French class, stopping at the teacher's desk, eyeing where she and Ian usually sat. Why were Sebastian and Vincent sitting at their table when they usually sat with either Vega or Greg? She eyed Ian sitting in the middle of the room, wanting him to fix this. This was the only class they could sit together, their only time to plan. But instead of waiting for her, he sat with Vega and Greg. She felt abandoned.

He locked eyes with her, mouthing, 'I had no choice.' Tilting his head in Sebastian's direction as if he were blaming Sebastian for this new seating arrangement. Ha! No, this was Vega's fault. That stupid TikTok had destroyed her precious gossip time with her bestie and left her with few places to sit. She scanned the classroom twice, spotting one empty chair at Vincent and Sebastian's table. There was no other option. She'd have to sit with her crush. *Awkward.* Her hand tightened around her pineapple, shoving the last juicy chunk in her mouth. There went all her comfort. What if her crush brought up the auditions? Telling the truth felt like too much information. She had disappointed her favorite teacher, and now she wasn't sure about auditioning anymore. Sebastian would dislike her answer, and then she'd have disappointed two people she admired. Failure doubled.

Sebastian's cameramen filmed her from the corners of the classroom. If she had known this would happen, she would have rehearsed cool topics. She would have worn a cute dress and went with eyeshadow that popped. Her outfit was too blah, screaming, 'Today's another boring day,' and not 'Camera, lights, Sebastian, now!'

How could God do this to her? How could Ian? Couldn't they see she needed her third-period gossip time, especially after forgetting Mrs. Sehar's homework assignment? Especially when she needed to strategize how to get an invitation to Greg's party? She felt like she was losing control of everything.

She slid into her seat.

Vincent said, "Sup?"

She croaked out a reply. So Frog-Leg Zoey. Embarrassed, her eyes danced to Ian. He exchanged whispers with Vega. When he felt her staring, he turned around and blew her kisses.

Her cheeks grew hot. She glanced away, deciding to make the best of this awkward situation. "How are auditions?" she asked Sebastian.

"Hard."

She waited for him to elaborate. He didn't.

"Man, I don't even know why you're stressing," Vincent said. "Cast Mahogany and call it a day."

Zoey bit her lip. Mahogany would be the perfect partner. She sat with Polly and Marc, looking like success covered in chocolate. Chocolate was so delicious. Zoey wished she had some now to sweeten the realization that there was no point in competing against Mahogany. Sebastian wouldn't choose her, Vega would make fun of her, and CLASH-mates would call her Frog Legs forever. Her senior year known as Frog Legs. Eewww. She rubbed her forehead, feeling pathetic.

Sebastian must have thought she looked terrible cause he tried to make conversation. "Don't you dance?"

Zoey's eyes widened. "I salsa and bachata. How'd you know?"

"I did a deep dive on your IG the first day of school. I was curious cause my mamá dances Latin styles."

Oh yeah. She remembered Sebastian checking out her feed because of her outfit. That's when he followed her account. She started feeling herself just a little, loving his compliment.

"You're fun to watch, and it'd be cool to explore your skills further. Can you come by tonight?"

"You mean to audition?"

"Yeah, you should. You have something different that excites me."

That excites you? Wow. Warmth filled her chest, simmering her doubts into a stew of gushy confidence. She still wasn't sure about auditioning, but she liked him too much to tell him that. "I want to audition, but I can't tonight. I'm not ready."

"I'm a good judge of ready."

"I have this fashion project. It's huge." She grimaced, regretting her words. Even if she wasn't sure about auditioning, she didn't want Sebastian thinking she couldn't balance dance with her homework. "I mean, I want to give it my all. It means so much to me, so I'm thinking the last day."

Sebastian didn't like that answer.

"*Bon journée*," Mme. Marie sang. Saved. Her teacher entered class late with a purple boba tea. It was perfect timing. Zoey slouched against her chair, relieved.

"Get into groups of two or three, please," Mme. Marie said. "I'd like you to work on a dialogue about your upcoming weekend plans, in French, of course."

Her relief turned to horror. She didn't want to be in a group with Vincent and Sebastian, not when Sebastian was determined to convince her to audition tonight.

She rushed towards Ian, clinging to his arm. "Be my partner."

Ian sought permission from the SG gang. Greg's face said no, eyes bouncing from Sebastian and Vega. There was no way he could be in a group with the twins, but he also couldn't team up with his usual faves, Vincent and Sebastian, not with him having to stay loyal to Vega. Oh God, the CLASH social game at play. That left Zoey and Ian as his safest choices, but Greg looked hesitant, not wanting to spearhead teaming up with an outsider.

"Ian, Val, let's partner up," Vincent said before Greg opened his mouth. "Mahogany, you good to team up with Polly?"

"Polly, you can be our partner," Vega said.

Mahogany obeyed Vega, kicking off a strategy communicated entirely through body language. Zoey watched, both amazed and confused, wishing to be a part of this silent game of musical chairs so she too could glide into a group. But she was an outsider who needed permission to join.

The game ended with Sebastian sitting between two empty chairs, the only empty chairs left.

No! She looked at Vincent, at Mahogany, at Ian (the biggest traitor of all), at Vega. Had they all known? Greg hadn't. He looked as startled as she felt but nowhere near as intimidated. She watched Greg regain his composure, joining Sebastian's table, leaving her standing alone. Greg and Sebastian looked at her, waiting. They wanted her to sit, with them, two big dudes with powerful jaws and athletic bodies. They were perfect for lead roles in Miraculous Ladybug while she was Marinette without the cool job of saving the world.

Sebastian pulled out her chair.

She channeled strong, just like her mom and dad, just like the people of Compton. Sharing a table with Greg and Sebastian wouldn't be a big deal. On the bright side, this was an opportunity to ask Greg for an invitation. She slid into the chair, and Sebastian squeezed her shoulder.

"Such a lady's man," Greg snickered. He looked like danger, his blue eyes narrowed on Sebastian, his body leaning away from Zoey. He was not interested in her, and that made Zoey feel dirty, like begging for a couple dollars when all she desired was acceptance.

It's not desperate to ask for an invitation. It's part of the assignment, and you have to go for what you want. She breathed. Her tongue felt thick. She didn't want to get rejected in front of Sebastian, but she wouldn't have any more chances like this. "Aren't you having the Back-to-School Bash this weekend?"

"Sure," Greg shrugged. He held out his hand to Sebastian, waiting for the pen and paper. Then he wrote his name and scribbled, *J'ai un fête.* I have a party. He steered the conversation to Sebastian. "What about you? How are auditions? Are you holding them over the weekend?"

"You know how they're going." Sebastian studied Greg, distrusting.

"I didn't have anything to do with that video."

"Did you ask her to take it down?"

Greg grew irritated. "Dude, you guys fight all the time, and it's pretty abusive. Did you apologize to her and get her to take it down? Try being the nice guy for once."

"Love how guilty you're feeling, but don't," Sebastian said. "I expected you to take her side."

Greg sighed. "Let's focus on the assignment."

"Okay, Gregory. Damage control. I think that's *gestion de crise*. So, about your big party? Invite list includes Vega, SG minus me because you choose sides."

"I'm not choosing sides," Greg said. "You're mean. Admit you were wrong, apologize, and she'll take the video down."

"Those are your conditions? For us to be friends?"

Greg reclined in his chair, clasping his hands behind his head. It was as if he loved knowing that Sebastian still wanted his friendship. "Apologize to your sister, *excuse-toi auprès de ta sœur*, but wait, you'll have to do that on Thursday before invitations go out Friday, so I guess your plans are up in the air." Greg wrote, *Sebastian n'a pas encore de plans pour le week-end.*

Zoey didn't like Greg insulting Sebastian, not when Greg was clueless as to how it felt to be trashed on social media. Even if the twins were to kiss and forgive, CLASH wouldn't then join hands and sing, 'Fighting evil by moonlight as one big FAMILY.' Not this thirst trap of a school! Unless Sebastian pulled off a brand makeover, he was going to be the abusive brother, and people would avoid him so they wouldn't become the next social media scandal. She felt like she and Sebastian were the same.

"I'm sorry Vega invited everyone into your business. People probably don't want to audition for you now. I get it," She said. "Frog-Leg Zoey is a thing from seventh grade."

She watched the tension in Sebastian's body drain, loosening his grip around the table. Watching him relax made her feel warm. He wasn't alone. She was on his side.

He smiled her fave smile. "Write this, '*Parce que j'aime les grenouilles, je prévois d'en attraper des jolies ce week-end.*'" Because I like frogs, I'm planning how to catch pretty frogs this weekend. He was flirting with her, and he didn't care what Greg thought. She liked him even more.

"*Cinq minutes de plus,*" Mme. Marie announced. Five more minutes.

An office attendant entered, whispering in Mme. Marie's ear.

"Sebastian," Mme. Marie waved. "The principal needs to see you in his office."

Zoey stiffened, the class growing silent. There were only two reasons CLASH-mates got called to the principal's office. Either they were getting an award, or they were in trouble.

Sebastian shoved his chair backward. The sound of metal scratched her ears.

It was most likely the latter. Dad had probably seen Vega's TikTok, and the school had a strict "no bullying" policy. Air quotes cause obviously Vega was still in power. She was the real bully, not Sebastian.

Zoey grabbed his hand. "I'm excited to audition—I mean, *ce week-end je me prépare pour tes auditions de danse et je suis excitée. À bientôt.*" I'm preparing for your auditions this weekend. I'm excited. See you soon.

Sebastian squeezed her hand goodbye.

CHAPTER 19

SEBASTIAN

he hated disappointing people. That's why he worked tirelessly to obey the rules, going above and beyond expectations. A prodigy—that's what CLASH called him—and prodigies didn't get called to the principal's office. Not for social media scandals. He hadn't watched the TikTok. It was a waste of his time, a dumb effort on Vega's part to annihilate him, but now he wished he had as he walked to Principal Raine's office.

The walk felt long. His feet sometimes refused to move. The film crew had to love every time he stumbled, especially Amy. She was probably noting in her iPhone, 'Stumbling down hallway defeated. Add to the rough cut.'

He wished Papá had warned him becoming a star would make him a spectacle. Papá had to have known from years of international stardom that people would love watching his demise. It would have been nice to be clued in. That way he could have mentally prepared. Papá had worked hard to find a partner to make stardom bearable, committing to Mamá early on. Sebastian wished he had someone to commit to. He used to have Vega, but Vega wanted to gut him.

He pushed himself through the Alumni Corridor and into Principal Raines' office.

Mamá was there, listening to Principal Raines. She gripped her necklace so tight her hands reddened. She stared, disbelieving, her giant gray eyes begging Sebastian to tell her it was a badly planned skit he and Vega created for views. Lying wasn't a skill he developed, unlike Vega, so he stood frozen, absorbing all of Mamá's horror, growing angrier and angrier.

Vega would not continue to deface him in front of his parents. He had sacrificed too much to make them proud.

When Principal Raines demanded he sit, Sebastian sat with his back so straight it hurt.

Principal Raines loaded Vega's video on a giant monitor behind his desk.

Sebastian refused to look at it. Instead, he stared out the gigantic windows overlooking the statue of a stingray leaping out of the fountain. Past that was the CLASH gardens paved with violets. Vega's insults diminished its beauty. The Stingrays' track and field stadium towered just beyond. His sister's cries reduced its majesty.

He had missed out on so many sports events. Missing a basketball game wasn't an option. He had to support Vincent. Other than that, he was too busy working to have a social life. Vega acted like she had all the time in the world. She pranced around CLASH with Gregory, taking selfies at the stingray fountain and pretending to pray in the chapel. It was all to please the thousands of followers that she wouldn't even have if it weren't for him. He had sacrificed so much so she could have a brand, and how did she repay him?

The video ended. He was shaking uncontrollably.

"This is pretty damaging," Principal Raines said from behind the desk. "But I want to hear your side."

Mamá and Principal Raines believed the video, and he didn't want to waste his time convincing them that the video was a lie. That was what Vega wanted him to do, beg for reprieve, but he refused.

He shifted his gaze to Principal Raines' framed football jersey, number fifty-five. It was next to eight-year-old Zoey smiling from a picture frame. Dressed in overalls, she blew bubbles, her enormous eyes filled with wonder, her dimples round and deep.

Principal Raines walked around the desk. He was gigantic at six foot six with bulging biceps, but he sat on the front of his desk, trying to look friendly. "I got time, Sebastian." Principal Raines phoned his secretary. "You'll have to hold my calls and clear my calendar."

"Are you sure?" The secretary answered back, worried.

"As sure as a stubborn ballet dancer."

He could see Amy whispering in headphones to go tighter on Principal Raines.

"I want you to know I've been where you've been," Principal Raines said. "I'm one of five kids, four boys, and one girl. We all played sports, and we fought like rabid dogs."

Mamá tensed beside him. "Vega and Sebastian have small disagreements, but they normally get along."

"Let me get to the point, Mrs. Bautista. What I'm saying is I understand sibling rivalries, so you can talk to me, Sebastian."

Sebastian concentrated on the Zoey museum that was Principal Raines' office. Each Zoey photograph revealed something new; He learned her favorite color was orange and that she loved pineapple, even in her ice cream.

"You're really going to let me suspend you without saying anything?" Principal Raines asked.

"Suspension?" Mamá gasped. "No. That's unacceptable."

"Bullying is unacceptable. CLASH has a strict no-bullying policy."

He could see Amy smiling at the fact that she was finally getting the conflict she needed for this scene to work.

"Sebastian, say something, please. We want to understand why you would try to hurt your sister."

He looked at Mamá, shocked she would ever accuse him of hurting Vega. "I give her so much of me, but she hates me. And I told you she hates me." He stood. "I told you that, but you had to see it. Well, there's the proof. Vega's spreading lies to destroy me. And now you see it. The whole world sees it." He turned to leave. His flesh was burning.

He needed to escape. "I don't want to talk about this any-more. I have auditions for this film."

The cameramen zoomed in on his face.

Mamá blocked his exit. She was small, hardly reaching his shoulders, and still, she trapped him. The giant office closed in. His vision blurred along with his thoughts. He had to break free. Gripping Mamá–

"Sebastian Silvian Bautista!" Principal Raines barked.

He snapped out of his haze, startled, releasing Mamá. Red fingerprints were tattoos on her tiny wrists. He had done that. He had hurt Mamá. Shame squeezed tears from his eye sockets.

Mamá hugged him.

He recoiled away, not wanting to be held or told he was okay. He wasn't okay. He was a monster.

She tried guiding him, and he stumbled to the chair, collapsing forward to hide his face. Vega stole everything, his reputation, his control. His sister spat at his pride, but Mamá didn't deserve his anger or the bruises he left on her wrists. He heaved snot and tears, feeling Principal Raines' gigantic hands massaging his back along with Mamá's tiny ones. Their hands were a poorly coordinated effort, making dysfunctional circles over his shoulder blades, up and down his spine as if they could rub love into his flesh like lotion.

"He's under a lot of pressure, Mrs. Bautista, and I know pressure. Back when I played for the Rams, I was blinded by pressure and blew out my knee, ending my career when I was at my prime. That put a stop to all my dreams."

"I don't want that to happen to him."

"This might feel like a punishment, but he needs to step down from SG and his Class Lead roles and take some time for himself."

"No," Sebastian said, the tears muddling his voice. He hated how he sounded.

"Yes," Principal Raines said.

"I'm the best dancer in Level III. I earned Class Lead. Vega doesn't do anything. She sucks at dance. Make her choose something else."

"Your sister may not want to make this her life, but you can't devalue her efforts just because she doesn't want what you want," Principal Raines said. "That's not good leadership. Good leadership leads through love–"

"Vega doesn't love. She destroys. I'm not letting her destroy me."

"She's not your enemy. Leading isn't easy. It's a skill. You have to learn to lead when others fail, especially when people don't look at the world the way you do."

"Principal Raines is right," Mamá said. "You'll have to learn to love your sister where she's at in her dance journey. I regret letting you fire her off the doc."

"Love her?" Sebastian recoiled. The very idea that he had to accept Vega's blatant disrespect for the craft made him want to puke. She probably spent an hour creating that one two-minute TikTok, smudging her makeup, frazzling her hair, deciding on flat lighting and dutch camera angles. That was way more time than she would spend rehearsing with him. He needed someone who would rather be rehearsing instead of thinking of his demise. "Vega can audition if she really wants her spot back."

"Fair," Principal Raines said, "But that doesn't resolve the conflict. I'm going to assign you to write a five-thousand-word paper on the importance of 1 Corinthians 13 when it comes to leadership. And, I will discuss rearranging Vega and Sebastian's schedules with the dance faculty. It's a good idea to separate them to minimize conflict. Sebastian, I want that paper by the end of next week."

He'd write that paper with generative AI and delete it as soon as he finished so he wouldn't ever have to remember Vega was the reason that paper existed.

Mamá walked with him, arm in arm, through the blue hallways. Her flats thumped the tiles. Dressed in black leggings and a matching cami, she looked and smelled like she had just been training. He loved seeing Mamá dressed for the studio. It reminded him of his legacy.

"*Extraño a tu papá, a veces me siento sola,*" Mamá said. I miss your papá. Sometimes, I'm lonely. She squeezed his hands. "*I dance, and I dance, and when I stop, my son's off making a documentary, my husband's in Madrid running a company, my daughter's off with her boyfriend. And here I am alone, almost fifty, reconciling with a hard truth: dance is part of me, but it is not human.*"

"*I won't stop, promise. Not even when I'm fifty.*"

She laughed, wiping her tears. *"That's what I'm afraid of. You'll dance your whole life away, marry a beautiful woman, and make her lonely."*

He knew she was talking about Papá, and it hurt him. He hadn't noticed Mamá was unhappy. She got up every morning and ate breakfast, and then . . . he could only imagine her life after that. He never saw her much, especially now that he was always filming. Before, Papá had forced them all to hang out on the weekends. It was the morning beach trips, the family rehearsals, and the dinner parties with the neighbors that had all ended when Papá moved back to Madrid. They stayed with Papá every year, alternating summers and winters. And his parents looked happy. They were always kissing and touching, and maybe that was only teasing Mamá, not satisfying.

Sebastian hugged Mamá as if she were breaking and he could hold her together.

"No te olvides de ser humano," she whispered. Don't forget to be human. She left him feeling so empty.

He lifted his head, breathing deeply until he no longer felt the tears behind his eyes, then he sent a text.

Sebastian: I want to go to Gregory's party. Can you make sure I'm on the guestlist?
Vincent: You pulling some espionage-type stuff?
Sebastian: Correct.

Vincent texted him a Bronny James dunk GIF.

CHAPTER 20

IAN

he wanted to know how Vega felt about Sebastian getting called to Principal Raines' office. She wouldn't talk, so he was left guessing. Sadness? No. Worry? Would worry make her freakishly controlling? She was supposed to collaborate with him and Mahogany on Mme. Marie's assignment, but Vega didn't want their input. She grinded her pen into the paper, mapping out SG's weekend schedule in French. That wasn't the point of the assignment, but okay. They'd arrive early Saturday morning and work until the Back-to-School Bash started. Sunday, they'd meet to review the party's successes and failures. Vega read the paper, so he and Mahogany could identify any errors. There were none, so she slammed her pen on the table.

Agitated. Vega looked agitated, but why?

Vega pulled out her phone and went to DoorDash.

"What do you want for lunch?"

"Order whatever," Ian said. "You think Sebastian's going to get grounded? For getting suspended?"

"I don't know. I'm not my parents." She jumped up and ran to Greg, standing at his side like a baby poodle. No, it wasn't agitation. It was guilt. She was feeling guilty.

"Sebastian's parents are going to freak." Mahogany stuffed her notebook in her bag, readying for lunch. "He has a career to think about, not just CLASH."

"Right, this is so headline news." Ian didn't want Vega feeling sorry for Sebastian and backtracking to make things right. He was so close to securing rank one, and her guilt could halt his rise. He was never certain about Vega. She was as unpredictable as rain in Los Angeles. One moment, she'd rain on Sebastian's reputation, and then, when least expected, she'd radiate sunshine.

He drifted behind Mahogany to lunch. CLASH-mates were talking. Exams, sports tryouts, Sebastian. So many people thought Sebastian was a loser now. Vega could easily change all that. She could launch a campaign and push out Sebastian-fandom until everyone dressed in his merch.

He entered the cafeteria. Plantains and jollof rice hit his nose. He squashed the urge to hop in the lunch line, heading straight to the SG table. Vega was missing in action even though her sashimi tray was opened and her chopsticks laid in soy sauce.

"Where's Vega?" he asked Greg.

"She got called to Principal Raines' office."

"Wait, what?"

Greg shrugged, self-absorbed and uncaring as always.

Ian texted Vega when she didn't arrive to debate class. She ignored him, or worse, she couldn't answer because she was in trouble. He was so worried about her he showed up to Modern III on time. He hated showing up on time. Being late was how he maintained some sense of individuality, but Modern III was the last class of the day and his only chance to uncover what happened to Vega.

He paused at the entrance to the dance studio. Sebastian stretched at the barre while his camera crew filmed. So, Principal Raines didn't suspend Sebastian. Great. Ian continued scanning the studio. To the right of Sebastian, Mr. Nureyev studied a manual, and to Mr. Nureyev's right, there was Vega stretching with Mahogany.

He ran to Vega, scooping her up and whirling her around. "What happened to you? You disappeared."

"Obsess much, stalker?" Vega laughed.

"Drama King, maybe. Stalker? Hmmm . . . too busy."

"I was stuck arguing for my life. Principal Raines wanted to put me in Level II so I would never run into Sebastian, but I was like, hell no! I don't deserve that."

"So your schedule's staying the same?"

"You're stuck with me, bitches."

"And Sebastian?"

"Yeah," Vega whispered. There was that guilt again. She glanced at Sebastian's little corner. People tried their hardest not to warm up too close to him, afraid to look like Sebastian sympathizers.

"Maybe Sebastian will apologize," Mahogany said. "And things can go back to normal."

"Being an asshole is his norm. I'm glad you stuck up for yourself, Vega. He deserves whatever he gets, and you shouldn't feel bad about calling him out. Especially after how he embarrassed you in front of the world."

Vega glanced at the cameras. "Yeah, he's not sorry. He only cares about himself." Her guilt shrunk, and Ian felt a little less threatened.

He rested his leg on the barre, leaning away until he felt a pleasant stretch up his side. The stretch felt as nice as the certainty that Vega wouldn't backtrack. The fall of Sebastian could continue, and so could the rise of Ian.

"Ian," Mr. Nureyev called. "You're leading warmup starting today."

Ian lowered his leg. Did he hear that correctly? He looked at Vega and then Mahogany.

Vega shoved him forward.

It was happening. He was leading warmup, just like he deserved. Walking to the center with his chin raised high, he savored the feeling of being seen. Then he led the class through the same warmups he did in his house early mornings whenever Mahogany didn't sleep over. Pliés stretched into tendus, limbs rose with développés. He walked around the class, gently adjusting his peers' technique, showering a compliment here or there. He was kind, empathetic, not Sebastian the vampire.

Sebastian danced mechanically, his body facing away from the class. Ian didn't need to see Sebastian's face to know that he hated his demotion, but Ian didn't let Sebastian's hatred sour his mood. He owned every minute of class, each bead of sweat proof of his gratitude. The bell rang. His CLASH-mates started readying to leave, but he savored his rise a bit longer.

"You're a hot mess." Mahogany shoved him towards the door.

"You like it messy." He grabbed her hands, guiding her through the crowded hallways, past the dressing rooms. His sweaty dance clothes felt like a gold medal that he wasn't ready to take off yet.

"Not this messy. I hate watching them hurt each other. It's like watching someone cut their wrists. And I don't get why you're out for Sebastian when he's your friend. He literally pays your bills. You wouldn't even be here if it weren't for him."

"Which makes him my boss and not my friend." He kissed Mahogany's chin. "Can you be my boss instead? We could run the world." Mahogany wrapped her arms around his neck. She held him as if he were the barre, helping her balance in this hateful world of Bautista chaos. He kissed her, loving how his fingers tangled in her hair.

He felt someone tapping on his shoulder and knew it was Zoey. She was the only one who would interrupt his make-out sessions. He teased her about it. "Want to join?"

She rolled her eyes. "We have to get home so we can practice and hopefully wrap by nine. I don't want to forget to do my homework."

He curled his lip, annoyed. Zoey shouldn't audition, especially now that Vega had implemented the fall of Sebastian.

"What are you practicing for?" Mahogany placed her hands on her hips.

"Sebastian's auditions."

"Really? You're not scared?"

"Vega's already trashed my reputation." Zoey shrugged.

"Of embarrassment, like, are you even on his level?"

This was absolute gold. He was going to use this catfight to his advantage. "Come over tonight. Help Zoey get on Sebastian's level," he said.

"Can't, Sebastian and I are meeting up. I'm his pas partner, and we have to work on a routine." Mahogany texted Sebastian before showing off his response, three black hearts. "You two have fun." She walked in the opposite direction of Sebastian's locker, too scared to be seen at CLASH with him. The social game was at play.

"You think Mahogany auditioned?" Zoey asked.

"Yeah," he said, even though he wasn't sure. He hoped Mahogany didn't. That would make her Team Sebastian when he was Team Vega. And no one could be both. Vega would make them choose. That's why he didn't want Zoey to audition.

"Do you think I still have a chance?" Zoey asked.

"She's kinda perfect." He hated seeing Zoey sad, but he really, really didn't want her to audition. "We can do something else to destress from all this drama," like grab organic ice cream at The Glen Centre or visit The Getty Museum before grabbing ramen in Brentwood. They could even grab a veggie burger and get lost in Long Beach. All of that would be way more fun than prepping Zoey to join forces with his enemy.

But Zoey wasn't the type to give up easily, something he loved and hated about her. She wanted to go home and train, so they sat in traffic on the 101 South, creeping slowly to Compton. They arrived home after sunset. Ma Raines sat on the front porch grading papers.

"You two want dinner?" she called to Zoey and Ian as they climbed out of the car.

"No, we have to practice," Zoey said, dragging Ian to his studio. He would have preferred some dinner, but Zoey was all business so he followed her lead.

As soon as he stepped into his studio, he channeled his inner CLASH dance instructor. Few of them smiled. They stood in the center, yelling corrections. He became that for Zoey, working her through the toughest warmup and center routine that her body could endure. He forced her to stand on relevé and complete rond de jambes into developés. He made her do that until he noticed she couldn't lift her leg without wincing. Then, they practiced turns until her calf muscles cramped. When she couldn't take anymore, she hobbled towards his mini-fridge, grabbing pineapple and collapsing into exhaustion.

"It hasn't been a full hour," he said. "We have to keep going. Sebastian would want you to keep going," which wasn't a lie. He had witnessed Sebastian's evenings when spending nights at the Bautista mansion. Sebastian would train endlessly, only stopping when his Ma prompted him to take a break.

"Everything hurts," she said.

"Training with Sebastian hurts." He collapsed down beside her. "Now you know why Vega made that video."

"Do you think I have a chance? I can't even get through a tough rehearsal. And if this is how hard Sebastian trains–I mean, I don't know."

His plan was working. She was doubting herself. He just needed to intimidate her a little more. He pulled out his phone and showed her Mahogany's TikToks. "You see how good she is?" He showed a couple videos of her dancing with Sebastian.

"They dance together a lot," Zoey whispered.

"I mean, they're friends. And they look perfect together. It's normal."

"I think I may be wasting my time."

The rise of Ian could continue.

CHAPTER 21
ZOEY

last night was rough. Ian led her through a rehearsal that almost killed her. She had been so tired when she got home that she fell asleep on top of her homework. She woke up late and fell asleep in first period. By lunchtime, she was dragging her feet through the cafeteria, dazed and wondering, could she last another week? Should she continue with her suffering now that Mahogany was competition? What was even the point? Mahogany was perfect for Sebastian.

Zoey needed to stay on her low carb diet and eat a salad today, but her emotions craved oily bread covered in cheese. And the cafeteria had the best pizza Fridays. She spotted the pizzas glowing on silver trays from the front of the lunchroom. The smell of dough and tomato sauce hugged her stress away. The culinary students were so good, so good. Michelin needed to stop playing and give all the cooks stars cause their cooking skills helped her survive the CLASH rollercoaster. Up and down, CLASH tossed her emotions, whipping her vertically and horizontally until she puked all that she had, including her soul. She needed a break. Just one slice of pineapple pizza, and then she could return to eating salads.

CLASH-mates buzzed about the Back-to-School Bash. Oh, yeah, today was also Invitation Friday. Her heart sank a little, fearing she wasn't successful in getting her name on the list. A big, juicy slice of pizza bejeweled with pineapple shined. She grabbed it, heading to the gardens, to the big cherry plum tree. There was still hope that she made the list. Maybe Greg felt terrible about acting like a jerk during their French assignment. Maybe Ian bribed Greg to make her waitstaff and hadn't told her yet. She crossed her fingers, squeezing her eyes tight. *Please let me make the list. Please, God, please!* It would take a miracle, but miracles happened.

Sebastian sat at a stone table close to her favorite cherry plum tree. Seeing him there alone, typing on a Macbook mini, his lunch half eaten, was weird. Now that Vega had demolished his social life, he wasn't a part of SG, so he wouldn't be working on party invites. His film crew would be his only friends.

Vega had turned her own brother into a social menace. How unthinkably cruel. Like, did Vega sleep at night, or was Ian right, and she was a vampire? That would also make Sebastian a vampire, a good one that Zoey could join forces with to end Vega's evil once and for all.

A rush of excitement shot up Zoey's body as she considered pitching Sebastian the idea. They would make a great team, with them already being food cousins. Sebastian chewed a teriyaki steak dotted with pineapple while she had a pineapple pizza. Fate.

She stepped closer, then stepped back, then stepped closer, and then stepped back. She didn't want to distract Sebastian from his work, and the film crew didn't look that friendly either. They were all skinny men with bulging biceps and huge cameras. Amy was the only woman, and Zoey couldn't depend on Amy to rescue her if she choked on her pitch.

Sebastian looked up from his laptop, eyes settling on her.

She had his attention. There was no turning back. "What're you working on?" *Lame.*

"An essay."

"On what?"

"How First Corinthians Thirteen can make me a better leader."

Actually, that isn't lame. "How can it make you better?"

"ChatGPT said I basically suck at loving leadership, so ..." he shrugged, closing his laptop and standing. "Suck less, I guess. I'm not a big Bible person." He cleaned up his trash.

"What class is it for?" She felt pressure to keep the conversation alive even though she felt its death was near. Sebastian was done with lunch. And he wasn't even looking at her as he zipped his bookbag.

"None. Principal Raines forced me to write it as a way to address the Vega TikTok."

"Sorry for that. Is she writing a paper, too?"

"That's not a punishment to her. She'd write the paper and create social videos about it, trashing the Bible and CLASH for assigning stupid papers."

She laughed. Classic Vega. "She loves weaponizing her social media. Maybe . . ." she blushed, calling on her spirit animal, "We can team up and take Vega down. Like, you know, a superhero duo."

"Like Ladybug and Cat Noir? Or Sailor Moon and Tuxedo Mask?"

Sebastian had studied her IG. She smiled into his gray eyes, bouncing on her toes and forgetting all about her pizza. It slipped right off her plate and into the grass. "Oh no." She tried to pick it up, but Sebastian beat her. He held up the remains. The camera crew zoomed in for the perfect insert. Half the cheese was gone while most of her pineapple glittered in the grass. There went her five-dollar lunch.

"I'll buy you another one."

"You don't have to. This is my life."

"I have enough to buy you a new life."

Only a CLASH-mate would say that. It had to be all that selfless leadership training the school pumped into their brains. It made the wealthy feel like their money gave them powers they could use to save scholarship kids like her. She had a dictionary-sized list of comebacks for when people made her feel like her family's wallet wasn't enough. None she could use right now on Sebastian. His confidence wasn't exactly belittling. There wasn't a trace of 'you need to do better' in his demeanor. More like he wanted to share, and she wanted to share everything with him. Biting her lip, she accepted his offer, following him through the gardens and into the crowded lunchroom.

CLASH-mates looked up from their tables to watch them. Their stares were worse than the cameras. She felt so vulnerable, standing in the pizza line while Sebastian didn't seem bothered. This had to be what it would feel like if Sebastian chose her. Everyone would watch her, waiting for her to do something interesting. If she didn't do something interesting, they would make up rumors about her. Wasn't she tired of rumors?

Sebastian said something. "What?" she asked.

"Your papá has your photos all over his office," he repeated.

"He takes a ton of pictures of me. I thought the school would have a rule, like no showcasing off your daughter, but I guess they don't."

"They shouldn't, ever. I like eight-year-old Zoey."

Was he grinning? Was this still her moment? "Why?"

"She seemed brave. Free. Like a superhero."

"Oh." As opposed to sixteen-year-old Zoey who was a creeper. "I'm still brave."

"Do you still eat a lot of chocolate ice cream?"

"Tons."

Sebastian nodded. "We could be a Willy Wonka duo."

She laughed, drowning in his grin and his eyes and his lips. "Willy Wonka is kinda not a superhero, but I guess."

"He's my favorite superhero, but we can be the Timothée Chalamet Willy. That means you have to audition."

"Sure," she said, desiring to say yes to him always, "but that means you have to choose me."

"It probably does. Maybe we'll superhero-duo it, maybe we won't." He was rejecting her, but his body leaned towards her in an I-want-you way that stirred her curiosity. She wanted him to keep flirting with riddles, loving how his words washed over her and mixed into the lunchroom noises.

A girl's scream pierced through the noise.

Zoey looked at the girl waving her phone, jumping. Another phone buzzed, sparking another scream, then another, and another, filling the entire lunchroom.

It was happening. SG texted out phone invites. Zoey squeezed her phone, praying for it to buzz.

Sebastian's phone rang. He answered. She zeroed in on Sebastian's conversation, selfishly hoping he wasn't getting a personalized invitation.

"Yeah, I considered it," he said to Greg. "But for Vega, I'm sorry, not sorry."

Greg said something she couldn't decipher.

"I CC'd you both on an essay I had to write for Principal Raines. Sort of explains why we fail as friends. Maybe we can discuss it after your party. You know where I live." He hung up the phone and looked at her. They were the only ones in the cafeteria not invited. They were outsiders, together.

She took the pineapple pizza from him, raising it in solidarity. "I guess we're both free that night." She took a giant bite.

"Not really. I have to train."

Oh. She was still alone. Her shoulders folded forward, eyes lowering.

Sebastian grabbed her wrist, and her eyes snapped up. She watched him bring her hand close, grease dripping from cheese to fingers to wrists. The tail of the pizza slid past his lips. He bit down. And she felt a tingle in her stomach as if the pizza were her tongue, the grease on his lips her saliva.

Her heart raced. They had shared a pineapple pizza kiss. She felt so warm and gooey like her pizza.

"See you at auditions, Noodle." His grin matched hers.

CHAPTER 22
SEBASTIAN

sebastian was sneaking into Greg's party. Amy wanted him to drip style but not too much that he'd attract attention. She needed a fashion connoisseur to style him just right, so she called in a favor from Robé Pak. Robé was her brother who graduated from CLASH, and CLASH-mates stayed loyal. If the devil were an Asian stylist, he'd look like Robé, six feet tall and slender with black hair looped into a manbun. He had two assistants with skin midnight black, just as tall and modelesque as him. They dragged clothes racks into Sebastian's dance studio, covering his floor with designer brands.

The clutter stressed Sebastian out.

"This'll only take an hour. Promise," Amy said while texting.

Robé started with a Fendi silk shirt paired with Tom Ford jeans.

"Go bigger," Amy replied.

He replaced the jeans with Dolce & Gabbana cargo pants with poppies decorating the legs. Amy thought it was too big. The hour morphed from eight in the morning to ten.

Vincent strolled in with his basketball, sweating from his morning workout. He sat in the corner, cracking jokes with the assistants about the brands until he announced, "Have to help Greg prep his party. Don't show up looking too brand new." He threw up deuces.

Sebastian wished he could leave with Vincent, but Robé was nowhere near done with styling. Robé took his time matching the shirts with the pants and the shoes with the jackets. He consulted with his assistants. They whispered. Then an assistant would add a scarf, then remove a scarf, and then add a belt, then remove a belt. Sebastian learned their names were Tonto and Ini, and they were two Nigerian sisters.

Mamá stopped by to drop off a salad. She couldn't resist a good fashion show. She watched the Oscar de La Renta blazer go from a Fendi short sleeve to a Balenciaga fitted v-neck. Then eleven turned to twelve, and even she had to leave.

"I love the minimalist look. It's very vampire," Amy said.

Sebastian looked confused, so she showed him Vega's Instagram. Vega had posted photos of vampire teeth surrounded by dead roses. "It's the theme."

In that case, Robé insisted he wear baggy Jonny Cota cargo pants and a Balenciaga fitted v-neck with solid silver vampire fangs. The La Greca Barocco flower-patterned sneakers would draw the eye down his physique.

Robé held up a Versace crossbody bag. "This'll get all the fashion stalkers vlogging."

Sebastian was okay with decorative sneakers, but he was not doing a murse. "Hard pass."

"You must push past your comfort zone," Amy insisted. "For the likes."

"Want likes?" Sebastian replied. "Auction it off on IG and give the money to charity."

"Love it." Amy gave a thumbs up.

Robé slipped the Versace crossbody on him long enough for Amy to snap a few photos.

His phone vibrated, SG Rebellion flashing on his phone.

Vincent: I snuck you, Amy, and your film crew on the guest list. You're all good for tonight.'

Amy texted back a panda emoji.

Sebastian could always depend on Vincent. They'd been best friends ever since he arrived at CLASH and discovered Vincent dribbling alone on the basketball courts. Vincent was quiet and so nice he had shared his basketball without Sebastian asking. And Sebastian liked sharing quiet moments filled with basketball drills up and down courts. Their friendship grew under hoops and in dance studios. They pushed each other athletically, making each other better. He had his best friend; now, all he needed was his best dance partner. Tonight had to go well.

Sebastian drove past the mansions glowing along Beverly Park Terrace, slowing when he spotted the line of cars waiting for the valet.

He gripped the steering wheel with sweaty palms. Amy kept going over the plan even though the plan was simple: He would lie low and wait for the right moment to seize the stage. Then Vincent would queue up a remixed version of *Baianá* with Pablo Fierro.

He asked Amy to play the song while they waited for the valet.

She refused. "I want it to catch you off guard."

"That stresses me out." He needed to visualize the movement to create a perfectly timed and controlled choreography. If he didn't plan, things could go wrong. And if things went wrong, he'd be another viral video. He tried to explain that to Amy when the valet opened his door, and Amy leaped out of the car, joining the crowds walking up the white carpet.

Sebastian's heart pounded, his emotions broiling. Amy abandoned him. And the vampire decor was nauseating, the themes of death heckling the fear building in his stomach.

He pulled up the hood on his jacket, glad to have a barrier that hid him from people. No one was looking at him, too busy flashing their vampire fangs for selfies. Catered food glistened from bowls. Supermodels flirted and drunk texted. Celebrities smiled with their relatives. This wasn't his vibe. He preferred weekends reading to chatting it up at parties, but no one could tell that back when he had Vincent and Gregory to lean on for social support. They had made him feel part of the CLASH elite, but that was before Vega destroyed his status.

Now, he couldn't trust anyone. CLASH-mates would rat him out to Gregory, so he kept moving through the bodies, never feeling safe enough to stand still. If he stopped, someone would catch him in his big lie.

He crossed through the kitchens into a hallway that opened into a study where Ian argued with Mahogany.

Sebastian froze, panicking. There was nowhere to hide.

Mahogany's hair was messy, sticking to her wet cheeks. Ian grabbed her, and she slapped his hand away. Sebastian couldn't hear a thing, but he guessed Mahogany was angry with Ian for being a manwhore, for his lackadaisical attitude toward school, toward dance, toward loving her. Why was she even wasting her time with Ian?

Ian glanced down the hall as if Sebastian's gaze had touched him.

Sebastian tensed. The hoodie covered his face, and it was so dark, Ian shouldn't be able to identify him. At least, he hoped.

Ian stepped forward.

Adrenaline shot through Sebastian's body. He didn't want to run even though he knew everything was at risk. His heart thumped louder with each step Ian took to close the gap. He could smell Ian's cologne, see the outline of Ian's fingertips reaching for his hoodie.

Sebastian gripped Ian's wrist.

The lights went black.

The classical hip hop faded out and became a remixed version of The Star-Spangled Banner, transforming the party's mood. That song meant Gregory was about to announce he was running for CLASH president.

Sebastian dropped Ian's hand and hurried towards the stage centered high in Gregory's living room. People struggled to fit, and those that couldn't, overflowed into the surrounding rooms. Principal Raines stood in a VIP section, networking with Gregory's papá, Charles Bradford. Seeing Charles was terrifying. He had enough power to expel Sebastian from CLASH and all of Hollywood. If that happened, Amy would capture it on the docuseries, and he would be a social pariah.

SG Rebellion popped up on his phone.

Vincent: DJ cued up the music.

Gregory stepped on the stage to welcome his guests.

Amy: Own this.

She sent three panda faces.

He couldn't even hear what Gregory was saying. Fear was rising through his body, blurring his vision. He had to get a grip. Squeezing his eyes shut, he struggled for happy images of anything: his family on the beach, Amy over pho, demi pointe on sprung flooring, eight-year-old Zoey squeezing a chocolate ice cream cone. The fear diminished as he pictured her dimples glowing.

He heard applause, his cue to jump on stage. He stood shoulder to shoulder with Gregory.

Gregory's jaw fell open, "What the heck?"

The lights went black.

Electronic Brazilian drums emerged from the speakers, becoming thicker until they throbbed throughout the room. The lights repeatedly dimmed from dark to bright, making the crowd gasp.

Sebastian stretched into an arabesque, whipping his leg into pirouettes. He succumbed to the drums and the chorus filling every particle of his body. The beat rippled through his muscles with a force he didn't recognize, leaping from fifth position into a grand battement that awed. He whipped around into fouetté turns, his hoodie falling back from the force.

Someone yelled, "Sebastian." The crowd hollered.

He rushed across the stage, facing off with Gregory just as the last beat dropped. He could see Gregory's pores, feel his angry breath on his face.

The crowd exploded. Camera lights flashed.

"Whoever auditions and becomes my partner," Sebastian shouted over the crowd. "Will dominate life with me. Audition!" He thanked Gregory for the stage time, running and back-flipping off.

Sebastian's heart thundered louder than the applause. The feeling warming his chest, a tingling sensation in his arms: It was joy. Joy had risen from the graveyard of his pain, bursting forth, taking him over, and freeing him to dance powerfully. He hadn't felt that free since … since…

Vincent pummeled him with a hug. "That was sick." He dragged Sebastian to his crew of basketball players to brag.

Sebastian soaked in the smiles, the laughs, his gaze traveling across the room. He met Vega's death glare. And suddenly, he remembered the last time he had felt that free. He saw his toes digging in sand beside Vega's, her toenails painted purple. He saw Papá and Mamá stepping through second into relevé. He could hear the waves and see the seagulls, taste the street tacos dripping on their fingers. Back when it was okay to love his sister, and his sister loved him, and they loved through dance. That was the last time he felt free.

He stared into her hatred, wishing she'd walk across the room and be happy for him.

CHAPTER 23
IAN

ian moped around greg's estate, watching Mahogany avoid him. She tried helping Greg manage the wait staff, and the cleaning crew, and the caterers, even though Greg and his padres managed without her help. The Bradfords chose vanillas, velvets, and golds as the party colors. A white carpet sprinkled with dead petals stretched from the driveway to the party entrance. Walls were lined in LED twinkle lights. Pastries inspired by dead roses were served on gold trays. The sun set, and the Bradford mansion became a vampire ball. No help required from Mahogany.

It was romantic, surprisingly, the perfect setting for scandal. Mahogany didn't want scandal with him. Whenever he approached her, she gave him her back, turning to Polly or Vega. It hurt, her constant rejection, so he eventually gave up, searching the party for new friends. He chatted up a few CLASH-mates and even bragged about dancing in The Fall Showcase with board members. Talking to adults got boring real quick. He had to wake himself up with moves on the dance floor. He tried not to take up space, weaving through the bodies, shoulder shrugging and bouncing his head. That's where Mahogany found him, two-stepping to remixed Mozart.

He tried to give her the same silent treatment, but he couldn't resist floating closer until her arms were on his shoulders and her vampire teeth pressing into his neck.

"We're the rebels," she whispered, waving around the party.

He knew exactly what she meant. There wasn't a lot of melanin in the room. "Want to do something extra rebellious?"

"Always down for trouble with you."

He led her away from the dance floor. Sometimes, he had to wonder how many other CLASH-mates snuck off to have sex in Greg's mansion. There were so many hiding places like the garden, the attic (his favorite), the library with its huge windows. He lifted Mahogany on the library's desk, positioning her under the moonlight. The music thundered so loud it shook the books and masked Mahogany's moans.

Mahogany smelled like citrus, and she tasted just as sweet. He soaked up her kisses, swimming through her limbs. She held him tighter when he felt her body tremble. Then, she pulled away as soon as the trembles ceased. That was different. They normally held each other for a while.

"What's up?" he asked.

"Why won't you commit?"

He groaned. *Not right now.* He didn't want to have this conversation, but he couldn't let her leave feeling like she didn't matter. He pulled her close. She came up to his chest, so she relevéd so that she was taller. "You mean the world to me," he said.

"You're sleeping with the whole school."

"I'm training for perfection."

"You're so LA it's disgusting." Mahogany pushed him. "Everything's so fake and Hollywood with you."

That wasn't true. She was the only one that mattered. All the other people were good times. They were quickies in lunch period, a rush to break up a heavy class schedule, but Mahogany was so much more.

He raced to beat her getting dressed, zipping up his pants and tossing on his blazer. She gave up on finding her panties, yanking on her gold cocktail dress. She smoothed the wrinkles out, rushing to retouch her makeup and comb her hair. He still beat her. A few finger swipes through his mohawk transformed him into party-ready. No one would ever guess he was the lover who had transformed Mahogany's perfect curls into an updo.

He grabbed her arm just as she ran into the hallway.

"I'm not lying to you," he said.

"You never commit. And that makes me feel like nothing. I don't want to feel like that anymore."

"My family's poly, I'm poly, I'm bi, you knew that when we first started hooking up."

"That's just it," Mahogany snapped. "I was never just hooking up with you." She pushed him away, and he stumbled, surprised by the pain building in his body. He felt someone's eyes and looked up. A guy wearing a gold and black hoodie watched him from the end of the hallway. He couldn't make out who it was, but Ian would uncover his identity before the guy ran off and spread rumors about him and Mahogany.

Ian advanced, and the guy stood his ground. Exciting. He liked playing these types of games. He lifted his hand an inch from the hooded guy. The guy stepped closer, sending a chill down his spine. Challenge accepted. He touched the hood. The guy grabbed his hand.

A remixed star-spangled banner burst through the house, signaling that Greg was about to make his grand entrance. The lights went black, and by the time Ian could see again, the hooded guy was gone.

He groaned. Greg's lame anthem had the excitement.

He trudged towards the VIP, where Vega would expect him to join her and the rest of SG.

Greg walked on the stage in the center of the living room. He thanked his pa and the CLASH executive board before launching into a speech that Vega wrote, again. Honestly, she should send Greg a Cash App request for speechwriting.

He shifted closer to Mahogany, and she moved so that Vincent created a barrier between them. Her tears had washed off her eyeliner, and she hadn't had time to fix it. He wished to kiss the smudges, reminding her she was who he loved. Mahogany always made him feel worthy while he kept failing her. His love wasn't enough for her. She wanted his worldview as if he could erase his childhood. He didn't even realize monogamy existed until he was ten, during a family barbecue. Ma and Pa Raines explained their marriage was monogamous, blowing his mind. Then the world started making sense when he noticed his CLASH-mates only had one set of padres. His padres were the weird ones, and he liked that weirdness. Being weird was fun; it made his padres happy. He thought he'd surely end up like them. Then, boom, he fell in love with Mahogany. She made him question his upbringing. It wasn't fair. He shouldn't have to deal with these life questions until at least forty.

The lights went black, cutting Greg off mid-sentence. The music went silent. What was up with the electricity? Greg wasn't creative enough to add lighting effects to his speech, and Ian could tell none of this was Vega's idea. Her body was too stiff.

He felt the crescendo of music, the pulse of base thumping in his chest. Was that *Baianá*? His mouth slacked, recognizing the hooded guy. Now, it all made sense. Greg hired a backup dancer.

Ian glanced at Vega. Her frown and crossed arms said it all. She hadn't known.

The hooded guy danced.

Vega stiffened as if the holy spirit whispered the dancer's identity in her ear.

Ian studied the dancer. No, that wasn't Sebastian. For one, Sebastian couldn't dance contemporary while this guy danced on the edge, anticipating every beat. The hooded guy dominated the unexpected, powerfully slicing the air with his limbs. Sebastian hated the unexpected.

Leaping and stretching into three fouetté turns, the hood flew off.

Ian couldn't believe it. Where the hell did Sebastian learn to dance like that? He texted Cody.

Ian: Have you been coaching Sebastian?

Cody: Who? The white Spanish boy you go to school with?

That was a hard no.

The crowd was going wild. Sebastian yelled, "Whoever auditions and becomes my partner will dominate life with me. Audition," and people went even more crazy. "Thank you, Gregory, for the stage time." He blew kisses at Vega.

"Wow! Sebastian!" Greg clapped. Ian was so confused.

"I'm bringing that kind of energy to class presidency."

Vega trembled, her small hands curled into fists.

Why was he even confused? Ian shook his head. This was typical Greg behavior. He didn't have to betray Vega for shock value. Especially when no one would waste their money or time running against a Bradford, but if Greg saw an opportunity to shine, he'd grab it.

Ian hugged Vega. "He should have asked me to dance." Her head pressed against his shoulder. She was crying, and he felt just as bad as she did.

Everything had changed for them both. CLASH operated on a twelve-hour news cycle. Vega's TikTok was last week's news. This week's? Sebastian reclaiming prodigy. Vega would have to get over her trauma, and Ian would have to return to the shadows.

He didn't know how he'd survive CLASH. He no longer had Mahogany. She thought he was Hollywood fake; and he was losing Zoey, she wanted to dance with his enemy.

CHAPTER 24
ZOEY

what was sebastian doing right now? She scrolled through his social media, stopping at his latest post. He modeled a Versace crossbody to raise funds for his scholarship. Even though the murse was so not him, his confidence sold her. She scrolled through the comments, her FOMO increasing the more bids she read. A thousand bucks! People in LA be rich, rich! She didn't have that kind of money to support him, but she wanted to join in the fun. 'You make murses mexy,' she typed, her thumb hovering over the send. Would he laugh and invite her over? They could celebrate being the only superheroes Greg didn't invite to his party. Her thumb shook. Her hesitation grew.

"Baby girl." Dad poked his head into her bedroom. "You sure you don't want to come with me?"

Zoey eyed her dad's boring gray suit. "You can't wear that." She grabbed his wrist and pulled him back to his bedroom closet, hoping to find something unique and vampire-like. She pushed through gray suit after gray suit, growing frantic.

His closet was a fashion disaster. How could she have let this go on for so long? "The royal blue silk shirt," she screamed, spotting it in the very back. She rushed to her room, grabbing the embroidered scarf she had stitched sophomore year, and placed it in his suit pocket. She wished she had some vampire teeth, but this was all she could do for him.

"You saved me." He squeezed her into a big hug. "You know I don't have to go."

"You're CLASH's first Principal of Color, and every powerful, wealthy parent will be there gossiping." And who knew what they would say? Less than five years ago, some local representative had called the school a breeding ground for white privilege, which sparked a CLASH initiative to recruit faculty and students from around the world. CLASH blamed its last principal for the bad publicity and fired him. Thus, Dad became CLASH principal. What if someone at the party started spreading he was a diversity hire? Tons of people wanted Dad's job and would say anything to get him fired. "You want to be there controlling the story." Even if she didn't get invited. It was important for Dad to mingle with the CLASH elite.

He didn't fight her, hugging her tight. As if a hug could heal her social status and make up for the lack of an invitation. Then he headed out.

She watched Dad pull out of the driveway before returning to her couch pillows. Her fingers ventured back to Sebastian's social feed, wishing to escape from her loneliness into Sebastian's life. She imagined dancing with him in

Beverly Hills and sharing desserts in Michelin-star restaurants. She liked a video of him facing off with Vincent on a Venice Beach court. The oceans waved behind Sebastian. He stretched his leg into a vertical split while Vincent dribbled defiantly. Basketball versus ballet.

'Love it,' she commented, feeling brave. She messaged a screenshot to Sebastian. Maybe he would reply. She grew nervous the longer she stared at her solitary message. Or maybe he wouldn't.

Mom plopped onto the couch. "What pizza do you want, baby girl?"

She snuggled inside her Mom's warm embrace, breathing in cocoa butter and lavender. "Nothing. I just want to sit here suffering from FOMO."

"For what? You know none of this matters, right? You don't need Gregory's party to get you into Fashion school."

"I know, but I want to get invited at least once."

"Don't you get tired of code-switching in Bel Air? Isn't that a lot of work?" Mom made a face. "I wouldn't want to do it," and she didn't have to code-switch as a middle school teacher working just down the street from their house. Her students were her neighbors, while her PTA parents were the same people attending their church, a church that didn't pry into Mom and Dad's relationship with Godmom and Goddad Cruz. Mom had a Compton tribe filled with friends who loved her for her. Zoey wanted to find her Bel Air tribe so that she could finally live her dream life, a life where Sebastian posted selfies of them captioned, '#couplegoals,' and Vega yelled, 'Frog-Leg Zoey is Fashionista Zoey!' She dreamed of code-switching her life around so that she would never again spend a lonely Saturday scrolling through social media while everyone cool partied.

Mom decided they should spend the night watching all of Gina Price-Bythewood's movies. They'd start with *Love and Basketball* and then *Beyond the Lights*. "This can finally be our mommy-daughter night. I'll make popcorn too."

"Can I get a salad?" Zoey waited till Mom was completely out of the living room before checking her phone. Her heart squeezed. Sebastian still hadn't texted back.

Mom put together a homemade kale salad paired with a bowl of popcorn covered in melted chocolate. All wonderful cures for FOMO. She grabbed a handful of chocolate popcorn, snuggling under a blanket. *Beyond the Lights* played to Mom and her commentary. Soon, she was laughing, and her FOMO was dying.

Her phone buzzed half-way through the movie.

Ian: I'm outside her phone.

It was barely eleven. She followed Mom to the front door. "What are you doing here?" she asked as soon as he was inside.

"I'm going to finish reading in my room." Mom flipped off the television. Ian's surprise arrival signaled the end of their mommy-daughter movie night. "Don't stay up too late talking."

"Good night, Mommy, Love you!" Zoey shouted, feeling a little bad, but she had to know. "Did you get kicked out of the party?" Or did Greg's house burn down?

"Let's talk at my place." Ian led her outside.

Ian's place was safer for secrets. Godmom and Goddad Cruz would spend the night in Long Beach, running their salsa club till four in the morning. That meant they could get tipsy and dance it up in the back of Ian's studio without worrying about parents. They ventured through his dark, empty house, laughing when they bumped into the furniture, searching his cabinets for Godmom Cruz's favorite apple cider beers.

He flipped on his studio lights and played reggaeton from his Bluetooth speakers. Soon, they were swaying in front of the wall-to-wall mirrors and throwing back apple cider beers. She giggled when her knees touched his, loving his dark eyes and wicked haircut. He was emotional support plus eye candy. She rested against his chest, thankful he was her friend.

"Sebastian danced at Greg's party," Ian said.

Zoey lifted her head. "He was invited?"

"I guess. I don't know. It doesn't make sense."

Her connection to Sebastian had felt so real, back when she thought they were the only ones not invited. Outsiders no one wanted, but they had each other. Them against the popular, but she guessed that connection was all in her head. She was the pathetic one who wasn't invited to another cool party. Monday would suck.

"And then he ends everything shouting some tagline, 'Dance with me, and you'll win at life,'" Ian continued. "He even blew kisses and thanked Greg before he got off stage."

"Blew kisses?" That didn't sound like a Sebastian activity at all. But then, what did she know about Sebastian? "He had this big plan to go behind Vega and Greg's back, and he didn't even say anything." She had been right there with him while everyone's phones were buzzing with invitation energy. He could have hinted, made her feel included. Her heart cracked a little. But why would he hint any big plans to her? She wasn't his girlfriend. She wasn't even his friend. She checked her phone. Still no text from Sebastian.

"What makes you think he had to go behind Greg's back?" Ian squeezed her, drawing her eyes back to him. "Greg doesn't care about Vega. He uses her all the time. She's a hot secretary who likes to satisfy."

"You would know about the satisfaction." Ian hooked up with Vega at one of Greg's parties last year. Lucky for him, Sebastian made sure his scholarship recipients received party invites. Gen Xers ran her scholarship, and they didn't care about her social life. Anyway, Vega became so intoxicated that she mistook Ian for Greg. Ian gave Vega the best oral of her life, and Vega promoted him from an outsider to the inner circle.

"Sex pays dividends. Crossing to the dark side?"

Zoey's eyes grew enormous. "I'm not sleeping with Sebastian."

"Duh. Sebastian will die a virgin, no shade to monks. We're going to have to find a way to push your boundaries."

"What do you mean?"

"You can't just dance. You have to be savage. Everyone in the world's auditioning now."

"You're right! Oh my God." Zoey panicked. "I definitely have no chance."

"Shh." Ian removed his shirt, completing a triple pirouette. The muscles in his abs flexed.

"I'm so drunk right now." She shouldn't be staring at him like that. "I'm sorry. I'm being a creeper."

"It's okay. I like it when you look at me." He pulled her body close, moving her hips against him.

She collapsed into his smell, his eyes, his limbs. "I feel like you're trying to seduce me. Are you trying to seduce me?"

"Sort of kind of."

"Iiiiaaaaannnn." She tried to pull away. He spun her into a turn, dipping her so low her head almost touched the ground. He pulled her tight. And she could feel his muscles against her skin. She wrapped her arms around his neck. She wanted to leave, but then again, did she really? Ian was fun. He wasn't judgy, he'd fight for her while demanding nothing in return, he'd text her back when she texted. Sebastian wouldn't text her.

The music soothed her heartache. Ian swayed her into a warm feeling filled with lots of colors. His kisses were sloshy like liquor. She smiled against his lips. He was such a good kisser.

"Ma always says, 'A good partnership feels like lovemaking.'" Ian's voice was extra deep.

She laughed. "How does that actually work?"

"Want me to show you?"

What the heck? "Yes." Screw Sebastian, and she'd screw Ian.

CHAPTER 25

SEBASTIAN

his phone kept buzzing at four in the freaking morning! He kicked off his sheets, staring at darkness. The only people ever awake this early were journalists. He knew that much from watching Papá navigate his career. Journalists were worse than producers, their hunger for a story transforming them into stalkers. His phone buzzed and buzzed, waking every cell in his body. If he answered one call, he'd lose control of his morning, and grabbing one hour in the studio was more important than the outside world.

He stretched upwards, his back cracking, slipping on sneakers and a thin shirt. The house was quiet, just like his studio. A few birds tested their chirping outside the windows, practice before sunrise. He kicked off his shoes, gripping the barre and pressing his feet into the sprung flooring. He needed this one hour of solitude before the world demanded he become their ideal celebrity. Last night had drained him.

He had been starving for reacceptance. And yet, the roar of Gregory's audience, all the congratulations, those were appetizers. What he really craved was Vega's approval. She was his blood. They were part of a legacy that mattered more than strangers. But Vega didn't feel the same. She spent the night glaring at him from across the room, her hatred burning him long after the party.

He completed degagés on both sides, lengthening back into cambré derriere.

Footsteps filled his space.

He sighed, noticing the camera crew hurrying into the room. Amy was bubbling over with joy, yapping away on her phone.

"It's *The Hollywood Reporter*," She beamed. "They want to know how you feel about J.Lo retweeting your video."

What are you talking about? He felt nothing. "How do I feel?"

"Inspired to be recognized by such an icon. Throw in your heritage." She shoved the phone in his face, snatching it back. "Do you feel ready to say that, or do you need a second?"

Cause a second was all she was giving him. He felt the peace draining from his body as he pressed the phone to his ear. "Hello?"

The reporter introduced herself, but he couldn't focus on her words. He had done interviews before, but Papá or Mamá or even Vega had always been there. Now he was alone, stuck acting like he was sophisticated. "I'm inspired.

Jennifer Lopez is a queen of dance with an extensive Hispanic heritage, and I'm trying to be a Spanish prince. So thanks, J.Lo, for lifting me into your court." That sounded horrible. He shuddered, handing Amy back the phone. *You couldn't come up with anything better?* Pictures of himself dressed as a court jester bombarded his mind.

He flipped onto his forearms, splitting his legs into a straight line. A headstand made him feel safe when the world felt upside down. As if balancing upside down was a proactive response to his world tilting out of control.

"How long are you staying like this?" Amy was worried.

Maybe till Vega left for school. Her ice-gray eyes replaced the memes popping off in his head. Maybe till he blacked out.

Amy pushed him over when he looked weak.

He fell to his knees, blinking the spots away.

"You're on top of the world. The world's not on top of you. Own this moment. Dress for this moment." She sounded like a self-help book, but he could either do as she said or shirk his responsibilities. And he was not about the latter.

"Own this moment," he chanted from the studio to the shower, from the shower to his bedroom closet. Dress for it meant a vanilla blazer, jeans, and matching Air Jordans. He felt overdressed, but Amy wanted it for the shots. She felt like this could be the climax.

Amy skipped behind him to the first floor, taking call after call, bragging about him with executives he'd never met. She owned his story and pitched it hard while he struggled to feel an ounce of her excitement.

He entered the kitchen, freezing. The camera crew zoomed in on his reaction.

Mamá and Vega ate breakfast at the island, watching Papá discuss Sebastian's social media video on *CBS Mornings*. Papá capitalized on the moment to sell his memoir. It bothered Sebastian. Papá's book was already an international bestseller; he didn't need to use Sebastian. But everyone wanted in on his rise, Papá included.

"J. Lo retweeting Sebastian brought him a flood of attention. The murse he auctioned on social last night sold for a hundred thousand," the reporter said. "That money will go to your family's foundation. That has to make you proud."

Sebastian cuffed his hands behind his head, exhaling. This was insane.

And like a pro, the reporter asked, "But, how do you feel about Sebastian auditioning dancers to replace his twin sister?"

His heart raced, eyes settling on Vega's back.

"I admire how my son has dedicated his life to the Bautista legacy, so I trust he won't settle for anyone who doesn't represent the Bautistas' dedication to the artistry of dance." Translation: Go back to Vega or choose a blood relative. If not a blood relative, then a future wife willing to live and breathe the Bautista mission.

Papá's words were heavy, setting off a battle between Sebastian's heart and mind. He wanted to please Papá, but he didn't want to feel like he did with Vega. He didn't care how great the dancer was; the dancer had to love and respect him as much as they loved the craft.

Amy screamed, pumping her fist in the. "They're talking about a father-son book!"

Sebastian wanted to squeeze her enthusiasm into a glass and down it like orange juice. Anything to ease his growing anxiety. He found the remote, changing the channel so he wouldn't have to listen to Papá's coded demands for Bautista perfection.

"I bet you think you're so perfect," Vega said.

"*Mi amor, se feliz por tu hermano,*" Mamá said. My love, be happy for your brother.

"Why?" Vega asked. "He's embarrassed me in front of the world." She raised her phone and pressed ignore, sending Gregory's call to voicemail. "He's destroyed my relationship with Gregory. Now I can't trust him."

"Good," Sebastian replied. "He's not trustworthy."

"So says the abusive dictator. I need a ride to school."

"Did you get my paper?"

"What paper?" She tilted her head, batting her eyes.

She knew exactly what paper he was talking about. He had emailed her his essay on love and leadership, installing a tracker that had alerted him when she opened it. Her expression told him she deleted it without reading. "You have a car," he reminded her.

"*Maneja tu hermana,*" Mamá ordered. Drive your sister.

He didn't want to squish into the same car with Vega for even fifteen minutes, but he always did what Mamá said.

"*Estoy muy feliz por ti, y Silvian está tambien,*" Mamá said. I'm happy for you, and so is Silvian.

"*Seguro.*" He grabbed his bag and headed out the door with Vega.

Vincent waited at his car, stoked about *CBS Mornings.* "You'll get a Season Two, probably even a feature. And you better let me compose your big-budget film." He pointed to the violin case sitting next to Vega in the backseat, covered in LA Lakers stickers.

"Why wait?" Sebastian asked, not wanting to kill Vincent's joy. "You can compose my docuseries as well."

"Dude, if Amy let me, I'd get no sleep, but I'd get it done."

Sebastian drove past a stop light, turning off Sunset Boulevard and onto Stingray Lane.

He slowed.

A crowd surrounded CLASH, bodies smashed together on the street. They were all dressed in leotards, holding posters yelling his name.

"This is insane," Vega whispered.

His thoughts exactly. He navigated through the bodies, using other cars to estimate a parking spot. There were so many people outside his window.

"This is all you," Vincent said. "Man. What does it feel like?"

Scary. Adrenaline pounded through his body. But right. Now that he had so many people competing for his attention, he could find someone that would make him and Papá happy.

Vincent reached for the door handle, locking eyes with him. "Let's do it."

"And die famous." Vega recorded selfies, using the bodies pressed against the car as her backdrop. "Ripped apart by stalkers obsessing over Sebastian, a *Dancing With the Stars*-wannabe."

"Shut up!"

"No fighting," Vincent snapped. "We have to focus and commit. Are we in or are we out?"

He took a deep breath. "In."

Vega grabbed Vincent's violin to use as a weapon.

Sebastian counted down from three. Then they slammed the doors open. He and Vincent surrounded Vega, struggling to ram through the people snatching at their clothes. He could feel his shirt ripping. Vega screamed when someone snatched her bookbag, and she bit and scratched her attacker until blood covered her purple nails. Then, she swung the violin like a crazy person until Vincent ripped it away. They were almost there. Sebastian locked eyes with Vega and Vincent, syncing his breaths with theirs. They counted down and pushed as hard as they could through the bodies, falling forward through CLASH's blue double doors.

Sebastian exhaled, staring at the ceiling lights. His white shirt barely covered his sweaty chest. He could hear Vincent laughing and repeating, "We almost died." The hall was filled with students, some crying, some in awe. He didn't know how Amy had gotten there safely, but there she stood in a corner, calling shots into her headphones. His camera crew filmed.

"Sebastian Bautista!" Principal Raines called down the hallway.

He dragged himself up, glancing at Vega to make sure she was okay. Her bra was showing, and her hair was a mess, but her nails weren't chipped, so a win for her.

"Sebastian Bautista!" Principal Raines shouted again, his nostrils flaring. "I need you and your producer in my office."

He followed Principal Raines, blood still pumping hard. That was the craziest experience of his life. Fans have never acted like that over his papá, and he was a megastar. Pride welled inside him, and he fought hard not to smile, paying extra attention to Principal Raines' rant on crowd control.

His phone rang, and he checked it. Papá was calling, but'd have to call later.

Sebastian: *Lo siento, no puedo hablar. Te llamo despues.*

He noticed Zoey's text for the first time, a screenshot of him facing off with Vincent on a Venice Beach basketball court. His smile finally won the fight.

He searched Zoey's social media, pausing to watch a video of Ian dipping her in a salsa club. Ian touching Zoey bothered him, so he continued scrolling, finding a video of Zoey dancing alone. Snapping a screenshot, he sent that to her.

Sebastian: Explain this. Not now. Face-to-face.

"Are you listening?"

Sebastian slid his phone into his pocket. "My producer handles these kinds of problems."

"I can make some calls to enhance our security," Amy quickly offered.

"You better, or you'll have to find another academy to film." Principal Raines waved towards the crew. "CLASH doesn't have the manpower to protect these students."

"My mamá and papá are on the board," Sebastian mentioned.

Principal Raines' face hardened.

"I'm not threatening you," Sebastian said. Not that he could easily threaten someone born and raised in Compton. He'd never been there, but he'd seen contemporary dancers choreograph pieces about its gang-violent history. "I meant my mamá and papá can help you get whatever you need. I want this to work for both of us."

"Good," Principal Raines said. "This is our livelihood, not solely your reality show."

ZOEY

her phone startled her from sleep. She slapped hardness, grabbing it. Why was her bed so hard? She squinted her eyes at her phone's screen, her heart skipping. Sebastian had replied to her message, sending her a screenshot of her at El Famoso.

She hearted the message, falling backward onto hardness. Wait. That wasn't her ceiling. She sat up, panicking, fingers brushing glass beer bottles, and a chest, and then a leg. Forcing her eyes left, she cringed. There was naked Ian. She slept with Ian. Again! How could they have let this happen when they made a rule promising not to let this happen, which Ian obviously didn't care about. He was wide awake, texting, unphased. "Good morning." He tried to kiss her.

She palmed him right in his chest. "We made a vow." Her head throbbed. Everything hurt. Why wasn't Ian in pain?

"I know, but you needed freeing."

"We're a horrible couple."

"Stop stressing. Didn't I make you feel great? You said you wanted it."

"Yeah, but ..." She couldn't think of a comeback. He had made her feel so good, washing away all of her insecurities until they had created a rhythm that was all their own.

"A dance partnership should feel like great sex," Ian whispered in her ear.

She closed her eyes, breathing him in. He still smelled like apple cider beer.

"Maybe you can convince Sebastian to relax and come on over, baby, to the dark side."

She laughed, wincing from the pain.

"I'm serious. If you can make Sebastian feel like I made you feel, you'll have awakened something he's never felt."

"Dancing together and having sex are two different things."

"Why?" he asked.

He can't be serious. She snatched her shirt over her head. "Ian!"

Her body went stiff. Her godparents were standing with their tech nerd and hippie lovers, all dressed for a morning salsa class. How embarrassing. Godmom and Goddad Cruz had witnessed her and Ian's colossal fail at #couple-goals and were extremely worried. Her godparents dragged them to the kitchen and stuffed bagels down their throats while lecturing them on excessive drinking and unsafe sex. Getting lectured by her godparents, plus Tech and Hippie Nerds, was too much. They all had different opinions on sex with friends. And Zoey thought that was weird because the

Cruces were on the cutting edge of marriage. They should have agreed that sex was fun and random, but no, they needed an outside opinion.

The worst. Zoey begged them to keep this secret, but her godparents dragged her home. Mom and Dad were finishing their coffee when arguments about sex and boundaries overwhelmed their kitchen.

Mom zeroed in on Zoey and Ian. "Didn't you two say you weren't doing that again?" Mom didn't believe in random hookups. When she told Mom she lost her virginity to Ian, Mom took her to a gynecologist for birth control before coaching her and Ian on the rules of dating.

Dating Ian was her first lesson on love. She loved Ian to death. He was super fun but very distracting, and he never took anything seriously, skipping class and enjoying sex way too much to be human. Her GPA dropped, and she gained four pounds from all the candy bars he bought her. She broke up with him and told Mom and Dad she could never date Ian again.

"I know. It was a mistake." Feeling embarrassed, she pinched Ian to get him to talk.

"Sure." Ian struggled not to laugh.

"I know you two are sixteen, living your best love lives out in these wild streets of LA, exploring yourselves sexually and whatnot. But, Ian, remind me, what we discussed about a woman's body?"

"A woman gets pregnant, and she has to do lots of things to prevent pregnancies that I don't have to do as a man."

"Can I get an amen?" Mom asked in her best preacher's voice.

"Amen!" Ian replied.

"Now that's settled," Dad waved his phone, ready to move on from a conversation that was working on his nerves. "Get mentally prepared for what I'm predicting will be a crazy Monday morning."

"Why? What's happening?" Zoey stepped closer to Dad's phone. He watched a YouTube clip summarizing *CBS Mornings'* interview with Silvian Bautista. A clip of Sebastian dancing played. She loved his outfit. The yellowish-gold, baroque-inspired patterns offset his black cargo pants. It was so hip-hop, matching how his body snapped to the beat unpredictably. He looked so powerful. No wonder J.Lo retweeted it.

Zoey's hands shook as if she had emerged from deep prayer. "I've never seen him look so–I don't know … alive." Everyone watching this would audition for Sebastian. The competition would be intense.

"You auditioning, Ian?" Mom asked.

"I wish he was cool enough to transcend gender norms, but he's not. Zoey's auditioning."

"Sebastian's under a lot of pressure," Dad interjected. "You sure you'll have time for him and fashion?"

Zoey wasn't sure about anything now that Sebastian's auditions had made national news. She should reprioritize fashion and not audition. It would free up her Sunday morning so she could spend the time getting lost in fabric stores to destress a little before tackling her homework. She was so behind. "I think I'm going to hit up the Arts District."

"No way. We have to focus," Ian said. "This is the opportunity of a lifetime. You can't quit now."

Her heart ached. She hated the word quit, so she gave in to Ian's demands, spending her entire Sunday training in his studio. Whenever she became too exhausted, he reminded her that they were no longer training for themselves. They were training for the higher call to make love through dance. A ridiculous call to action, but she pushed harder, stretching longer, and lifting higher late into the evening. She had felt the sweet high of exhaustion. Sleep was so good that night, and yet, exhaustion's sweetness stayed with her even on her drive to school.

Dad had predicted school would be crazy Monday morning. And he was right.

Zoey's car rolled closer to CLASH. Dancers surrounded the premises, filling the lawns and spilling out of the parking lot on the street.

Ian leaned forward in the passenger seat, excited.

She circled the lot, afraid she'd hit someone. After making a lap through the crowd once, she gave up and located a parking spot a mile away. They had to walk up a hill in ninety-degree weather. She was sweating through her blouse by the time she approached the school. She felt like a mess. "Maybe we shouldn't go," she told Ian.

"No. You have to audition today."

"Do you see me right now?" She waved at the sweat stains under her armpits, then gestured to all the perfect bodies dressed in ballet core.

"You're not competing against them. You're competing against yourself."

She rolled her eyes at the CLASH-ism. Mantras made of clichés.

"I'm serious. Remember what we talked about?"

"What did we talk about? Dance partners and sex?" She didn't even really agree that dancing should feel like sex, and she would not apply his crazy philosophy to her life. "No." She headed back to her car. "I'm taking a mental health day."

"Oh my God," Ian pulled out his phone to play Sebastian dancing. "Look how happy he is. It's like he's making love to the beat."

Watching Sebastian jolted her spirit and made her want to dance just so she could feel constant spirit jolts.

"Sebastian doesn't need another traditional dancer. He needs someone who'll challenge him to dance this freely each and every time. You know how it is to feel free. You showed me that last night."

"Pineapple pizza is also freeing," and so was sex with Ian even though she wasn't telling him that, "And dancing salsa and bachata. We can do a pizza and clubbing night." Anything to avoid applying his crazy "make love through art" philosophy.

"I'm talking about pushing this guy to go deeper in his artistry, and you're pitching me a date night? Come on, Zoey, think bigger, Paris big."

Zoey recognized that sinister look burning in his eyes. Ian wanted her to break rules, push boundaries, shock. All things she was pretty sure Sebastian hated. In fact, Ian hated everything that Sebastian loved. That's what made them enemies. "Are you sure?" She grew suspicious of Ian. "Why do you want me to dance with Sebastian so much? You hate Sebastian."

"I do, but I love you way more than I hate him. And you really, really want this."

She didn't believe him.

"When have I let you down? I even put my sex life on pause for you."

Until last night, but that was neither here nor there. She couldn't think of one time that he ever intentionally let her down. "Fine, I'll make love through art."

CHAPTER 27
IAN

he entered the studio, warmth and sweat attacking his senses. Mrs. Agnes led the dancers through *The Nutcracker*'s party scene. Nothing new, perfect. He slid into a line of boys, skipping to the beat of the trumpets when the bell rang.

Sebastian glared at him, shouting, 'Do better, human,' with his eyes.

He turned his back on Sebastian, facing Mahogany.

She packed her duffle bag at the barre. "Why don't you try arriving early for once?" Her words cut him, a nerve in his chest. Anyone could criticize him harshly, not Mahogany. Her opinion mattered too much.

He closed in on her, filling her space and claiming her focus. He could smell her perfume soured by sweat, so he knew she could smell him. "Stop being mean." He leaned close enough to feel her lips tremble.

"Ian, I need to speak with you," Mrs. Agnes called.

Mahogany grinned, savoring an ego boost. "Start caring, and I'll stop being mean."

"I do care." Why can't you see that? He showed up to this crappy, bougie academy and gave his ninety-five percent like everyone else. CLASH had his mind and body, but he refused to give it his soul.

"Ian," Mrs. Agnes called.

Mahogany could have his soul. She owned his feelings, and she made him feel as disgusting as day-old tights.

He sat in Mrs. Agnes' office, a little homage to Paris. Paintings of French immigrants hung. Some were Cameroonian, like Mrs. Agnes, some were Middle Eastern, and some were Asian. "This is your second tardy, and we're barely into the fourth week," Mrs. Agnes complained.

He considered lying. His ma got sick. The car broke down. Mrs. Agnes could handle those lies better than his truth. He didn't care about showing up for school when he'd rather drop out and train with Cody. Cody would hook him up with some auditions. Then, he could dance in music videos with other brown-skinned dancers from similar working-class backgrounds. Dancing with Cody would make him feel included, wanted.

"If you're late again, I'll reassign your solo to someone else. Principal roles in *The Nutcracker* are a privilege. They aren't for CLASH-mates who can't be bothered to be punctual."

"I'll do better. Dancing here means a lot to me, and I would love the opportunity to dance the Nutcracker this year."

"Faculty already decided on roles. They're posted outside of class."

"I would like the opportunity to audition and prove I can dance the Nutcracker better."

"Start by proving you can be punctual." Mrs. Agnes was done with the conversation.

He could predict his roles for The Fall Showcase, but he wanted to read the cast list anyway. The white paper was taped to the door. Sebastian would dance an orchestrated piece honoring the Bautista contribution to dance excellence. Then Sebastian would dance the Nutcracker with Mahogany as Clara while he was stuck again dancing Drosselmeier and the cavalier. Just like last year. *Lame.*

CHAPTER 28
SEBASTIAN

vega and gregory tried to ruin him and failed. One viral video catapulted him back to god status, and CLASH-mates were in awe. They pretended not to watch him while Mme. Marie lectured about Earth in French. He pretended not to notice, enjoying the attention.

His short stint at the bottom taught him he couldn't stomach being a pariah. Dominating the top was in his nature, and he'd do whatever it took to maintain god status. And getting help from SG was not an option. They were users, and he wanted to erase them from his life. Sharing a classroom with them was unbearable. Looking at the backs of their heads made him sick, knowing how little he could trust them.

"Fall's coming, an exciting time for us all," Mme. Marie passed out handouts. "The Fall Showcase, the fall fashion, the parties. And winter, my favorite. Let's pair off into groups of two and discuss changing seasons."

He got up to ask Vincent to be his partner, but Gregory blocked him, allowing Vega to partner with Vincent. She still wasn't speaking with Gregory.

"Let's work together," Gregory said with that greasy smile.

You're the last person I want to work with. "Choose someone else." He scanned the room. Zoey was working with Ian. Mahogany was working with Polly. No one else was free. He was stuck with Gregory when everything about Gregory made him nauseous: his cologne, his eye color, his outfit.

Sebastian chose a desk in the back, shoving his chair as far away from Gregory as possible while still reaching the desk to write.

"Great job Saturday night. My dad keeps congratulating me on the successful show. I mean, I tried to tell him it was all you, but he wouldn't listen. No one believes you crashed the party. Vega doesn't."

"You and Vega need a break anyway."

"You destroyed my relationship."

He wrote Gregory's words down. "Fall equals me destroying your relationship. Hopefully, Madame Marie gets it. What about fall to winter?"

"Your Dad call you yet?"

"Why?" He felt defensive.

Gregory pointed to Amy standing in the back of the room with the rest of the film crew. "Your producer hasn't said anything?"

"Just say it."

"She can really keep a secret."

This was the way Gregory liked to wield power, dripping information in bits and pieces, toying with his emotions. He pretended not to care. "So fall to winter. Any thoughts?"

"My dad'll be so busy this winter. He always has to be involved in everything, even getting behind your project. I'm like, Dad, do you have time for that?"

That's why Amy hadn't mentioned the news. She knew he'd see it as a threat. Gregory's family was behind BGM, one of Hollywood's oldest studios. He used to go with Gregory and Papá to walk around the lot with Charles Bradford. They'd introduce them to stars and point out all the locations where classic movies were filmed. Gregory's papá would take them to the flashy offices where studio heads worked. That's when Sebastian learned celebrities didn't have power. It was the studio heads, and he didn't want Gregory's papá having power over his docuseries. Today's docuseries could become tomorrow's shelved project if Gregory felt like convincing his papá to kill it.

"Don't look at me like that." Gregory pulled his chair close to Sebastian, throwing his arm around his shoulders. "I've missed you. We rarely get to hang out now that you dropped SG."

Gregory missed controlling his life. SG and dance, that's all he used to do, following SG everywhere, dressing the way SG wanted. And now that he was out, he didn't have to ask SG permission to do what mattered to him. "That gives me an idea. How about we discuss my new season without SG? "

"If my dad can find the money to make your project successful, I think you can find the time."

"Tell your dad thanks, but no thanks."

Gregory laughed. "You're nothing like Vega. You always need some type of coaching."

"I've changed. I'm not interested in SG. It has nothing to do with dance. It has nothing to do with me. I was only doing it because we were friends."

"We're still friends, and you need my friendship to protect you from my dad."

Sebastian gripped his pencil.

Mme. Marie circled closer to their desk, noticing they weren't working on the assignment. "Is everything okay?" She scanned Sebastian's writing.

"We're brainstorming," Gregory said. "We'll have it done."

"Vous avez quinze minutes." You have fifteen minutes. Mme. Marie turned and announced the same to the class.

Once Mme. Marie was out of earshot, Gregory dropped his smile, and returned to business. "Rejoin SG, and I'll make sure my dad loves your project."

"You don't want me back."

"You have the Bautista legacy. I have the Bradford legacy. The Bradfords win student body president, no questions asked. And now that you're dripping popularity again?" Gregory shrugged.

"You just don't want to look used," Sebastian said. "Like toilet paper." And that's what Gregory would be if the truth got out. 'Sebastian wiped his butt with the Bradford party,' CLASH would gossip. 'So he could reclaim god status.' Gregory would get talked about for days, and Vega would seize the opportunity to ruin his campaign. And somehow, in Gregory's twisted, tiny mind, it'd be Sebastian's fault.

He gripped his pencil tighter, the wood softening in his palms. He saw no other way to keep his docuseries alive. "I'll rejoin SG on one condition."

Gregory smiled. "I'm up for negotiations."

"Dance takes priority."

"Sure. I get that."

"I'm doing SG on my terms. You don't own me."

"I didn't know you felt like that. I'm looking forward to this brand new honesty."

The pencil snapped in his grip.

CHAPTER 29
ZOEY

she needed a miracle, and CLASH was the perfect place to find miracles. The School of Religion housed an Islamic prayer room on the third floor. Luckily, it was open to all cause she was the only girl there when she arrived. She tried to stay invisible, finding a spot in the back where she could copy the boys' movements without bothering them. Knowing when to kneel and sit up was hard, but she figured it out before traveling to the second floor to learn Jewish prayers. The Rabbi initiated the Barechu, some kind of opening prayer, at least that's what he told her. He wouldn't let her leave until he completed several prayers in Hebrew. The Buddhists were less strict. Quietly tiptoeing into their room on the first floor, she received a pillow and a blanket and sat with her eyes closed for maybe ten minutes. She wished she had time for a sound bath, but she couldn't stay at the School of Religion all day. Lunch was only an hour, so she skipped it for a quick prayer in the chapel.

Sitting on the benches, she felt this urge to change. As if the Holy Spirit whispered, she wasn't about to stir Sebastian's spirit with sweaty armpits. Thank goodness for spiritual counsel. She rushed out of the chapel and into the L&L, entering the storage room in search of something minimalist that popped. A white lace bodysuit dangled in the back. *Such a find! Sebastian would love that.* She paired it with rose-embroidered leggings and a crop top. It was so edgy but just innocent enough to feel pure. A splash of purity, but not too much. Sebastian was never too much in his style.

He could choose you, you know? A jolt of miracle energy dashed up her body while she examined her reflection in the mirror. She felt ready. No matter what was about to happen, she knew she looked good.

Joyously skipping down the Alumni Corridor, she blew a kiss at Sloane Magnolia's portrait. A cool breeze caressed her. The stingray fountain sparkled. She felt like God and The Universe were setting the scene for her miracle. Even Sebastian appeared as if summoned. Walking calmly through the gardens, he chewed a peach, his camera crew filming as always.

This was her chance, ready or not. She took a deep breath, rushing up beside him. "Perfect weather for a peach."

"What else is it perfect for?"

Her spirit did a happy dance. It took everything in her not to get lost in his gray eyes and the peach juice coating his lips. "Dancing together. Maybe even impromptu auditions."

"I'd love to, but I have to work on this solo. We're already prepping for The Fall Showcase."

"You have months for The Fall Showcase. We only have now now."

His eyes sparkled. "Good point." He opened the doors to the Dance School, guiding her to studio D125, a large room with giant glass windows curved upward as if in worship. He sat under the barres. The sunlight fell through the leaves, through the windows, and onto his white sweats, creating a glow. He gestured for her to head to the center.

Zoey's spirit alarm went off. He wanted her to sustain her miracle all alone, in this empty studio with his entire camera crew focused on her. "Don't you want to make this audition a little more fun? Like a pas de deux?" She extended her hand.

"I want to see a prepared routine, so I can judge your technique."

"That's so boring. Isn't dancing supposed to create an emotional experience. Like making love?"

Sebastian's eyebrows raised. "Where'd you hear that?"

"Ian."

"Do you and Ian dance together a lot?"

She had to answer that question carefully, especially since Sebastian had scrolled through all of her videos to find the one video of her dancing alone. "Ian's family taught me how to dance, so he's like a brother–" a weird, incestuous brother "–We dance every weekend. You should join us."

"Maybe." Sebastian stood, grabbing the barre. "Ian makes everything about sex. That works for a salsa club, but not for me."

Her miracle faded. She had to fight to keep it alive, or she'd fall back into fear. Then she'd have to limp back to Ian and tell him she failed. Ian wouldn't let her fail. He'd force her to try again, and she didn't have it within her to do this twice. This was now or never.

She slid into the spot facing Sebastian as he relevéd from fifth. She felt the heavy weight of the camera lenses zooming in close.

"I could have sworn Ian said that's what you're looking for," she began. "He showed me that video of you at Greg's party. He said it was like you were making love to the beat. You were so free in that moment, so he guessed you were looking for someone who'd challenge you to dance freely like that all the time, but maybe Ian got it wrong."

Sebastian stilled, eyes like lenses. He took in her curves, her wild, kinky hair, and bronze skin. "Alright," he said, ending eternity. "Make love to me."

She slid her hand into his, and her spirit went wild. Or at least she thought it was just her spirit. The ground shook under her feet, and the trees waved. She gripped Sebastian tight as the studio rumbled, growing loud before dissolving into nothing more than his breathing.

"Did we just have an earthquake?" she asked.

"Maybe a miracle."

She laughed, looking into his gorgeous eyes. How did he know? The earthquake exhilarated her. They looked around, and seeing no damage, Sebastian went to bluetooth music from his phone. He let her choose what song to play, and she chose her favorite bachata remix of Alesso's *Cool* with Ryan English. He joined her in the center, and she froze. Everything Ian had taught her fled her mind without a goodbye. She couldn't stay scared, so she surrendered to what was natural, moving her hips into a four-count bachata rotation.

Sebastian spun her against him, their hips moving in time to a relaxing movement that became fiery when he spun her onto relevé before folding her into a dip. She locked eyes with him, a heat washing over her. She curled her leg into an attitude before he danced around her into a pas de basque. He lept into the air, spinning back into her, pulling her close, and shoving his leg between her thighs. He led her by her neck under his arm, and he spun her into an arabesque.

All of the training she completed with Ian, where she was left drained and sore, led to this miraculous–no–majestic moment of shared heavy breathing in a dance studio.

Sebastian traced his thumb down her jaw as the song ended. His arm tightened around her waist. She prayed to God he never let her go, but what was never to the Infinite?

He rested his forehead against her forehead, closing his eyes and then releasing her. He returned to the barre to stretch.

She really wished she had the power to read his mind. "I didn't know you knew bachata." She tried to get him to look at her.

"My mom's a ballroom champion. I know some of that world."

"Cool." Duh! She knew that. She had stalked his social media enough to know. Her nervousness grew as the awkward silence increased. She needed to know what he thought of her audition. "So?"

"You need a lot of work."

That was harsh. His words iced the warm sensation inside her. But maybe it was true. Her eyes drifted to a hummingbird fluttering past the windows.

"What kind of work?"

"I don't know what I'm looking for. I have to finish up the auditions."

"Do I have a chance?"

"I don't know. Maybe," he said. "Maybe not. I don't know."

"I'm definitely up for your kind of yes … once you figure out your maybe." She sounded confident, even managed a wicked grin, but his words had killed her mood.

CHAPTER 30
IAN

zoey had one shot with Sebastian, and he worked hard to push her past her limits for her one shot. Some nights, she had limped out of his studio, but winning required pain. And she wasn't the only one feeling pain. His love life was beaten bloody and close to dead. Mahogany was ready to cut off life support, and he had to make things right before she did. He hit up Cody.

Ian: Help me shop for an apology gift.
Cody: Bet

They landed on the Westfield Culver City mall. He was about to book his Lyft when he received the dreaded text from SG, 'EMERGENCY MEETING.' *Darn it.* Groaning, he typed, 'For what?' before erasing it. He was just going to have to cancel with Cody.

Ian: Never mind. Have to go to an emergency meeting.

He booked a Lyft to Bel Air. The traffic felt unbearable, the sun set a glossy bitch taunting him as it lowered over the Bel Air mansions. Bel Air was so beautiful, so perfect, so not his mood.

The car slowed at the top of Greg's driveway. He slammed the door on accident, apologizing. It wasn't the Lyft driver's fault he had to be there. And he couldn't enter the meeting in the wrong head space anyway. Calling on all the mindfulness techniques CLASH taught him, he reduced his negative vibes. A lightness rose within, and he flipped on his codeswitch before entering Greg's enormous living room.

"And Sebastian's work proves he cared, that he made a mistake," Greg continued, waving at Ian.

He waved back, grabbing a slice of pizza before squeezing between Marc and Polly.

"I spoke with him, and he apologized. That's why I want to vote him back in." Greg looked satisfied with his speech.

This! This was why he canceled his plans and spent fifty bucks on a Lyft. Ian forced his smile to stay on his face. A four-hour shift at El Famoso would go to covering the cost of that Lyft when he could have simply texted a yay or nay. He scanned the room. Sebastian wasn't here, and no one looked like they wanted to vote Sebastian back in. This was a complete waste of time.

Mahogany handed him a pencil with a slip of paper. He tried to make eye contact, but she wouldn't look at him, still mad. He should have continued with his plans and brought a gift, a card, or flowers, but no, he had rushed here thinking it was an actual emergency.

"Don't write your name," Greg instructed.

Duh! He scribbled, 'No,' siding with Vega so she wouldn't feel alone. Tossing his vote in the bowl, he hopped on his phone to shop for Mahogany. He was usually good at picking gifts but couldn't buy her another blouse or water bottle. A teddy bear looked lame.

Mahogany tallied the votes, and they came out as Ian expected. Two people voted no, and five people voted yes. They were all such Greg-pleasers. He locked eyes with Vega so that she knew he was the other no. Then, he went back to online shopping. He found a Fenty Beauty gift set. Fifty bucks, another four-hour shift. He'd do it for love.

"Vote for me cause I'm a leader that unites." Greg smiled, satisfied.

Yeah right.

"Hhmmm … I don't like it." Vega stood, moving to the center of the makeshift circle. "I think I have a better slogan, so I've decided I'm running for president."

What? Ian looked up from his phone. Was it happening? Finally?

"We told everyone you're running as my VP," Greg said, which wasn't actually true. People just assumed that's what Vega would do.

"And we can tell everyone I'm not. Now that you guys know, you have a few weeks to pick a side. Ballots are finalized mid-September." She smiled. "That's all from me."

He had been waiting for this moment for so long, so tired of watching Vega slave away while Greg took all the credit. And now she was dumping him. Ian smashed his lips hard to keep from laughing, his mask firmly in place. If he had to choose sides, he was Team Vega for sure. Greg was nothing without her. She wrote his speeches, planned his meetings, picked his clothes, and helped him with his slogans.

"You can't change your mind," Greg shouted.

"Double standards much? You kicked Sebastian out cause he broke the rules."

"I'm leading through love."

Vega burst out laughing.

"First Corinthians Thirteen. Sebastian's paper?"

"We read it together." Vega turned to them, "And Gregory wanted to delete the email without opening it. I'm the only reason he even read it."

"She's lying."

"You're fake, and I don't want to be VP to Gregory the Fake."

"You're such a bitch."

"I'm a boss. I'm a bitch. I'm a boss bitch." Vega grabbed her bag and left.

Awkward silence. He waited for Greg to regain control, but Greg wasn't good at codeswitching cause he never had to do it. People diminished their personalities to make space for him, not the other way around.

Greg choked out an embarrassing "S-sorry for my outburst" and rushed out of the room.

Meeting adjourned. It was all worth it. Five-star review. He'd pay the fifty-dollar Lyft ride again.

He joined a group hug, mainly for the opportunity to touch Mahogany. She mourned the death of their friend group. He was happy he wouldn't have to pretend anymore. Greg was a horrible leader, and he didn't like Greg with Vega. Vega worked for wifey while Greg only contracted her as his administrative assistant.

Ian followed Mahogany to her Lexus. She tried to outwalk him without being too obvious.

"You want to come over?" he asked. The night air felt icy.

She didn't answer. He thought the wind blew his words away.

"Just to talk."

"I don't want to talk. I want a boyfriend."

"I want a boyfriend too, but I really, really like you."

Mahogany's footsteps slowed. "Then why won't you be with me?"

"Why can't you accept how I love?"

"Cause how you love is all over the place. It's just like you and dance. You're naturally talented at putting on a show, but there's no commitment. I don't want a one-night-only performance. I want commitment."

He hated that she saw him like that. He was passionate about dance, but dancing at CLASH didn't speak to him like salsa and bachata. CLASH-mates rarely looked like him or understood him. It was painful and lonely, but he trained past the pain. Like any serious dancer would. But he didn't want his love for her to be anything like dancing at CLASH. "We're not Vega and Greg."

"At least they commit."

They really weren't on the same page about love if she thought Greg and Vega had reached #couplegoals status. He threw up his palms, surrendering. "I really like you and want you to be with me, but you don't have to."

"Good cause I'm Team Sebastian. Whoever he chooses, I choose."

CHAPTER 31
SEBASTIAN

dancing with zoey felt like connecting with a force bigger than himself. His body tingled with Zoey sensations, his mind with Zoey thoughts. At night, he'd hold auditions in the CLASH studios, searching for a dancer to impact him like Zoey. The dancers were from all over California. They had their own flare, surpassing Zoey in technique, form, and grace. And not one dancer stirred his spirit like Zoey. Instead, they simply reminded him too much of Vega, and that was traumatizing.

Friday night, midnight came. He danced his last pas. His heart pounding, nerves wrecked. The last dancer left him staring at emptiness. Black sky poured through the studio windows. His aloneness reflected in the mirror. A panic overcame him. He still hadn't found what he was looking for.

He went home and couldn't sleep, so he trained until the black sky transformed into blue. Amy showed up early. She dragged him to the family office on the third floor. Mom waited with a hug. She knew this was a big day for him.

Gregory and Charles showed up with their assistant, carrying bagels and coffee. The film crew set up four cameras, transforming the office television into a video conference. Studio executives popped on screen, one by one. The executives waited for Sebastian to pitch them a dancer. He didn't know who to pitch, the choices a messy thought cloud with Zoey dominating his head when she wasn't the best dancer. And he should want the best.

Amy flipped through the gigantic photo stack, holding up the first dancer. The first assistant camera loaded the image on the screen, playing the dancer's audition.

The executives discussed it, asking Sebastian for an opinion.

He didn't have opinions, and that was the problem. Each dancer was beautiful. If not muscular, thin. Their technique was precise. He could dance with any of them, and they would make him look good, but so what? Vega made him look good but feel empty. He shuddered. No way was he feeling like that ever again. Charles' assistant tossed each "no" into the trash.

He glanced at the clock. It was almost one. Amy asked, "What are you thinking for lunch?"

"I'm good," he said.

"Can we order sushi?" Vega asked, strolling into the room with Vincent. His sister sat down at the front of the table with Mamá. She ignored Gregory's waving.

Vincent squeezed between him and Amy. "You need to eat, man. Sebastian never turns down Korean-fusion tacos."

Amy ordered from Sebatian's favorite taco truck. Vincent was usually right, but the smell turned his stomach, and their chewing bothered him. He tried to close his eyes, but he could still see their teeth mashing food soaked in spit.

Breathing steadily, he let his mind wander back to Zoey. Her brown eyes and wild hair calmed him, her touch, her hands on his body. She was thick with the perfect curves.

"Oh, I love this girl!"

His eyes snapped open, focusing on Amy holding Mahogany's picture.

"She goes to CLASH. We already have a ton of footage of her."

"Play her audition," Charles demanded.

They watched Mahogany dancing like LA, seamlessly fusing hip hop and ballet. She was bold, and her boldness was commercial. That's what the executives liked. Her picture went into a separate yes pile that no one else made it in. They started combing through the maybe pile to find another dancer to compete with Mahogany. Sebastian knew he needed to speak up about Zoey, but what if her audition looked stupid?

Mamá squeezed his shoulder. *"Di lo que tienes en la mente."* Say what's on your mind. She wanted him to be brave like she had been. She started off in ballet, dancing with Papá at the family company until she discovered ballroom. Leaving ballet had to be scary. Papá probably fought her. And then Abuelito was tough. He didn't like when people surprised him with a no.

If Mamá could fight for what she truly wanted, so could he. He coughed, unlodging the words stuck in his throat. "There's another dancer." They looked confused. That sounded illogical when there were tons of dancers on the table.

Amy suddenly clapped her hands. "Oh, yes! We filmed that audition. It's on the cloud storage."

A crew member loaded up the footage, revealing Zoey illuminated in sunlight. She shook with nervousness, melting when Sebastian touched her. Tingles crawled up his arms, his legs, as if he were reliving the dance. Television him looked happy. And that happiness was contagious, stretching through the screen and filling the room with energy.

"You have a crush on Sexy Panties?" Vincent laughed.

"Shut up."

"Yo, load Zoey's TikTok," Vincent yelled. "She got tons of dance videos on there."

A crew member scrolled through Zoey's feed. Charles reviewed the videos like he would any rough cut that reached his inbox. He critiqued Zoey's pacing, demanding the executives envision the emotional story.

Someone asked if she was Afro-Latina.

"Does it matter?" Sebastian knew the answer was no, but he felt like saying no would ruin Zoey's chances.

They stopped at a video of Zoey dancing bachata with Ian. Ian spun her away to dance alone. She ran, jumping, and Ian lifted her above his head. The caption, '*Dirty Dancing* remixed,' flashed up.

"*West Side Story* meets *Dirty Dancing*," the youngest executive said.

"Oh my god," Amy shouted. "I can already see the campaign."

Charles stared, unconvinced. "I'll think about it. What was the other dancer that you liked, Amy?"

Amy held up Mahogany's photo. Charles made the crew replay Mahogany's audition back-to-back with Zoey's.

Sebastian grew doubtful with each watch. He liked Zoey, but she wasn't exactly Bautista material. Papá would reject her if she auditioned for his company. Shouldn't he?

"Let me mull over this until Sunday." Charles thanked everyone for their time.

Each executive's screen went black.

Sebastian wished the film crew would also go black, and maybe Vega as well. She thought Zoey making the final two was hilarious.

"Please pick Frog Legs," Vega said. "Maybe we can have a watch party with Papá. We can invite all our friends."

Vega knew Papá would want Zoey's hair straight and pulled into a bun. He'd want her lines long, her frame thin, her feet arched. Everything Zoey was today went against Papá's standards. And that made Sebastian sick.

CHAPTER 32
ZOEY

she sat at the kitchen island, staring at her phone. Sebastian text now. A second went by. No text. She tossed her head back, groaning. All she wanted to know was, did I make the cut or not? That wasn't too hard to text, but Sebastian was taking forever. She couldn't enjoy Sunday family brunch waiting for him. Mom and Dad cooked the best veggie omelets of their lives while Godmom and Goddad Cruz shimmied to salsa music, chopping up fruit. The atmosphere felt vibrant. Tech and Hippie Nerds argued with Ian about spirulina. She didn't know what that was, but it sounded interesting. She should want to argue about spirulina, but she felt sluggish. As if she had overeaten and couldn't get rid of onion breath. She inspected her omelet. Nope, no onions. Maybe in the salsa.

"We're about to leave soon." Dad pointed to her pajamas.

She was the only one not dressed for church. "Can I stay home? I have a lot of homework," which was true. She was behind in her fashion design classes.

"You can do homework after church."

And the argument was over. She paired a hoodie with ripped jeans, dressing for her sluggish mood. The sun shined bright as if it hadn't gotten the memo that today was kind of depressing. Her family wanted to walk so they could enjoy the birds singing Sunday melodies.

She walked past the pride flag waving on the front lawn, following her family into the small brick building. The auditorium had faded walls where a Latin Jesus hung and purple seats that were too modern for its old Bibles. Pastor Carter believed in radical love, and Zoey could only guess he was preaching on some version of that. She wasn't listening, her mind drifting from homework to Sebastian back to homework.

Mrs. Sehar wanted her CLASH-Mates to create a skirt inspired by Christian Dior's new look from the 1950s. Zoey loved a tea-length skirt and could spend hours in the attic, seeing what old tablecloths she could use. That would keep her from thinking about Sebastian.

Her phone vibrated, causing her heart to leap. It was only Ian texting so their parents wouldn't know they weren't listening.

Ian: You look sad.

Zoey: Sebastian didn't text me.

Ian: Is he all you think about? He's not even that interesting.

Zoey: He's supposed to update me on auditions.

Ian: He's a jerk. He's probably going to wait till midnight.
Zoey: #survivalmode.
Ian: How about we go out?
Zoey: On a Sunday?'
Ian: I know, but we can go somewhere you won't think about Sebastian.
Zoey: Sold!

They'd have to wait till their parents were asleep. Mom and Dad called it a night around eight. The Cruces left for El Famoso after nine. Ian came over shortly after that, texting Cody, 'Where you going tonight?'

The basement was under an apartment building turned studio in North Hollywood. The place was packed. Music banged until the walls shook and alcohol bottles wobbled. Zoey opted not to drink cause it was a school night. Ian would have to be her buzz. He pulled her to a spot between sweaty bodies, grinding against her. Beats pulsed through their bloodstream. Cody squeezed Ian, and they locked lips.

She kept dancing, dancing with so many strangers, the beat becoming an extension of her soul. Dance gave her life like it gave Sebastian life—no, she wasn't thinking about him.

She danced back to Ian, snatching him out of his lip lock with Cody, and forcing him to dance bachata. She handed Cody her phone for a video, one she hoped Sebastian somehow saw so he could see she wasn't waiting for him.

"Check us out, CLASH," Ian smiled. "We're too savage for CLASH rules."

"We're too wicked for curfew."

"Man, screw CLASH, screw those rich, egotistical pricks," Cody yelled.

"That doesn't rhyme," Zoey said.

Ian burst out laughing. "Yours didn't either." He snatched the phone from Cody, holding it in an awkward close-up. "Screw CLASH, screw dance, screw rich, egotistical pricks." He chanted it over and over again. Zoey joined him, copying Ian when he stuck out his tongue and blew kisses to the camera. He tossed the phone back to Cody, spinning Zoey in a circle, making her body move to the rhythm and dipping her so low she could see behind her. He brought her up so that their noses touched.

Cody tagged the video with Sebastian's name.

She watched it upload, growing scared as the percentage neared a hundred.

"Don't!" She reached for the phone.

Cody jumped back. "Screw CLASH, screw dance, screw rich, egotistical pricks."

Her heart raced. What would Sebastian think?

Ian dragged her out of her fear and onto the rooftop. She shivered when the cold air hit her sweaty clothes. This feeling's the best. Wet hair stuck to her face.

"We don't have to go back," Ian said. "We could drop out."

She breathed North Hollywood. It smelled like urine and day-old tacos, but its black skies looked like adventure. She was so thankful for Ian and Cody. She could survive any fear with them.

"We're not running. We're graduating and moving to Paris to live our dreams." She held out her pinky. "Two Compton kids in Paris. Vow renewal?"

Ian reached for her pinky, stopping an inch from touching. "How about we'll stay if Sebastian chooses you?"

"And if he doesn't?"

Ian smiled wickedly. "I hope he doesn't." He curled his pinky into hers.

CHAPTER 33
SEBASTIAN

mahogany or zoey? he stared at their headshots. A manila envelope lay beside the photos. Cameras filmed him from every corner of the studio, and Amy watched. He had an hour before midnight.

He looked out his windows. The sky was as black as an empty theater. Papá would want him to choose Mahogany. If he chose Mahogany, Papá would fly her to Madrid and train her.

Sebastian reached for her photograph.

Mamá knocked, leaning against the door frame and holding up her phone. Eleven-fifty-five glowed on the screen. It was a cue he needed to get to bed.

Papá used to pick fights with Mamá when she first left ballet. Then, after months of trying to persuade her, Papá gave up and accepted the new Mamá, the happier Mamá.

Sebastian reached for Zoey's photograph. He could be fearless like Mamá, and eventually, Papá would accept his choice.

He almost had Zoey's photo in the envelope when his phone vibrated, notifying him that Ian had tagged him in a video. Ian was so petty. He had nothing to do with Ian or Zoey drunk dancing, but Ian wanted him to know that he was a rich prick.

How could Zoey be so stupid? CLASH would be all over that video, and the faculty would retaliate. Not to mention Vega. She'd use this trash against him when he had just survived her attacks.

He snatched Zoey's headshot from the manila envelope, hand hovering above Mahogany. Should he even care about what people think? Mamá hadn't cared. She chose what she loved.

His phone alarm went off. He had missed his deadline, so there was no point in torturing himself. Grabbing the photos and heading to bed, he fell asleep and dreamt about Zoey and Mahogany. Their bloodied toes spun on brown floors. Vampires licked the blood off their cuticles. Disgusting.

Sunlight hit his eyelids, and he jumped out of bed, shaking. Thinking about Zoey and Mahogany sucked his energy. He just had to make a choice, or there wouldn't be peace. He grabbed the headshots and, closing his eyes, tossed them in the air. Searching the floor till his hands brushed one, he slid it into the envelope. Problem solved. Now, he could spend an hour in the studio.

He worked till he was too mentally exhausted to point his toes. Then, he dragged himself downstairs for breakfast. Coffee and pan dulce hit his nostrils. His stomach grumbled as he slid into a seat beside Mamá at the island. She looked at him, surprised. Breakfast was a last-minute habit for him, but this morning he needed fuel.

Mamá checked his forehead while he reached for a roll. *"Comó te sientes?"* How do you feel?

"Bien." Well.

Chef Ramón handed him a plate filled with eggs and bacon. He scooped eggs into his mouth. Chew. Swallow. The food was thick in his throat. He was on edge, and the camera crew wasn't making him feel better.

Mamá pointed to the manila envelope that rested beside him. *"A quién elegiste?"* Who did you choose?

"El destino decidirá … o El Señor." Fate will decide … or God.

She laughed. *"Quizás tenga que sacarte del CLASH."* I might have to take you out of CLASH.

A part of him was starting to hope God existed, though he'd never admit it to his family. He was tired of making decisions alone.

Mamá's phone rang with Papá calling.

"Don't mention the documentary." He didn't want to admit he was letting fate choose his partner. Papá would think he was crazy and choose for him.

Mamá answered the video call, blowing kisses at the screen.

"Voy a volver para el Showcase de Otoño," Papá said. I'm coming back for The Fall Showcase.

"Genial," he replied, kissing Mamá and hurrying out of the kitchen before Papá could bombard him with questions he didn't have answers for.

He grabbed his bookbag and messaged Vincent, heading to his car.

Sebastian: Meet me outside.
Vincent: Done.

"You chose Sexy Panties, didn't you?" Vincent said as soon as they were out of the driveway.

"I'm leaving it to fate."

"Wait. What?" Vincent looked confused. "You talking about rolling dice and flipping coins?"

"Exactly."

"That's crazy. You really like Sexy Panties."

"Zoey's not trained."

"Yeah. It's tough, man, I get it. I'd probably just let my dad choose, but I already know how you feel about that."

Vincent put on Bach's *Cello Suite No. 1 in G Major*, and Sebastian drove to school in silence, thinking about Vincent's relationship with his dad, Mr. Dixon. Mr. Dixon was tough on Vincent, but he believed in failure. The tattoos 'Sweat. Play hard. Grow' came from Mr. Dixon's life philosophy. The great Silvian Baustista believed in 'Pain. Perfection.'

Amy wanted the unveiling of Sebastian's decision to be as dramatic as possible, so she orchestrated a meeting in Principal Raines' office. The entire dance faculty was there, surrounded by cameras. Principal Raines sat at his desk, his face expressionless.

Sebastian laid the manila envelope on his desk. It looked scary, but he had faced scarier things, like the adagio between Spartcaus and Phrigia. He had lost sleep over those rehearsals. If he could survive Spartacus, he could open a manila envelope.

He pulled out the photograph. It took a second to register the dimples, the big brown eyes. He couldn't believe it. Warmth filled him, a smile stretching across his face. He felt like he did during Spartacus' curtain call.

"Is that your daughter?" Mrs. Agnes pointed from the headshot to the photographs hanging around the office. The faculty's whispers increased as they connected the dots.

"Indeed." Principal Raines didn't believe it himself. "Do you have a second choice?"

"No," Sebastian said. "I surrendered to fate."

"Fate? Fate doesn't bring championships. You know anything about football?"

"I know that hard work doesn't always bring the win. Otherwise, everyone would have a Superbowl ring." He gestured to Principal Raines' framed jersey. Raines probably worked harder than most of his teammates, but fate neutralized hard work all the time. That's how Raines ended up at CLASH.

Principal Raines' eyes narrowed.

Sebastian regretted mentioning how fate blew out Principal Raines' knee when he had been on track for a Superbowl ring. "I'm sorry."

"Zoey's my Superbowl ring. Don't break her heart."

"As long as she commits to my vision, I won't give up on her. Promise."

Principal Raines believed him. Hunger recognized hunger. Drive recognized drive.

CHAPTER 34
ZOEY

"zoey! i thought you said you weren't doing this again!"

Her eyes popped open, and she shot up straight in bed.

Mom stood at her bedroom door, fists pressing into her hips and legs spread into a superwoman stance.

"We didn't have sex." Otherwise, they would have awakened in the back of the Basement. She was for sure. Sex with Ian was never practical enough for a bed.

"Whatever is going on with you two, fix it. This is the third time you're late to school, and I don't want this mediocrity sleeping under my roof."

"Actually, do we have to go? I'm not feeling well."

"Don't play with me. You better come dressed correct."

Zoey rolled out of bed, her head heavy. She struggled to match her clothes and comb her hair. "We're not staying out till four on a school night ever again," she told Ian. And Ian agreed while following her to the kitchen.

Mom fed them pancakes and burnt bacon while lecturing them about their tardiness. She got more worked up the more she paced, waving her spatula as she multitasked lecturing, praying to God, and washing dishes. Suddenly, she stopped, pointing her soapy hand at Ian. "Zoey's only ever late because of you. You're a bad influence. I hate to say it."

"No, he's not."

"Don't defend him, Zoey." Mom grabbed Ian's chin. "Do better, you hear me? I can't stand mediocrity, and I'm not having this conversation again. Do better."

Eyes lowered, Ian nodded.

Mom decided all this lecturing was sweating out her blowout, and she didn't want to be late for work. "You finish the dishes." She left the kitchen.

Zoey sat frozen, afraid Mom would rush back, ignited with more grievances. When her phone buzzed with Sebastian's name glowing on the screen, she ignored it. She wasn't ready for another morning dose of strong personality.

Ian pressed the answer button.

Oh my god, I could kill you. She forced her voice to sound chipper. "Hey, you!"

"Hey, yourself. Where are you?"

"On my way, technically … I never miss school." Which was true. She might arrive three hours late because of Ian, but she never missed it entirely. And after that lecture with her mom, she might never be late again.

"What time?" Sebastian asked.

I don't know. My life's such a mess. "By lunch."

"I need you here before the end of first period. Can you make that?"

She glanced at the time on the microwave. She'd have to run every red light to make that happen. "Why? What's the rush?"

"Life's a rush. Can you make first period?"

Why not? She could break laws, get tickets, get arrested, live in the fast lane. "Sure." She slid off her stool and grabbed her book bag.

"Exciting. Be ready cause I am."

What the heck did that mean?

Sebastian told her to share her location with him so he could track her ETA, and then the phone went dead.

She looked at Ian and screamed, "We have to go, we have to go," before tossing dishes recklessly into the dishwasher. Glass shattered, and she hopped over the white shards. "Mom! There's glass on the floor, and I can't clean it up. My life's about to change."

She ran past Mom dressing in the living room and burst onto the front lawn with Ian close behind. He barely had the car door closed when she pulled out of the driveway and sped down Rosecrans Avenue toward Interstate 110 North.

"Why are you driving so crazy?" Ian leaned forward, in love with this fast and furious moment of their lives.

"I have to make it by the end of first period. Sebastian said, and I quote, 'Exciting. Be ready cause I am,' end quote. What did he mean by that?"

Ian squeezed her hand.

Her heart somersaulted. "Do you actually think it means what it means?" Ian would know. He was a master at deciphering Sebastian's cryptic messages.

She ran through the red light on Stingray Lane, barely missing a BMW. Parking, she jumped out of the car.

Ian rushed around and squeezed her tight. His hug felt more like a goodbye than a congratulations.

"Our friendship isn't ending," she said against his chest.

"I don't know, it might. You know how CLASH is."

"You just don't like him, but you can try. We can all talk it out at lunch, or I can invite him to El Famoso."

"He's an asshole, and CLASH is so political. One lunch therapy session will not change that, but I don't want to bog you down when this is the opportunity of a lifetime. Protect yourself. He's cutthroat, and he'll break your heart into itty bitty pieces and stab you with them. Develop boss bitch armor."

She shivered.

Sebastian waited for her at the school entrance with his camera crew, dressed in ripped jeans and that gorgeous hoodie embroidered in gold baroque patterns. His hair combed neatly into a man bun contrasted with her messy curls. She wished she dressed in something other than a boyfriend shirt and leggings. Her imposter syndrome raged, but she kept walking, picturing Dad and Mom, her godparents, Tech and Hippie Nerds, watching her walk into her new future.

"You made this bold statement when you auditioned for me," Sebastian said.

Please don't talk about making love.

"Superheroes have to be bold."

She felt relieved. "Bold's becoming my new practice, so does that mean we're superheroes?"

He grinned, "Yeah," unzipping his hoodie and putting it on her.

His hoodie felt like a wedding ring. She breathed in his scent, savoring her spirit dancing on the inside, filling her with warmth. This was everything she wanted: Sebastian choosing her, her life elevating, everyone seeing her worth.

Sebastian grabbed her hand, rushing her through the main building and out past the fountain. *This is so wicked.* A drone filmed above, a crow in the sky. Not a sparrow. Sparrows were peaceful. She stumbled into the dance studio, face widening. So many people squeezed into the room, surrounding Dad, CLASH-mates and faculty that she didn't know. They clapped, except for Vega. Vega glared, the model of a resting bitch face.

Zoey took a blue duffle bag with CLASH written on the side. Dad handed her a schedule. She scanned it—Dance, debate, lunch, French, science– Where were all her fashion classes?

She looked at Dad. "This has to be a mistake–" She couldn't finish her sentence with a dance instructor pushing her into a locker room where a stylist waited for her. Everything happened in a blur. She was forced out of her jeans and into tights and a leotard that completely hugged her curves the wrong way. She tried voicing her disdain, but a producer hurried her into the studio for a photo session at the barre. Her mind raced, struggling to decipher the photographer's instructions. He spoke quickly, like New York City, Spanglish quick, coaching her to relax and breathe.

She was achieving none of those actions, not with all the eyes. And then Vega loudly consoled Mahogany for everyone to hear. "You're better than Frog Legs," and "Sebastian will regret his choice," Vega spewed. So obnoxious. Could someone please shut her up?

Ian tried coaching Zoey from across the room. 'Go for a splits,' he mouthed, sinking into the floor.

No. She shook her head. That would make everyone look at her more when she wanted to disappear.

The photographer tossed up his hands. "*Venga,* come." He waved at the faculty and CLASH-mates. "Join us."

Thank you. She leaned against the bar, grip loosening. Now, she could hide. It was much easier to pose when she could copy her CLASH-mates' hands and legs. And whenever there was an opportunity, she scooted further behind bodies. She would have made it to the back if Sebastian hadn't found her and repositioned her in the center. Her cheeks bloomed red, feeling his hand on her hip. He could just touch her as if she were already his.

"You've accomplished a feat, Zoey," Mrs. Agnes said between camera clicks. "We're spotlighting both you and Sebastian at our Fall Showcase."

What did spotlighting mean? Sebastian had a segment dedicated to the Bautista Foundation that opened for the dance department. Was she going to be forced to dance a solo during his segment in front of an audience filled with agents, and celebrities, and supermodels when she was supposed to be living her best life backstage dressing supermodels?

"This has to be a mistake." She approached Dad. She hadn't wanted her whole life to change, just minor improvements: a few friends at lunch, a fun class schedule where pre-calc and biology were swapped for dance, not her fashion classes. How was she supposed to achieve her dreams now?

Sebastian looped his arm around her waist, making her the center of attention again! The photographer readied his giant lens. If only she could rub Sebastian's confidence on her like deodorant, cover the stench of terror fuming from her pits. He was smooth, his skin pressing against hers, his chest, his arms. They all felt as cozy and warm as her fashion studio. She relaxed. Why keep fighting this goodness? She rested her head against his shoulder.

The photographer whispered, *"Bueno."* Good. His face lit up.

Sebastian guided her from pose to pose, his confidence seeping into her blood. She faced him, wrapping her arms around his neck. His forehead pressed against her forehead, making her spirit dance. If dancing with Sebastian always felt this incredible, maybe she wouldn't miss fashion.

"You only need to lose fifteen pounds," Vega reassured Zoey in the dressing room. "Don't stress it. Sebastian'll work you so hard, he'll break you. You'll drop all that fat in no time."

Zoey hugged her boyfriend sweater to her bra, looking at dancers with their toned bodies. Her heart ached. No. She'd miss fashion a ton.

CHAPTER 35
IAN

he had to make a decision. Who was he walking to class with, Zoey or Mahogany?

Zoey needed a pep talk. Her photo shoot was a disaster, producing awkward photos he hoped never got posted to IG. And then there was Mahogany, jealous and alone, mourning her loss to Zoey. They both needed a hug, but group hugs weren't an option. They hated each other, and there was only one him.

"Ian, Sebastian, Zoey," Mrs. Agnes called, including Marc, Vega, and Mahogany. "I need you in my office."

Now what? He groaned, following his CLASH-mates into the cramped office. His teacher's harsh expression caused stress to build in his shoulders. He wished he chose standing over sitting at her desk. Shoving his chair back, he knocked into Zoey. There wasn't enough room with his CLASH-mates and the camera crew squishing him in the center.

Mrs. Agnes loaded a TikTok on the television monitor hanging on the right wall. "Screw CLASH, screw dance, screw rich, egotistical pricks," he and Zoey yelled. Embarrassing. He slouched further into his seat. This was so ironic. Just weeks ago, Vega was here, shaming Sebastian with her TikTok. And the new shame of the week? He and Zoey.

"I'm really sorry I have to have this discussion with you," Mrs. Agnes said. "The entire faculty saw the video. Principal Raines saw it, and they're deeply upset."

And what sparked this quasi-SG meeting? Were they voting on his punishment?

Vega raised her hand. "Besides the fact that I had nothing to do with this, I feel like we're being overly policed. They made this video outside of school hours, off CLASH premises."

"CLASH is world-renowned, and you are our highest-ranked dancers in Level III," Mrs. Agnes said. "You'll go on to have illustrious careers in a competitive industry, in which you'll represent various brands. Right now, you represent CLASH. And every story you release to the world shapes yours and CLASH's narrative. This is the second damaging video connected to this department that has gone viral."

"And there will probably be more."

He bit his tongue to keep from laughing at Vega's remark.

"Therefore, we are taking action." Mrs. Agnes shifted her gaze. "Marc, you'll dance the roles of the cavalier and Drosselmeier."

Those are my roles. He sat up, panicked. "What will I dance?"

"You'll sit out of The Fall Showcase this year."

He struggled to blink the spots away, feeling the weight of everyone's eyes. Mrs. Agnes didn't have to humiliate him in front of everyone. Mahogany looked at him as if he could never get his life together. Her disappointment sliced his heart. Marc looked sorry, Vega could care less, and Sebastian? Typical asshole thought he deserved it.

He felt a hand squeezing his shoulder. It was Zoey, glowing with kindness, reminding him of Baby Jesus in the chapel. He could always count on her, his Compton bestie. He squeezed her hand.

"Zoey joining our dance department will increase our visibility," Mrs. Agnes continued. "And she'll need your support …"

Mahogany hated him, and Zoey was all he had. Compton before Bel Air always.

He caught fragments of Mrs. Agnes' speech. "Exude leadership" and "We're in this together" sounded like false advertising. CLASH claimed they were in this together, but if that were true, why was he the only one punished? Mrs. Agnes talked about the importance of helping Zoey succeed as Sebastian's partner. And it all started making sense. Zoey had played the social game and won the esteemed role of the dance department mascot. From here on out, she could do no wrong. As for himself, he didn't matter.

Time blurred like the words in Mrs. Agnes' speech. Zoey's hand fell from his shoulder, bodies left. The room grew bigger and bigger while remaining claustrophobic. He gripped his chair. He couldn't leave yet. Grounding his feet, he prepared to fight. "I don't care that the world's watching." His words sounded soft. He hardened them with confidence. "Let them watch. My viewpoint is diverse and has a right to be expressed."

"You can express your views without verbally assaulting your CLASH-mates and our reputation. I suggest you find creative, productive ways to do that. If you feel CLASH-mates are pricks, get in conversation. Stop hiding."

Stop hiding? Was she kidding? This school would devour him if he didn't wake up with codeswitching on the brain. Chew him up and spit him out like day-old frog legs. Sorry, Zoey. "I took one moment to speak my truth. Leaders speak their truth all the time."

Mrs. Agnes pointed at the photographs of her family working in vineyards around an estate in Southern France. Ian guessed that's where she grew up, taking private lessons to prepare for the Paris Opera Ballet.

"You want authenticity?" Mrs. Agnes asked.

"Who doesn't?"

"You flounce around, coming late, dancing a B-average when you can ace every move. And it makes me so angry. You have so much natural talent, and that's not enough, but you refuse to focus and commit. Why?"

"Survival mechanism?" Playing the CLASH social game was exhausting. He danced with people who didn't look like him and struggled in AP classes with people who didn't think like him. Then he had sex, went home, danced, slept, got up, and danced again. CLASH drained him.

"You know I can never get my hair to lay how I want in a bun."

And that relates to me how? He stared at her hair. It was big, curly, and thick. None of those descriptions seemed bun-friendly. Punishment for being so mean, he guessed. Eventually, everyone danced with karma.

"I used to spend hours straightening my hair, burning my ends till it broke off to my ear. I grew so tired of trying to fit in that one day, I shaved my head. The director was mad, but he couldn't throw me out cause, at the time, I was one of the only Black Muslims in the company. However, he wanted every woman, not just me, every woman to know dancing in principal roles required beautiful, straight hair worn in a bun. Yet, I was defiant. I walked around with a shaved head for two years till I grew tired of being passed over for principal roles. I had to learn if I wanted to succeed, I had to commit to being the best and obeying the rules."

So Mrs. Agnes wasn't just another nepo baby. He misjudged her when he should have known better. Ballet wasn't afro friendly. It wasn't friendly at all. It was demanding, requiring full commitment of his mind and body. And the thought of obeying every rule till he graduated made him want to shave his head. "Thanks for sharing. It must have felt so lonely, and I'm sorry they made you feel that way, but I can't." He rambled CLASH-isms, words from empathy classes that sounded more like 'It's me, not you.' But that was his truth. "I love dance, I love learning from you. I wouldn't be the dancer I am today if it weren't for you, but

I clash with CLASH, and I need to find my tribe so I don't end up shaving my head."

CHAPTER 36
SEBASTIAN

he wasn't sitting next to Zoey during debate. He didn't care about Amy's shot list. It was easier to watch Zoey from across the class. And he wanted to watch her in wide shot, not close up.

The debate teacher, Mr. Dean, announced they needed to form teams of two.

A group of CLASH-mates bombarded Zoey, wanting to team up. He grinned when she pointed at a skinny boy with a chessboard on his t-shirt. Cool choice.

Amy: That should have been you.

He ignored Amy's text, glad it wasn't. Zoey's team had to go against Vega's, and he didn't need the crew filming Vega ripping him and Zoey to shreds while they argued against abortion rights.

Back when they swapped reads, Vega would slide in a trending feminist book. She loved reading women's studies literature. And from the looks of this debate, he guessed that wasn't true for Zoey. This wasn't a debate. It was a slaughter. Vega quoted maternal health statistics like she would a Taylor Swift song, punching Zoey's gut with her rebuttals, calling her Frog Legs in between her low blows to the pussy. He grit his teeth when Vega snapped, "Did you skip all of the reading requirements sophomore year?"

Zoey's lips trembled, looking frail.

"Maybe you need to review *The Second Sex* and *The Handmaid's Tale* cause you obviously remember nothing."

Sebastian stood, ready to defend Zoey.

"Alright." Mr. Dean clapped, waving Sebastian forward. "Your team can go next."

It was a good thing Mr. Dean misread his actions cause he was ready to pounce on his sister. He swallowed his rage, a spicy rawness that scratched his throat. There was no point in confronting Vega now. He popped the muscles in his neck, joining his partner at the front. Arguing for abortion rights, he was on autopilot, quoting the feminist books Vega had shared. And he felt ill, relying on a knowledge base that he wouldn't have without his sister. Trending feminist books weren't exactly his first choice. So much of him was so much of Vega. That's why they used to be so close, back when she had a heart.

The bell rang.

He rushed out of class, chasing his sister down the hall. "Are you still jealous?"

"Of Frog Legs relying on you for her self-worth? Absolutely not. I'm done relying on men." Vega handed out posters as she walked. He didn't get a good look at what the posters said, and he didn't care.

"You're always reading feminist books, talking about women supporting women. And then you trash Zoey cause you're jealous."

Vega rolled her eyes. "Love does not envy–"

"Love does not envy? You? You're reading the Bible?" *Or did you read my paper?*

"When would I read the Bible? I don't even have time to envy you and Frog Legs, who isn't even on my level. So why would I envy her? She can't dance. And she needs to read some, I don't know, Roxane Gay."

Vega continued taping posters to lockers.

He studied the posters centering his twin dressed in a business suit, wearing a shirt that read, "Vote Boss Bitch Purple." There was no mention of Gregory.

He studied his sister, looking for any signs of the breakup. There was no heartbreak, more determined to win than hurt. And he recognized that determination. It existed within him. She'd push past any pain, too focused on working harder to overcome any obstacle. And he figured Vega had identified Gregory as enemy number one. She wouldn't cry over him. She would mount a campaign to take him down.

Vega was popular, but she couldn't take down Gregory alone. The Bradfords had run this school for the last three years. Electing another Bradford was tradition, and CLASH loved traditions as much as gossip. She would need his help and even Zoey's, no matter how much his sister hated it. People started to like Zoey now that she was his partner. He pointed to Zoey entering the hallway with a group of girls.

"Zoey and I have a lot of influence. What if Gregory taps that influence?"

Vega's eyes narrowed. "You'd choose Gregory?"

"I don't vibe with bullies, and most don't. CLASH has an anti-bullying policy."

"You would know, wouldn't you?"

"Yeah, you taught me just how much people hate bullies." He pointed at Zoey's locker. "Just look …" his words faded, noticing the green gift wrapping decorating Zoey's locker. Pink frogs dotted the paper. "Congratulations" glittered in gold letters. It wasn't unusual for CLASH-mates to decorate lockers as a way to celebrate each other, but those frogs felt wrong. He didn't know why, but he had to run.

Zoey spun her locker combination from the first number to the second.

"Don't open–" He stopped breathing.

Zoey pulled the door, and a bucket of green slime spilled all over her, evoking a scream that chilled his bones.

He could hear Vega laughing. She recorded the whole thing for social. As if they hadn't begun their day listening to a speech in Mrs. Agnes' office.

He grabbed Vega's arm so hard she winced. "What did Mrs. Agnes say? Delete that video now and apologize to Zoey."

"I didn't do it, asshole."

"Who did it then?" She was always in the know. People gave Vega their secrets, hoping in vain their secrets would earn them social status, but Vega wasn't a giving person.

"I'll tell you this. Frog Legs' a great target. She's easy to hate because she's so weak and fun to pick on. Perfect for viral content. The best thing you can do for Frog Legs is make sure she doesn't suck. Otherwise, she'll stay trending. Mrs. Agnes can't punish the whole school." She was preaching, but she was right.

He felt sick. Everyone in that hallway recorded Zoey waddling by, zooming in close to film the green trail of slime she left behind.

He ran up next to her, grabbing her hand. "I guess I'm the frog prince," he shouted, waving to people's camera phones.

"Thank you," Zoey whispered.

"We're in this together." He wanted CLASH to know when they attacked Zoey, they attacked him.

It took a long time to get to the L&L. Zoey's body seemed weighed down by the layers of slime. They wouldn't make lunch, so he ordered her DoorDash and had it delivered to the office. He wasn't hungry. The painful events destroyed his appetite and made him want nothing more than to train. Dance was his only weapon to protect Zoey from CLASH.

He grabbed the barre, slime still wet on his palms. Pressing his hands against his white sweatpants left palm prints reflecting in the mirrors. The barre felt more secure on the second grab, and he let the silence become a rhythm for his pliés. Peace overcame him. His breath deepened. Tension slowly dissolved in his shoulders, and then Amy gasped.

Ignore her. She gasped again, making him tense. He glanced at her reflection.

"Oh no." Her hands pressed against her chest, approaching him with her phone outstretched.

He watched Vega's latest post. There he was, shouting, "I guess I'm the frog prince." The video cut to Vega. "You know my twin loves donating his money to kids that can't afford CLASH." She stood in the chapel, the perfect setting for a lie. "Now, he's donating his time to Charity Case Frog Legs. It's self-sabotage. She's going to destroy his career–" The video cut to Zoey yelling, "Screw CLASH, screw dance, screw rich, egotistical pricks!" His sister's gray eyes pleaded with her followers, "My twin chose Frog Legs cause he felt sorry for her–"

Amy sighed, sinking to the floor. "I feel bad for poor Zoey. Don't you?"

"Let Vega say whatever she wants. I'm going to prove Zoey's great."

"How?"

"By pushing her to be great."

"Oh no, that's the exact opposite of what Zoey needs. Remember how Vega felt? She needs you to be kind."

"I was kind to Vega."

"You were tough. Don't be tough. Not at the first rehearsal, at least. Be nice."

He wasn't tough on Vega. He held Vega to the same standards Papá held them. She just wanted him to treat her like her CLASH-mates, like a celebrity at a West Hollywood spa.

He couldn't stand how people crowded around Vega as she walked from lunch to French, taking her posters and promising they'd vote. He couldn't stand it when the teachers let Vega break the rules. She'd blurt out answers, eat cinnamon chips in class, and draw hearts in her textbooks. No one ever told Vega to pay attention, but Zoey? If she so much as spoke without raising her hand, the teacher would call her out. She was just as smart as Vega and even showed the same passion, but it was clear she was not Vega.

The basketball team carried Vega's books to her Waymo. She always chose expensive ride-hails even though she had a car. He hated that. Zoey walked alone to the dance studio. People avoided her, afraid they'd catch invisible slime. Kindness wasn't what Zoey needed. She needed respect. And he'd train her to be so great people would bow down to her. That would be kindness.

CHAPTER 37
ZOEY

she scrubbed her skin red, but washing off this green slime wasn't easy. It was a thick concoction of vanilla pudding, pineapple, and oatmeal. And it preferred sticking to her flesh versus washing down the drain to only God knew where.

Her hair was a green mess of tangles. She tugged at the strands in the mirror, lips trembling, but refused to cry anymore. Whoever did this–and she definitely blamed Vega–would not ruin her day. This was the day Sebastian chose her, and no matter what, she would keep her joy, especially after all of those long, painful rehearsals and then that time when she forgot her homework. Mrs. Sehar had been so disappointed. And then being stuck on this low-carb diet sucked. No bully was making her quit. Not on her dreams or on Sebastian, her frog prince.

Zoey smiled, remembering Sebastian holding her slimy hand. He had made her feel like a goddess. And no guy ever made her feel so powerful–Ian didn't count. That's why she couldn't disappoint Sebastian. She had to walk out of this locker room exuding goddess vibes.

She looked at the outfit she discovered in the L&L. An oversized football jersey that would make a good boyfriend dress paired with leggings. It was cute, but getting dressed seemed like a lot of work. She hugged her towel tighter, eyes settling on the bench. *I can rest there for a bit.*

The hardwood felt good against her back. *Maybe I can stay here forever.* She imagined Ladybug and Sailor Moon teaming up to fight off Vega and her CLASH-mate minions. The silence covered her like a blanket. Vanilla shampoo lingered from her shower. She would have stayed there if a short office attendant didn't enter the locker room and announce her DoorDash was getting cold in the front office.

DoorDash? She hadn't ordered DoorDash. Growing curious, she dressed and then followed the office attendant to administration, where a white bag holding a turkey burger with sweet potato fries sat on the front desk. Sebastian, her frog prince, had ordered it for her. The fries glowed her favorite color, and the burger was fat with fresh lettuce as green as new fabric. Taking a bite, she closed her eyes. Grease and salt coated her tongue. So delicious.

"Charles Bradford's waiting for you."

Zoey's eyes popped open. The office attendant stared as if she was supposed to know this.

"You're late."

Late was a strong word when no one told her about this meeting. She stumbled backward, the attendant scooting her into her dad's office with her burger still wedged between her lips. Dad conversed with Charles' lawyers and executives from BGM Studios. All intimidating men who looked like they worked in boardrooms.

They gave her a crew of two women camera operators, Tayo and Rebeeca, and a sound mixer. Tayo was from Nigeria. She earned her chops in Nollywood. Rebecca grew up in Los Feliz, and Jeff, the sound guy, was from Michigan.

She left that meeting understanding little, except every moment of her life would be recorded and used for future embarrassment. But the good news was her camera operators were women, and she would get paid. She'd have enough money to pay for fashion school in Paris. Yay, right?

She stopped outside at the stingray fountain. Water flowed like the sparkles that danced around Marinette transforming into Ladybug. *I wish I were Ladybug right now.* Then, she wouldn't feel like returning to that bench in the girl's locker room. She wished she had a sidekick like Rena Rouge. They'd fight off green slime and Vega. They'd devise tactics to survive her first rehearsal with Sebastian. That way she wouldn't feel so scared. She didn't even want to enter the dance building. It looked too much like Colt Fathom's hideout.

She didn't have Rena, but she did have Ian to text. But she already knew what he would say: 'Didn't you ask for this? Suck it up and go.' Like she needed to hear that.

She dragged herself into the dance building. The halls were empty and so clean. Studio D120 was right in the middle. Taped to the side of the door was a poster of Vega. 'CLASH girls unite. Vote boss bitch purple.' That was her slogan? Unite? More like terrorize.

She ripped it down and spotting more, she ripped those down too, ripping the posters to shreds and tossing them into the air. She kicked the pieces into a pile, scooping them up and sprinkling them into the trash. She was never voting for Vega. NEVER!

The camera operators stepped closer. She forgot they were there. Feeling embarrassed, she rushed inside D120. Her eyes widened. It felt like a hundred degrees. Sebastian defied gravity mid split, shirtless and covered in sweat. His energy surrounded her, and she was filled with heat. He was gorgeous. She tried not to stare at his abs. His body, his skill, all perfectly unreal.

"Are you nervous?" He grabbed a towel, patting his face.

She nodded her head. Why lie when it was obvious?

"Good. Channel that into energy."

"Is that how you deal with fear?"

"What's fear?"

"A handbag."

He smirked, grabbing the barre. "Is this your first time seriously training in ballet?"

"Ian trained me a bit, and then before that, I did it when I was six for like a year." She remembered hating ballet. It took her away from her room filled with dolls and toy dresses. "I think that's how I decided to create fashion and live that life. It was those moments with the dolls."

Sebastian nodded. She wasn't sure he was listening. "So this is first position." He put his legs together, rotating his feet out.

She tried to copy him. He lifted her chin and straightened her back.

"Try and keep your spine neutral." He spread his legs so they were outside his hip bones. "This is second position."

She copied him. He readjusted her shoulders. Then he showed her third, and then fourth, and then fifth. Those positions hurt her upper thighs, but she didn't want him to know.

He lifted up in his torso, sliding his right leg forward and pointing his toe. "This is a tendu. We'll do this in first, second, third, and so on. Got it?"

She nodded.

"To music." He put on classical music and then he tendued away. His movements were smooth, his toe brushing the floor before curving into an arc.

She tried to be like him, but her feet didn't like arcs. She wanted to ask him about her feet, but he wasn't in a mood for talking.

He straightened her legs and tapped her on the small of her back to remind her to tuck her pelvis and lift. He was so different from Ian. Ian couldn't dance twenty minutes without launching into a story that inspired exploration and play. And she missed that play. It made her feel comfortable.

"This is a tombé pas de bourée." Sebastian extended his right foot forward and fell into tombé before lifting.

She did the same, wobbling. It was harder than it looked.

Sebastian had her repeat it.

She tried not to look at his harsh expression while she wobbled. The more nervous she felt, the harder it was to balance. "When's this supposed to get fun?" she joked.

Sebastian rested out of fifth position. "You don't have time for fun. There's a lot at stake."

"We're creative leaders that play, explore, and create genius," she quoted the CLASH-ism, hoping he'd tease her for being lame. Ian would, but it seemed Sebastian didn't like lame.

He headed for a towel, pulling his shirt over his head. "If you're tired, just say it."

"I'm not tired." That was a lie. "I'm messing around."

"CLASH is watching. And they want you to fail, but you can't fail. My family's legacy is resting on this. We can't suck."

His words squeezed her, popping teardrops from her eyes. She turned her back, raising shaking fingers to her wet cheeks. It was the first rehearsal, and he already regretted choosing her. All she had wanted to do was create art with someone as inspiring as him. Then maybe CLASH-mates would see her as more than Frog-Leg Zoey, but of course this was bigger than CLASH. This was Sebastian's career. And she was destroying it.

She shuddered when he touched her. "I don't want to suck. I'm made for greatness." And she didn't want to hold him back when he could find a better dancer. When the tears became floods, she rushed out of the studio.

"Zoey, I'm sorry." His apology exploded in the empty halls.

CHAPTER 38
IAN

he planned to tell his family he was dropping out, but he needed backup.

He texted Cody, praying to God one of his friend's clients got sick.

Ian: You free tonight for Salsa 2.
Cody: Yeah, I'll swing by.

His insides screamed while entering Ma and Pa's packed Salsa 2 class. Tech and Hippie Nerds danced up front. They were the cutest, flirting with each other between dance moves. Everyone thought he was so lucky to have two sets of progressive padres, but no, he felt like every conversation was group therapy. And then they would take each other's sides.

Cody showed up near the end of class. After the last student left, he walked with Cody and his padres down to the empty booths on the second floor. He stared into their sweaty faces, wishing Tech and Hippie Nerds would disappear. That would make this conversation easier.

"I landed a feature starring Usher. It's a musical," Cody said.

Ma and Pa's eyes lit up, jumping into a bunch of questions. They loved Cody, finding his backstory inspiring. They'd adopt him if they could. Cody began dancing at the Boys and Girls Club when he was eight, working at fast-food restaurants to help his padres pay for extra dance classes. Beyoncé gave him his big break. Then, he was traveling with Usher, Ne-Yo, and Chris Brown. He even danced on Broadway before returning to LA to open his dance studio at nineteen. He did all this without completing high school.

Ian hoped his padres saw Cody as proof that he didn't need CLASH. He wanted to dance somewhere spicy and look into mirrors that reflected faces from diverse backgrounds, just like he did when he took Ma and Pa's classes. "I need a better fit for my career so I can land an agent and be like Cody," he said. "So I'm dropping out."

"*Te quedarás a CLASH hace muertas,*" Pa shouted. You will stay at CLASH until you die.

"*Sí, Sí!*" Ma agreed.

That didn't make any sense. "They're kicking me out at eighteen." He waved at Tech and Hippie nerds, growing annoyed at their stupid pity faces. "Why are they even here?"

"They're family," Ma said. *"And they believe you should stay in school."*

Tech and Hippie Nerds nodded.

"We're Mexican," Pa shouted. *"America thinks we're lazy. They think we're criminals. We have to prove America wrong, and we have to look out for the next generation. You need to be a role model for your cousins."*

"So now I have to be a martyr for my people?" he resisted the urge to launch into Spanish so Cody could follow the conversation even if this conversation took a left turn into madness.

"Don't be like Juan," Ma shouted.

"Unbelievable. Juan's not a bad person." So what Juan dropped out at sixteen and got two women pregnant? The only family Juan had growing up was poverty. And that had landed him in jail on a drug possession charge. After a few years of being homeless, a cousin hooked Juan up with a social worker who got him a job as a janitor. He had worked that until someone hired him to run a gas station. It wasn't the dream, but Juan was happy and cared for his kids. But that wasn't what people talked about at the family barbecues.

"I'm not trying to be like Juan," Ian said. "I want to be like Cody. He didn't finish high school. He went straight into the industry and got an agent. And he's going to hook me up. I have a plan."

"You dropped out?" Pa asked Cody.

Cody rubbed his low fade and shrugged. "Technically, yeah. They home-schooled me, and then I got my GED." Cody raised his hands when Pa muttered, "No, no." "I'm not here to disrespect you or wreck Ian's life. Thing is, my mom and dad were all in on my dream. They pooled their resources together to make sure I succeeded, and I did. Ian's simply asking you to do the same."

Ma and Pa went so silent Ian could hear their hearts cracking. He knew his padres dreamed of him dressed in Mexican colors, walking across CLASH's giant stage to grab his diploma. They had even purchased a two-hundred-dollar frame, confident that his photo would hang in the Alumni Corridor one day. That was their dream. His was loving life.

"We love you, so if you want this, we'll support it." Ma rubbed Pa's shoulders.

Pa wouldn't look at him.

"But you need to figure out what you want and commit," she continued. "No more trying to have it all cause you're afraid. CLASH is one of the best dance schools in America, and you're throwing it away. Make sure that's what you want."

CHAPTER 39

SEBASTIAN

it was so cold he could see Vincent's breath. That's how it usually was at six a.m. in Bel Air. He was so numb he couldn't feel it. His heart pummeled like the basketball pummeling the cement. He was losing four to eight. Vincent shoved him out of the way and dunked. Correction, four to ten. He turned away as the camera guy pushed closer.

"La culpa está destruyendo tu partido," Vincent said. Guilt's destroying your game. *"No estás enfocando. Quieres descansar?"* You're not focusing. Do you want to rest?

No. Whenever he stood still for too long, he saw Zoey's face scrunched with tears, and smelled vanilla pudding and shampoo. He'd think about making her cry. He should have listened to Amy, his mamá … Vega. He held the back of his neck, staring at the back of Vincent's house. *Maybe Vega's right. I'm abusive. "Soy gilipollas."* I'm an asshole.

Vincent threw him a water, re-racking his basketball.

"No terminamos el partido. Todavía nos quedan doce puntos." We haven't finished. We still have twelve points left.

"Bro, the game was over when you stepped on the court all angsty and unfocused. Let's eat. Mom and Dad's making waffles." Vincent trained like he trained, but unlike him, Vincent would end practice early and still call it a win.

He didn't want to return home and switch into actor mode, but he supposed he had to prepare. Charles was transforming his dance studio into a film set for today's livestream, and he'd have to become Sebastian the Influencer, introducing all of his followers to Zoey. That would take a lot out of him. Zoey didn't have camera experience, and he wasn't sure she'd feel confident about today after he hurt her. Still, he had to make sure she looked confident, no matter what. She would leave this day feeling like she was his perfect match.

He felt Vincent's arm flop over his shoulders. "You're eating, man." His friend squeezed him.

He didn't want to eat, not with Zoey's suffering on his mind.

The kitchen smelled like batter and eggs, making him want to puke. Swallowing the saliva flooding his throat, he hugged Mr. Derek and Mrs. Courtney. They were a big hug kind of family. And they liked big breakfasts. Waffles, turkey bacon, and eggs decorated the yellow tablecloth that matched the walls. A pitcher of orange juice reflected the sunlight falling through the kitchen windows. Mrs. Courtney and Mr. Derek made him a plate when he didn't. He forced food down his throat, knowing Mr. Derek would pull out a scale and weigh him if he didn't eat.

"How was practice?" Mr. Derek asked. "You getting rest and taking care of yourself?"

He couldn't lie. Mr. Derek knew nothing about ballet, but he knew what good training and rest looked like. "I haven't been able to sleep."

Mr. Derek put his fork down, leaning forward. So did Mrs. Courtney. They waited.

"Am I–" An asshole? A jerk? Was Vega right? Did he hurt her, and that's why he could hurt Zoey? How was he supposed to say what he felt? Principal Raines forced him to write a whole paper on leadership and love. First Corinthians Thirteen listed out these traits, and none of those traits described him. He lowered his eyes, his tongue pinned down with shame.

Mrs. Courtney whispered something to Mr. Derek.

Mr. Derek jumped up. "Shoot, Mario's playing in Atlanta, and we about to miss it."

"We're going to watch the game and leave you two to finish up." Mrs. Courtney squeezed Sebastian, resting her chin on his head before kissing Vincent.

He watched them hurry out of the kitchen. They were lying. Mr. Derek's assistant made sure he never forgot. As soon as they were gone, gravity lessened, making Sebastian's shame lighter. His tongue unlodged, and he asked Vincent, "Am I abusive?"

"To Vega? Man, she exaggerated a lot of things."

"So it was half true."

Vincent made a so-so motion with his hand.

"Amy told me to be kind to Zoey cause she thought I was mean to Vega. She said I was tough."

"Amy said that? She your therapist now?"

"I'm asking you what you think."

Vincent shrugged, looking away. "You're straight-up mean. It's like you shut off all emotion when you're working, and I mean, I do the same thing, but I feel like you never stop working. I have to remind you to hang out, sometimes to eat. Do you even go to the bathroom? Should you go now?"

He sank lower in his chair. No wonder Vega hated him. "I'm an abusive, evil person."

"Vega never practiced, so she was holding you back, so you upgraded to Sexy-Panty Zoey, who isn't a ballerina, and that's pretty confusing seeing that you dumped your sister in front of the whole world. But Sexy Panties clouded your judgment."

He shoved Vincent. "Stop."

"Bruh, who you lying to? I see the way you look at her."

He shoved Vincent again, fighting a smile. None of this was funny. He was an asshole, and Zoey could end up hating him just like Vega. But Vincent was the only person in the world who could make him laugh when he wanted to be serious.

"Zoey's hot, so I get why you're into her. But she's messy. And you don't like messy."

He didn't, but her quirky personality made him feel unstoppable. And the way she looked at him? It was like she believed he was a master of his craft, and he loved that.

"I like her and want to dance with her without making her feel like I'm beating her up."

"Then prince charm those sexy panties. Be nice. And I'm talking extra, extra, extra times infinity nice. Don't go into that livestream today being you."

Being nice wasn't him. Nice was Papá the actor on red carpets, the Papá who donated himself to anyone that asked. Sebastian was more like Papá the dancer, an introverted perfectionist.

He returned to his bedroom, rehearsing kindness in his mirrors while Robé's two assistants completed his hair and makeup. His first attempts at kindness rang false, so he dug deeper. He pictured Mrs. Agnes coaching him, Papá and Mamá praising him, his sister sharing her books. He lived for their compliments. They inspired him to achieve more. He wanted to inspire Zoey to achieve.

Amy called shots while the cameramen filmed Robé styling him in an Alexander McQueen beige and ivory sweatshirt that matched joggers and dance sneakers. He surrendered to this kindness, thanking Robé, and hugging the assistants. His mood lifted when he entered his studio and noticed Zoey's outfit matched his.

She looked amazing, dressed in a beige tube top and ivory leggings. Her wild fro hung straight down her back. "I love this," he fingered her hair. "But, I miss your afro already."

"Well, they didn't ask me what I wanted to do with my hair cause then they would have known I don't do straight."

"Whatever look you're into, I'm into. Next time, tell them." He looped his arm around her waist, shifting her to face the photographer. He could feel her tense when the camera clicked. "Breathe."

Her shoulders rose and fell, but she was still stiff.

"Be a bubble."

Zoey giggled. "A bubble?"

"Weird, right?" He tickled her, holding her tight when she fell forward. "I landed my first commercial at eight. It was for Gap. And the director wanted me to be happy, like a bubble, but I was scared. My papá kept making these funny faces to cheer me up. And the director loved it. It ended up becoming this father-son shoot. Papá claimed we were the best bubbles."

"I love that. We can be bubbles." She raised her phone when it vibrated with an alert. "They posted the pictures." She showed him the post. It announced that they were going live in thirty minutes. "I can't believe this is happening. Are you sure you want to do this with me?"

"Till death do us part." He was all in. There was no going back.

Amy guided them to directing chairs in the center of the four-camera setup. They had an onset picture editor that would switch between cameras. The cinematographer completed the lighting while Gregory and Charles observed from video village. Vega entered wearing a purple sweatsuit, an omen that transformed Zoey's mood from awe to fear.

"Do you want me to ask her to leave?" He didn't want anyone there making Zoey feel unsafe.

Zoey shook her head. "She's your sister."

He bit his tongue. Love did not kick twin sisters out of dance studios. "I'm sorry about everything that happened," he said, trying to draw her focus from Vega.

"It's okay. You can't control Vega."

"Me yelling at you and making you cry."

"Oh."

"I was such an asshole, and I don't want to be that with you. This has to be magical, so we can create great art, whatever that looks like."

"Same." She smiled. "I'm an amazing artist. You've seen my work. I play-create hard."

"You do." He admired her confidence when she'd been through so much.

The sound recordist hid lavaliers down his costume and gave him an earpiece so Amy could direct him during the livestream.

"Set's ready," The First AD announced.

Everything went black except for the lights focusing on him.

"Rolling," the cam ops and sound recorders announced.

Amy said, "Action!"

This was it. His nerves became fire. "It's crazy early in LA. Anything before noon on a Saturday is early, so thank you lots for joining me. Not to mention all the likes and comments you've been throwing at my posts about my search for a new dance partner. Hundreds of you auditioned, and you guys are crazy talented. I wish I could dance with all of you. It was a hard decision to make, but one dancer stole my heart, my mind, my everything–" He tossed it to Zoey, but Zoey froze, focused in Vega's direction. She couldn't see his twin. There was no way, not behind the bright lights.

He squeezed her hands. 'Bubbles,' he mouthed, turning back to the cameras. "This is Zoey Raines. She's scared right now, but I'm asking her to think bubbles–free, airy, fun–so guys, can you help her get into this bubble mindset by sending her love in the comments?"

A bunch of hearts floated up the screen.

"Zoey, I think you're artsy, cool, happy, all the reasons why I chose you, but how would you describe yourself?"

"Be bubbles, be bubbles." She breathed. "A fashionista turned dancer, I guess. I study–I mean, I studied fashion before CLASH faculty swapped my classes for ballet, and I'm hoping I can do both, but right now, all that matters is learning you and your style."

'So she's not even a dancer?' user XOXO202 typed in the chat.

That was strangely negative. He answered it so people wouldn't doubt Zoey. "You dance salsa and bachata, right? You incorporated that into your audition, and it reminded me of my mamá. All my fans know this cause I post about it a ton—love you, Mamá—but the great Catalina Bautista is a competitive dancer, dancing International Latin ballroom styles all over the world. And, so, I'm so drawn to you. How'd you get into Latin social dances?"

"My best friend Ian Cruz's mom and dad own a Latin club called El Famoso in Long Beach. And I was there all the time growing up cause his mom would babysit me. My mom and dad had crazy work lives. My mom—her name's Janet Raines—is a teacher, and my dad, Frederick Raines, was a football player who had to go back to school when he got injured. Ian's mom taught me salsa, bachata, merengue, the tango."

"You tango? We have to tango."

"It's my favorite dance. You must know so much about these dances cause you're Spanish, right?"

"You're taking control and asking questions. I like it."

Zoey brushed her shoulders off. "You know, I guess I'm getting a little cozy."

He laughed. "Lit, so you're right, I'm Spanish, a first-generation immigrant, actually. Mamá and Papá moved here from Madrid when I was eight."

Spanish flags floated in the chat. Then, stupid user XOXO202 typed, 'Is she Afro-Latina, or is she cultural appropriating?'

Who the heck? He crushed the urge to whip out his phone and uncover XOXO202's identity. "I think XOXO202 is trying to burst our love bubbles with hate, but let's attack hate with kindness. First, are you Afro-Latina?"

"I took a DNA test last Christmas, and I'm eighty percent African and twenty percent European. My family's been in

Compton since my great, great granddad, but Compton's majority Hispanic now. Does that count?"

"*Supongo ...Te hablas Español?*" I suppose. Do you speak Spanish?

"*Un pequito,*" Zoey laughed nervously. "Whatever Ian and his fam taught me."

"*No te preocupes.*" Don't worry. "I'll teach you, so that leads to my next question, which I think is a dumb question cause, news flash, ballet's French, not Spanish, and Latin social dances stem largely from Black culture, but I digress. Are you culturally appropriating?"

Zoey shrugged. "I'm not Afro-Latina and don't speak Spanish, but Ian's family is Hispanic from Guadalajara. Ian and I were born the same year, and he grew up right next door to me. And his parents started teaching us dance before we could even ask. Ian's parents were competitive ballroom dancers who used their prize money to buy their studio. They probably beat your mom in a few competitions."

"Probably not. Mamá drips gold medals."

"Like mom, like son, I guess." Zoey's smile faded when she read Rebel_4_Duarte's comment, 'Is learning Spanish that hard when LA's majority Hispanic?' BlandM0nday stated, 'Latin dance isn't ballet. I don't get it.' A few fans tried to defend Zoey with, 'I like her. She's super cute and down to Earth,' but XOXO202's comment ruined everything. 'You must want to get in Zoey's sexy panties cause there are tons of actual LatinX ballet dancers or even Black ballet dancers like Mahogany Baker. Why didn't you pick a real ballet dancer? Were you afraid of being outshined by a BIPOC?'

XOXO202 had to be a CLASH-mate. *Vega's dead.* He stared at the blinding lights, hoping to catch Vega in the act. His eyes burned. *I'm not going to find her.* And even if he did, what could he do about it now? Giving up, he yanked Zoey from the director's chair. "I have a surprise for you."

"Not yet!" Amy yelled through his earpiece.

Screw you! Where was she when he needed her? All Amy cared about was a good story, but he wasn't coasting while XOXO202 cyberbullied Zoey. He hoped Amy got her Emmy, but he was jumping in the driver's seat and speeding to the next plot point, Zoey's big surprise.

The production team parked a cherry red Volvo right on the street, so it was the first thing he saw when he stepped out of the house.

Zoey stood on his lawn, confused. He had to pull her closer to the car.

"Your first brand sponsorship," he said. Charles had a friend who was best friends with the CEO of Volvo, and they were all in on sponsoring him and Zoey with a new car. It felt weird to throw a new car at her without asking. As if he were a daytime special, but he didn't have time to ask her if this would be okay.

She touched the paint with her fingertips, forcing a smile, a fake one. Her real smiles were goofy with dimples that dripped gold. Her fake smiles were dry.

"Thank you," she lied. She wasn't looking at him. She was staring at Charles, and Amy, and Gregory, and Vega, and the crew.

"You deserve it." He kissed her cheek.

Her eyes floated to his. He soaked in her curiosity, his eyes outlining her soft pink. Why not shock her? Why not shock the world? He kissed her lips. Pause. He could feel the cameras pushing closer. He kissed her lips again. This time, she kissed back.

His world ignited.

CHAPTER 40
IAN

ma and pa agreed he could meet Cody's agent at World Wide Creatives under one condition: They could make his life a living hell until he made enough money to move out. Living hell meant working weekends, mopping the floors, taking out trash, and cleaning the bathrooms–a job he absolutely hated. Every human should make it their mission to improve janitors' lives by learning to piss and poop outside. He was so busy with hell, he missed Zoey's livestream. His phone blew up with gossip, and he had nothing to add to the conversation.

Cody was driving him to WWC Monday morning, and he planned to listen to it then. As soon as he climbed into Cody's Corvette, he asked, "Can I put on Zoey's livestream?" It was an hour's drive to WWC. They could finish it on the way there.

"Naw, you late. I already sent you my thoughts, and we have to work on your elevator pitch."

Darn it.

"You're entering big dog territory, and Jamison isn't signing you just cause you're sleeping with the owner's daughter. So, why you? Sixty seconds."

His first attempt at an elevator pitch failed, but Cody drilled him hard. By the time his friend's Corvette turned onto the Avenue of the Stars, he was flipping dance credits off his tongue with ease. WWC's concrete skyscraper shone under the sunlight, and he felt important, watching Cody hand keys to the valet. He followed Cody into this architectural composition of little squares, ready for this life where he had an agent who sipped ginger tea while typing emails on an iMac behind a glass wall.

Riding the elevator to the tenth floor felt so right that he had to check himself when Cody asked him to wait on a bench outside agent Jamison's office. That reminded him real quick, he was an outsider wanting membership. He sat on the bench.

Why did the office walls have to be made of glass? There were no secrets, and it was unnerving watching Cody sell him to Jamison. Jamison's resting bitch face could win UFC fights.

He pulled out his phone. This was the perfect time to watch Zoey's livestream. His bestie's face filled his screen. She was nervous, but her style was giving, and he was ready to buy. Her hair, her outfit, and as much as he hated to admit it, her new plaything, Sebastian, everything, whatever idea they wanted to sell him, he was ready to swipe his credit card and go in debt. Their chemistry was so cute, making the vampire look almost likable. Okay … unexpected.

He grimaced, reading, 'So she's not even a dancer?' *Hold up. Who's this bitch XOXO202?*

Sebastian's answer made matters worse. Like why couldn't the vampire just check his massive dick energy for once?

Ian shuddered, watching the onslaught of hatred intensify as Sebastian egged on the troll, playing Vampire the Hero when he should have been playing Beyoncé the Hate Deflector, ignoring that last question, 'Were you afraid of being outshined by a BIPOC?'

That question stank of Vega. Ian texted XOXO202's comment to Vega.

Ian: Did you write this?
Vega: I'm not the only one that hates Frog Legs. Try a private investigator.
Ian: But you're the best investigator money can buy.

He searched social media for user XOXO202 and uncovered a profile with fifteen posts. He texted what he discovered.

Ian: It's a fake account.

He hoped she'd fill him in on what she learned. If she hadn't trolled Zoey, then she would have spent the weekend calling and texting people till she found the culprit. She stayed in the know, and that's what made her powerful.

Vega: Want to sell your soul?

He laughed. *You're such a bitch.* But he couldn't be mad at her. Bitchiness and coconut chips were kind of his faves.

Ian: You already own it.

She texted a link to the culprit behind XOXO202, some skinny vegan who drank spirulina and had a butterfly obsession.

He couldn't believe it.

Ian: This basic Level II ballerina?
Vega: A jealous nobody. Anyway, I have my own problems like running for SG prezy …

She sent him a purple heart, done with this conversation.

'You're still to blame,' he typed, erasing the letters. He didn't care Vega was now too busy to bully Zoey. She was the reason his bestie was such a social disaster that no CLASH-mate wanted to see her win. But what was the point in calling Vega out when that would only make him her target?

"I can't escape you."

He looked up.

Mahogany stood over him, and the atmosphere changed. The bland walls looked vibrant, but Mahogany had that effect on atmospheres. She entered a space and made it electric. "Run faster," he whispered, taking in her ocean ballet shrug, leotard, and matching leg warmers. She looked so kissable. He leaned away, fighting her magnetic pull. "School let out early?"

"My dad's taking me out to lunch. He wanted to cheer me up about Sebastian."

Like you would do if you were a good boyfriend. That's what she wanted to say. "I'm sorry I didn't text you. I had to work."

She shrugged. "You know you skip class way too much."

"I've never skipped dance."

"So. All the teacher's talk."

"It doesn't matter. I'm dropping out of CLASH." There wasn't any point in hiding the truth. She would find out anyway, and it would hurt less if he broke the news. "I'm here to meet with Cody's agent so I can land work."

Mahogany shook her head. "You would drop out. You're so non-committal. Maybe you should just drop out of life."

"That's not it. I could already be dancing backup to Olivia Rodrigo or someone savage like that, not trying to impress old teachers who gave up on their careers."

"You don't have to leave CLASH. Look at Sebastian. He does both." Mahogany didn't fight the tears rolling down her cheeks.

"I'm not Sebastian, and I don't want to be." Sebastian didn't need fun to survive, so he spent every waking moment training, but there was more to life.

"I meant try like Sebastian tries. You're just as talented. The only difference is Sebastian commits. He says yes to dance, and you're all over the place. And it's so sad. Like being your friend and watching you never commit to anything is sad."

"I don't want to hurt you."

"Then say yes and stop telling me no."

"I never told you no." He just couldn't be what she wanted cause he didn't quite understand it. Even though he grew up with the Raines family and saw that a monogamous coupling was possible, it was like taking a course. Ma and Pa with Tech and Hippie nerds were his every day. They raised him to be open, to love both men and women without questioning, as if there were no limits to love. Monogamy was a life lesson he learned when he left home, an interesting textbook he closed when he grew bored. "You've told me no." His hands shook.

"I told you I wanted to be your girlfriend. I gave you my body."

"Thank you. I love your body. I love everything about you, but you think I'm disgusting."

"No, I don't."

"You do. I'm queer. And some queer people are made for monogamy, but I don't think I am. I want to commit to you, but I'm not normal." He'd crumble if she left him crying in the middle of this giant office building with assistants looking at him sideways, as if he were a reality show, another C-list celebrity hungry for a come up. He turned to find a restroom where he could clean himself up and switch back into the confident Ian, ready to sell himself for representation.

Mahogany pulled him back. And he couldn't resist hugging her, pressing his nose against her scalp. He needed her smell, her body. She mattered to him and made him feel real when, sometimes, all he felt was fake. He didn't kiss her, unsure if she wanted his kisses anymore.

"I don't want normal. I want you, and I need to know if you can prioritize me a little? I just don't want to feel so worthless all the time."

He cuffed her cheeks. "I'm so sorry, truly."

She kissed him.

He squeezed her, lifting her tight against his chest. Her kisses were as delicious as a carne asada burrito. That first bite was always the best but never as fulfilling as Mahogany's lips. He wanted to stay locked in her lips, her arms, her legs, savoring all that Mahogany was, his girlfriend. But then pushy drama overcame his bliss. Balancing Mahogany with one arm, he grabbed his vibrating phone.

Zoey: Where the heck are you?

He read her words, and his heart ached.

Mahogany peered over to see. "Glad to know I'm not the only one you're neglecting."

"My work schedule's consuming me." He let her hop down, sure they gave everyone a show.

Cody stepped out of his agent's office, grinning big. He had seen it all, and so had Jamison. "Jamison's ready if you're ready."

Ian said nothing, experiencing major technical difficulties with his codeswitch. He wasn't getting stuck in an office with two Black men riding him for being in love. Cody and Jamison would have a comedy pilot by the end of their meeting.

"Tell Jamison we gucci," Mahogany answered.

Relief filled him as his girl pulled him to the highest floor, where the big dogs prowled.

CHAPTER 41
ZOEY

terrified, zoey gripped her phone in the CLASH parking lot.

Zoey: Where are you?

She waited for Ian's text, dreading entering CLASH alone. How could she walk those halls and look at her CLASH-mates while they all made fun of her, calling her Frog Legs the Colonizer? Alone. And she never had to suffer this humiliation all by herself. Ian had always been there. But now what?

She groaned, rubbing her head against her car window. GoPros filmed inside the Volvo. A camera crew surrounded her car. They were human bodies, but they weren't the one body she needed. Her phone vibrated with mentions. Someone tagged her in another post. '#saveSebastian from Fake Ass Frog Legs.' Laugh faces and hearts liked the post. Her lips trembled. Still no text from Ian. He was ghosting her, probably ashamed.

She reloaded the dance department's website. A big class photo stretched wide. This was her third time looking at it, counting one, two . . . twenty-seven people of color–no, she missed the guy in the back—twenty-eight out of two-hundred and sixty-seven. Hello! It was right there, the complete lack of diversity, and yet she'd been walking around sleep. XOXO202 had to slap her awake for all of CLASH to see. It was so awkward even Ian was ghosting her. And she deserved it for being a sucky friend. He complained all the time about being the only Chicano, but she had ignored him cause there were hella people of color in the fashion department. There was even a white boy from Big Bear selling "Red Necks for #BLM" merch on Etsy. And her faculty stayed recruiting Black beauty from Paris and Ghana. So, admittedly, she hadn't even been thinking about Ian and his diversity crisis. And her willingness to stay sleep now made her the problem.

She had to tell Sebastian to choose Mahogany. Mahogany had trained her entire career to represent LA only for her opportunity to get snatched away by a ballet newbie. And for what? A boyfriend? No, ruining a girl's career wasn't worth it.

Zoey didn't want to face CLASH feeling so awful, but she had dressed for her public shaming, wearing leopard-print sunglasses, a matching corset with ripped jeans, and heels.

"There she goes, Fake Ass Frog Legs," a CLASH-mate yelled. Eyes lifted from phones, the hallway erupting with laughter. Zoey shielded her face as she shoved through the bodies. There was nothing to do but keep moving. She was Monday's hot topic, and she would stay the butt of everyone's jokes until Sebastian dropped her.

Her gut tightened, noticing a group of fourth graders waiting outside of the dance studios. *Now, I have to get mocked by babies.* Their tiny bodies jiggled excitedly. She turned to run, stopping, remembering her film crew. What if the fourth graders chased her, and they caught it on camera? She squared her shoulders. It was better to confront them.

"Can we have an autograph?" a fourth grader asked, her face bright with joy. Her friends unleashed a flurry of questions: "Was that your first kiss?" "Are you guys dating?" "Did he buy you the Volvo?" "Is he mean? He looks mean."

They were cute, and she laughed, wishing she were nine again when all she cared about were kisses and cherry red, expensive gifts. Not the dirty looks CLASH-mates gave her when she entered Ballet III to start stretching.

Zoey scanned the class for Ian, but he wasn't there.

Sebastian stretched in the back of the studio alone, lengthening his back leg along the barre. He seemed invincible, the sunlight falling around him like God's chosen one. She joined him under the sunlight, hoping to be a chosen one. She wanted to be like him, wealthy, successful, and so good-looking he had the power to transform sunlight into a hate blocker. CLASH-mates were talking about him, and he wasn't bothered. She wanted to be unbothered. But she wasn't anything like him.

Sebastian reached for her leg to help her stretch. "You're tense." He squeezed her muscles.

"I'm trying to relax," but it was immensely hard with everyone talking about them. She felt like all the dancers were XOXO202 impersonators.

"How can I help you relax?" She felt him step closer, his waist touching her hip, exciting her senses and turning her hot. His fingers traced her knee, and then he tickled her.

She gripped his hand, fighting back a smile. "Not that."

"We're supposed to make laughter or love, I forget."

He was making her knees weak when she needed her knees to survive this class. She searched for Mrs. Agnes to save her from this overly confident, privileged boy who claimed spaces with audacity. She was never good at resisting a spirit of play. The play dancing in Sebastian's eyes called her, and she hungered for his type of play, so much that she knew the longer she danced with him, the more challenging it would be to quit. She had to tell him now. "Sebastian–"

"Ian?" Mrs. Agnes called.

Ugh. Her head fell back. *So close.*

Mrs. Agnes scanned the class for Ian and then waved to Sebastian. "Please lead the warmup."

Sebastian puffed out his chest, reclaiming his spot in the center. Heads turned, and mouths closed, waiting for Sebastian to lead.

Zoey tried to keep up with her CLASH-mates. They moved in unison, copying Sebastian as he progressed from small and controlled into big, complex feats. She was left behind, wondering, how was she supposed to keep up?

"She should start with the kindergartners," Vega whispered to Polly.

The CLASH-mates laughed, proof no one thought she belonged. It was so infuriating. Sebastian was the reason she was taking the class, but like Vega said in her TikTok, people weren't mad at him for his charity. They were mad at her for accepting it. No one was coming to her rescue. She would have to save herself.

Mrs. Agnes asked them to find space to work on their solos for the annual showcase. All Zoey wanted to do was find some water and retreat to the chapel, where she could cry about her life under White Baby Jesus.

Mrs. Agnes motioned for her and Sebastian to step forward. "Have you two been practicing your opening?"

What opening?

Mrs. Agnes observed Zoey's confusion and then motioned to Sebastian. "The sugar plum pas de deux." She fluttered on pointe, resembling the peacocks walking through Bel Air neighborhoods. She took Sebastian's hand, and he balanced her as she glided through each turn, extending into arabesque, looking as delicate as a strand of yarn.

There was no way Zoey would be able to dance like that by the first week of December. That was less than two months to prepare.

"You'll dance a modern interpretation," Mrs. Agnes said.

"Cause she can't do it," Vega pointed out.

The class laughed, ignoring Mrs. Agnes' commands to stop. Why shouldn't they laugh? Now that she wasn't in fashion anymore, her life was one big joke. The Nutcracker used to fill her with excitement. Ian's interpretation of Drosselmeier was simply enrapturing. And Sebastian? She couldn't take her eyes off him whenever he entered the stage. His Nutcracker Prince was so romantic. And most of all, she loved designing his velvet jacket, embellished with gold braids and appliqués. Her designs had made him look good, and yet her dancing would not. She couldn't humiliate him, that's why he had to choose Mahogany.

She rehearsed her speech in the dressing room, trying to decide on a good opening. "XOXO202 was right" didn't sound convincing, so she experimented with different versions of "I'm sorry." Her eyes flickered to the cameras, wishing Tayo and Rebecca would help her improve her speech. But they stayed silent, following her down the hall to Mr. Dean's debate class. Maybe she shouldn't start with I'm sorry. Like why was she apologizing? She played with "You're the best dancer ever, and I hate holding you back," but that didn't hit right. Sebastian could easily counter that one.

She pulled out her journal in the back of Mr. Dean's class. Her teacher talked, but she didn't hear a word. 'To every beginning, there's an ending,' she scribbled. Scratch. She needed to go artsier. 'Even Tuxedo Mask says goodbye to

Sailor Moon.' But Sailor Moon never quits on him. Scratch. 'Mahogany would make a better Noodle to your Wonka.' That. She smiled. That one was cute, and it hurt. She doodled ladybugs and lunar moons surrounded by lots of sad faces.

"Sad faces? That's your mood?"

She slammed her book close, looking up at Sebastian. He looked scary, studying her so intensely as if his superpower was secret absorption.

She jumped up. "Are you heading to lunch? Can I sit with you?" she asked even though she didn't want to sit with him. He would sit with Vincent, and they spoke their own language. Watching them would make her feel lonelier now that she didn't have fashion or Ian.

"I was thinking we could rehearse," Sebastian said. "Maybe order DoorDash after."

"Sure," she croaked, following Sebastian to the dance building. He took a long way, circling through the parking lot, past the sting ray fountain, and through the gardens to the football field.

It was weird, but walking the campus calmed her nerves. Outside felt warmer, kinder than inside a dance studio, where the floors were too clean, the walls too plain, and the mirrors a reminder that her body was thicker and weaker than the other dancers. She had to face those mirrors when Sebastian finally entered the studio. She ignored them, hungering for the blue sky and the trees outside the windows. Fun. Outside those windows was her fun.

Sebastian extended his hands.

She hesitated. Inside the windows was this gorgeous boy she deeply admired even though he scared her, but she didn't want him to know just how much. So she grabbed his palms, standing face to face, body to body.

"Were you writing a poem: Mahogany would make a better Noodle, and even Tuxedo Mask says goodbye to Sailor Moon?"

She squeezed his hands like she would if she were sitting in a dark theater on Halloween. He had read her opening lines. And now he questioned her with their eyes locked, their breaths synced, their life force pulsing through their palms.

"More like letters to a god you don't believe in," she teased, feigning boldness. He couldn't have made this conversation harder. There was no looking away. "XOXO202 was right about me. I don't deserve this opportunity when dance is so competitive, and Mahogany worked so hard. She should be your dancer. She's more talented."

"And then what?"

"I'll go back to fashion. We can pretend this never happened."

"That's what you want?"

"Yes."

"And everyone's going to forget and be your friend? That's why you're quitting, right? Vega will stop hating you?"

She cringed at the word quit. "I'm not quitting."

"You're quitting. That's what all your sad faces are about."

"I'm appropriating ballet."

"You can't appropriate ballet. You can retrain, rethink, rediscover, and persevere."

Unbelievable. She barked a laugh. You're quoting the freaking CLASH handbook. A whole chapter was dedicated to praising grit while shaming quitting. They took a class on grit in sixth grade, where it was essentially drilled into their heads that it was better to fail a thousand times than to quit. "I know all the CLASH-isms by heart, thank you."

"I chose you cause I want to tell a story of growth and love. That's the story I want to tell, not the story of a quitter."

"Tell it with someone else," she snapped, tugging at her hands.

"You want to quit on a chance to change your life all because of a troll."

"Let go!"

"The whole school will remember that you quit. Some little girl that looks like you will see you and see a quitter."

"I'm not a quitter."

"Then don't." He cuffed her face, staring at her till her eyes became his eyes. "I need you not to quit on me, on us."

Her heart pounded, and she felt so seen God could have parted the clouds and looked her in the eye. Sebastian should not be able to see her like this, but this was his superpower, seeing her beyond flesh and blood to the thoughts that made her quiver. Not only did CLASH drill it into their heads never to quit, but her parents hated quitting. Her mom refused to quit on Malcolm X Primary even though the pay was low and the kids were rough. Dad hadn't quit either, not on success, not on Compton. So how could she quit on Sebastian and feel good about herself?

His thumbs massaged her tears into her cheeks.

She couldn't unsee him. "I don't think we work."

"I'm never quitting on you. Please don't quit on us."

CHAPTER 42

SEBASTIAN

zoey quitting is a great plot twist. Charles and Amy said that, laughing over red wine and salmon. She hadn't been able to cut it, and that ups the competition factor. His docuseries had become *Step Up* meets *So You Think You Can Dance*. The world would love it.

Sebastian gripped his dining room table, fighting the urge to flip it over. The more Charles and Amy laughed, the more his stomach turned.

Mamá massaged his shoulder blades. She was the only one who noticed his fight with madness.

"Zoey can't quit," he told Mamá once Charles and Amy were gone. She wasn't just a story beat in his life. He rubbed his forehead. If he could call it a life. It all felt fictional, constructed for the cameras and sound filming from the dining room corners. His crew always showed up early and stayed late. Exhausted, bored, frustrated or not, they were his only stability, and he didn't even care to know their names. He cared about Zoey. *"I'm not letting her quit."*

"You can't force her. Remember you promised to be kind?"

Yeah, I remember. He already broke it. Reading Zoey's journal made him so desperate that he walked her around the school until he created a plan to intimidate her. He knew if he stared her in the face, studied every speck of dead skin, he'd uncover her secrets. She had an aversion to "quit." That four-letter word became a boxing glove, and he punched her with "quit," "quitter," "quitting" till he knocked her out of the studio.

He was such a jerk, but he needed her to dance with him, and he didn't know how to make her stay without being abusive. He considered asking Mamá for help, hesitating. She'd ask what happened, and he wouldn't be able to lie. The truth would scare her to tears, and he was done making women cry for the month.

He kissed Mamá's cheek, pretending he was going to put in another hour of work, but instead wandered to Vincent's gym. It was arm day. He grabbed a set of twenty-pound dumbbells off the rack. Vincent glistened in the mirror. Standing next to his best friend, he looked like less of a monster.

"Qué tal?" Vincent asked between bicep curls.

"Me odio mi vida." I hate my life.

Vincent laughed. "You? Mr. Worldwide?"

"Zoey wants me to choose Mahogany. I'm thinking cause of XOXO202's comments."

"Man, that livestream was rough. Except that kiss scene." Vincent loaded a video of the kiss filtered in pink and covered in glowing hearts. The kiss played over and over to a Rod Wave track. The video had a million views.

"Did you make that?" Sebastian asked.

"Naw. That's weird."

"It's weird you have that on your phone."

"Then all of CLASH must be weird cause they're commenting on this video right now." Vincent went back to his dumbbells. "The amount of texts I got about your livestream over the weekend was crazy. Everyone is talking about how you should have picked Mahogany."

"Should I have?"

"I mean, Mahogany's dad owns one of the biggest agencies in the world, but do you need her? Does she need you?"

"Facts."

"I told them if they want to stay friends with me, keep your name out of their mouths cause if they were really about it, they'd point out Mahogany isn't starving like Sexy Panties." Vincent threw down his dumbbells. "It's messy. CLASH-mates are all about the likes and laughs."

"How can I tell Zoey that?"

"You haven't told her that already?" Vincent stared him down. "Don't tell me you went in there being you."

"I messed up."

"Bruh, what happened to love and kindness?"

"I think I'm handicapped, psychotic, maybe."

His friend jumped back, shaking his head. "Do you hear yourself right now? You went from zero to one hundred. You just need a reset. My dad's always saying if you miss the shot, go grab the ball and make another. You lose the game, train hard and show up to the next."

"The Dixon philosophy to life. Got it, but Zoey's a little more complicated than a basketball game."

"If you want to get literal, you need to speak with some-one who talks to Sexy Panties like that. I don't know her, and obviously you don't, but who does?"

"Ian." He shuddered. The last person he wanted to talk to.

"My man, Ian. He knows every girl like that." Vincent burst out laughing. "Text him right now."

Ian wouldn't answer his text. "I don't want to talk to him."

"You pay his scholarship. He owes you."

"He hates my guts."

"Well, I don't know what to tell you. Ian's the only one I know who talks to Sexy Panties like that. Maybe you can try showing up at her house and talking to her mom."

He didn't like that idea either. He sank to the bench. I'm going to lose Zoey. When she had auditioned for him, he felt a warmth that rose from his stomach, filling him with an energy that consumed him. He needed that energy to overpower the long, painful hours of the craft. "I'm good at enduring the pain," he whispered.

"Naw, bruh, we don't quit." Vincent examined his muscled body drenched in a sweaty glory. "We play-create genius."

"Have Ian laugh at me or suffer alone? Suffer alone."

"How bout you text Ian first and go from there? If he laughs at you well, you know, love and war." Vincent kneeled like a coach delivering the play in the fourth quarter of a losing game. "But if he doesn't, and you win the war, you win Sexy Panties. And maybe convince Sexy Panties to launch a balletcore, sexy panty line."

He laughed.

CHAPTER 43
IAN

his feet tapped rhythms while waiting to speak with Pa Raines in the school's administrative office. Having this conversation would suck. Honestly, he would skip telling his godpa about dropping out if he thought his padres wouldn't break the news behind his back, allowing Pa Raines to derail his plans.

That left Ian with no choice. He either faced Pa Raines and maintained control of his narrative or lose. *I hate this.* CLASH made everything so serious. Do or die should be its slogan instead of play-create genius. It was hard to sit still. The office felt too clean, and the black and white photos of sports coaches weren't friendly, just like Pa Raines. He loved his godpa, but he was strict, the kind of man who hated grandiose ideas. Instead, Pa Raines wanted summaries with result clauses, a blueprint to the perfect ending. And Ian had a blueprint of how his life could go, but Pa Raines would wrestle for control of his blueprint. And he couldn't lose power.

He examined the coaches' photos. Why not google them? They were there because of Pa Raines. The last principal had a food fetish, and paintings of cupcakes were too cute for a man like his godpa. He googled Tara VanDerveer, a women's basketball coach. Cool. If he lost control of the conversation, he could lighten the mood with sports trivia.

Vega plopped into the seat beside him, squeezing a stack of "vote for me" posters. He assumed she was there to get Pa Raines' sign-off on her candidacy. *"Yo deseo que no te vayas. Podríamos dirigir la escuala juntos."* She kissed both his cheeks. I wish you weren't leaving. We could run the school together.

He felt a little sad. He'd miss Vega's bitchiness, and he'd miss watching her take on Greg and Sebastian. She'd try her best to destroy them, and being in the midst of that drama would be fun. *"Mahogany te dijo?"* Mahogany told you? Not like it should surprise him. It was hard to keep things from Vega. He wouldn't miss that about her.

She paused, gaze shifting.

Tension bunched in his shoulders, his eyes traveling the carpet to Pa Raines' brown shoes. Great. Pa Raines heard everything, and having survived Malcolm X Primary, he knew Spanish.

Ian made a mental note to cut his speech's opening and head straight into his plan. He'd treat this conversation like an opening night. Shows didn't always go as planned, but he could always trust his body after hours of rehearsal. Taking a deep breath, he strolled into Pa Raines' office.

The door slammed behind him.

He jumped.

"What do you mean you're dropping out?" Pa Raines demanded.

Don't lose control. "I already discussed this with Ma and Pa, and we agreed I'd complete my GED so I can still qualify for the Paris College of Arts. And then, I'll focus on getting an agent and booking auditions. I'll also work full-time at El Famoso to have money."

"You're studying in the number one arts and science academy in the country for free. And you want to settle for a GED?"

"I'm jumpstarting my career." He made sure not to bring up feeling like an outsider. Pa Raines would counter that with his own success story of surviving a drug and gang-infested neighborhood. He'd tell him to stay committed, don't quit, survive. And for what? Dance wasn't fun anymore, and why live if it wasn't fun? "It may sound like I'm quitting, but I'm re-strategizing, like you did when you damaged your knee."

"You mean when my body failed me and forced out of the NFL?"

"You could have turned to coaching, but you started over in a different career. I'm not even doing that. I'm sticking with dance."

"You know how hard that was for me? I had a family. I had you to take care of. Life commitments, and I don't break my promises." Pa Raines leaned forward in his seat, eyes narrowed.

Ian braced for the attack.

"What promises are you breaking?"

Accountability, right. He thought he mentally packed for the Pa Raines guilt trip, but an onrush of faces filled his mind: Mahogany's lips; his padres' disappointment; Pa Raines, who looked pissed; Sebastian, who he didn't care about. His heart clenched. Zoey. He promised her he'd finish, and he threw that promise in the trash, along with his black cape, mask, and roses. He couldn't be her Tuxedo Mask or her Cat Noir. His mood tanked, feeling like the worst friend on earth, but he grasped for control. "I was reading about Tara VanDerveer–"

"We're not playing this game, Ian," Pa Raines cut him off. His face softened. "Sorry, I love you, and I always have your back, but I can't let you sabotage yourself. That's why I'm not signing off on this."

"Ma and Pa said yes. It's done."

Pa Raines flexed, reading him like a billboard. "Why you in here if it's done?"

He swallowed, hating this. "I need your permission."

"Exactly. And you're not getting that unless you bring me evidence your chosen path is better than a free ride at CLASH. Good luck."

she didn't want cameras filming her beg her way back into her fashion classes, but the cameras were always filming every mistake, even her farts.

She found Mrs. Sehar in the back of the classroom, scribbling notes on concepts for The Fall Showcase. The top three designers would lead this year's theme. *That should be me. My concepts should be there.* If she had time for her homework, not to mention brain power.

"Mrs. Sehar," she whispered.

"Zoey," her teacher beamed, extending her hands.

She squeezed them. Her teacher's hands were soft and smelled like lavender. Kindness emanated from her palms. She missed Mrs. Sehar's gentle, creative guidance, a complete contrast to her dance teachers' cold, ruthless instruction.

"How's dancing with Sebastian?" Mrs. Sehar said his name with such energy.

She felt ungrateful, admitting, "Hard."

"I bet. He's highly respected. The dance teachers brag about his talent often, and he already has a career that you'll be a part of. Such a dream, Zoey. I'm so proud of you."

She felt weird watching Mrs. Sehar express an excitement that she had as well but found extremely scary. Sebastian was her mind and body's favorite addiction. She could be exhausted from dance, too drained to pick up a pencil to sketch a design, but her brain still could muster the energy to picture Sebastian. He was the sugar and salt that kept her going, and fashion? Oh, that was salad. "I really, really like Sebastian, and that's the problem."

"What do you mean?"

She blushed. He's excellent and inspiring, but he consumes all my mental energy. Not to mention, she didn't think she had a right to work with him. Her CLASH-mates also thought she was a fake. Could she and Sebastian be lovers instead of partners? Mrs. Sehar stared at her sincerely. She opted for admitting something less emotionally messy. "I just miss being a fashion design student."

"It's tough to do both. You have to take so many dance classes."

"I'm thinking of dropping those so that I can come back. I don't want to dance with Sebastian anymore."

Mrs. Sehar sighed. "You've missed so many assignments, and we're prepping for the showcase, which is a huge part of your grade. I don't know if you could catch up."

"I'll work really hard."

"There aren't enough hours in the day, I'm afraid. You'll have to stick with dance."

But I don't wanna.

"Embrace the new challenges." Mrs. Sehar squeezed her hands. "I'll make sure your CLASH-mates design you a beautiful bodice and tutu for your showcase debut."

A beautiful bodice for a meh dancer, dancing next to Sebastian the Great. All of his glamour and excellence, and there she would be, Les Arts Décoratifs on discount.

CHAPTER 45
SEBASTIAN

he watched zoey order pineapple pizza for lunch before heading to the chapel. Those were signs she was upset.

He texted Amy.

Sebastian: Can you order Zoey some cheesy gift? Flowers or something? Make it cinematic.

Searching the cafeteria, he spotted the table where SG used to eat. It was empty, like a memorial. CLASH-mates were still too hesitant to claim it out of respect even though Vega had taken a stand. She had demolished the false sense of SG community, leaving behind nothing but raw loyalty. Vincent and Marc stayed loyal to Gregory, sitting with him at the basketball table. He tried sneaking by, but Gregory spotted him and wouldn't let him leave without a 'Leader That Unites' campaign sticker and shirt.

He tossed the shirt in the trash, walking into the gardens. That's where Mahogany and Polly stayed loyal to Vega.

There was no Ian. He frowned. Ian was never where he was supposed to be.

He sat beside Mahogany at the stone lunch table. "Hey."

"Gregory's inside." Vega pointed at his sticker.

He eyed the stack of 'Vote Boss Purple' stickers, tucking one in his pocket. "In case I change my mind." He ignored his sister stuffing the rest in her bag. "Have you seen Ian?" he asked Mahogany.

"Why?"

"I really, really, really need his help."

"He's at an audition."

"An audition?" He eyed Mahogany, confused.

"It's not for school. A music video for Lola Ross, a new independent artist."

"He's skipping school for a nobody? Mrs. Agnes already took his solo? The faculty's going to kick him out."

"He already dropped out. He's tired of competing."

"We're dancers. We're always competing."

"Let me rephrase that. He's tired of being the only one who looks like him competing in a space he thinks he's not wanted." Mahogany took a bite from her mango salad, acting strangely calm for someone so in love with Ian. She would lose the swapped secrets and shared giggles, the shared plantain chips, and hallway hugs. There'd be no more passionate pas de deuxs, no more random hookups in empty classrooms. Sebastian would kill to have that kind of existence with Zoey, albeit way less messy, but if he had just a sliver of their magic, he would hold on tight. "Why are you letting him leave?"

"Believe me, I've tried talking him out of it. I even recruited my dad to help, and you know Ian. He won't listen, and he's super persuasive. Eventually, my dad caved and hooked him up with an agent."

What a waste. Ian's scholarship could have gone to someone else. Sebastian checked his inbox for an email from Ian stating he forfeited his scholarship. It would have taken five minutes to write, but no, that would have been professional, and Ian was talented, energetic, but not professional.

"Thinking about your little foundation?" Vega cooed.

His jaw flexed.

Vega batted her lashes. "You'll raise more money."

"Can you guys quit it?" Mahogany asked. She could already see where this was going. "I shouldn't have told you anyway."

"No, I need your help," he said. As annoyed as he was, he couldn't take it out on Ian. He had to find the strength to be kind. Mrs. Agnes once asked him to imagine himself as Ian, a brown hue blurred against a palette of whites. He knew what it was like to feel lonely and have it weigh down his artistry. Zoey relieved that heavy feeling for him, and Ian did the same for Zoey. Zoey needed Ian, and he needed Zoey. "Can you help me convince Ian to stay? He's leaving cause he thinks he doesn't fit, and we need to show him that's not true." He told Mahogany to collect videos of

CLASH-mates shouting their love for Ian and post them on social.

Mahogany gave Sebastian the address to Ian's auditions so he could drive to Sunset Boulevard. He used the time stuck in traffic to visualize himself acting kindly towards Ian so he wouldn't call him out for throwing away his scholarship money.

The dance studio was narrow, and the hallways were filled with dancers. None of them Ian. He passed the sign-in table and stepped into an elevator big enough to fit a cameraman and a sound person. After checking the third floor, he found Ian warming up with sissonnes. Bad Bunny played from Ian's cell phone, and he stretched limbs into lines that evoked a sense of forever. And Sebastian had chosen that sense of forever to represent his scholarship. He didn't want to choose the third-best dancer in the school when he could have Ian.

Ian slowed out of a pirouette into a la seconde, frowning. "What are you doing here?"

"*Necesitamos que te quedes en* CLASH," he replied. We need you to stay at CLASH.

"I don't understand your dialect."

"*Don't be a prick.*"

Ian gave in. "*Who's we?*"

"*We're all over social media.*"

Ian pulled out his phone, his mouth falling open. There must have been fifty videos filling his social feeds. He scrolled through them, deciding to play a video of a middle schooler dressed in a leotard with pink tights. "My favorite was watching Ian dance Sancho Panza in *Don Quixote*. It's like I can watch him for days …" he clicked on another girl screaming, "No way, he's leaving? He can't leave." Another video played of Vincent and the basketball team making fun of how perfect Ian was with … everyone. "There isn't a girl in this school that doesn't want to get with Ian. Shit, guys want to get with Ian." Vincent yelled to the camera, *"Oye, Ian. No te vaya."*

The videos kept rolling in, and Ian's expression morphed from confusion to awe. Teachers raved about Ian the social butterfly with the perfect tours en l'air. "I do wish Ian would arrive on time," Mrs. Agnes said in her office. "But, when Ian earns a principal role for the Paris Opera, I'll take my family to see him." Principal Raines said, "Diversity matters, not just skin color, but economically. So thank you, Sebastian, for making it affordable for a genius like Ian to be at this school."

Ian slid to the floor, his hands shaking as Zoey's video played. "You're leaving? Why didn't you tell me? My heart's breaking right now. Maybe that's why you're not answering my calls or texts cause you know how much it hurts to hear that you, my best friend, my only friend in this school, is abandoning me. We made promises to each other. And I need you to keep that promise. And I love you so much. And it's not just me. Mahogany showed me all the videos she made for you. The school loves you. You're perfect. And I need your perfection around me every day to survive. I don't know if I can make it here without you." Mahogany appeared in the video. "Me neither." She hugged Zoey.

"*You're such a shit,*" Ian said, scrubbing his tears with his shirt. "*How'd you get all these?*"

Sebastian shrugged. "*Mahogany. I guess she goes hard in everything she does.*"

"*She does.*" Ian covered his face with his hands. It was like he was hiding himself from the camera filming them.

Sebastian sat beside Ian so he didn't feel so embarrassed.

"*I can't go back to that school,*" Ian said. "*Mrs. Agnes took my solo. And I told Pa–Principal Raines I'm dropping out. And he'll come after me if I don't start booking gigs.*"

"*Don't drop out. Earn your solos back.*"

Ian shrugged. "*Like that's possible. You think I deserve it anyway.*"

"*I mean, I invest a lot in you. What more do you want? A wedding ring?*"

"*You're such a dick. I'll pay you back your money when I make my first million.*"

"*That's not why I'm here.*"

"*Why?*"

Sebastian hesitated, his ego flaring up. "*Dance with me and Zoey*" was easier to say than the truth. He didn't want Ian laughing at him.

"*Mrs. Agnes won't say yes to that.*"

"*We don't need her permission.*"

Ian examined him. *"Someone's Mr. Brand New, breaking hearts and rules. You know, it's better for you if I stay gone. Wouldn't want to destroy your god status."*

He threw his head back, exasperated. *"I messed it up with Zoey, and I need your help to fix it."*

"I thought so." Ian cracked up, making Sebastian's skin crawl. His patience thinned the longer he had to sit there, listening to Ian's cackles.

Finally, Ian's shoulders bounced one last time, sighing satisfied. Facing Sebastian, he extended a fist bump. *"I love breaking rules."*

CHAPTER 46
IAN

sebastian discovered how to make him doubt everything. That detail-oriented prick knew him so well he couldn't stand it. His CLASH-mates shouting their love for him were cute, but that Zoey video had gutted him. He couldn't drop out and abandon his bestie. Compton before Bel Air always. And he never would have realized how much he needed to stay if it weren't for Sebastian. Surprise, surprise.

He didn't feel like riding in Sebastian's expensive Jeep while the camera crew filmed the emotional wreck that he was, so he returned to Compton. Ma Raines welcomed him inside her kitchen with hugs and kisses. She fed him leftover chicken and gravy. He ate it feeling so grateful that he had two mas and two pas, plus parental advisors Tech and Hippie Nerds.

He wandered to Zoey's bedroom and rummaged through her closet filled with her crazy beautiful dresses. His favorite was a black cocktail dress with an orange, beaded Siberian

Tiger stitched into the back. He fingered the beads, pressing the fabric against his body. She had to make him a matching suit. They'd wear this on their first day in Paris.

"Ian?"

Zoey entered the bedroom, carrying tulips and a stuffed ladybug. Those gifts had Sebastian's name all over them. Only a guy so laser-focused would know to buy Zoey a stuffed ladybug. He contemplated teasing her about the gifts, but she looked like she needed to be held, so he asked, "Can I get a hug?"

Zoey dragged herself into his arms. "Always."

He rested his chin on her head and rocked her side to side, digging his nose in her hair. His poor, poor Zoey. Ballet had changed her smell from scents of linens and glue guns to rosin and day-old deodorant. Ballet had changed her body. She was thinner. It had even changed the way she dressed. Her black leotard and jeans looked safe, like the CLASH elite.

"I'm so mad at you," she whispered. "You hurt my feelings so much I don't know where to start."

He hated apologies. No matter how much he practiced the words, they never came out right, so instead of saying sorry, he said, "I felt like I needed to run away."

"I want to run away too. It's so embarrassing."

"But we can't."

"Why not? You're so good at running."

"That's a flaw, not a positive." He tugged her to the bed so they were at eye level. "I'm also good at thinking people hate me. I felt like such an outsider. And I was sick of always competing against Sebastian. But then I saw your goodbye video and realized I didn't want to abandon you."

"You don't have to abandon me. We can run away together."

"We can't run. That outsider feeling is all in our heads. Everyone wants us there."

"Except XOXO202."

Ian pulled out his phone. "XOXO202 isn't some leader in DEI. She's just another jealous dancer trying to make you feel bad." He showed her the Instagram account of the skinny dancer showing off her butterfly tattoos. She was the typical CLASH stereotype, dressed in brand names, drinking smoothies, and advertising for her next hookup with scantily clad selfies. All of CLASH needed to know who this girl was. He created a post with the dancer's face, captioning it, 'I need real DEI leaders challenging my bestie @Compton-ChicFashionista, not basic bitches like @humbleBragHannah appropriating wokeness, *cough, cough* @XOXO202.'

Zoey laughed when she read it. "Nice."

"We're hot shit. People come at us for daring to be great. We can't take it personally."

"I can take it as a critique and rethink my life choices. And XOXO202's right. I'm a fashion designer stuck in a dance class. My whole life's upside down, and I want to flip it."

"You're taking life advice from a hater when Sebastian's putting everything on the line for you? No one else."

"Sebastian's insane."

"And that's what you want. The more insane, the better in bed–"

"I'm not trying to have sex. I'm trying to be a great artist."

He pushed through her resistance. "And CLASH will remember us as the insane ones, not the normal ones. The ones that took risks, made bold moods, and did the unexpected. Just think, Sebastian could have chosen a prima ballerina, but you inspired him–" He jumped up, eyes becoming huge. "You inspired him to make love through dance."

"Oh my god, this is a thing with you! Are you having wet dreams about us?"

He leaned into the energy firing through his body. "If you stick with Sebastian and blow our minds, we'll all be having wet dreams about you. No one will be thinking about Frog-Leg Zoey cause you'll be a star, shining in Paris." He felt like he had her. He just had to land his grand jeté. "We can't give up. We can't quit."

Zoey recoiled at the word "quit," and he knew he made a mistake. He couldn't zap the word from her memory. It attached to her neurons, spreading from her mind to her muscles. "I love the analogy, the complete vision, and I wish I could commit to it. Sebastian called me a quitter, and now you. I'm not quitting. I'm finding a new strategy."

God, I lost her. Damn it. Enthusiasm had overwhelmed him, and the word popped out. "Strategize away then," he said. At least he knew when to quit. He just hoped Sebastian landed the grand jeté better than he did.

ian's speech about making love through dance was exhilarating, but for real, if she and Sebastian were making love, she'd be having way more fun. Making chaos was more like what they were doing. And she was tired of creating chaos.

Sebastian went all of Monday without mentioning his search for a dance partner, and she would not let the day end without following up with him. Approaching him at the end of their Modern class, she asked, "Have you spoken to Amy and the faculty about a new partner?"

"How about we take a break for the week and revisit next Monday?"

"Isn't there some kind of process?" She pointed to the camera crew she wanted gone as soon as possible so that she could have her privacy back.

"Sure, we'll discuss that Monday, unless …"

"Unless what?"

"Unless you just want to quit now. If so, I can make an announcement in the paper."

"About me quitting? I'm not quitting. I'm re-strategizing."

"What do you mean?" He looped his arm around her waist, pulling her close. "How so?"

Her body warmed, her cells vibrating energy. His touch. It was satiating. Her tummy loved his hands on her like it loved chocolate-covered pineapple. Her eyes loved his face and her nose his smell, so calming, a salty sweat mixed with mint. Ugh, he was so dangerous but delicious.

"What's your new strategy?" he asked again.

Her thoughts swam in his warmth, and she had to will each word into a cohesive sentence. "Let's break until Monday." She forgot whatever else she planned to say, but Monday felt logical. There was always a Monday. It wasn't like she remembered what she wanted to say anyway. His gray eyes, and his lips, and his proximity made her forget that life was cruel.

He tensed, fighting the urge to make her confess plans she couldn't tell him with her mind so fuzzy. She needed space to refocus. In his arms, the world felt so possible. He could be her fantastic boyfriend and they could make love through art. And she so, so wished she could surrender to this desire, but she knew that beyond his loving embrace existed a reality where these feelings couldn't thrive.

He kissed her cheek and whispered, "Sure," leaving her in the empty dance studio.

I'm so thirsty for him. Her body tingled with his essence. This like, it was overwhelming. *If I don't act fast and leave him now, I'll never leave.* She pulled out her phone and typed an email to Mrs. Agnes and Mrs. Sehar, cc'ing Dad and Sebastian.

Subject: Meeting request regarding grades

Hello, All,

Since enrolling in the dance department, I have experienced undue pressure causing my grades to slip. I would love to discuss strategies to correct this, and see if there's opportunity for me to rejoin the fashion department where I feel like I'm my best artist self. Can we schedule a meeting for Monday?

Sincerely,
Zoey Raines

She squeezed her eyes shut and pressed send.

CHAPTER 48
SEBASTIAN

he wanted to rip Zoey's email to shreds. He stood in the hallways, anger raging. How could she do this? He ran towards Modern III, stopping, roaring like a beast. She's a coward. He wanted to spit each syllable in her face, but what would that get him?

He texted Ian and Vincent.

Sebastian: Zoey wants out, and she has a plan.

He would create his own, but not alone. Three heads were better than one. His friends reminded him to make Zoey feel safe, whatever he did.

Vincent: Show up like you would the fourth quarter, two points down. Give it your all.
Ian: Yeah, play hard, flirt harder. Make love through art.

Vincent filled the screen with laugh emojis.

Vincent: Bruh, get P. Raines to put that in the handbook.

Sebastian laughed. They were so dumb, but their dumbness was nice, better than the anger burning inside, better than his thoughts blackened with smoke. He could think straight now. If Zoey wanted to "strategize" a beautiful quit, fine, she could try, but she would fail.

He requested the meeting happen in Mrs. Sehar's classroom thinking that would make Zoey feel safe. He chose a costume, pressed jeans and a white polo with matching Converse. The white would make him look less intimidating. Monday arrived, and he stepped inside the sewing lab, ready to win.

A realization hit him. This was his first time in a sewing lab. His eyes surveyed the class like the cameras filming. Zoey's world was so different, and it smelled like–he breathed–erasers, pencil shavings, and glue. Walking by the desks, he touched the sewing machines and picked up the colored glues placed beside sketch pads. He pictured Zoey sitting at one of these desks, sketching her next fashion statement. And he wished he had asked her about this world. Her mind had to overflow with fashion genius. It showed in the way she dressed, or at least it had before she became his partner. Now, she wore black leotards like the other dancers. Regret filled him. He had somehow dimmed her individuality, and he never once thought to ask her about fashion, too worried about making her fit into his world. *I've been so selfish.*

Meats marinating in pineapple overwhelmed the class-room. He glanced backwards at Amy leading a team of caterers through setting up a taco lunch. Food wasn't allowed in classrooms, but he scheduled the meeting during lunch cause Zoey was a foodie. Ian had told him to order the tacos from her favorite restaurant. A big sign that read 'Mami's' was displayed on the table, surrounded by rasp-berry-filled chocolates, another one of her faves.

Mrs. Agnes and Mrs. Sehar arrived first, then Zoey with her camera crew following. His eyes stitched to her. Even her stomach rumbling felt loud. She chewed her lips, watch-ing Mrs. Sehar and Mrs. Agnes filling their plates. Then, she opted not to eat. And that's when he knew he had to make his plate. He stuffed his taco shell like a burrito with globs of meats and veggies, sitting across from Zoey so she could see the juices running down his fingers. Sauce got on his cheeks, and he licked his lips, feeling her eyes on his mouth. He loved the way she watched him eat, as if he were a com-mercial, selling her with each bite until her stomach could no longer take it. She wanted what he had. He licked his lips. She wanted him.

Her face grew hot, and she jumped up as if to hide her desire.

Mrs. Agnes finished her first taco, savoring it, and start-ing her second. "So Principal Raines confirmed he wasn't coming? He said it was a conflict of interests?"

"Correct." Mrs. Sehar wiped her mouth with a napkin.

"Is Dad–I mean Principal Raines allowed to do that?" Zoey asked, returning to her seat.

"He can. He wants to make sure the outcome of this meeting doesn't feel biased," Mrs. Sehar said. "And do we need help coming up with a supportive solution?"

"We don't," Sebastian cut in. He was glad Principal Raines opted out. Having Zoey's Dad present would have pushed him to step up his performance. And for Zoey's sake, and his, the less intensity, the better.

Mrs. Sehar held up her taco. "Thank you for this wonderful lunch. Mami's has the best tacos in LA. Hands down."

"Have you been to Papi's or Guerilla Tacos or Guisado's?" Mrs. Agnes asked.

"It's something about the pineapple. But LA has endless places for great tacos. One reason why I love it here, but I digress," Mrs. Sehar waved to Zoey. "You called this meeting, right? You wanted to discuss your falling grades and steps we can take to support you?"

Zoey dropped her taco, flipping open her notebook. There were pages of scribbled speeches marked with crossed-out lines. He counted the pages, wondering how many hours she had spent preparing, wondering if she had called Ian to rehearse.

He leaned forward, the pain welling in his chest. He wanted them to win together, not apart. He'd train extra hours, go without sleep, take sponsorships he didn't care about so he could invest in her. And she was writing speeches about leaving him.

"First, Sebastian, you've sacrificed so much–"

Make her feel safe. Make her feel safe.

"While a fashion student, I had straight A's. I felt like I was in my element and shined. As a dance student, I feel unable to complete the work."

She's not attacking me.

"I'm a fashion designer. That's why it's so important for me to rejoin the fashion department. I even have a strategy on how I could make up assignments." Zoey handed them each a schedule.

He scanned it, balling it up, catching himself, and then smoothing the wrinkles. Her schedule demanded every waking hour plus bonus assignments to make up for missed tests. Impossible. He shoved the paper under his plate like a napkin, confused as to why she'd rather suffer than dance with him.

"This seems like a lot," Mrs. Sehar said. "Almost unreasonable."

I'm tired of this bullshit. "Are you afraid of me?" he asked.

"No." Zoey wouldn't look at him. She was.

"It's okay if you are." He kept his voice soft. Like Papá with Mamá. Not like him with Vega. Zoey wasn't Vega. She wouldn't fight back or tell him to knock it off. And he was glad. When someone pushed him, he pushed harder. And he didn't want to push Zoey, or come to think of it, Vega anymore. "I admit I started off tough, and I'm sorry I didn't make you feel safe, but I want you to feel safe so we can create excellence. I'm really good at creating excellence, and you are too. That's why I chose you. What can I do to make it easier for you to trust me and the process so you can, I guess, become an A-dancer, if that's even possible?"

"It's not possible. I'm a fashion designer stuck in the dance department."

"So you feel like you stopped being a fashion designer?"

"Yes!"

"But that's not true," Mrs. Sehar said. "By now, you have a strong fashion foundation, and this opportunity to dance could create new inspiration, which is actually better for you and more reasonable than this demanding schedule you created. Your schedule doesn't account for surprises. And life always has surprises."

Mrs. Agnes smiled. "It's okay to be scared, Zoey. An outsider even. I've been an outsider too."

"Me too," Mrs. Sehar chirped. "I'm a hijabi-wearing fashion designer."

"Being a Muslim at CLASH?"

"They give us the third floor of the school of religion, a small floor that could fit every Muslim student inside. We're outsiders."

"We're superheroes," Sebastian said. "Zoey's Sailor Moon, and I'm Tuxedo Mask."

Zoey blushed, a soft pink mixing in with gold. Her blush reminded him of dancing amidst sunrise.

Mrs. Agnes observed him, soaking in his expression and his body language, aspects she had shaped over years. "You know, I think you make Sebastian better. He's much kinder with you, more willing to play. Play's what was missing from your artistry, Sebastian." She glanced at Mrs. Sehar. "What do you think was missing from Zoey's?"

"Such a good question." Mrs. Sehar chewed thoughtfully. "I have to say Zoey was working from an obvious comfort zone. And now that she's no longer in it, she's forced to face insecurities. And this may be a question for you to explore, Zoey. Can we really be great if we never face our fears? Remember that speech from Magnolia, about working with artists that inspire and challenge you to create great art?"

Zoey looked at him, her mind sketching answers to Mrs. Sehar's question. He couldn't gauge how scared she was. But at least she was facing him. He rubbed his foot against her foot, rubbing his knee against her knee. She didn't pull away, and he knew her answer before she spoke, "No." Electricity flew up his legs. He needed her to face him.

CHAPTER 49
ZOEY

i'm facing my fears *and becoming a better artist*. She made room in her home studio, shoving her tables from the center. That gave her enough room to practice. She loaded a video of Sebastian and Mrs. Agnes dancing the sugar plum pas. Mrs. Agnes danced parallel, and still, Zoey struggled to copy her movements. She développéd her leg to meet the height of Mrs. Agnes'. *Ow! This hurts so much.* Her leg flopped down, and heaving a breath, she willed her body to complete the attitude. Her torso twisted, fighting her leg until she fell out of the position. I'm giving up. It was eleven at night. I'm going to bed. Not like she could scream "moon, prism, power" and transform into Sebastian overnight.

She hobbled into her room, her mind and body shutting down as soon as she saw her covers. The pillows felt soft. The cold air became her blanket, drying her sweaty clothes. She wasn't ready for sun. Her eyes squinted open, abhorring the light. Her tongue flapped around a mouth that was dry and sour. When would ballet stop hurting?

She rolled over and dragged herself into the bathroom. Stepping onto the scale, red numbers blinked, 'One hundred and fifteen pounds.' She'd lost thirty pounds without even trying. No surprise there. Ballet was eating away at her identity; why not her body?

"Zoey!" Mom knocked on the bathroom door.

"I'm hopping in the shower."

"Your breakfast is ready, and there's a bunch of boxes waiting for you in the kitchen."

"Yay." She figured it was a gift from Dad to cheer her up. He often surprised her when he felt life was giving her an undeserved whooping.

She entered the kitchen, her feet slowing. Nothing felt innocent about those boxes stacked on one another according to size, each wrapped in paper dotted with gold ballet slippers. She searched the kitchen. "Where's Dad?" Tayo and Rebecca were there early, filming away while Jeff recorded the sound. Ian ate pancakes and eggs next to Mom. There was no briefcase, no third plate half eaten.

"He had to attend an impromptu meeting with donors." Mom gestured toward the boxes. "Are you going to open them?"

She hesitated. Dad' would be there if he bought them, and she was sure Mom didn't get them. Her love language was service, and her godparents were messy gift givers, the type of people who didn't remove tags. Ian's wallet couldn't afford it. Those boxes screamed wealth. She knew only one wealthy person. Thanks, but no thanks. She couldn't start her day obsessing over him. "I'm starving." She walked to the pancakes.

"Can you just open them, please?" Ian asked. "I'm dying."

"You open them."

"I can, but then Sebastian will think you hate him when he watches this footage and sees you couldn't even stand opening his gifts."

She groaned. Why did Ian have to be right about everything? Stomping towards the boxes, she yanked the card down, waving it so they all saw Sebastian's name. She read the note, "Text me so we can have dinner tonight." Her heart fluttered. Can't control my heart, but I have to control my mind.

"Are you going to open the boxes?" Mom asked.

"I'm opening them!" Geez, they were so impatient. She pulled the lid off the first box. It held a bracelet with ballet trinkets swinging from the chain. "I think you're so charming," the note read. Cute.

She opened the next box, pulling out a book with a Black ballerina on the cover. "I get misty-eyed thinking about you. My heart can't cope. Ha! Ha! Misty Copeland, get it." She chuckled as she noticed the gold pointe shoes snuggling matching ballet flats. "Goals," she read aloud. Ian and Mom released, "Aaaawwwww." Her heart bounced when she looked into the last box. Fabrics surrounded a sewing kit, smelling fresh. "Never forget where you come from," she read. He gets me. She pressed the card to her heart.

Mom elbowed Ian. "You going to step up your game?"

"It's not a competition. It's a blowout. Sebastian's a vampire, so I have to be out here competing with myself." Ian asked Zoey, "So, where's the dinner?"

"I don't know. Should I text to confirm? I don't know. Is he like asking me to dinner as a date or as an apology?"

"Both," Ian replied.

"No, no. You don't know that," Mom interjected. "It's best to confirm and then talk to him when you get there."

"Do I have to go?" she asked Mom.

"Never, but do you want to go?"

She chewed her lip.

"Are you thinking about saying no?" Ian asked.

"People will say Sebastian chose me because we're sleeping together."

"And what's wrong with that? Sebastian really likes you. And you really like him."

"I do not!" she shouted too quickly for it to sound truthful.

"Sure you don't. Dad and I are going to have a little date night to celebrate your brand-new romance." Mom texted Dad.

"I haven't even said yes!"

Ian bit into some turkey bacon. "If you want to say no cause you want to quit and break Sebastian's heart cause you're afraid of gossip, then do that."

"I'm not afraid," she snapped.

"You better not be cause we don't do fear in this household." Mom looked up from her phone, joining Ian. They stared Zoey down, daring her to text Sebastian.

She huffed a breath.

Zoey: Excited for dinner. Thanks for the gifts.

Typing a bunch of emojis, she pressed send. Then she showed the message to Ian and Mom. "See."

"Okay, poop emojis!" Ian gave two snaps.

Oh no. She gaped at the poop emojis.

Zoey: Those were supposed to be hearts. The orange ones.
Sebastian: Jajaja. Can't wait to see you.

He sent his home address, and she clicked on it, enlarging it on Google Maps. His mansion sat in the Bel Air hills amongst pixelated trees. This meant she was going to meet his mom and sit with Vega. "I have to be Black Excellence." She couldn't give Vega one thing to post about. Otherwise, the night would be a bunch of poop emojis.

"Done," Ian said. "Black Excellence, dripping now."

Compton had changed over the years. Gang families had moved out along with much of the Black community that had grown tired of the crime, replaced by people with more money and bigger dreams than the renovated homes. But nothing in Compton could compare to Sebastian's mansion.

Driving past the gate, she drove up a paved pathway, parking in one of the six garages.

She had dreamed of attending parties in homes just like this, and now her dreams were coming true. She should be dancing into the house, but thoughts of Vega kept her locked inside her car. There were so many evil things that witch could do to ruin this night, like give her diarrhea, or lock her in the closet, or turn her into a drunken hookup. A night filled with regrets and dirty secrets that would turn into CLASH's next gossip fest. *Maybe I can leave.* Zoey glanced in her rearview. No one was there. She could text Sebastian, 'Sorry, flat tire.'

Someone knocked on her window.

She jumped, rolling it down.

"Nervous?" Sebastian asked.

Everything about him made her nervous, his looks, his smell, his wealth. His house was three of her houses. She didn't know how to say that without sounding like she hated him and his family.

"I can have food brought out here," Sebastian said. "We can do our own drive-in movie, maybe play *Dirty Dancing* or *Crazy, Stupid, Love.* I'm down for either."

She laughed, "No."

When he extended his hand, she took it and followed him inside.

"I'm really excited to be here, meeting your mom."

"My pa flew in," he whispered.

She tripped, and Sebastian gripped her arm so she didn't fall. She had only mentally prepared to meet Sebastian's mom. How was she going to get through this night without saying something stupid?

"I'm nervous too," he said.

"Why?"

"I'm terrified I'll say something mean to mess us up."

"When we get together, emotions fly. That's our thing."

"I become this asshole around you, and I hate that."

"It's not your fault. We don't make good dance partners."

"No. We make good everything. We just haven't figured out how to turn that good good into greatness."

She laughed. Good-good greatness. The words were smooth in her head, froyo coating the nervousness that receded just a little as she entered the living room.

Vega sat on the sofa, hand wrapped around a purple mug, watching her parents dance a pas. It reminded Zoey of when Señor Silvian Baustista debuted his memoir A Family Legacy: Defying Gravity in a photo essay for the Los Angeles Times. Sitting in her bedroom, she and Ian had devoured the black and white photographs of Señor Bautista posing with his wife against a white backdrop, loving the one where Señor Bautista dipped his wife while her leg stretched towards the sky.

'Sebastian's parents are gods,' She had told Ian.

'Or vamps that live off babies' bodies to stay young,' Ian had replied, 'and suck each other's blood,' which had been the first time he had mentioned that stupid theory.

Señor Bautista focused dark gray eyes on her. *"Zoey Raines, finalmente, nos conocemos. ¿Cómo estás?"* Zoey Raines, we finally meet. How are you?

"She studies French," Sebastian said.

"Oui, ça va bien?" Señor Bautista said.

"Très bien, Merci. Enchanté," She replied. Señor Bautista was as handsome as Sebastian and as tall. Maybe Ian was right about his vampire theory.

"Moi aussi. Avec plaisir," Señor Bautista said. Same, with pleasure. "You received our gifts?"

She showed off the gold ballet flats she had paired with a matching halter and a black tulle mini skirt.

"Beautiful. Did you bring the pointe shoes? I would love to see you dance."

"Zoey hasn't learned pointe yet," Sebastian jumped in to save her.

Señor Bautista's mouth dropped, looking at the cameras, then at Amy, then at his wife, and then Vega, who laughed and said she thought the whole thing was also stupid. "I'm confused. Aren't you starring in a docuseries about our family's influence on dance?"

"The story's evolved, and it's not like she can't dance. She dances Latin social."

Señor Bautista waited for Sebastian to continue, but his son didn't, allowing the silence to grow and grow until Señor Bautista said, "Well, since you refuse to explain, Zoey can show what she's been learning. I'm curious."

Sebastian marched past his dad.

She followed through the backyard. The cold air felt brutal. She rubbed her arms, passing a glowing pool and heading into Sebastian's dance studio. She'd only seen it in the day. At night, the white walls looked icy and unwelcoming.

Sebastian extended his hand. She rose to relevé, her ankles wobbling under the weight of Señor Bautista's glare. His judgment weighed down her movements, making it hard to lengthen or lift. She accidentally locked eyes with Señor Bautista's disappointment, toppling over just as Sebastian caught her in a dip. He twirled her into a tight embrace. His heart pounded against her back.

Señor Bautista stared hard, chin resting on his right fist. It was a while before he asked Sebastian, "Can I talk with you?"

They left her alone, eyeing herself in the mirrors. The shadows clung to her frail body. *Where is all my fat?* How had she gone all this time without noticing her clothes clinging for dear life to a body that, right now, felt like it didn't belong to her?

Señora Bautista squeezed her shoulders.

She looked into kind gray eyes, the complete opposite of Señor Bautista's. "You bring something so unique to dance."

Well, that was one way of putting it.

Zoey let Señora Bautista pull her away from the mirrors and lead her back into the house. The smells hit her nose before she saw the food on the dining room table. It all smelled so vibrant.

Señora Bautista named each dish while the crew filmed. There were huevos estrellados, or fried eggs, and cocido madrileño, a traditional stew comprised of potatoes, vegetables, and meats. Then there was also calamari and squid. There was ceviche sitting beside a bread basket, and oh, of course, paella de marisco, a Spanish rice mixed with shrimp, mussels, and wine.

"You'll eat a little bit of each," Señora Bautista said. "Or everything, I don't mind. I couldn't decide what to serve, so I served the whole country. If you gain five pounds, you can always lose it, right?"

Zoey thought back to her reflection. "I don't really have to lose the five pounds."

Sebastian entered, frowning, signs that his talk with his dad didn't go well.

"What did your dad say?" she whispered, afraid of his answer.

"Choose whatever story I want to tell, and you're the story I'm telling." He forced a smile that didn't make her feel better.

He danced for his dad, didn't he? She examined the Bautistas. He danced for his legacy, and what a beautiful picture of legacy, their thick, black hair and gray eyes, their athletic bodies, and exfoliated skin. Then there was she with her peanut butter likeness and wild curls. She didn't fit. Her existence conflicted with Sebastian's mission. How come he couldn't see that?

He squeezed her hand under the table, reminding her to eat. She scooped a bit of the ceviche in her mouth with her free hand. Seafood and spices danced on her tongue. "This is really good." She took another bite.

"Good like you?" he asked. "Maybe not as good."

"You're so weird."

"Duh, that's why I chose you."

She laughed. She wanted to drink her glass of lemonade, but she couldn't with him holding her hand. "You know, I'm right-handed, so you have to let go."

"What if I can't right now?"

"What if I spill something?"

"I'll help you clean it up. Always." He squeezed her hand one more time, and this time she squeezed back.

She managed to get through eating and drinking with her left hand. It was a challenge, like trying to stay on relevé. She had to focus a little more, which enhanced the spices in the food. She slowed down her eating. Her life was spicy right now, and if she paid more attention, she could enjoy the flavors of the moment, even if those flavors hurt a little bit.

Vega bragged in Spanish to Señor Bautista, but it didn't look like her dad was interested. He wanted to know, "*¿Qué te parecisteis tus bailes? ¿Estáis practicando suficiente?*"

Zoey didn't know what Señor Bautista asked, but Sebastian answered by lifting their hands onto the table so that his dad could see their fingers interlaced.

Enjoy the spice. She breathed. *Enjoy the spice.*

"She has her campaign and her Harvard dreams," Sebastian said.

"Stanford," Vega cut in.

"Stanford. She doesn't have time."

"I had time. You hated dancing with me and dropped me."

"Why would you do that to your sister?"

"You're so late, Pa," Vega groaned. "I've moved on to competing for student body president. I don't have time for Sebastian."

"See? She never did. That's why I chose Zoey."

That was spicy.

"You know, loves, we can argue after dessert," Señora Bautista said.

"Exactly," Vega said, waving to the server. "I ordered something special."

The server emerged from the kitchen carrying a box with gold ribbon.

Zoey prayed the server tripped and destroyed whatever was inside, but that didn't happen.

Amy instructed a camera person to get a close-up of the box. The server undid the ribbon. Each panel fell open, revealing a cake shaped like a frog with a gold crown and ballet slippers. Zoey's lips trembled. 'Welcome to the fam, Frog-Leg Zoey,' sparkled on its back.

"Princess Tiana, anyone?" Vega asked.

"Thanks, I guess." She tried not to look hurt.

Sebastian jumped out of his seat. "Stop picking on her cause you suck at dance."

Vega stood. "And she doesn't? Frog Legs had never danced a step of ballet, and you picked her over Mahogany, who is the best."

"I picked her cause she brings me life. You make me feel dead. You kill off everyone you know with your rumors cause you're unremarkable. Everyone knows it, and that isn't Zoey's fault. It's yours cause you won't practice."

"You're a horrible brother. I hate you so much." Vega stormed out of the room.

She had never seen Vega cry real tears. She didn't think someone that cold even had emotions, but Sebastian's superpower was making people cry. He had made her cry twice.

Señora Bautista sipped her wine, waiting for her husband to speak. When he did, he demanded Sebastian apologize to his sister.

"Why?" Sebastian replied. That meant no.

Awkward. Zoey tossed her napkin on the table, thinking she'd give Sebastian space. No one even noticed her leaving.

She wandered down the halls, ending up in the kitchen, drifting past the dirty dishes. The wait staff were outside talking about the craziness happening inside. Tayo filmed her as she opened the fridge. She didn't know why she opened the fridge or what she hoped to find. It was a habit she would do at home when she felt sad.

The Bautistas had a fridge of life goals, overflowing with veggies and fruits. There were stewed meats, and sweets, the healthy kinds, and kombuchas, so many kombuchas.

She stood there, dreaming, not wanting to return to the dining room.

"I'm so, so sorry," Sebastian said. He hugged her.

She really liked his hugs, his smell, his face. Her likes were endless. She liked he was a masterful artist, that he chose her. But, she couldn't keep dancing with him when it was hurting Vega, who was crazy jealous. "I think you hurt Vega's feelings when you dropped her."

"She doesn't want to dance."

"I think she's jealous."

"I promise this has nothing to do with you. She hates me without ballet."

"She doesn't hate you." Come to think of it, Vega's actions made sense. She lived in a perfect family with a massive legacy, and to add to the pressure, her twin brother was a god. Who wanted to live that life? "She wants to be like you just like I want to be like you. And that's not easy. It's hard. And it hurts a lot. And you never acknowledged your sister's pain. You dropped her. That's why I think you should say sorry."

Sebastian's eyes widened, shocked.

"I know I'm like the last person who should be Team Vega, but I'm really Team Love."

"You're trying to get out of dancing with me."

"Uhmm, not really. I just want her to stop being so angry. And if you were nicer to your sister, she'd grow a heart."

"I'll say sorry if you promise not to quit."

Now, this was spicy. She breathed in the flavors of the moment. Vega could reject his sorry, but at least it'd be a step towards neutrality. Neutral ground was what she needed for her dream to flourish. Then she could focus on creating art that challenged with the guy of her dreams, just like Magnolia had advised. She closed her eyes and said a quick prayer. "I promise?"

He smiled big.

"I mean, anything for a happy ending. And it's the only way she'll stop torturing me."

"Can I kiss you?"

Wait, what? Her heart thumped. He had already kissed her, but the first time he did it, he hadn't asked. She remembered standing in front of her cherry-red car, his lips against her lips. It had been a magical moment, the stuff of great social media videos. But him kissing her now? "I totally get why you kissed me at the livestream. It was a new car, and all these emotions were going, but if you kiss me now, it's giving romance. You'll have to be friends with Ian. I'll have to be friends with Vega."

Sebastian shrugged. "Deal." He kissed her.

CHAPTER 50
SEBASTIAN

their second kiss changed the atmosphere. Zoey relaxed so much that he felt like he could ask her to rehearse another hour.

She shrugged, "Why not? Burn off all the food."

He led her through a simple barre exercise. When he noticed Papá watching them, he asked for privacy. Papá was already too embarrassed about their dinner argument to make a big deal out of his request.

He coached Zoey, explaining that ballet was a constant lengthening toward a sense of infinity, from their toenails to their fingertips. And yet, most movements were atoms of conflict, painfully pushing and pulling towards art.

"Like us," she said, landing an unexpected kiss on his chin.

He laughed.

She did it again, this time landing a kiss on his shoulder. He couldn't predict her kisses or where they'd land. Sometimes on his nose, once on his knuckles, his cheek. Her kisses were soft wonders dotting his skin, morphing their rehearsal into an hour of play.

"Let's grab the cake," she suggested while breaking, tugging him out of his studio and into his kitchen. She pulled the cake out of the fridge and snapped a picture to post on social with the caption, '@B0ssyG0als called me Princess Tiana, so I guess we're frienemies…' Vega would see that post and hate it.

They passed the living room where his family played chess. Zoey asked if they should join. Chess was more of Vega's game, not his, and he didn't feel like losing while Zoey watched. Winning was Vega's life mission, and so was his. That's why he didn't see his sister accepting his apology when they both knew pain was the cost of winning. It was better to return to the studio and think about his sister later.

They ate the frog cake on his floor, forgetting time had limits when Papá knocked on the studio entrance with a reminder. "Time for bed." Papá tapped his watch.

He fought the urge to ask if Zoey could sleep over, instead walking her to her car. He wanted one more kiss, but she stuck out her pinky.

"Vega apology for a sugar plum pas?" she asked.

"Deal," he spit in his palm.

"Eeeewwwyyyy." She spat in her palm.

They slapped hand to hand, their goodbye kiss for the night.

His heart thumped, watching Zoey drive off. A Vega apology. He glanced at Vega's bedroom window, a yellow glow against a black sky. Maybe apologizing would time-travel their relationship backward to a time before they started hating each other. Back when they swapped jeans and skateboarded along the beach to sneak into random bars. Back when they watched local bands they either loved or hated. Back when he knew all her secrets, and they were so in sync, he could predict she would need a tampon.

He knocked on Vega's bedroom door, nervous. She didn't answer. He looked around the quiet hallways, noticing the cameras for the first time that night. How many Bautista fights had they already filmed? Did he want to give them another? He turned to leave, stopping. This is for Zoey. He knocked again.

"*Estoy ocupada.*" The door muffled her words. I'm busy.

He opened it anyway. She was lying on her stomach reading Cosmopolitan while finishing a bag of cinnamon chips. Busy? Yeah, right. "*Can I have a few seconds?*"

"*One, two, times up. Close the door on your way out.*"

"*I'm sorry.*"

She frowned, looking up from her magazine. "*Say it again.*"

He took that as a sign she wouldn't snap off his head if he sat on her bed. She made room for him. There was a time when he could sit in here for hours and breathe, and that would be their conversation. She had to miss that time even if their schedules had changed, and he couldn't see himself doing that now. "*I'm sorry for how I've been treating you. I've been stupid.*"

Vega rolled onto her back and looked at the ceiling. *"Who made you come in here? Mamá? Papá? God? Santa?"*

"No one."

"You've been treating me like crap the whole year, and suddenly you've had an epiphany?"

He wouldn't tell her Zoey put the idea in his head. He wasn't there to argue about Zoey. *"I wanted tonight to be fun. It wasn't."*

"Cause you yelled at me for no reason."

"You bought that frog cake to hurt Zoey's feelings, and you know it."

"Did I?" Vega showed him Zoey's social post. It had a ton of likes. Then she went to his page. Amy had already posted photos of him and Zoey eating the cake in the dance studio. His whole life was a freaking livestream. "Looks like you and Zoey were having fun. Did you two spend the night talking about me until you felt so crappy you had to come up here and mutter a fake apology."

He cuffed his neck, growing irritated. Talking to Vega was like yelling at a shattered mirror. His eyes wandered to the U2 merch on her wall. Looking at the framed shirt was easier than looking at his sister.

"You don't care about me. You don't even like me. You'd rather be downstairs making out with Frog Legs. So go do that."

They saw U2 live when they were twelve to celebrate Papá's birthday. He remembered what it felt like being there, laughing with his sister at The Hollywood Bowl. They had decided *Beautiful Day* was their favorite song, choreographing a birthday dance to show their Papá.

"I just want us to be a beautiful day."

His sister glanced at the U2 shirt. She knew what he was talking about. *"What you want is your beautiful day. Me? I'm whatever. That's why you chose Frog Legs over me. That's why you'll choose Gregory over me—"*

"Actually, about that. Principal Raines had me write this paper on loving leadership based on First Corinthians Thirteen—"

Vega groaned, reaching under her bed and pulling out a purple shoe box big enough to fit knee-high boots. Under her tampons, condoms, and birth control was an essay, his essay.

She had read it. He took it from her. 'B-' glittered in purple gel above a note, *'Overly reliant on ChatGPT, plus Beth Hooks over Bible quotes any day.'* He flipped through the pages. She had left questions and doodles in the margins, just like they used to do back before Papá left.

"Happy, beautiful day," she said. *"You can save me the recap."*

At least it wasn't a C. She would have given him a C if she wanted to insult him. *"You didn't let me finish,"* he said. *"I was going to say, I'm not exactly loving, and you're not either, but I'd rather love-hate you. You're my sister. And I want you to win. "*

Her gray eyes locked with his. *"Prove it."*

CHAPTER 51

IAN

"wait, you want sebastian to lie to Vega?"

He stopped dead in the dance school hallways, eyeing Zoey. They'd been talking non-stop about her drama-filled dinner with the Bautistas, and then she threw a plot twist at him. She wanted Sebastian to say sorry. To Vega. He examined his bestie for signs she was joking. "Like sincerely apologize?" It didn't make any sense. "Did you almost die? Is that what happened? Did you hear from God?"

"I'm tired of hating Vega and Vega hating me. And now that I'm stuck being Sebastian's partner, there's no way I'm getting rid of her. Might as well forgive and forget."

Forgive and forget!? No way. If he had a sister who came at him like that, he would choke her with garlic and staple a cross to her face. He thanked God that he was an only child. Watching Sebastian and Vega forever scarred him. He hoped his parents never had another baby.

He continued to Mrs. Agnes' class, hesitating, not sure if he was ready to become a student again.

Zoey entered first. The camera crew waited behind him, but he couldn't move. What if everyone thought he was returning cause he couldn't land work? CLASH-mates would make fun of him so bad, loving a failure story. And he wouldn't be able to defend himself. Telling the truth would wreck his plan to help Zoey. *I'll send an email announcing my return.* That way, he could gauge the response. Turning to squeeze by the cameras, they pushed him into the classroom.

His CLASH-mates eyed him. And his codeswitch went haywire from all the judgy faces. Their masks, thin and regal. He hadn't missed feeling judged.

Vega rushed him and jumped into his arms.

"He's back," Marc yelled, also running for a hug.

Thirty dancers, minus Sebastian, squeezed him, and he felt their hearts beating against his body. Vega wanted a selfie with Mahogany and Polly included. Then Mrs. Agnes asked them to take a group picture so no one felt left out. Sebastian didn't mind being excluded, and that was probably for the best. They had to keep everyone thinking they were enemies.

He danced with his CLASH-mates, buzzed from all the love, the piano music flowing through his hands and feet. I was so willing to give this up when they were all so beautiful, the best of the best. Imposter syndrome was real. He pas de cheval, lifted. And how funny for Sebastian to be the one to help him find a cure. Life was a beautiful surprise.

And he overflowed with thankfulness. He wanted Zoey to overflow with such belonging.

His bestie struggled to sous-sus soutenu, toppling over. Every now and then, someone rolled their eyes at Zoey. And she would get further lost in her head. At one point, she stopped moving. Sebastian had to tap her shoulder, a reminder to complete her frappes. Her face burned with embarrassment.

My poor Zoey, sick with imposter syndrome. He knew the side effects. Self-sabotage, self-hatred, mediocrity. And his bestie hated mediocrity. She would destroy her opportunity with Sebastian to save herself. Today, she might love dancing with the cool influencer, but as soon as imposter syndrome flared, she would quit. Or, in her view, "re-strategize."

He could not let that happen.

Mrs. Agnes instructed them to rehearse in the Spear's Theater so their bodies could become familiar with the space. Crossing the grand stage, he surveyed the hundreds of empty blue seats. He always felt this theater was too fancy for a school, but even if it was, who cared? He belonged.

Joining Marc, he assumed the role of the attentive understudy, which was laughable. He could dance Drosselmeier with a broken foot, having danced the same old role since Freshman year. It was extremely boring. He had to make the role a game of surprise. A little magic here. A little spontaneity there. People loved it, but this year's Drosselmeier would suck if Marc danced like a schoolboy volunteering at a community theater.

I'm going to have to coach the shit out of him, which as Marc's understudy, wasn't his job.

He mentally checked out, his gaze traveling upstage to Mahogany. Her dance was powerful, her technique a painful reminder that he had been so ungrateful, so unfocused. Guilt formed in his chest. He rubbed the spot, looking away, past Vega's petit battements en pointe to downstage left where Sebastian and Zoey rehearsed.

His bestie had improved, remembering to tighten so her body had a fighting chance against gravity. She looked stronger, more like a ballerina. Her dancing, though, felt like a newbie dancing with her first kiss. Sebastian, of course, was a pro. It was embarrassing watching him overpower Zoey. Ballet still wasn't her thing. If only she were dancing salsa and bachata. She'd slay, and she wouldn't look boring.

Ian's brain sparked. "That's it."

Marc lowered his attitude. "You think?"

He completely forgot about his SG buddy. "Yeah," he lied.

Cody thought Ian was wild for collaborating with Sebastian, betting on Sebastian laying the groundwork for the ultimate betrayal. And Cody wanted to witness it, so he let Ian borrow a studio in the Valley.

Sebastian wasn't the nicest person, but he was honest, so Ian highly doubted betrayal was in his future. Zoey's kisses had reminded the vampire of his humanity, and Sebastian was so in love he would do anything to maintain access to her heart, even if it meant apologizing to an evil twin or accepting a combo of Zoey with a side of his frenemy. At least, that was what Ian had been stupid enough to think.

He entered Cody's studio, tensing. Three unexpected guests huddled together at the barre, swapping secrets. No one was supposed to know about this rehearsal. That's why he and Sebastian were rehearsing all the way in the Valley instead of Long Beach. Lyft was expensive.

He felt the cameras pushing close on his shock. His eyes locked with the lenses briefly before bouncing back to the three strangers, suddenly remembering their faces from Sebastian's social feeds. They were the masterminds behind the outfit Sebastian wore while ambushing Greg's Back-to-School Bash. He swallowed nervously. This could be another ambush.

Sebastian danced an adagio to Tokischa in the center. Ian waited patiently, not wanting the vampire to know how pissed he felt. Sebastian was calm. The vampire was always too calm.

"Come look." Robé waved for Ian to join the huddle, handing him an iPad.

He studied the digital sketches. Sparkling halters screamed, 'Vote Boss Bitch,' in purple sans-font. Cody was right. This was a trap. Sebastian was Team Vega and would find some weird way to force Zoey into promoting her enemy's campaign. Ian had to warn her. He'd gather as much intel as he could, sneak photos of the sketches, and present them as proof that Sebastian couldn't be trusted.

The vampire completed his sisson fermé, approaching the huddle.

"What are these?" Ian asked, making sure no one saw him press record on his phone. Zoey needed to run and never look back.

"Costumes for The Fall Showcase. Zoey promised a sugar plum pas for a Vega apology."

"I don't get it."

"Vega's jealous of Zoey, and she won't stop attacking her unless I apologize. And I'm tired of fighting her anyway. I miss her, and what's the point? She's my blood. If I win, she wins."

"I'm here for this Sebastian 2.0, and I get why you'd dance in Vega merch. But why would Zoey? Are you making her?"

"I haven't told her yet. I wanted to run the idea by you first."

There was no way in hell he'd help Sebastian use Zoey to push Vega propaganda at the biggest event of the year. He hadn't sacrificed his plans to drop out only to return to CLASH and lose his bestie. "I have nothing to do with this. I want you to make that very clear to Zoey. This is all you."

"We have to go big with Vega."

"No, you have to go big, but Zoey doesn't."

"If Zoey did this, she'd earn Vega's respect. And you know her respect pays dividends."

Did Sebastian have to throw everything in his face? Sure, his social status was a product of Vega's respect. But Vega didn't donate her respect to the needy. "If you want Zoey to promote her enemy's campaign at the biggest event of the year, you're going to have to beg. I mean, at least let Zoey design the costumes. That's her domain." And that would give his bestie the opportunity to exact revenge if she wanted.

"Yeah, good point. I'll work on my pitch. Hopefully, she won't freak."

He was one hundred percent sure Zoey would freak, but Sebastian was too laser-focused on the end result to see that. This "Vega apology" was Sebastian's idea, or what he defined as a control-freak quirk that Sebastian exhibited (however annoying) with the good intention of seeing an individual push past his or her limits to achieve success. And this Sebastian-ism could potentially push Zoey into a breakdown. He had to throw Sebastian a lifeline. "Think, what would Sloan Magnolia do?"

Sebastian grinned, turning on the music for the sugar plum pas. Great, Sebastian understood. There was hope.

Harps and strings floated from the speakers, grating on his nerves. Visions of a stiff Zoey dancing in front of a packed audience filled his head. "Now that we figured out costumes, let's talk choreography," Ian said. "I'm thinking we need to make this sugar plum pas more Zoey-friendly?"

He watched Sebastian in the mirrors. The influencer's frown showed he struggled with the same idea.

"What are you thinking?"

"We morph the dance into Bachata as soon as possible."

"That's breaking too many rules. Mrs. Agnes will already be pissed about us including you in the dance."

"I'm not saying completely do away with the choreography. Adapt it." Sebastian wasn't buying it, so he used a Sebastian-ism. "We must push Zoey past her comfort zone so that she embodies the sugar plum pas. We can do that if we dance steps Zoey knows. She lives and breathes bachata, so if she freaks, we can do damage control, freeing her to dance her best self."

"So ballet meets bachata," Sebastian whispered, chewing on the phrase.

CHAPTER 52
ZOEY

why did wealthy people have to go bigger? Every year CLASH held the showcase at the Spears Theater. It was free with ample parking. But did Sebastian's dad care about ample parking and free? As Sebastian put it, his papá went to a Lakers game with Gregory and Vincent's papás. Beer and basketball flowed, and soon Papá was joking about upgrading the showcase to Bautista legacy status. Why not host it in the Dolby Theater? It's the perfect setting for a star's ending. Charles took that idea and ran, fast.

It felt insane, her sitting with Ian in this iconic Hollywood space of gold statues and celebrity glory. Stars like Lupita Nyong'o and Timothée Chalamet had walked where her feet would dance. And she'd done nothing to deserve dancing with the stars.

Mrs. Agnes led dancers through rehearsal. Production designers constructed sets, and Zoey was on the verge of a panic attack. "What if this all ends very badly?" She covered her face, hiding from the Arri Alexas zooming in on her fear. "What if this all equals destruction?"

"I can't hear you," Ian leaned close. "Are you freaking out?"

I am. She didn't want to whine or sound ungrateful. Especially when she knew he deserved to dance there and couldn't. The faculty still refused to let him participate.

"Wonder, fun, like flurries of snow," Mrs. Agnes yelled at Mahogany as she bounced towards Sebastian. Zoey's heart clenched. They were snow, Christmas white snow in New York on vacation. Not the dirty black snow. Her dancing was dirty black snow. Her fashion was Dolby Theater grandeur. "I'm a designer." And no one would get to see my true talent.

"You're freaking out!" Ian was so close, his head brushed her lips.

She buried her head in his hair, pulling him close. "I don't want to dance," she groaned.

"Zoey! Sebastian!" Mrs. Agnes called from the stage.

"I guess you're up," Ian whispered, helping her stand.

She didn't want to release him, but he was stronger, easily twisting out of her fingers. At least he walked her to the stage.

Amy stood at the backstage curtains, commanding Rebecca and Tayo to zoom in close.

Zoey held her breath. The stage felt humongous, and the rows of seats felt endless. There would be hundreds on showcase night, but today, her audience was her CLASH-mates plus Sebastian's family. His dad sat in the front row with his wife and ballet company. Adorned in black, their outfits contrasted with her multi-colored ballet-core.

Tchaikovsky's music floated from the speakers, and she took Sebastian's hand before lifting to passé on relevé. Once she was moving, the power she felt dancing with Sebastian overtook her insecurity.

She hadn't noticed when her fear of dancing with Sebastian transformed into comfort. That must have happened sometime between that awkward family dinner and their second kiss. Sometime between when her feet started remembering the steps and her mind recognizing the counts. By that time, Sebastian had stopped demanding her hips stay level and her legs straight, his demands evolving into 'good,' 'better.' Each tiny improvement, all her hard work, it culminated into her lifting into attitude with squared hips and shoulders on the Dolby Theater stage.

I did it. I actually did it.

Sebastian breathed against her ear. The music faded.

Ian bellowed, "Great dance, Zoey!" His words echoed throughout the theater.

Zoey eyed Sebastian's dad. He looked bored. And she felt insecure once again.

Sebastian and his dad spoke a silent language, their eyes intensifying the longer they glared. Finally, Sebastian kissed her cheek. "Good job. You did great."

You're lying. His definition of great was a verb meaning, impress my dad. She followed Sebastian to the wings, watching his dad take the stage with his wife.

Tango music played. Señor Bautista guided his wife to the rhythm, accenting the beat with his feet.

Sebastian studied his parents, his jaw clenched, arms crossed. He wanted to be better than his dad. And he looked like he was strategizing how. An eerie feeling slid up her body. Somehow, she felt Sebastian was including her in his strategy.

Señor Bautista tossed his wife toward the ceiling, her legs slicing the air.

What if Sebastian tried to make her into his mom? Dancing the tango wouldn't be a problem. She had that solid. She could even kick as high and as strong as Sebastian's mom. It was the idea of surrender. Señora Bautista submitted to her husband, and he dominated her, lifting her and dipping her, spinning her so fast she blurred.

The lights went black. Zoey's body trembled. Submitting to Sebastian like Señora Bautista submitted to her husband seemed impossible. But that's what Sebastian wanted, and Zoey wanted to be whatever he needed, but what if her body held her back?

Sebastian hurried on stage, accompanied by his dad's ballet company. They were performing the next number. From what Sebastian had explained, it was a piece about a vampire's search for meaning in a human world. Very meta.

Sebastian struggled for connection on the black stage illuminated by icy blue lights. Dancers dressed in gray floated by him while he reached for connection and grasped for nothing. A goddess wrapped in red lowered from the roof. The dancers closed in on Sebastian, lifting him towards the goddess, but no matter how much he lengthened, he could not touch her. Curling up alone under a white spotlight, the stage faded to black.

So beautiful. Her hand curled around the veins pulsing in her neck. She felt Sebastian's pain, his loss. And what had she made people feel? She looked at Señor Bautista sitting in the front row. Boredom.

She begged Sebastian to come home with her so they could practice. She was nervous about bringing him back to Compton. At night, the city looked as dangerous as the movies made it seem. But she promised herself to bring him back during the day to show him the quiet places she liked to sit and listen to the birds.

She figured they would practice in Ian's studio, but Sebastian had no interest in dancing on enemy territory. "There's nowhere else," she whispered, afraid her parents would hear her whining in the front yard.

"Show me your artistic hideaway."

She knew what he was asking. "We don't have time." She headed towards Ian's studio, hoping he'd follow.

Sebastian continued in the opposite direction and knocked on her parents' door.

She ran across the yard to pull him to the back of her house before her parents opened the door. Mom could not know Sebastian was there. They couldn't have any distractions.

Sebastian entered her studio first, walking around the tables, eyeing her sketch pads, running his fingers along the sewing and serger machines. He played with her easels and fingered the wools and the silks, the denim, and cottons. He stopped at her designs mixed in with sketches of Sailor Moon and Miraculous Ladybug. Turning towards her, he bowed low to the ground.

She grinned, tugging him upwards. "Can we go now?"

Sebastian held her. His chest felt warm and comforting, like her studio, his nose in her curls, his arms around her waist. Slowly, her rhythm matched his rhythm, and the desire to never leave spread through her.

"I apologized to Vega," he whispered.

"How'd she take it?"

"She hates me only a little now, not a lot."

"Baby steps, you know Paris wasn't built in a day."

She could feel his lips curving upward.

"Can I show you something?" He pulled out his phone, holding it out before snatching it to his chest. "Promise me you won't get mad."

"I want to see," she whined.

They were costume designs, white leotards with matching tights that sparkled. She loved everything about them except for the purple letters shouting, 'Vote Boss Bitch Purple,' across the chest. "Amy's brother designed these. But they're not quite hitting. I was hoping you could help me create something better so Vega will forgive me."

"You want me to design Vega merch?" Even the question grossed her out. "No."

"I mean, you're kind of a genius." He approached her mannequins, each dressed in a different fashion category. One wore a swimsuit. The other wore her annihilated back-to-school outfit. "Do you believe in God?" he asked.

That's suspicious. "Yes. I thought you didn't." She wasn't sure where Sebastian was going. She never knew where he was going.

"Your artistry makes me believe in God more than all the stories of death and miracles."

"You're such a poet."

"No, really, your artistry makes me regret stealing you from your first love."

He knew how she felt even though she worked hard to hide her truth. "No regrets," but why lie when he could read her? Dancing with him consumed her. Just months before, she designed every day. And now she was lucky if she found time to watch a fashion video on YouTube. When she wasn't training, she was thinking about him, his lips, his eyes, his perfection. Sebastian lifted her chin, his nose circling her forehead, then her cheek. He smelled like mint. "Are you sure you have no regrets?"

She kissed him, unable to wait. When presented with deliciousness, she had to bite. "Sorry."

"Not sorry." He nibbled her lips.

But I am sorry. He was teasing her, and the kiss would have been more intense if she had waited, but waiting wasn't her thing. She was impulsive and even tossed her fashion career in the garbage just so she'd have room for him. And she hadn't thought it through, but she wasn't making the same mistake twice. Designing for Vega would be a lot of work. And even though returning to her first love was tempting, she didn't want to design for Vega. At least not for free. "Vega cost me my social life."

"That's a lot. How much does she owe you?"

She regretted bringing up money. "Nevermind. Designing campaign wear is a little blah. I don't like politics."

"How much would Sloan Magnolia charge?"

She laughed. "Magnolia owns a global fashion line."

He navigated to Sloan's website on his phone. "Looks like she's selling three to four hundred an outfit."

"That's crazy."

"I'm good for it, and if Jesus can die for your sins, I think I can foot the bill for my sister's."

"Okay, god status. I see you."

"And you'll be helping my sister win, and that'll help me win with her, which would be huge for me and you."

She didn't believe it'd be that big for her. "I don't know if I want to risk it. We have less than two weeks, and I don't have time to waste designing a peace offering."

"Amy's brother can help."

Okay, she'd get paid and get to work with Robé Pak. The dream. She'd be crazy to turn that down, but "What if it doesn't work? Vega could say thanks, but no thanks."

Sebastian grinned, "Then we fail together."

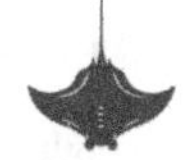

CHAPTER 53

SEBASTIAN

today was the fall Showcase, and he planned to train, but Charles murdered those plans with chicken and steak lunches. He tried to get out of lunch, but Mamá and Papá coaxed him out of his dance studio and into the packed kitchen. Vincent was there with his parents, Gregory with his. It felt nostalgic, like the days before Papá moved and Vega started dating Gregory.

He scanned the kitchen. Where was Vega? He texted her.

Sebastian: You're missing family lunch.
Vega: Greg makes me want to vomit. Hard pass.

Sebastian approached Papá talking with Charles and Mr. Derek at the Island. "So Vega gets to skip, and I can't?"

The three responded with mantras like "rest and food are a part of training" and "enjoy the moment," irritating the heck out of him.

He returned to stabbing his fork in his steak salad, forcing the meat down his throat with iced coffee. It was bitter and salty, the strange mixture almost enough to wake him. He was exhausted while his family was electrified. Mamá joked with Mrs. Courtney, Charles sold big ideas, Amy practiced Korean with Robé. She grunted whenever she needed help with a word. As if this kitchen was her apartment. As if she didn't have a shot list she needed to review. Was he the only one that had to prepare? Swallowing his last bit of coffee, he made another, but none of that American watery stuff. More a cortado, like his papá often brewed in Madrid. The stronger, the better.

He had spent the last couple weeks pulling double-duty rehearsals, working with Zoey till she felt confident. Then, he would sneak to Cody's studio to rehearse with Ian. Then, around three in the morning, he'd drive the thirty minutes back to Bel Air. It was the hardest he'd ever worked in his life. There were moments he didn't think he'd make it, but he loved pushing himself to his breaking point.

His phone buzzed with a text.

Zoey: Happy show day. Costume preview.

His mind exploded. He loved her designs.

Sebastian: Can't wait to dance in them.

"Ahí está mi sonrisa grande que me encanta." Mamá hugged him and kissed his forehead. There's my big smile that I love.

Mrs. Courtney also hugged him before Vincent threw his arms around him. It was a love fest, and they wanted to know, "You feeling okay?"

He reassured them he was, showing his empty salad plate as proof.

Their worries softened, yet still, they didn't want him to leave even though they knew it was customary to arrive at the theater three hours before showtime.

He downed another cup of coffee and headed to his room, tossing ibuprofen and protein bars into his duffle bag. Then he snuck out of the house, fearing someone would notice that he could actually spend another hour hanging out in the kitchen.

Gregory rushed after him down the driveway. "Want to ride together to the Dolby Theatre?"

"That's okay. Vincent's riding with me," he responded as if his Jeep didn't hold three people in the back. He pointed to Vincent running up to them with his violin swinging at his side.

Vincent slid into the passenger seat. "That was rude as hell. What happened to kindness?"

"I need another cup of coffee."

"So your kindness battery on low? That's what that is? Do you have time to pull into a drive-through? Wouldn't want you messing it up with Sexy Panties."

"Relax, we'll no longer be friends with Gregory after today."

"Why do we have to stop being friends with Greg?"

He pulled out his phone and showed Vincent pictures of Zoey's costumes for the performance. Vincent studied them as they drove past the UCLA campus.

"So you're Team Vega? And you haven't told Greg yet?"

"He'll get the message when he sees us on stage."

"Dang, man, you're ruthless. We've been friends almost our whole lives, and you're just going to let him down like that? We used to be the Marvel universe."

Sebastian shrugged, turning onto Hollywood Boulevard. Their friendship had dried up when Gregory became his sister's yes-man. "He doesn't need me to hold his hand." He turned into the Dolby Theater parking garage, handing the valet his keys. Vincent grabbed his violin from the trunk.

"So, do you need help with the Sexy Panties surprise?" Vincent asked. "I feel like Ian's plan is risky."

"We're the opening act. Ian just has to be at the entrance, stage left at curtain rising. Then it'll be smooth from there." At least, that's what he was hoping.

IAN

the end was near. CLASH-mates ran around backstage in a panic, teachers snapped, actors cried, and dancers cursed. To add to the pressure, Charles had hired a famous director whose indoor voice stayed at a ten. He barked orders at his crew, waving his hands to make up for his height at five-foot-four. The drama was delicious, the atmosphere set for rebellion.

Ian felt alive. He breathed in the backstage musk, taking in the set, a *Holy Nights* meets Nutcracker theme that was so artsy it clashed with taste. Candy canes surrounded the manger scene, and music-mates played a weird blend of *Holy Nights* and Tchaikovsky.

"What are you doing backstage?" Mrs. Agnes asked.

His smile dropped. "I'm helping with props." He pointed to the skinny fifth grader manning the station, hoping Mrs. Agnes would give him a break. He needed to be backstage so he didn't miss his entrance.

"We already had this conversation. You're not participating in the showcase this year."

"Props is severely understaffed. I felt bad."

"No exceptions–"

"Excuse me, Mrs. Agnes, but do you intend to give Ian an A for sitting and staring while kids like Eric oversee props all by themselves?" Pa Raines climbed down from the catwalk.

Mrs. Agnes looked stuck. She didn't agree with Pa Raines, but Pa Raines was her boss. And his management style was more NFL coach than corporate collaborator. "Fine, you can help with props." She waved Ian off, storming towards a dancer struggling with her bodice.

Saved. He fell back on his heels. The proximity to death heightened his excitement. Those moments right before getting caught, those moments made breaking rules exciting.

A text flashed across his screen.

Sebastian: Just parked.

He ran through the backstage exit, hoping to meet Sebastian, but then he discovered Baile Madrid's dressing room. The dancers looked elegant, powdering their shoes in rosin and balancing their lattes while stretching. He imagined himself one of them, dressed in gray, sitting in a split while balancing his Cafe Americano.

"*Oye!*" Sebastian called from the dressing room entrance. "*Debemos que apurarnos.*" Hey, we have to hurry.

Ian followed Sebastian and the camera crew into a separate dressing room. Robé and his assistants had readied their costumes. Zoey had designed Ian a see-through mesh shirt with tapered joggers. Purple paint splats decorated the words 'Vote Vega' along his left pants leg while Sebastian's right pants leg read "Vote Brand New."

"Zoey's stuck in traffic, but she'll be here in thirty," Sebastian said.

Robé's assistants dressed Ian before pulling him into a giant chair for makeup and hair. He couldn't believe he didn't have to do his makeup this year. This could definitely be his life.

His phone vibrated.

Zoey: I'm almost at the theater.
Ian: Have to sit with the faculty. Mrs. Agnes doesn't want me participating.

She texted back a sad emoji.
"She's here," Sebastian said. "You have to leave."
Robé threw a coat over him.
Let the end begin.

ZOEY

where was the coffee? Why wasn't there any coffee?

She searched backstage for a hint of brown roasted beans and paper cups, her feet leading her deeper into darkness. She could barely see, but she could feel wool and sparkles … these were clothes, not coffee. Her feet had led her to the costume department. She rested her head against a wool jacket. Home. The clothes rack felt sturdy enough for two seconds of sleep.

The last two weeks were a struggle. If she wasn't training with Sebastian, then she had been working to transform her crazy thoughts into fabulous leotards. And even though working with Robé had been everything she'd ever dreamed of, his help hadn't nearly been enough. Like always, she had to do way too much.

"You're late!"

Zoey's eyes flew open, landing on Amy. "I need coffee."

"There's coffee in the dressing room."

Thank goodness. She followed Amy, hints of overly roasted beans guiding her nose. The brown carton sat next to the dressing room door, and she almost felt its warmth before someone yanked her backward into a chair.

"Coffee, please," she begged Robé. He made her a cup.

She sipped it while Tonto picked out her hair, using gel to slick her afro into two puffs. A homage to The Lady of Rage's hit song *Afro Puffs*. It went with the whole design. She had told Robé that even though she was a Sailor Moon-loving, Miraculous Lady-bug vibing, French-speaking Black girl, she was still a Compton original with the fashion sense to match. She had to find ways to celebrate hip hop. Robé supported that, helping her create a nude mesh leotard with "vote" on the legs and a baggy halter hoodie with Vega's face printed on the chest. Written on the sleeves in giant, purple cursive letters were the words "Boss Bitch."

When Ini finished her makeup and handed her a mirror, Zoey screamed. She loved the glittery purple eyeshadow dotted with hearts along her brow bone. She lowered the mirror. "Vega doesn't deserve me right now."

Sebastian laughed.

"I'm serious. She better say thank you–no, she better swear allegiance to me."

Sebastian joined her in the mirror. He wore a see-through mesh that showed off his abs and tapered joggers. She took extra time to embroider lip prints along his arm sleeve. For Ian, she did violets. Her little "love you lots" to her favorite boys.

"Can all the parents take some time to clap for them-selves?" Dad's voice erupted from the TV. Dad walked from the wings, wearing a blue suit, looking like money. The speakers boomed with audience applause.

Zoey felt a wave of excitement. They were about to go on.

Everyone hugged her, whispering, "Break a leg," before sending her out the door. Sebastian's hand was hot with sweat, but feeling his flesh against her flesh kept her sane. Pressure built from her knees. The sounds were intensify-ing. She saw the stage entrance. It looked big and black. She freaked, turning to run.

Sebastian tightened his arm around her waist. "I'm with you. We're dancing together."

"Just a quick meltdown." Or maybe a slow meltdown. No, no. She wasn't freaking out. Ian and Sebastian sacrificed so much, and she wasn't just dancing for herself anymore. She was dancing for her best friends. Mom sat in the front row with Godmom and Goddad Cruz, and Tech and Hippie Nerds. She was dancing for her family. Everyone else didn't matter. Not even the journalists dotted throughout the the-ater, hungry for drama.

"I was afraid when I took over for Principal McGee," Dad said. He stood at a podium, center stage.

Sebastian's chin rested on her head.

"I was the first person of color to take on leading an acad-emy that produced the most billionaires in the world. And I alone felt responsible for continuing this school's track record. That was a heavy burden, but then I realized I'm surrounded by leaders who want me to succeed. Every day a CLASH Stingray actively decides to empower not just myself but the community."

I hope my dance is empowering. As if Sebastian heard her thought, he pulled her closer, his muscles firm against her back. She pressed her nose into his shoulder. Tonight, he smelled like froyo. Pineapple. Chocolate. Her stomach stirred. He was enough. He could be her community.

"I made a decision when I said yes to this position," Dad continued.

Her decisions could win a Crazy of the Year award. She had taken one look at Sebastian's gorgeous face on a poster and went mayhem, tossing her grades in the trash, switching up her career. She kissed his shoulder. His mouth met her mouth. And *I'd do it again … Almost.*

"Tonight, I'm honored to present the culmination of our decisions, our risk, our genius."

The audience erupted. The lights went black.

Oh, no. Sebastian entered the stage, taking all of his froyo goodness with him. Her heart thumped with terror, but there was no turning back. She took a step, then another, her legs forming croisé derriere. The lights rose. Someone shouted, "Vote Vega." Her heart pounded in her ears, drowning out Tchaikovsky's music crescendoing to full volume.

She was supposed to move. She couldn't.

Sebastian waved for the lights to lower. They were going to start again.

I have to move.

The lights brightened, and the piano grew louder. Then the strings played. She forced her shaking legs forward. Sebastian smiled. Oh, yeah, that's what sugar plum fairies did. Lifting to him, he extended his hand. She grabbed it, and he spun her into a circle. Her leg developéd while he twirled her into an attitudé, and she tightened her gut. Don't wobble.

Tchaiksovky's melody morphed into something familiar. Her smile faltered. Was that … was that a bachata tempo?

Sebastian dipped her.

Her eyes bulged.

His grin was wicked. "Trust me."

Trust you!? What the heck is going on?

He lifted her, and she came face-to-face with Ian.

She screamed.

Ian dominated her body, and she willingly surrendered so that when he moved, she moved without questioning. A good thing happening cause she was freaking the heck out.

Ian improvised with the beat, changing his timing, spinning her, and grabbing her pants leg. It unraveled, revealing her sparkling white leotard. 'Vote Vega' glittered across the front.

The crowd gasped.

Sebastian caught her, rocking her hips and folding her over.

Her brain cells were haywire, but her feet kept moving. Answering Sebastian's call to play, she mimicked his tempo changes.

It was hard to predict when Sebastian would become Ian or Ian Sebastian. They were a blur of hands and chests and legs. When finally they surrounded her on either side, she touched their shoulders just to ground herself. Relaxing into the musicality, she took the lead. They shimmied when she shimmied and paused when she paused.

"Ménage à trois, Ménage à trois," echoed over the speakers. The Lady of Rage's *Afro Puffs* boomed. Her mouth dropped. This was the craziest remix ever. It touched on so many aspects of her identity.

Sebastian spun her into Ian's arms, leaping and slicing the air with a split. Ian, then, had to show off a double turn en l'air. When Sebastian pulled her close, her heart jolted. He smashed his hips against hers, and they became one with the rhythm. Ian slid up behind. Sparks exploded all over her body. Her brain was on fire. Sebastian's hands and Ian's lips, their sweat her sweat. "Ménage à trois, Ménage à trois," beat from the speakers. The Lady of Rage roared.

The crowd screamed.

She could see her Dad offstage. He was pissed.

They were all in so much trouble.

SEBASTIAN

the house shook with applause.

He rushed off stage, high-fiving Ian and kissing Zoey. "You're phenomenal." She had felt so alive, making him feel like he could do whatever he wanted. And he had.

Flushed red, Zoey struggled to speak. He licked her sweaty lips, fighting the urge to eat her alive. *I have to dance.* Baile Madrid took their places on stage, and he joined them.

He tried his best to dance lonely and disconnected, but it was hard to do when he felt so alive. Kinetic energy overflowed, and that worked for when the corps lifted him toward the goddess of love. He stretched with so much hope, and that hope didn't leave when they abandoned him. Papá's commentary on social isolation became a peaceful acceptance of loneliness.

The audience gave him a standing ovation, proof people didn't read the program. He gave himself a pass. This was the worst he ever danced, but that was his and Papá's secret.

He ran to the wings, his steps slowing.

Principal Raines waited for him. "We need to talk."

The cameras and sound followed him into an empty dressing room Principal Raines had converted into an office. Mrs. Agnes was there, and so were Ian and Zoey with their parents. Ian had too many parents for the small dressing room, forcing Principal Raines to leave the door open so Papá and Mamá could slide in with Vega.

"Tonight was supposed to be about our spirit of collaboration," Principal Raines said. "You hijacking our showcase and making it about you was disrespectful to your faculty and your CLASH-mates."

Vega raised her hand.

"Yes, Vega."

"Those 'vote for Vega' costumes were all Sebastian, and I didn't know he was going to do that, so can I go? I'm hungry."

Principal Raines ignored her. "Wipe that smile off your face right now, Mr. Bautista."

He sat up straight, shocked he was smiling. It was the dopamine still pumping.

"Well?" Papá demanded.

Well, what? He wasn't saying sorry. That would only make Zoey feel worse when she was already looking guilty. "The sugar plum pas didn't work for Zoey."

"I adapted it for her," Mrs. Agnes said.

"Sure, but I could tell that wasn't enough. And, I showed leadership by creating a routine that championed my pas partner," making her into a legend.

Principal Raines glanced at Zoey. "Why didn't you speak up and request accommodation?"

Zoey's eyes went big. "I didn't know I was supposed to."

"Sir, are you really going to call her out like that?" Vega asked. "I mean, isn't it our responsibility as the people in power to create safe spaces where everyone can visualize a loving mindset? That's the new philosophy you're exploring to include in our CLASH manual for next year at the behest of your leadership."

Sebastian couldn't tell if Vega surprised Principal Raines with her knowledge, but then CLASH knew about his sister's reputation. She had spies in kindergarten and spies in the faculty. Principal Raines had to already know.

Charles squeezed into the crowded room. "Sorry, Frederick, but we have to be in Beverly Hills in less than an hour. Big people are waiting."

CHAPTER 57
IAN

his family could turn a group hug into an argument. Ma sided with Pa Raines. Dad disagreed. Tech and Hippie Nerds stayed neutral. No one asked for his opinion, knowing he was the culprit, guilt-free and ready to yell, 'I'll do the time.'

He had finally claimed his space, creating a dance that represented him—no thanks to CLASH faculty—and represented Zoey. She had slayed. And he couldn't be happier.

"Can we please?" Ian tried to wiggle out of the hug. They were going to be late.

Ma and Pa looked at each other, sighing. They'd been arguing about him for a while. He could tell.

"You're becoming an adult," Ma said. *"We have to let you make your own mistakes."*

"But we don't have to fund your mistakes," Pa emphasized. *"You're free to be your own man as long as you can afford it. And we're learning to be okay."*

"Just don't end up in jail."

"The boy danced. He didn't commit a crime," Pa replied.

They were arguing again.

Ian jumped out of reach so he wouldn't be looped back in with a group hug. "I'm riding with Zoey. See you guys at the restaurant." He hurried to the dressing room. As much as he loved Zoey's outfit, he wasn't about to wear a nude mesh to a restaurant in Beverly Hills.

He halted in his run when he spotted Vega and Mahogany switching into their dresses.

"Don't guys have their own dressing rooms?" Vega quipped.

He kissed each of her cheeks. "Sure. But it's never as clean."

"Besides, he's seen us both naked," Mahogany said, leaning into the mirror to finish her blood-red lip gloss, the perfect color for a newly turned vamp.

Vega giggled.

Ian grew alarmed, testing them both. "Christmas ménage à trois?"

Vega and Mahogany locked eyes, laughing.

Yep. Vega converted Mahogany. He guessed Mahogany had opened up to Vega about how much she hated that he was a school slut. That probably freed Vega to admit that she had slept with him. A dirty secret she had kept from Mahogany for a while.

He would have to be very careful with them both. If Vega turned on him, he would lose Mahogany. "You joining us for dinner?" he asked.

"Can't," Mahogany replied. "My dad planned a family and friends gathering in Brentwood. Speaking of which, Dad loved you guys. He sees big things for your future."

"Cool," he replied. "That was all Sebastian. He's a big thinker."

"You guys besties now?" Vega asked.

"I suppose. You guys besties now?" He gestured to them both.

Vega and Mahogany shared a look. Then Vega approached him. Tall, slender, she could kiss him without forcing him downward. Mahogany relevéd, her kiss replacing Vega's.

What is happening? They giggled, their eyes filled with play, fucking his emotions. And it was exciting. Women united were dangerous, and danger was his favorite game to play.

CHAPTER 58
SEBASTIAN

so this is what disappointing Mamá and Papá felt like. No wonder Vega was jealous of him. He wished the cameras and sound weren't there, recording his parents discussing possible reprimands with Principal Raines. They talked as if they had overlooked a mental illness. Principal Raines suggested sixty hours of community service. Mamá suggested therapy. He flinched. Nothing against therapy, but none of this was making the cut.

He wasn't crazy. He broke the rules to create a safer world for Zoey, not to be a jerk. "I regret nothing," he said. *I shouldn't even be punished.*

Principal Raines hesitated. "It's complicated, I get that, and I respect what you did. I'd have done the same if it were me and my wife. However, there's rules. There's people you hurt. Recognize that."

Unbelievable. "CLASH is always challenging us to push beyond the comfort of the status quo," *and I'd done just that.*

"Imagine if you choreographed a piece, and then a dancer tossed it out, hired a DJ, and did whatever?" Papá demanded.

His papá's words slapped Sebastian's face. He lowered his head, unused to disappointing his parents. And all he could think about was escaping. "I'm going to be late," he said, using the dinner party as an excuse. The words scratched his throat. Not like he wanted to go anymore and face all the gossip. He'd rather go train. No one could hurt him while he trained.

Papá pulled him into a hug, kissing his forehead.

He tensed, feeling unworthy, his papá holding him till he relaxed."We trust you'll make better decisions next time," Papá whispered. Mamá rubbed his back, and he fought hard not to cry.

He embarrassed them, and it felt disgusting. Everything he did was for his family legacy, and he sacrificed so much. That familiar loneliness slithered in his chest as he meandered down the cold hallways. And he didn't want to feel lonely on this night. So he searched one dressing room after another until he found Mrs. Agnes cleaning the last of her makeup. She noticed him in the mirror.

"*Je suis désolée*," he said. I'm sorry. He could apologize to her.

"*For what?*" she asked. "*Being a hero?*"

He shrugged, jumping to sit on the counters. "*I'm not really sorry. I just feel like I should be. My parents think I need a therapist. Principal Raines thinks I need punishment.*"

"You know, if I had someone stand up for me like you did for Zoey, I'd have stayed dancing in Paris." Her words rooted inside him, reminding him he wasn't some rebel leader trying to take down the system. Just the opposite. He loved CLASH, but CLASH was cruel. It didn't love the weak, so he led Zoey and made her strong.

Mrs. Agnes squeezed his hand. It was weird how much she understood him. In another life, she could be his aunt.

"I don't want to go to the party," he said, and she shhed him, promising him people would celebrate him instead of shame him. And he believed her, finding enough strength to head to the parking lot.

He groaned when he spotted Gregory waiting at the parking lot entrance. The guy seriously needed to learn to take a hint.

"So what now?" Gregory asked. "Are you choosing Vega?"

He shrugged. "She's my sister."

"So. We're best friends."

"Je suis désolée." I'm sorry.

"She hates you, always has. She talked so much crap about you while we were dating. And I ignored it cause we were friends. I chose you. You owe me. I saved your film. Your film wouldn't do anything without my dad."

Sebastian kept walking, pointing to Vincent and Vega standing next to his Jeep shining blue. "Those are my friends. That's where my loyalty lies. You? Go make real friends."

Gregory pushed him.

He pushed Gregory back, only to end up with a busted lip. Returning the favor, he punched Gregory, wrestling him to the ground and turning his face raw.

Vincent yanked Sebastian off Gregory.

"Man, we don't have time for this," Vincent yelled, shoving Gregory so hard he stumbled and fell. "Get in your car before Sebastian and I both jump you."

"I'm never speaking to him again," Gregory yelled into the night air.

"Who are you telling? We're done." Vincent pulled Sebastian's arm. "Man, what did you think you were going to tell Greg's dad when you showed up at the restaurant?"

"I don't know." He touched his busted lip. The blood was sticky. Now, he had to show up to dinner looking like an animal. All cause of Gregory. His eyes raced across the parking lot, ready to finish what he started.

Vega threw her body against his.

He braced for an attack, mind frazzling. Pain never came even though she squeezed tighter. She was hugging him, not choking him. He relaxed, remembering how to hug her. One arm around her waist. Then the other.

She knew the exact length of time she needed to hold him silently. *"Gracias por un día hermoso."* Thank you for the beautiful day." Her gray eyes, his gray eyes, brightened. *"My phone hasn't stopped blowing up."* She showed him the texts that people were sending. They thought she was responsible for the costumes. *"There's no way Greg's going to top this. He knows that."*

"Show no mercy," he said. And they didn't. He and Vega were so alike. They went hard against their obstacles. And he was glad she no longer saw him as an obstacle. He was tired of fighting.

"I'm sorry for all the stuff between me and Frog Legs. I'll try to be nicer."

"Nice isn't really our thing, but Zoey will love your kindness."

"And Charles will love us arriving before nine," Vincent said. He raised his phone up to remind them that they needed to hurry.

"Let's get a selfie." Vega pulled them both cheek to cheek, snapping a photo. It was slightly blurry and poorly lit, but she posted it with the caption, 'Beautiful day.'

her **CLASH**-mates were actually calling her Zoey. Not "Frog-Leg Zoey," or "Sexy-Panty Zoey," or "Ménage Zoey." Just Zoey.

She felt woozy, dancing with Ian to her Volvo, giggling with her bestie. She'd gone from straight-A student to scandalicious, forever known for having a ménage à trois at the Dolby Theatre. The faculty were livid. Her CLASH-mates screaming for more! And it was exhilarating. She laughed with Ian, safe in her car, where Dad couldn't hear. His angry glare was tattooed on her brain, and eventually, she would have to face him. "Can you tell Dad you and Sebastian planned your R-rated sugar plum fairy so he doesn't ground me?"

She navigated into the traffic, slowing down when she spotted a blue Jaguar. It looked like Dad's car, and she didn't want to risk it.

"Stop thinking teenage broke girl and start thinking teenage star unlimited. The school wants to be you. Sebastian got the dopest ending for his film, and my godpa oversaw CLASH creating a global doc. You're welcome, Principal Raines."

Ian was right. Their bold actions were elevating their lifestyles. Last year, their afterparty was them eating soul food at a Compton diner. She remembered ordering the baked chicken with a side of yams. This year, they were celebrating in Beverly Hills.

Cameras filmed her and Ian easing on down the road into their private party. It felt glitzy. Mom and Dad talked to studio executives. Champagne sparkled with hors d'oeuvres. A cake shined with her and Sebastian's names. Her real name. Finally. She squeezed Ian's hand.

"Charles has big news," Amy called, spotting them.

Zoey wasn't ready to face Mom and Dad yet. "Can we wait? I want to take everything in?" And try some bruschetta before Dad kills my appetite.

Ian grabbed a glass of champagne even though they were surrounded by adults. "When in Spain, right?"

She rolled her eyes. "We're technically not in Spain."

"Who knows where we'll be next year? So many possibilities."

She could see the stars of her future.

They continued easing on through the party, smiling at every compliment, only stopping when they found Sebastian huddled with Vincent and Vega.

She leaned in close, noticing his busted lip. "What's the story behind the battle scar?" she teased.

"Gregory."

She followed his scowl to Greg standing with his dad. He shared the same bruised lip along with a dirty shirt and ripped jacket. "Were you guys fighting?"

Sebastian shrugged, embarrassed.

She didn't want to make him feel bad when he was supposed to be feeling like, 'Cameras, lights, Paris!' So she stepped closer, whispering, "What's it like to kiss a battle scar?"

"I don't know. You tell me."

She stood on her tippy-toes, his scar scratching her lips. "Like kissing glitter."

His eyes shined, kissing her again.

"Make that orange glitter," Ian joked.

Charles clinked his glass with a fork. "Can I have every-one's attention?"

"Let's head out back for a second," Sebastian whispered.

She'd always choose alone time with him over a Charles thank-you speech. Even if that alone time included a camera crew. He led her to the rooftop with a pool. She could see mansions sparkling in the hills, and squinting her eyes, the Hollywood sign. Hollywood, here I am, standing on a roof-top with the guy of my dreams. It was so cool. "Are you happy?" She studied him, his hunched-over shoulders and battle scar.

"Crazy happy. How about you? Has your heart stopped racing?"

She shook her head. "When do you think it'll stop?"

"Honestly?" He pulled her closer. "That's what I want to talk about."

She was nervous, so she rambled. "My Dad doesn't hate you. I'm sure once he sees how happy everyone is, he'll forget about trying to punish us."

"I know. He's probably in there listening to Charles explain where all this is headed."

"Where do you think it's headed?"

"Somewhere big. Charles sees our docuseries becoming a manga and then a script, and he wants to push the romance angle hard."

I love a romance.

"He thinks fans will eat it up, but I don't want to force you into anything you're not feeling."

"I like you."

"Same."

"So let's just make love." She felt her boss bitch armor growing solid.

Sebastian laughed. "Maybe in Paris."

"Or Los Angeles," she teased.

"Or Madrid."

"Your dad's in Madrid."

"So are my aunts, my uncles, my grandparents."

That's scary. "Or Los Angeles." There was something about kisses on Hollywood rooftops that sent her heart singing. Looping her arms around his neck, she felt high. His lips tasted sweet, like hot chocolate, and his body a cozy blanket for a winter night.

She danced to the dinner table, hoping the tapas tasted warm and good like Sebastian's lips.

A seat sat open next to Vega. Can I sit there? Ian would say, 'When in Spain.' Besides, she wasn't the old Zoey anymore. She was a fashion designer who rose from the year's biggest social disasters to become a ballerina showing off in packed houses. Life was different, and yes, she was brand new.

Vega smiled wickedly, a sign the social game was about to begin. "How was rooftop sex?"

"We didn't–"

"I know. Sebastian's not reckless."

"Oh." Where can I go from there?

"He's into you, that's obvious." Vega sighed. "So I guess I should apologize for making fun of you so we can be friends."

"Friends, not frienemies?"

"Whatever's more exciting. So, did he ask you out?"

She hesitated. "Kinda … not officially." She supposed she couldn't call him boyfriend.

"Cute," Vega reached for her fork. "Welcome to my circle."

She's joking. She has to be.

Vega leaned over for a selfie, posting the picture with the caption, '#friends or #frienemies? XOXO, @ComptonChic-Fashionista, AKA Zoey.'

Wait! Stop! Senior year, she would be frienemies with CLASH's first girl president. Now, this was spicy. Fifteen years later, her gray-bearded dad would stand at a podium talking about her legacy. 'My daughter started out a social disaster, but she refused to let that define her. She took a risk and changed it all. Now, she's a successful Parisian fashion designer with a book deal, a docuseries, and a lead role in Miraculous Ladybug. You, too, can be like Zoey Raines.' Her picture, bedazzled in a gold frame, would hang in the great Alumni Corridor next to Sebastian Bautista's. How exciting.

She looked around the table. Dad was listening to Charles, his eyes big. Mom blew kisses at her. Godparents sampled ceviche with Tech and Hippie Nerds. Ian talked excitedly with Vincent. Sebastian listened to his mom and dad, his eyes finding hers. She faced him, unafraid. How had he managed to make it so their loves no longer clashed? It was mind blowing, but Sebastian was a genius, her genius.

Her eyes twinkled. She was about to redefine her legacy with lots of dancing, lots of fashion, and wink, wink, orange glitter. And she would do it with the boy of her dreams, an A-team gone global. Yas, #blessed. She was ready.

Loves Clashing

follow me at:
instagram: lawwrites
threads: lawwrites
tiktok: rainewheat

visit:

www.cinemalattecreative.com

ACKNOWLEDGMENTS

This book wouldn't be what it is without the beautiful humans who read early drafts and gave me their honest, generous notes.

To my mom, Debra Fletcher—thank you for always being down to read and critique my work. Your faith in me is loud, constant, and so full of love.

Kelli Herod, Kiara Walker, Xander Bernstein, and Donald Bull—thank you for the feedback, the encouragement, and the gentle (and not-so-gentle) nudges to keep going. You each brought something special to this story.

To my writer's group, thank you for the magical moments that fuel me as a writer.

Huge love to The Anaphora Arts Publishing, Cinema Latte Creative, and The Periplus Collective—thank you for giving writers like me room to grow, mess up, and create something beautiful.

And thank you God for the creative spirit that and the wisdom and love to write.

www.ingramcontent.com/pod-product-compliance
Lightning Source LLC
Chambersburg PA
CBHW070201310726

48976CB00001B/172